BLACKFOOT AMBUSH

Zach saw a Blackfoot ride a Crow woman down. The warrior's tomahawk flashed in the day's first slant of amber sunlight. The weapon swept down and came back up dripping scarlet. Zach heard the keening whine of a bullet. The ground all around sprouted a crop of Blackfoot arrows, but he paid no heed to the danger. A mounted Crow ally galloped past. The next instant found the warrior falling, riddled with arrows, his pony veering off. Zach hurdled the dead brave and kept running.

Then he saw her.

She was racing through the trees with the grace of a gazelle. In hot pursuit were a pair of mounted Blackfeet, one some distance ahead of the other, both closing fast. She was quick, but stood no chance.

Morning Sky! Zach screamed inside.

He hiked the rifle to his shoulder and tried to steady his aim. So this was what it meant to be a trapper. . . .

HIGH COUNTRY

HIGH COUNTRY

by

Jason Manning

A SIGNET BOOK

SIGNET
Published by the Penguin Group
Penguin Books USA Inc., 375 Hudson Street,
New York, New York 10014, U.S.A.
Penguin Books Ltd, 27 Wrights Lane,
London W8 5TZ, England
Penguin Books Australia Ltd, Ringwood,
Victoria, Australia
Penguin Books Canada Ltd, 10 Alcorn Avenue,
Toronto, Ontario, Canada M4V 3B2
Penguin Books (N.Z.) Ltd, 182-190 Wairau Road,
Auckland 10, New Zealand

Penguin Books Ltd, Registered Offices:
Harmondsworth, Middlesex, England

First published by Signet, an imprint of New American Library,
a division of Penguin Books USA Inc.

First Printing, August, 1993
10 9 8 7 6 5 4 3 2 1

HIGH COUNTRY

Chapter 1

For Zach Hannah, St. Louis was a true wonder.

Never had he seen so many people congregated in one place, or so many buildings stacked so closely together. The sights and sounds and smells were overpowering. He'd spent his twenty years running the ridges of the Appalachian Mountains in Tennessee, and none of his experiences there had prepared him for this.

Zach was tall and rail-thin, his shoulders as wide as a wagon's singletree. He wore a long-tailed buckskin shirt that had seen better days and leggins dark with grime. A wide-brimmed woolen hat covered his head.

Until yesterday, flax-colored hair had brushed his shoulders. Upon arrival in St. Louis, one of his first stops had been a barbershop, where a mincing Frenchman with a girlish voice had cropped his hair close to the scalp and shaved the bristles off his face. Rose oil had been generously applied to his hair, and French quinine to his cheeks, and even now, a day later, Zach thought he smelled like a high hillside covered with wildflowers.

He stood with his back to a rawboard wall and watched the hustle and bustle of a street in the Vide Poche district. He gawked at well-to-do fur traders passing by in their ruffled shirts, beaver hats and blue claw-hammer coats, with shiny brass buttons flashing

in the bright April sun. Proud Spaniards from Santa
Fe swaggered beneath tall sombreros. Brawling rivermen staggered past, reeking of strong spirits, reminding Zach of his Uncle Simon's Copper Creek still—and
of Uncle Simon himself.

About twice a minute he glanced with wonder and
admiration at the brand-new percussion rifle cradled
in the crook of his arm. He'd traded his trusty old
flintlock and fourteen dollars for this .53-caliber work
of art at the shop of the gunsmith brothers, Jacob and
Samuel Hawken. The Hawken rifle had a thirty-four-
inch octagonal barrel and weighed twelve pounds.
Fifty paper cartridges, secure in Zach's beaded bullet
pouch, had been included in the transaction. Each
cartridge contained a half-ounce lead ball and two
hundred and fourteen grains of black powder.

This morning, in the heart of the city's French district, it seemed to Zach as though the population of
the whole world moved up and down and across the
muddy streets. Bearded bullwhackers cracked twenty-
foot whips of braided rawhide over the backs of plodding teams of oxen. Painted Indians wearing blankets
and breechclouts and scalp locks rode by on their
painted ponies. Indian children played naked in the
puddles. A farmer rode by on a trundling wagon, his
woman in the box beside him wearing bonnet and drab
gingham dress. Younguns hung over the wagon's tail-
gate, gaping at the sights.

Seeing a pioneer family like this inevitably reminded Zach of his own folks, not' long dead and
buried, and a heart-twisting emptiness welled up inside him.

Yesterday he had roamed the length and breadth of
St. Louis, wandering aimlessly from the rowdy waterfront on the west bank of the Mississippi River to the
hillside mansions of the rich and famous. Wealthy

American fur merchants, known locally as "Bostons," competed with their French counterparts in erecting these lavish palaces, each spending a fortune to make his dwelling more outrageously opulent than the next fellow's.

Zach had seen William Clark's residence and had been informed by a local passing by that Clark's "council room," a chamber over a hundred feet in length, displayed an astonishing array of Indian artifacts collected by the legendary pathfinder during his trek west with Meriwether Lewis. Zach could scarcely imagine a room of such dimensions. Why, it could hold the log cabin in which he'd been born, and a couple more besides!

No question but that in the last two days he had seen sights a body could write home about—had he known how to write. Zach didn't know how, nor did he have anyone to write to. He'd sold the homeplace and the forty mountaintop acres it stood on for sixty dollars, paid his last respects at the graves of his father and mother, and struck out alone for the promised land.

Now he stood, a gangly backwoodsman, on the brink of a human current flowing every which way at once, and it struck him as odd that a body could be amongst so many folks and still feel so all-fired lonely. Most of these people spared him not a glance. Being by nature shy and reticent, Zach found it impossible to strike up a parley with a total stranger. Besides, everyone seemed to be in a mighty big hurry, with no time to spare for small talk.

He'd seen St. Louis from one end to the other— figured he'd walked a good hundred miles of city streets—and now he didn't rightly know what to do next. One thing was certain: He was feeling the itch to yonder. Zach Hannah had never been able to stay in any one place too long. His pa had seldom been able to keep him on the farm, and the schoolmaster had fared just as poorly keeping him after his studies. Uncle Simon had often looked at him with a twinkle in his rheumy eyes and made the comment that a rolling stone gathers no moss. Zach figured no moss would ever latch onto his gaunt frame.

For him, St. Louis was merely a means to an end. This city was the gateway to the frontier, the Far West, that vast and virtually unexplored region acquired by the Republic some years ago in the Louisiana Purchase. *Pays inconnu*, the French *voyageurs* called it. The unknown land.

This trackless wilderness beckoned in come-hither style to Zach Hannah. The urge to *yonder* owned him like Satan held title to a sinner's soul. With no kin left save old Uncle Simon, and no hearth and home, he kept his steps bent toward the setting sun.

Yes, he was bound for the promised land. Zach didn't know exactly what he was looking for, but he had a gut hunch he'd find it out west. All he had to do was get there.

The most sensible way across the trackless prairie was to venture up the wild Missouri River, but the Big Muddy was more than one man alone could handle. He had the inclination to take his chances and strike out overland. The inclination, but not the means, He didn't have the funds to outfit himself with a good horse, sufficient provisions, and at least one reliable pack animal. St. Louis was chock-full of wily horse traders, but nary a one would qualify as a good samaritan, willing to donate to the cause of a footloose frontiersman with less than forty dollars to his name.

A haberdashery stood open for business across the street, and Zach had an idle notion to find out exactly what kind of critter a haberdashery was, but it looked as though swimming the mile-wide Mississippi would be an easier proposition than trying to cross this busy thoroughfare. So he started north, sticking close to the buildings, shrugging his pack onto a shoulder. The sidewalks were crammed shin-to-shoulder with people, and it took him but a moment to realize he was not going to make much progress through this jostling throng.

An alley opened on his right. Zach slipped into it, relieved to be free of the crowd. The narrow passageway had a rank outhouse odor to it. The street at the other end appeared to be measurably less popular than the one he had just quit. So he bent his steps that way, brown muck grasping at the heels of his moccasins. St. Louis, he decided, was a fine place to visit, but no fit place to live.

As Zach reached the end of the alley, he wasn't paying enough attention to what was going on around him. When the man came around the corner at a dead run and careened into him, Zach was caught completely off-guard. The collision hurled him backwards. He tripped over his own feet and sprawled in the mud.

Zach Hannah's temper was only a shade longer than a flea's leg. He didn't mind getting dirty, but seeing his brand-spanking-new Hawken rifle lying in the chocolate-colored slime burned his bacon.

"You clumsy ox!" he railed, leaping to his feet.

"Pardon!" called the man over his shoulder. He didn't break stride. Zach had a quick impression of long flowing hair redder than rust and bare feet slapping into the muck; of a linsey shirt, a belt of braided hemp, and patchwork calf-length dungarees, considerably frayed at the ends.

The man ran like a deer, and Zach hesitated a fraction of second, debating whether to give chase. Before he could decide, two more men galloped around the corner and ran full-stride into him. Zach heard them cursing blue streaks as the ground rushed up to greet him. This time he winced as a booted foot slammed into his shoulder.

The men ran on without a by-your-leave.

Zach lifted his face out of the sour mud. His teeth flashed white in a snarl a wolf would have been proud of.

The first man, the one in the disreputable dungarees, came to a skidding halt halfway down the alley. Zach looked beyond him and saw why.

Two more men were blocking the only way out. Like the pair who'd trampled Zach, they had the look of rough customers.

Uncle Simon had sailed with Decatur during the War of 1812, and he talked the talk of an old seadog. Zach had often heard him judge men by commenting on "the cut of their jib." As the toughs closed in on their victim, like dogs moving in on a cornered fox, Zach decided he didn't like one bit the way their jibs were cut.

The last couple of days he'd seen their kind before, for the most part on the rough and raucous levee. Rivermen, mean as alligators and tough as an old harness. Brawlers and braggarts, many of them. Big talk and big fists.

Zach picked himself and his rifle up out of the mud. The rivermen paid him no heed. The cornered man spared him a quick glance, but did not cry out for help. His eyes were bright, but not with fear. He grinned at the four toughs surrounding him, and inching ominously closer.

"Now, gentlemen," he said, dryly, "you're sartin the odds aren't too tall for you . . . ?"

The man's cool courage impressed Zach. Or was it sheer bravado? The four river rats clearly meant to do some damage. Just as clearly, the red-haired man had no chance against such odds.

Zach was on the verge of interfering when he remembered his father's advice: *Mind your own business and no one else's.* Still, four against one offended his strong sense of fair play. Maybe the rivermen had good reason to want Red Hair's hide. But two wrongs didn't make a right.

And then one of the toughs pulled a knife.

Chapter 2

Zach was moving in a heartbeat, his lanky frame suddenly possessed of gazelle-like grace. He closed in before the rivermen could react, and raised the Hawken to drive the stock between the shoulder blades of the nearest, who happened to be the one with the knife.

At the last possible second he held back. By gad, the Hawken wasn't just any old rifle. It was his prized possession. It had cost him fourteen dollars, and his old flintlock besides. Now here he was fixing to use it like a dern ax handle!

His intended victim spun to face him, swinging the knife in a vicious stroke. Flinching, Zach fell back, desperately bringing the Hawken around to block the swing. The blade clanged against the barrel. The impact almost struck the rifle from Zach's grasp. Once again he fell into the viscous mud. He kicked blindly. By some miracle, the kick connected. The man with the knife howled and went down.

Quick as lightning, and just as dangerous, he was up again, spewing profanity. Zach stopped worrying about his new rifle. On his feet again, he rammed the stock of the Hawken into the man's snarling face. The point of the crescent-shaped butt, encased in brass, smashed into the riverman's mouth. Spitting scarlet blood and yellowed teeth, the knife man collapsed.

Another tough launched himself at Zach. Zach drew his legs up, wedged his knees in the man's breadbasket. Rolling back onto his shoulders, he catapulted the man over his head and into a wall.

The river rat plopped into the mud, rolled slowly over, and sat up, stunned. Zach stood, shrugged off his pack, and tilted the Hawken with great care against the wall. Then he selected one of several empty barrels stacked near at hand, raised it high, and brought it down with all his might, and no small sense of satisfaction, on the man's skull. Staves shattered, and the riverman flopped on his back, arms and legs akimbo, wearing the barrel on his shoulders.

Zach's blood was up now. A sober and soft-spoken young man in general, he became a two-legged wildcat in a scrape. When he fought, it was in the mountain way: no holds barred. Kick, gouge, bite, and use anything within reach that even remotely resembles a weapon.

The red-haired man was grappling with the two remaining rivermen. They had the upper hand, and were pounding him with their fists. He took the punishment without a sound, and got in a few licks whenever the opportunity presented itself.

Zach remembered the skinning knife sheathed to his belt. Drawing it, he stepped in to grab a handful of greasy hair and wrench one of the rivermen backwards, at the same time laying the knife's well-honed edge to the man's throat. The man stopped struggling when he felt the caress of sharp steel on his Adam's apple.

Zach spoke softly and earnestly in his ear.

"Mister, I'll see to it your head is buried in the

same hole as the rest of you. You've got my solemn oath on that.''

The riverman's eyes rolled as he looked with utter disbelief at his two colleagues sprawled unconscious in the alley mud. How had this scrawny, wet-behind-the-ears yokel dispensed with two of the meanest characters on the waterfront? It just wasn't possible. One's face was caved in. The other's head seemed to be knocked clean off.

The riverman was all brawn—the Mississippi did not spawn weaklings. He was as tall as the backwoodsman, with twice the heft. But he felt Zach's whipcord strength and knew he'd met his match, so he let all the fight drain out of him.

"Don't slice my gullet!" he begged. "For the love of God, don't kill me!"

Zach didn't intend to kill anybody. Fighting was one thing, killing another entirely. He removed the knife from the man's throat and gave him a hard shove. The tough stumbled, then broke into a shambling run. He didn't look back.

The red-haired man was finishing off the last of the river rats. A jab in the gut, an uppercut to the jaw, and the riverman reeled. A kick in the groin doubled him over. Red Hair took vicious pleasure in delivering the coup de grace, a kick that tore his opponent's ear half off and pounded him into the muck.

Bruised, bloody, and grinning like a fool, Red Hair opened one big fist and offered his hand to Zach.

"Lucky for me I run into you!"

The ruckus over, Zach's hackles smoothed out. His shy reserve fell instantly into place. He shook the proffered hand with diffidence.

"Weren't nothing."

"Is to me. These fellers would've skinned me alive,

or my name ain't Sean Michael Devlin." Counting bodies, he frowned. "Say, where's the other one?"

"I let him go."

"How come you went and done such a foolish thing?"

Resenting Devlin's reproachful tone, Zach sheathed the skinning knife and turned away, tight-lipped. to fetch his pack and rifle.

"You'd best come with me," advised Devlin.

"Why for?"

"That one you let go'll be back with half the keelboat men on the river. You'll wind up gator bait, and that's sartin."

Zach grimaced. This was his reward for ignoring his father's advice about minding one's own business. Why did he have such a difficult time learning his lessons? It was this kind of meddling that had put his whole family under.

Ma's heart had done it, bless her gentle soul. Smallpox had come to Copper Creek, and Ma just hadn't been able to sit up on the Hannah mountainside while her neighbors fought for their lives. Of course, Pa had declared it wasn't Hannah business. But Ma hadn't listened to him, and the plague came home with her.

"We'd best git, if we're going," said Devlin.

"Where to?"

"Why, up the river, natcherly."

"I'm pointed west."

"Likewise. I'm talking about the Big Muddy, friend. God's meanest river. I aim to make me a fortune in brown gold."

"Brown gold?"

"Beaver. There's what they call an 'expedition' all set to make for the Shining Mountains, and I have it in mind to volunteer."

Excitement surged through Zach's veins. Here was the solution to his problems, the means by which he could reach the promised land.

"Reckon I'll do the same," he said.

Chapter 3

Zach left the alley with Devlin and they were swept away by the torrent of humanity flooding the street. That their donnybrook with the four river rats had not drawn a curious crowd astonished Zach. Back in Copper Creek, a good fight would've brought the whole county running. Mountain folk liked nothing better than a ruckus, with the possible exception of a foot-stomping hoedown. It wasn't so much that they hankered to see eyes gouged and bones broken and blood let. They just wanted to make sure the participants lived to fight another day. Back home, the folks usually intervened before a scuffle turned ugly and murder was done. Here, it seemed, the people were too busy to bother, or just didn't want to get involved.

Zach let Devlin take the lead, as he apparently knew his way around St. Louis. They put some distance between themselves and the alley before Devlin broke free of the crowd and paused in the refuge of another back passage.

"Why were those men after you?" asked Zach.

Devlin pulled a pouch from the rope-belted waist of his dungarees. With a devilish smile, he tossed it in the air a few times, relishing the rich jingle of coins.

"You stole that poke, didn't you?" said Zach. He wasn't really asking a question; he knew the answer as surely as he knew the ways and wiles of woodcraft, and his conscience nettled him so ferociously that he began to feel sick to his stomach. He'd become a thief's accomplice.

"Aye, I did," nodded Devlin, without a trace of remorse. "If it's any consolation, I stole it from a man who stole it from others."

Zach said nothing. He wasn't consoled.

"Look here," insisted Devlin. "The man's name is Tyree. A flamin' cardsharp, a bottom-dealer. He's been fleecing the passengers on the *Independence,* the sternwheeler I was working on—until today. Friend, I've swabbed my last deck. Today I struck it rich, at Mr. Tyree's expense. They call this part of the city 'Vide Poche.' That's French for 'empty pocket.' Well, I've been *vide poche* for as long as I can remember, and now my luck has changed."

"Who knows how many rivermen are after your scalp—and you call that lucky?"

Devlin shrugged. "You have to take chances if you're going to get ahead in life. And the men who get ahead play by their own rules."

Zach shook his head.

Devlin returned the pouch to his waistband and took a folded piece of paper from under his linsey shirt. As he unfolded it, Zach realized it was a page torn from a newspaper. Devlin smoothed the page out against a wall, then pointed at something printed near the top of the page.

"These are last week's notices in the *Missouri Republican.* See this? That's why I done what I done."

"I can't read," confessed Zach, his ears burning.

"I can, a little. Never had proper schoolin', but one of my old skippers was kind enough to teach his poor dumb cabin boy all he knew. Here, I'll read it for you.

" 'To enterprising young men.' " Devlin grinned. "I reckon that's us. 'The sub . . . subscriber wishes to engage one hundred young men to ascend the Missouri River to its source, there to be employed for one, two, or three years. For particulars, inquire of Major Andrew Henry, near the lead mines in the county of Washington, who will ascend with, and command, the party; or of the subscriber near St. Louis. William H. Ashley.' ''

Devlin folded the page and put it back under his shirt.

"Who is this Ashley feller?" asked Zach. "And this Major Henry?"

"No better man for the job than the Major. He was the field captain of the Missouri Fur Company's first expedition up the Big Muddy. He give up on trapping beaver and went in partners with Ashley, mining lead. Looks like the Major's got a hankering to get back into the fur trade."

"But why steal the gambler's money?"

"I got to get outfitted. I aim to sign up as a trapper, not a flamin' boatman. I've run the river my whole life, and I'm needin' a change. Now, I don't know beans about trappin' and such, but I can look the part, and the Major won't need to know the difference." Devlin looked Zach over. His gaze came to rest on the Hawken. "I'll buy me some skins to wear, and a couple of good knives, and a long gun like the one you got there."

Instinctively, Zach tightened his grip on the Hawken. He sensed that when Devlin was in the vicinity no man's possibles were safe.

"You been up the Missouri before?" queried Zach.

"I know the Mississippi like the back of my hand. I been up and down the Ohio a time or two. In fact, I was born on the Ohio, in the stern of a Mackinaw boat, off Point Pleasant, where the Lewis Brothers fought Cornstalk and a thousand screaming Injuns in '74.

I been up the Red to Captain Shreve's landing. But I ain't yet made the Big Muddy's acquaintance. She's a downright unfriendly girl, or so I've been told. Which is one more reason I'd liefer hire on as a trapper than a keelboat crewman.

"Besides, there's a fortune to be made in brown gold. One day I'll have me one of those big houses on the hill. I'll pay Tyree back, with interest. And if he ain't content with that, why then we'll just have ourselves a duel on Bloody Island, in the manner of gentlemen. As it stands, he won't soil his lily-white hands on the likes of me, and hires wharf rats to do the deed. So what do you say, scout? Are you primed for big adventure? If so, stick with me, and we'll get our share, and more besides."

Zach wasn't too sure he could trust Devlin. This one was a thief and a scoundrel; that was clear as mother's milk. But he didn't want to miss a golden opportunity, and if he didn't stick with Devlin, he might not find Ashley or Henry in time.

"I'll tag along," he said, with some reluctance.

Devlin suddenly became very serious. He clapped a hand on Zach's shoulder and looked Zach square in the eye.

"You saved my life back there, and I don't even know your handle."

"Zach Hannah."

"Well, Zach Hannah, I'll not be forgettin' what you've done. We whupped four rivermen, and if we stick together there ain't nothin' we won't be able to step over. We make a fine team, Zach, you and me. I'm willin' to offer you my friendship, and a solemn oath to watch out for your scalp, if you'll consent to do likewise for me."

"I reckon," said Zach, disconcerted.

"Then we have each other's word on it, and we'll

seal the bond between us with our blood. It's the way on the river. Give me your knife.''

Without pause, Devlin sliced the palm of his left hand. He didn't flinch. Zach tried not to, either, as he took back the knife and cut himself.

They clasped hands. As their blood mingled, Zach considered the ritual and all it signified. For better or worse, he had a friend. Heretofore friendless, he took the oath very seriously. And as he studied the other's solemn features, he could only assume Devlin did the same.

Chapter 4

Though river-born and river-bred, Sean Michael Devlin wished to present himself to Major Henry as a bonafide backwoodsman, and Zach accompanied him that afternoon as he prepared himself for the new role he was about to play.

Devlin was fortunate to have Zach along. When Devlin selected his buckskins, Zach persuaded him to buy loose-fitting garments. Devlin didn't much care for the way the buckskins draped his lanky frame, but Zach warned him that leathers were prone to shrink considerably when wet—if the shirt and leggins fit snugly now, they'd have to be cut off with a knife after the first frog-strangler.

Considering the rags Devlin had been wearing before, it surprised Zach to learn that his newfound friend was vain about his appearance. Zach reasoned that it was precisely because Devlin had been forced by circumstance to dress so shabbily that he now wished to look the best he could. For himself, Zach had never been one to worry about appearance.

Devlin bought himself a pair of beaded Osage moccasins, and Zach sent him back to buy two more. ''You wear 'em all three at the same time,'' he advised. ''You could carry an extra pair in your pack if you wanted, but you never know when you and your pack might part company. Best to wear 'em all on your feet, in case you have to go day and night in a hurry and afoot over rough country. Besides, you'll walk mighty quiet.''

"I heard tell of a mountain man named Colter," said Devlin, eyes bright with excitement. "Captured by Blackfoot Injuns. They took his weapons and clothes, and told him to run for his life. Way it's told, Colter outrun 'em all except one, and that going barefoot across cactus flats and rock fields. He killed the one he couldn't pull away from. Run him through with his own lance. This Colter, he went seven days without food, they say, and traveled two hundred miles. Reckon you could do that, Zach?''

Zach thought it over, shook his head. He'd been a couple of days without food, but never seven, and he wasn't at all sure he could handle a passel of hostile Indians in the bargain.

"I don't know," he said, dubious.

"I could," said Devlin. "If I had a bunch of blood-thirsty savages on my tail.''

"Well, just don't go gettin' cornered in an alley.''

Devlin laughed at that. He laughed again, a little later, at Zach's expression when he presented Zach with a brand-new knife, just like the one he now carried under his own belt.

"It's yours," said Devlin. "My way of thanking you for what you did today.''

"I ain't never seen such a knife," murmured Zach, wonder-struck.

The double-edged blade was a good twelve inches in length, an inch and a half wide, with a quarter-inch rib. The handle was staghorn, the crossguard a straight steel plate. A blood trench extended from the base of the blade to within two inches of the point.

"It's balanced for throwing," said Devlin. "The man says it'll turn over once every ten feet.''

It all but broke Zach's heart to give the knife back.
"I can't take it."

"Why not?"

"It was bought with stolen money."

Devlin's expression turned dark. He spun and hurled
the knife. It sailed over and through a half-dozen people on the boardwalk in front of the blade-master's
shop and struck one of the uprights. A woman cried
out in alarm. A man swore gruffly. But no one took
issue with the two well-armed young men. Zach stared
at the quivering knife, the blade buried two inches into
the post, and then at Devlin's back as Devlin marched
away.

"If you don't want the flamin' knife," said Devlin,
"you can't be leavin' it there."

For the first time, St. Louis paid heed to Zach Hannah. He discovered that he didn't much care for the
attention. The passersby were giving him a wide berth,
staring at him in a less than friendly way.

Mumbling apologies, he retrieved the knife and hur-
ried to catch up with Devlin.

"I call that mighty reckless," he said, crossly.

"What?"

"Throwing a knife in a street full of folks. What if
you'd missed that post?"

"I never miss," replied Devlin. "As we haven't
been long acquainted, and you don't yet know me well,
I'll forgive that remark."

Devlin next paid the Brothers Hawken a visit, and
purchased one of their highly regarded percussion rifles. Even then, after buying leathers, three pairs of
moccasins, two knives and a long gun, he'd scarcely
put a dent in Tyree's money.

They made their way to the waterfront, at the north
end of town. Zach began to throw anxious looks
around, expecting at any moment to see a swarm of

toughs with blood in their eyes and knives in their hands.

The Mississippi was running high and strong, and the current swirled vigorously against the sharp prows of two large keelboats. The vessels were built exactly alike, with a long, man-tall cargo "box" amidships. Square sails snapped in a breeze on forward masts. The boatmen's poles and oars lay neatly stacked on narrow runways, port and starboard. Great sweeps swung ponderously on the stern as the river toyed with untended rudders.

The keelboats were moored snugly to the wharf, fore and aft. Half a hundred men were hard at work, streaming like ants back and forth between the boats and piles of crates on the dock, using bow and stern gangplanks.

"Hope they load heavier forward than aft," remarked Devlin, watching the preparations with a critical, knowing eye. "If they don't, and we strike a sandbar, we'll run aground so high we'll never get her shoved off."

Zach made no reply. He was woefully ignorant on the subject of river navigation. He'd come part of the way from Copper Creek on a flatboat going down the Ohio, and that was the sum total of his experience. Gazing now upon the mighty Father of Waters, he was awed by the sheer size and scope of the river. Steamboats churned up and down, trailing plumes of dense black smoke, trying to avoid a multitude of smaller craft—canoes, rafts, and rowboats. He could scarcely see the opposite shore, and decided that all the rivers in Tennessee laid side by side would not be as wide.

A sudden commotion drew his attention back to the wharf. A boatman had stumbled, dropping a crate, and a florid, barrel-chested character wearing a cock's feather in his scarlet tam-o'-shanter descended on him with a vengeance. Bull voice roaring, the red-faced man cursed and kicked the careless boatman with ruthless expertise, and the most extensive repertoire of profanity Zach had ever heard.

"Know who that is?" asked Devlin.

Zach said he had no idea.

"It's Mike Fink. King of the Keelboat Men, they call him. Major Henry's hired himself the best—as well as the meanest—man on the river. I can't think of a better reason to be part of the fur brigade, rather than one of the boat crew. Besides, looks to me like most of the boatmen are pork-eaters."

"Pork-eaters?"

"Aye. *Mangeurs de lard.* French-Canadians. Hardly fit company for an Irishman like yours truly."

"Reckon any of 'em been told to keep an eye skinned for you?"

Devlin shook his head. "If I know Mike Fink, he's kept them busy as bees since sunup, and well away from the grog shops. The taverns are where the one you were foolish enough to let go will look for reinforcements. Come on. I see the Major."

A crowd of spectators had gathered at the riverfront, and Zach followed Devlin through them to a group of men supervising the loading of the keelboats.

Two of the men had the well-fed, well-dressed look of city merchants. The third was a tall and slender man clad in buckskins and beaver hat. Sun-dark and steely-eyed, he was the type of person who stood out in any crowd—a man of presence and authority. He carried himself as though he were still an army officer; this, Zach felt certain, was Major Andrew Henry.

"We are sublimely confident you will succeed, Major," one of the others was saying, as Zach and Devlin came within earshot. "You have the requisite knowledge and experience to make the Rocky Mountain Fur Company a splendid success.''

"My thanks, Mr. Tracy,'' replied Henry. "And to you, as well, Mr. Wahrendorff. Without the financial backing of your mercantile firm, none of this would have been possible.''

"Your partner, Mr. Ashley, is a very persuasive individual,'' said Wahrendorff, chuckling from the depths of his prodigious belly. "Would you expect any less from the first elected lieutenant-governor of the state of Missouri? Still, I seriously doubt we would have so easily parted with thirty thousand dollars without Ashley's assurance that you would be in charge of the expedition.''

"You gentlemen flatter me,'' said Henry.

"If I may say so,'' ventured Tracy, "we're a trifle surprised. We thought you had retired for good from the fur trade.''

Major Henry's smile was wistful. "I thought I had, sir. I was quite content to spend the rest of my days enjoying the creature comforts which civilization provides, to read my books and play my violin. But alas, gentlemen, the call of the mountains is a siren's song. Now, if you will excuse me, I must have a word with Mr. Fink.''

As Henry broke away from the merchants, Devlin intercepted him.

"Major, my friend and I have come to join up.''

"Have you now?'' Henry gave Devlin a long look, from heel to hairline, and then did likewise with Zach. "You have the look of a woodsman.'' His gaze flicked back to Devlin. "You, sir, do not.''

Devlin's jaw dropped. His neck reddened. Then his ears. Then his whole face. Zach was afraid Devlin would scotch things up. His mind racing, Zach stepped recklessly into the breach.

"Major, I'm from Tennessee," he said, stumbling over the words. "Up Copper Creek way."

"Mountain-born," said Henry, nodding approval.

"Yes, sir. I'll bear witness for Devlin here. Neither one of us will let you down, sir."

Henry was silent a moment, lips pursed.

"Boys, my partner and I needed thirty hunters. We've signed on twenty-nine. Mike Fink has a full crew. Colonel Ashley is in charge of the cavallard, fifty half-broke horses, which will accompany the boats overland. I believe he has all the hands he requires to see that task through. I suppose the long and short of it is this: I have room for one of you, but not both."

"Which one?" blurted Devlin.

"I'll let the two of you decide that between yourselves. But don't be long about it. I plan to be under way within the hour."

He left them, striding across the dock in Mike Fink's direction.

"We'll flip a coin," decided Devlin.

Zach didn't like the idea of leaving it to chance. The Major needed one more hunter. Well, he'd been hunting all his life. He qualified for the job, and Devlin didn't. Perhaps he should go to the Major and tell him this. Tell him that Devlin was a riverman, not a woodsman. Maybe even tell him Devlin was a thief. That would certainly put Devlin out of the running.

"Zach, I know how you feel," said Devlin earnestly. "Believe me, I do. But if I don't get out of St. Louis right quick I'm a dead man, and that's a sartin fact."

Zach brushed past him. Mike Fink saw him coming, said something to Major Henry, who turned.

"Reckon he'll be going with you, sir," said Zach,

choking on his bitterness as he thumbed over his shoulder, indicating Devlin.

"What's your name, son?"

"Zach Hannah, sir."

"You sound less than pleased with the decision, Mr. Hannah."

Zach squinted upriver, into the hazy distance.

"I'll get there," he said grimly. "I'll get there if I have to walk."

Major Henry smiled faintly.

"That won't be necessary. You can both sign on. One more hunter won't present a problem. I admire loyalty. And I trust a man who will sacrifice himself for another. Fetch your friend, Mr. Hannah, and get aboard."

Chapter 5

As Major Henry had intended, they were off within the hour.

Zach stood with Devlin and a dozen buckskin-clad hunters on the afterdeck of one of the keelboats, out of the boatmen's way. The gangplanks were pulled aboard, the mooring lines cast off. The keelboat began to drift downriver. Zach braced himself against the roll of the deck and looked longingly toward dry land. He felt a little apprehensive without solid ground underfoot.

Mike Fink stood atop the cargo box, and cut loose a lusty yell Zach figured could be heard for miles.

"Set poles for the mountains!"

A half-dozen men located forward set to their oars. Twenty more, gripping iron-shod poles, gathered at the bow. Facing aft, they plunged the poles into the river, striking the bottom. Walking single-file along the running boards, ten to port and ten to starboard, they pushed with all their might against the poles, their shoulders firmly settled into sockets at the tops of the poles. The keelboat slowly began to gain way upriver, against the current.

Now manning the sweep, Fink gave a shout when the polesmen reached the stern. The twenty about-faced in unison, lifted their poles off the river bottom and trotted forward to the bow, there to repeat the process. The square canvas of the sail flapped and then billowed as it caught and held the wind.

On the waterfront, spectators cheered and shouted "Godspeed!" A rifle was fired somewhere in the crowd. Zach had a bad moment, wondering if it could be one of Tyree's hirelings, throwing lead after him and Devlin. Then, as other guns went off, and a haze of white powder-smoke drifted above the crowd, he realized the shooting was just part and parcel of a St. Louis-style sendoff.

They soon left the city behind. Zach caught a glimpse of the cavallard through the riverside trees. The horse herd was heading north, and making better time than the keelboats. He felt guilty, sitting here at his ease among bales and crates with the other hunters while the boatmen pitted brute strength against the river, muscling the vessels forward against the current. None of the other woodsmen seemed the least bit bothered. They lounged about in the keelboat's steerage, cussing and discussing, smoking their cob pipes or chewing their quids, and showing scant interest in the labor of the crew.

Nightfall caught them only a handful of miles north of the city, and Major Henry gave the order to lay to. Fink steered the keelboat close to the western bank. A pair of rivermen took up ropes fixed with grappling hooks. Iron sang through the air as the two whirled the ropes overhead before casting them into the trees. The hooks caught around stout trunks. Several other boatmen jumped in to help warp the boat to shore.

"Strikes me we would've done better to leave at daybreak," commented one hunter, disappointed in the first-day progress of the expedition, or lack of it.

"Major Henry knows what he's doin'," replied an older woodsman, who sat cross-legged next to Zach, leaning back against a crate full of traps.

This man looked to be older than Zach and Devlin put together. His hair and beard were as gray as river ice, stained yellow-brown at the mouth corners by tobacco juice. His buckskins were blackened with grime and fire smoke.

His voice rasped like two rough stones rubbed together. Pale blue eyes crinkled at the corners, and brown cheeks were creased with deep lines. Zach realized the man was smiling underneath that untrimmed face hair.

"You cain't trust these Frenchy rivermen," said the graybeard. "Come sundown, they're allus thinkin' about whiskey and wimmin. If the Major waited till mornin', why half the crew would be stinkin' drunk in some Pain Court grog house. It's too fur a piece fer 'em to walk back now, no matter how fierce they git to hankerin'."

The first hunter spoke again. "Reckon yore too dang old to think about whiskey and wimmin, Shadmore."

Shadmore grunted as several other woodsmen chuckled.

"I've had more of both than all you chillun put together, Sublette."

They disembarked and camped beneath the trees. Six men were chosen to hunt up some supper. Devlin was one of these. Zach regretted not being another. He was eager to show Major Henry he could hunt with the best.

Five of the woodsmen returned with a mess of rabbits and quail. Devlin emerged from the dusky gloom some time later, a chicken in either fist. The others had a good laugh at that. Devlin took the ribbing with good grace and a grin, for he could tell it was good-natured.

"Look hyar!" crowed a man named Beckwourth. "Sunday dinner on the hoof!"

'' 'Pears we got us a chicken thief on the payroll,''
remarked another.

"Why waste lead," asked Devlin, "when you can
do like the coyote does?"

"Coyote, he says!" exclaimed Shadmore, bent over
a crackling fire. "Throw me one of them thar cluck-
ers, Coyote, and I'll show you how one day the Blackfeet are goin' to roast you over an open fire."

The boatmen kept to themselves, around their own
fires, eating mush and sowbelly. Crickets and frogs
sang in chorus from the darkening woods, and the
great river murmured endearments to the night.

As the hunters sat around drinking coffee by the gal-
lon and taking their tobacco whatever way they preferred, Major Henry appeared and said he wanted to
have a few words with them.

"Gentlemen, as some of you know, in the spring of
oh-nine I came this way before, as field captain for the
first trapping expedition up the Missouri. We reached
the Three Forks, and I'll wager there is no better
beaver country. That's where we're going this time."

Henry paused as his audience rumbled approval.

"Now, I know a few of you were with me in the
days of the Missouri Fur Company, and I don't need
to acquaint you with the dangers awaiting us. But for
the benefit of the others, I wish to make a few remarks
regarding the greatest danger of all.

"I refer, gentlemen, to a tribe of Indians known as
the Blackfoot. Actually, the Blackfeet, Blood, Piegan,
and Gros Ventres are all related, and they all share a
keen hatred for the white race. They are cunning, brutal, and relentless. The other tribes fear them, and
rightly so. Their warriors are fierce fighters.

"Every Blackfoot is your sworn enemy. This you
would do well to remember. No one knows for certain
the reason for their animosity toward us. Some say it

is because a brave was shot and killed, and another
wounded, when a band of Piegans attempted to steal
the horses of the Lewis and Clark Expedition. Others
say it is simply the nature of the Blackfeet to take on
all comers. Whatever the truth, you can be sure that a
Blackfoot will stop at nothing to put you under.

"Unfortunately, the Three Forks region is in the
very heart of Blackfoot country. Twelve years ago, only
half our men could trap; the others had to remain constantly on guard against the Blackfeet. In spite of our
precautions, three trappers were ambushed and
slaughtered.

"With that said, I must admit to optimism. We made
a few tragic mistakes before. Hopefully, we have
learned from them. The price that beaver is bringing
has never been higher, the demand never greater. If
we are all careful, and look out for one another, the
cost to us may not be too high."

When Henry had finished, Devlin turned to Zach.

"If these Blackfeet are all we have to worry about,"
he said, "it won't be no hill for a stepper."

"Don't sell 'em short," advised Shadmore, sitting
on a nearby log. "They ain't nothin' like the tame
Injuns around this neck of the woods. They're two
shades meaner'n the Devil hisself."

Jim Beckwourth came over to borrow a twist of tobacco from Shadmore. In addition to his rifle he carried a fusil, a short-barreled shotgun, slung over his
shoulder. Zach was later to learn that Beckwourth was
the offspring of a slave girl and a Virginia planter's
son. The mulatto woodsman's features were craggy
and intense. Zach thought his piercing black eyes could
surely burn holes through a hickory post.

"Ask me," said Beckwourth, "the Major plumb
forgot to mention sumpin that'll kill you just as daid
as any redskin."

"What might that be?" asked Devlin.

Beckwourth had a mouthful of tobacco by now, so Shadmore answered on his behalf.

"He means the Big Muddy, I reckon. A thousand miles of her, with every mile worse than the one before. She'll be runnin' high, wide, and handsome this time of year, and as crazy-wild as a turpentined cat. Iffen we all git to Three Forks above snakes, I'll be one surprised pilgrim."

Zach wondered just how bad the Missouri could be. He was acquainted now with the Ohio and the Mississippi. Could the Missouri be all that much different from her sisters?

The fires flickered down. One by one the hunters rolled into their blankets, adding their snores to the night symphony of the crickets and frogs. Tired as they were, the boatmen engaged in a lusty songfest, Creole-style, accompanied by one of their own who had a knack for blowing a tune out of a mouth harp. Zach turned in and slept well, untroubled by dire warnings about the man-killing river they would reach tomorrow.

Chapter 6

The second day out of St. Louis, the Rocky Mountain Fur Company took on the Big Muddy.

They heard the river long before they laid eyes on her. The thunderous roar sounded to Zach like a hundred waterfalls heard all at once. He noticed a peculiar phenomenon as they neared the confluence. The Mississippi's water, generally, was green. Suddenly, only the eastern half of the river was green; the western half had become a murky reddish-brown. It seemed the Mississippi was reluctant to mix with the silt-laden waters of the Missouri.

Midday found them turning up the Big Muddy. Long before sundown, Zach began to wonder if any of them would make it to the mountains alive.

The sails had been of some use going up the Mississippi. Now the wind deserted them, and the useless canvas was furled. Quite often the current was so swift that the oars were rendered useless, as well. And sometimes the channel cut too deep for the poles. On these occasions all the men, save one remaining at the helm, were put ashore to tow the keelboats by means of stout cordelles attached to the masts.

The sandy banks were uneven and treacherous. The raging river was forever undercutting its banks, and they had to take care lest a ledge collapse beneath them. To make matters worse, thick brush and chest-high grass grew profusely right along the river. Several "bushwhackers" armed with cane knives would go in advance of the cordelle brigades, hacking out a path.

The Missouri fought them with its own special weapons. Fallen trees would anchor to the bottom with their roots and limbs, then bob like a cork just beneath the surface. These "sawyers" lurked unseen, and could surge suddenly upward to rip open a boat's belly. Hundreds of uprooted trees, mingled with the bloated, stinking carcasses of deer and buffalo, came swirling downriver. A thousand snags had to be chopped out, dozens of sandbars avoided.

But what raised the most alarmed cry from lookouts clutching the tops of the keelboat masts was the sighting of a "raft." These were log jams, caulked with mud and sand, that formed natural dams, forcing the river to plunge angrily through narrow spillways.

It was impossible to pole or even tow the keelboats up the spillways. Grappling hooks were employed, the lines attached to capstans at the bow. The hooks were hurled out ahead. A half-dozen men would strain at the windlass, warping the boat along the taut and humming rope. This was repeated time and time again. Inch by strenuous inch the boats crawled forward, the raging torrent battering the bows and washing the decks.

Just one day on the Big Muddy convinced Zach that the river was cursed.

Remarkably, they made steady progress. Zach gave most of the credit to the French-Canadians. The other hunters could look down their noses at the "pork-eaters" if they were of a mind to; he for one thought them to be, man for man, the toughest characters he had ever met.

Credit was also due Mike Fink. The patroon was everywhere at once, a rough and profane human dynamo, encouraging his men or berating them by turns, making jokes and singing at the top of his lungs when the going was the roughest. He did the work of two men, and did it well. The most hazardous tasks he saved for himself. He would not order anyone to do what he dared not.

Past the Gasconade they struggled, past the yellow Osage. Cote Sans Dessein was put behind them, and the Manitou Rocks. Wizard's Island gave them trouble for half a day, but could not stop them.

The days blended together for Zach into one long, exhausting fight against the river. The hunters had to do their share of bushwhacking, and take their turns at the capstans as the keelboats "grasshoppered" past the rafts. Zach had never worked so hard in his life. Compared to this, trying to scratch a crop out of a rocky Tennessee mountainside was child's play. He began to think he would have been better off striking out afoot across the prairie.

The Missouri called on its allies. Each morning found the sky clear, and as blue as a robin's egg. Inevitably though, thunderclouds would form later in the day, great towering white flat-tops, their bellies black with rain, and sometimes green with hail. They would fill the sky, blotting out the sun, and sometime in the afternoon, regular as clockwork, they would empty themselves on the Rocky Mountain Fur Company.

Swirling wind would drive the rain in sheets across the river. Jagged lightning bolts smote the earth with stunning cracks of thunder, and the rain chilled the hunters to the bone. Nurtured by the storms, the river surged higher and stronger, uprooting trees with contemptuous ease and flinging the flotsam at the keelboats with savage delight.

The Big Muddy, decided Zach, was an appropriate name for this river. Even on the calmest of days the water was so heavy with silt as to be undrinkable, and sometimes smelled so foul that the strongest stomachs turned. After a few days Zach found his clothes reeking of the Missouri's stench. His pores became so clogged with the river's filth that for the first time in his life he actually longed for a bath.

During the third week out of St. Louis, one of the keelboats was lost. A sawyer rose like a monster from the depths and smashed the sweep into so much kindling. The impact hurled the stern into the air. The deck tilted precariously, and men yelled for help. But Zach and his companions on the other vessel could only stand helplessly by and bear witness to the catastrophe.

The polesmen lost their poles, the oarsmen their oars. The rudderless boat began to swing around and around, enslaved by the malicious current. The sawyer bobbed, struck again, this time at the bow. Zach's heart missed a beat at the sound of deck timbers being rent into so much kindling. The keelboat dipped and plunged, like a wild horse at the business end of a catch rope. Men were flung overboard. Crates and bales came loose and were washed over the side. Striking a snag, the damaged boat lifted sharply at the stern. The Missouri seized its long-awaited chance. Water poured over the bow, and within minutes the keelboat had sunk to the bottom.

Mike Fink bellowed harsh commands, and the remaining boat drifted downriver to rescue the men of the wrecked vessel. More than a day's progress was lost in less than an hour of downriver running. Miraculously, every man was retrieved from the river. But half the expedition's supplies were lost. The Rocky Mountain Fur Company had seen its first major setback.

But by no means its last.

Chapter 7

Despite the loss of the keelboat and precious provisions, Ashley and Henry elected to push on.

The boatmen cursed the river. The river responded by giving them two days' worth of water so deep and so swift that the men had to tow and bushwhack an entire twenty-mile stretch.

The countryside began to change. Gone now were the deep woodlands. Only occasional groves broke the monotony of a sea of grass that stretched, gently rolling, as far as the eye could see. At times, ponderous herds of bison covered the golden prairie like an immense brown blanket.

Due to the sinking of the keelboat, supplies were severely rationed, and living conditions on the surviving vessel were almost unbearably crowded. Major Henry finally ordered a one-day layover for the purpose of killing a few buffalo.

Thirty-one hunters could kill enough shaggies to feed the entire population of St. Louis for months, so six were chosen at random, with the Major drawing names out of a hat. Zach was one of the six selected. It was his further good fortune to be paired with the graybeard trapper, Shadmore.

While the six hunters marched off with strict orders from the Major to kill no more than three buffs, the rest of the expedition spent a leisurely day on dry land, stretching their legs and battling a swarm of aggressive mosquitoes. The insects bit through their clothes and left them so covered with red bites that one of Ashley's wranglers, a Shawnee half-breed, arriving to deliver a message to Major Henry, galloped back to the cavallard in a blind panic, declaring in no uncertain terms that a plague had struck the company.

Zach had seen buffalo before; a few small herds hung on east of the Mississippi. But they were nothing compared to this herd, stretching as far as the eye could see, a slow-moving tide of brown beneath a haze of dun-colored dust. They were massive creatures, with beady red eyes and huge humps covered with a tangled mass of black-brown hair. Their presence left a distinctive musky smell that lingered downwind.

The three pairs of hunters moved in on the herd dead-on from the north, downwind and spaced well apart. Shadmore pointed out the herd's "pickets"—a dozen young bulls on the perimeter.

"They'll hurrah back into the herd at first sign of danger," said Shadmore. "Then the herd'll do one of two things. They might stampede. Or the cows and calves'll bunch in the center and the bulls will form a circle around 'em. This hyar is calvin' time, and the buffs git mighty protective."

They walked on across the wind-riffled grass, scattering crickets and hoppers before them. Zach made note of the way Shadmore used the prairie's undulating contours to the best possible advantage. He remarked on the small islands of antelope in the sea of buffalo.

"Them plains goats'll do that," nodded the old hunter. "Winter ain't long over, and the wolves are still hungry. The goats will graze right along with the shaggies. Guess they figure thar's safety in numbers."

Three hundred yards from the herd Shadmore called a halt, on the north side of a gentle swell. Here they could wait unseen until the bison, grazing slowly northward, came within rifle range.

"Reckon I'll let you make the shot," said Shadmore. "I advise you to aim for the head. Buff take a long time to die lessen you hit 'em in the brainpan, heart, or spine, and as they're comin' straight on, the brains are yore best chance. Iffen you don't kill him right off, he'll go to actin' up, and might spook the whole herd. They won't know what's happenin', seein' as how they cain't see nor smell us, so they might jis' go ahead on and stampede. Iffen they do *that*, they'll like as not run in the same dee-rection they been movin' all along."

Zach stared at him. "That's right at us."

Shadmore nodded, spat a stream of yellow-brown tobacco juice, and wiped his mouth and whiskers with a buckskin sleeve. He appeared blithely unconcerned.

"So I heartily recommend you make the first shot count." Shadmore grinned. "Soon as you drop him, we'll git up and mosey on down thar. 'Fore long they'll spot us, and either circle up or drift off in another dee-rection, if we're lucky. Put him down quick, and they won't even notice he's gone."

His Hawken loaded and capped, Zach crawled to the top of the swell and waited, belly-down in the short, curly buffalo grass, his eyes glued to the slow-moving herd. His palms were sweating, his pulse galloping. He had hunted all his life, but never before had so much hung in the balance. He was further pressured by the desire to prove to these frontiersmen that he could get the job done right. In fact, their approval meant more to him than the possibility of being trampled by ten thousand stampeding buffalo.

With the herd a hundred and fifty yards away, Zach picked his target, a young cow in the front rank. He calculated windage, range, and elevation, and wished he had taken more time in the past few weeks to practice with his new rifle. As he was shooting at a downward angle and into the wind, he aimed at a spot at the top of the cow's skull. Filling his lungs with air, he slowly exhaled half of it, then squeezed the trigger.

The Hawken spoke, kicked against his shoulder. Zach squinted anxiously through a drift of stinging white powder-smoke, and a shout of exultation welled in his throat. The cow was down, unmoving. He stifled the shout as another gunshot came from his left, followed in short order by a third from the right. Two more shaggies dropped dead in their tracks. The herd moved on, undisturbed, still grazing. Zach began to breathe again.

Shadmore strolled past him and sauntered down the slope. Jumping to his feet, Zach followed, reloading as he walked. He saw to either side the other teams moving in. Without consultation, they had all employed the same strategy.

Zach expected the herd to circle up, and looked forward to seeing this defensive maneuver performed by thousands of buffalo. Instead, it drifted somewhat west by north, veering away from the six approaching men.

"They ain't zackly got the eyes of an eagle," said Shadmore, pleased by this development. "They kin make us out by now, I reckon, but they don't know what to make of us, as they cain't git a scent. So they're playin' it keerful."

Each team set to butchering its kill on the spot. Zach and his partner rolled the young cow onto its belly, the legs spraddled to brace the carcass in that position. They made the initial cut from boss to tail, pulling the hide back and down on both sides, then chopped the ribs apart on both sides and hacked the spine in two, front and back.

The butchering had scarcely begun in earnest when

the coyotes showed up, appearing as if by magic. In no time at all Zach found himself surrounded by a dozen of them. Some circled, others sat with tongues lolling, and the boldest few darted in to pilfer pieces of bloody flesh.

"Dang-blasted pesky critters!" growled Shadmore crossly, throwing out an arm to scare off a coyote trying to abscond with the liver he had just removed from the carcass.

The hunters took the choicest cuts—the loin and upper portions of the hams, the liver, kidney, tongue, and brains, the meat from the hump. Shoving the carcass over, they peeled the skin off completely, and into this they bundled their selections.

They were finishing up when a member of another team cut loose with a shrill whistle to get everybody's attention, and then pointed north.

Three Indians sat their horses on the rise from which Zach had made his kill.

Their horses were fat with spring graze, still shaggy with the last traces of winter coats. The braves wore only breechclouts. Round hide shields were carried on their backs. Feathers on the shield rims and on their long lances fluttered in the wind. The lower halves of their faces were painted black.

Zach didn't realize he was holding the Hawken up tight against his chest until Shadmore laid a hand on his arm.

"Slacken off, son," he drawled. "Don't go actin' hostile."

"They're peaceful?"

Zach had seen plenty of Indians—Iroquois, Shawnee, Delaware, Cherokee. All of them had been peaceful; if not civilized by the standards of the white man, at least subjugated, their spirit broken, their tribal lands overrun, their traditions corrupted. Those Zach had seen before did not seem to even be of the same race as these three wild, magnificently savage-looking characters.

"Long as thar's six of us and them only three, they'll stay peaceable, I reckon," replied Shadmore, chewing his tobacco.

Zach turned his eyes from the three Indians and took a quick look around.

"I don't see any more," he said.

"If they mean mischief, you won't," said Shadmore. "Until they're liftin' yore hair."

Chapter 8

"They're Black Mouths," said Shadmore. "Arikaree soldiers. Come to scout us out. So just rack that firestick on yore shoulder, Zach Hannah, and commence to grinnin' like a half-wit."

Zach took another look around. The buffalo were still passing slowly to the northwest, less than a hundred yards behind them. The coyotes still tore at the carcass, their snouts red with blood, indifferent to this human confrontation a short distance away. Zach saw no sign of more Indians. But he was acutely aware of the fact that he and the rest of the hunters were cut off from the river by the three Black Mouths.

Shadmore held his right hand neck-high, palm outwards, the first two fingers extended upwards. He raised the hand slowly until it was level with the top of his head. This was the sign for "friend," and Zach was relieved when one of the Black Mouths responded in kind.

Extending his right hand out in front of him, now with palm inward and only the forefinger extended, Shadmore brought the hand slowly back to his face. He pointed at the Indians, and drew the hand several times toward his midsection, and followed this by pointing at the dead buffalo.

"I'm tellin' 'em to come take what's left, with our compliments," he explained.

"We got the best cuts," said Zach.

"Not to their way of thinkin'. They'll have a use for ever' part of the critter, from nose to tail. Now hoss, we're a-goin' to walk on by 'em. Don't go right at 'em, but don't appear to shy away none, either. And keep on a-grinnin'."

They walked unhurriedly up the slow incline and passed within thirty feet of the warriors, Zach carrying the buffalo bundle on his back. His face began to hurt, he was grinning so hard. The Arikarees watched them with the eyes of hawks, and the other hunters, as well, who were moving with all due circumspection toward the river.

As they started down the north side of the swell, Zach resisted the urge to look back, waiting until Shadmore did so, a hundred or so paces further on.

The Indians had vanished.

"Reckon they're down thar lappin' up buffalo blood with them other pesky critters," said Shadmore. "They'll drink the bile, too, and git as drunk as if it were corn likker." He looked off toward the river, bushy brows knit. "We'd best make tracks and warn the others."

"Just how peaceable are these Arikarees?" asked Zach, as the other hunters quartered through the tall grass to join them.

"Oh, tol'able, son. Tol'able. They ain't apt to pick a fight with us, like the Blackfeet would. It's our horses I'm afeared fer. We'll need mounts when we git to beaver country or we won't do much good. And next to the Crows, the Rees are the goldurndest horse thieves yule ever see."

Events proved Shadmore a sage prophet, for the following day the Arikarees stole by clever ruse every last horse belonging to the Rocky Mountain Fur Company.

For weeks the cavallard had traveled overland, staying close to the river. Colonel William Ashley was in charge of the horse herd. The forty-year-old Ashley was a Virginian come west, like so many others, to seek fame and fortune. Flamboyant, intelligent, and sociable, he was soon both rich and famous. Two years earlier, in 1820, he had become Missouri's first lieutenant-governor. He was also a general in the state militia, and Andrew Henry's partner in the Washington County lead mine.

All this was not enough to satisfy Ashley's ambitions, and so the Rocky Mountain Fur Company had been conceived. This was his first trip to the far frontier. He took his responsibilities seriously, and did his job passing well. The Company had spared no expense in purchasing the finest horseflesh available, and everyone knew the cavallard was a temptation the Indians could not resist forever. There was nothing more important to a Plains Indian than his horse; his very survival depended on a good mount. Ashley knew the success of the expedition depended on the horse herd, and he intended to keep it out of the hands of the Indians.

He took every precaution, posting scouts ahead, behind, and on the flanks while the cavallard was on the move. He nighted as close to the river as possible, so that those on the keelboat could lend their aid should the darkness breed trouble. Ashley was no fool; still, the Arikarees managed to fool him.

The day after the buffalo hunt, with the expedition again on the move, the Black Mouths reappeared. This time, there were five of them. The men on the keelboat saw them first, on a ridge beyond the horse herd. An alarm was raised, but the Rees approached in a peaceful manner, holding their ponies to a walk and shouting Arikaree pleasantries. Zach relaxed. He figured, as did his colleagues, that when Indians meant to make trouble they didn't make noise.

The horse guard fired their guns into the air. It was not proper plains etiquette to greet an Indian friend with a loaded weapon in hand. The Indian was apt to take this as evidence that he was not trusted. Ashley was well aware of this, and of how an Indian was quick to take offense at the most inconsequent slight. He was taking a chance, and knew it, but he didn't believe the five Rees would come calling in broad daylight if their intention was to steal the herd.

He was wrong.

The five warriors shook hands all around. They laughed and made friendly sign talk, and rode along with the cavallard for a while, passing the time of day and waiting for the proper moment to make their move. They knew precisely when that moment had arrived, as they were well acquainted with this stretch of the Big Muddy, where the channel suddenly shifted close to the opposite bank. This took the men on the crowded keelboat out of rifle range.

With perfect timing, a horde of Rees appeared as though out of thin air and descended on the herd. The horse guard didn't have time to reload their rifles. The five warriors among them knocked them out of their saddles. The herd, already made restless by the proximity of the first five Indians, broke and ran. The Rees followed, screaming like banshees and hazing the horses with blankets and buffalo robes.

Yelling in outrage, some of the hunters on the keelboat tried to reach them with their rifles, but their shots fell short. Before the horse guard could pick themselves up out of the dirt and load their own weapons, the Rees were long gone, with every last company mount in their possession.

The loss of the cavallard almost finished the Rocky Mountain Fur Company. Without horses, they could not adequately cover the Three Forks beaver country. Trappers afoot were sitting ducks for Blackfoot raiding parties. And they needed horses to carry traps and packs of plews. In fact, it was virtually impossible even to get to the Three Forks without the herd, as horses were required to transport the men and all their provisions around the Great Falls of the Missouri.

The discouraged expedition plodded on as far as the mouth of the Yellowstone River. Here Major Henry made another speech. It was short and sweet. They would build a fort and winter here. Ashley would return to St. Louis with most of the French-Canadians in order to purchase new supplies, another horse herd, and another keelboat. Next spring they would move on to beaver country.

This was unwelcome news for Zach. He didn't cotton to the idea of waiting almost an entire year to get to the mountains. They called to him, stronger than ever. Somehow he knew he wouldn't find what he was looking for—whatever that was—until he reached them.

A thousand times a day he gazed long and hard at the western horizon, longing to see the mountains, knowing full well he would see only the endless sweep of the plains. While he understood that Major Henry had made the best decision for the good of the Company, he felt it was not right for him.

Still, he had signed on to accompany the Major to beaver country, and had as much as given his word that he would not let Henry down. He wanted to strike out on his own so bad he could taste it. A loner by nature, he felt the crowd of trappers beginning to wear on him. But his sense of honor wouldn't let him go. To give in to the urge to yonder would be the equivalent of desertion.

Then he met the Indian girl named Morning Sky, and Zach Hannah's life was changed forever.

Chapter 9

The fort was built on high ground overlooking the confluence of the Yellowstone and the Missouri. Plenty of good timber grew in the ravines and river bottoms. With no horses for hauling, the cut and trimmed logs had been dragged up to the site by hand.

Two rows of cabins were put up, parallel to and facing one another. Each cabin had a stone chimney, earthen floor, and flat pole roof covered with a thick layer of sod. The other two sides of the fort were closed with upright posts side by side, from corner to corner of the cabin rows. This made a secure stockade which, Shadmore wryly remarked, was a fine place to keep all the horses they didn't have.

Dugout canoes were made, and in short order Ashley and his party were embarked on their descent of the Big Muddy. Those remaining behind were divided into "messes." Each mess numbered six men and occupied one cabin. Zach's mess included Devlin, Shadmore, and a young man Zach's age named Jim Bridger, as well as two boatmen. The latter pair, while landlocked, served as campkeepers while the other four hunted and trapped. For the past five years, Bridger had apprenticed in a St. Louis blacksmith shop; now he was placed in charge of the fort's smitty—an anvil, bellows, and grindstone had been brought up the river.

Game was plentiful: buffalo, antelope, deer, rabbits, a variety of fowl. On the high plains the winters were long, and Major Henry wanted to lay in a good supply of meat. That which they didn't immediately eat was distributed equally among the messes. Henry saw to it scrupulously that everyone got a fair share.

Devlin privately questioned this arrangement. There was, he argued, so much game that every man could do well enough for himself, and enjoy the choicest cuts of his own kills.

Shadmore begged to differ. "The Major knows what he's doin', I reckon. We're all in this hyar pot together, Coyote. It's all fer one and one fer all. That's how the Injuns try to do her, though they've sometimes fallen short of the mark in that regard. Thar's been blood shed over prime cuts. Whole tribes been split up over who gits a dang buffalo tongue."

The old leatherstocking went on to tell of how the tribe known as the Crows, or Absaroka, had once been part of the Gros Ventres, the Big Bellies, whose country lay west of the Wind River Range. A dispute concerning the rights to the first stomach of a fresh-killed buffalo had led to hard feelings and, ultimately, a falling-out among the bands, with the result being that the band now known as the Absaroka had moved east into the region drained by the Powder, Tongue, and Yellowstone Rivers, setting themselves up as an independent tribe. Zach envied Shadmore his wealth of frontier knowledge, and let pass no opportunity to question the gray-bearded mountain man about the land and the Indians who roamed across it.

By the Major's decree, hunters ventured from the fort only in pairs, and Zach spent a lot of time hunting with Shadmore. Shadmore seemed to derive satisfaction from taking Zach under his wing and educating him in the ways of the wilderness.

These late-summer weeks Zach considered well-spent. Though he wanted most of all to reach the mountains, he made the best of the situation, and learned a great deal that would later stand him in good stead.

Shadmore was pleased by Zach's progress. Once told, Zach did not forget his lessons. He was like a well-caulked barrel into which Shadmore poured the water of his lore; the old trapper did not spill a drop, nor did Zach leak a single one.

Still, though he kept busy, Zach longed for the mountains, and every idle moment found him gazing west. He could not see them but he could hear their call, from just out of sight beyond the curve of the earth. He did not miss his Copper Creek birthplace, but he missed the high country—the *pays en haut,* as the French-Canadians called it—and that was strange, he thought, as he had not yet ever been there. The mountains haunted him, like a dream after awakening, almost but not quite remembered.

His thoughts kept drifting back to the three Black Mouth warriors he had seen during that first buffalo hunt. They belonged to this untamed land in the way he wanted to belong—they were as much a part of this country as the immense herds of bison, and the swarms of passenger pigeons that could block out the sun for an hour when winging overhead, so great was their number. The Indians were as one with the sky and the earth and the constant wind scented by wildflowers that were swatches of pastel color in the sun-browned prairie grass. They *belonged,* as the ruffian wolf pack fleetingly seen lurking in the rocky ravines belonged. Zach wanted to belong that way, wanted it so badly he ached from the wanting.

The other hunters, Shadmore among them, taught Zach the Indian sign language. Zach applied himself with a diligence that a certain Tennessee schoolmarm would have thought impossible.

Being at its core eminently logical and largely idiomatic, the sign language was not difficult to grasp. It was a skeleton language honed down to convey elemental ideas with the utmost economy. There were no articles or adjectives to deal with—nouns and verbs by themselves carried the essence of the idea.

Zach was amazed at how simple and effective it was. Most of the signs were made with the right hand. To pass the hand outward from the chin meant to "speak" or "talk"; to cup the hand behind the ear meant to "listen." When the first and second fingers of the right hand were pointed out from the eyes, it meant to "see" or "look." Drawing the hand, partly closed, down past the mouth was to say "eat" or "food." Raising the cupped hand to the mouth was "drink."

It was a matter of equating word to concept. To an Indian, "good" was the same as "level with the heart," and so the sign for "good" was swinging the right hand, flat and palm-down, out in a semicircle from the heart. "Bad" was the same as "thrown away," and the sign was to begin with the fist held close to the chest and then thrust down and away, opening the hand while doing so. Man, "the upright one," was signed by holding the right index finger close to the face and pointing upwards. Passing curled fingers down over the hair signified "woman," or "she who combs her hair."

There were some variations among the tribes, but the basic vocabulary Zach learned in the course of that short high-plains summer enabled him to understand and be understood when he began to associate with the Indians.

Before the summer was over, there were plenty of Indians to associate with. News of a fort full of "hair-face'' hunters spread quick as a grass fire through the tribes, and their scouts came to investigate.

Out hunting a few miles west of the fort, Zach and Shadmore came upon the tracks of unshod ponies, and followed them to a ravine where wild rose and resin-weed sweetened the cool shade made by a point of cottonwood and willow. The horse sign was a day old. Zach counted four ponies. Willow thrush made their *whee-uuh* whistle from the hazel clumps, while orioles and towhees were fleeting flashes of color in the brush; their behavior inclined Zach to believe the Indians were long gone. Sniffing the air like a bloodhound seeking fresh spoor, Shadmore arrived at the same conclusion.

"Yule git so's you kin smell out the rascals," he told Zach. "Reckon they nighted down in that point, moved out at can-see. We'd best go in and have a look. But keep yore eyes peeled. Never kin tell about Injuns. They're sneaky as all git-out, and they've fooled me a time or three, I'll confess.''

They proceeded with all due caution, down into the trees and brush. No Indians were found—only the ashes of a recent fire, and a few moccasin prints in patches of bare earth. Shadmore hunkered down to give these some serious scrutiny.

"Huntin' party?" wondered Zach aloud.

Shadmore shook his head. "Scouts. Be more of 'em were they out a-huntin', and wimmin besides, to do the cuttin' and skinnin' on the spot. Amongst Injuns, wimmin do all the hard work, and leave the fightin' and huntin' and like sport to the men. I reckon if In-juns were farmers they'd have their squaws pushing the middle-busters. Warn't no wimmin hyar. They were all four Crow bucks.''

"How can you be sure they're Crow?"

"Taint none betern'n Crows fur workin' with hides.

Their moccasins are so well-made the print's 'most allus smooth, with no crooked seams and bulges and such not. And Crow moccasins are tanned top to bottom, and sewn at the heel. Now, Blackfoot sewin' will be at the toe, Sioux footwear ain't got tanned soles atall. With Cheyenne and Arapaho, the inside edge is straight and the point turns inwards.''

Zach was impressed by Shadmore's virtuoso sign-reading, and he filed this new information away for future use. He was a little dismayed, as well, for it struck him that there was so much to learn—more, it seemed, than one could possibly induct in a single lifetime. Shadmore sensed the young man's consternation.

''Out hyar, a man's a gone beaver iffen he don't larn such tricks. Yule larn 'em, Zach, don't you fret. You got the makin's.''

They made haste back to the fort and reported their discovery.

Two days later, the sun rose to betray the presence of two Indians, sitting their horses on a distant rise, just visible from the fort as black specks on the eastern rim, in silhouette against the flaming stroke of daybreak. Major Henry employed a brass spyglass to look them over. At length he announced that the two were Crows, and both were chewing on green sprigs. This was their way of indicating that their intentions were peaceful. The Major walked out to parley, accompanied by Jim Beckwourth. The two Crow warriors rode forward, and the palaver was conducted a few hundred yards from the fort.

The Crows—the Absaroka or Sparrowhawk people; the *gens de corbeaux* to the French—had always been friendly enough towards whites, and Major Henry returned with news that the summer camp of the Indians was a two-day ride downriver. The scouts had brought an invite, and Henry intended to pay a call on the camp and try to trade for horses.

All manner of trade goods had been brought up from St. Louis, and while some rested at the bottom of the Big Muddy, there was still plenty left with which to barter: blue and red cloth in bolts, iron kettles and frying pans, blankets, vermilion, knives and hatchets, brass buttons and finger rings, even a little powder and lead and some flints. No liquor, though, the consensus being that to mix whiskey and Indians, be they friendly or not, was a fool's play.

The problem lay in transporting these goods to the camp, as the Rocky Mountain Fur Company could not claim title to a solitary horse. The Crows provided the solution to this. A week later a larger party arrived at the fort, twenty in all, and half of them women. The latter rode horses fixed with travois, upon which the trade goods would be loaded.

One of the women caught Zach's eye. She was young and willowy, her complexion much lighter than those of the other women, and her features were finely sculptured, almost delicate, in marked contrast to the broad, coarse facial casts of her counterparts. Her hair was the black of a raven's wing, common to the Indian—so black that it gave off indigo highlights when touched by bright sunlight. Her eyes gave her away: They were the deep, smoky blue of violets.

"She's got white blood in her," judged Shadmore. "Taint unheard of amongst the tribes. Thar's been a heap of minglin' and mixin' and carryin' on ever since Lewis and Clark came through hyar twenty year back."

Zach was speechless, and he couldn't help but stare. She felt his eyes, and as she rode by looked his way with a shy smile. Zach's heart felt like it was going to gallop right out through his rib cage.

Shadmore squinted curiously at Zach's face and chuckled. "Wagh! You look downright lovesick, son. She's prime fixin's, I s'pose, iffen you like your wimmin all thin and bony-like. Like they say, beauty is in the eye of the beholder."

In Zach's mind, she had to be God's most perfect creation, and as he gazed at her, overwhelmed by potent feelings he'd never felt before, he no longer felt the pull of the high country.

Chapter 10

Regardless of how amiably the Crows might behave, Major Henry deemed it wiser to keep them out of the fort.

"You hitch your wagon to these wild'uns," said Jim Beckwourth, voicing his approval of the Major's caution, "you'll wind up in a ditch sooner or later."

The trade goods were brought outside the fort. Then the Crow women took over, placing the merchandise on the travois and lashing it down snugly with ropes of braided rawhide. The warriors supervised, sitting tall and proud on their painted ponies. The woodsmen stood apart, leaning on their rifles, watching the work—and keeping a wary eye on the warriors.

It did not seem right to Zach that all these able-bodied men—and himself, most of all—should look idly on while members of the gentler sex toiled, but he gathered that to partake in "squaw work" would be to expose a man to ridicule at the hands of the Crow braves. Indian males did much posturing, and put great store in image, and it behooved any white man who wished to deal with them to do likewise.

Zach could not take his eyes off the pale-skinned woman. Where the other squaws had coarse, copper skin, hers was the color of honey. She wore a doeskin dress. It was short, in the Crow fashion, ending above the knee, and the sight of such strong and shapely female limbs bewitched and embarrassed him. Her moccasins were decorated with dyed quills and adorned with tiny tin bells, so that with each step she made sweet jingling music.

"I'druther have a squaw with more meat on her," said Shadmore. "Strong as a mule and big as an ox. I had me a Flathead squaw oncet, a few winters back. Broke my leg—I larnt I warn't no bighorn sheep that can fall off a danged mountain, land on his head, and jist git up and go on about his business. Anyroad, this hyar squaw of mine carried me purt near ten mile on her back. I don't reckon that little punkin yonder could even pick you up, boy."

"What happened to her?" asked Zach.

"Huh? My squaw, you mean? Oh, she's gone under."

"I'm sorry."

"Why? You didn't have nothin' to do with it. It was a danged grizzly did for her."

Devlin joined them. "*There's* a good-looking blanket-warmer," he commented.

Zach realized Devlin was referring to the same young woman who had so beguiled him. He felt a sharp pang of jealousy. Devlin was watching her the way a coyote watches a field mouse just before attacking.

"What's wrong?" asked Devlin, becoming aware of Zach's glare. He correctly interpreted Zach's expression, threw back his head and laughed.

"It's one for all and all for one, remember, Zach? Besides, we're blood brothers." Devlin clapped him on the back, amused by Zach's consternation, and taking wicked delight in trying to nettle him. "Blood brothers are supposed to share."

Zach was too tongue-tied to respond. He didn't like to be laughed at; he felt his ears burning.

"I hear Crow women are free and easy with their favors," said Devlin, turning to Shadmore.

The old leatherstocking chewed his quid a moment, then spat a stream of yellow-brown juice and wiped his mouth and beard with a buckskin sleeve.

"Heard it said. In some tribes, a squaw'll git herself branded with a burnin' stick, or git her nose cut off, iffen she lays with a man that ain't her husband. Taint so with the Absaroka. A buck might trade off one of his wimmin fer a good blanket."

"*One* of his women?" echoed Zach.

"Yep. Most bucks got more'n one squaw. Thar's more wimmin than men among the Crow. Reckon that's 'cause the Crows are almost allus at war. If it ain't the Sioux it's the Cheyenne and their Arapaho cousins. And the Crows'll fight the Blackfeet any day of the week and twice on Sunday. The Crows are good fighters, brave as all git-out, but they kin git killed dead same as anybody, and with all the fightin' they been doin' fer all these years, well . . . ever' year thar's less men to go around. They's got to take more'n one squaw."

"Wonder could I get her for a blanket?" murmured Devlin.

Zach's hands closed into white-knuckled fists. Devlin's talk infuriated him. "Don't seem right," he said, strangle-voiced. "A person ought not to be traded like a . . . like a piece of goods. They ought to have a say in such things."

Shadmore nodded. "Mebbe. Life ain't fair but fer a chosen few." He gave Devlin's face a moment's grave study. "Coyote, you ought to keep yore blanket. Ask me, a woman in this hyar fort come winter is like a powder keg wantin' a match. Ain't nothing like wimmin to make trouble. Worse'n snake-head likker for gittin' men to actin' up crazier'n a horse with a bellyful of locoweed. 'Sides, I reckon that gal thar won't go cheap, iffen she goes at all. See, she's some different from the ordinary squaw. And jist like the Injuns put a lot of stock in the white buffalo, I'd bet a pale-skinned gal fer a squaw makes her husband feel like he's big medicine.''

''That must be him,'' said Devlin, his voice cast low.

One of the warriors maneuvered his high-stepping pony alongside the travois being loaded by the woman with the violet eyes. He pointed at the goods, spoke harshly, with sharp authority. Apparently he did not care for the way the young woman had packed the travois.

Zach took an immediate dislike to the warrior—a dislike so violent he tasted bile. There was no reason for the warrior's rudeness. She was doing the best she could, and a fine job, as anyone could tell. Zach got the impression the warrior was bullying her just for the fun of it.

The young woman took this scolding with a submissive nod and redoubled her efforts to pack the travois to the liking of her lord and master. Zach could scarcely refrain from jumping in to help her, and appearances be damned.

''Yep,'' said Shadmore. ''Looks like he thinks purty high of hisself. All decked out in his Sunday best. Likes to think he throws a long shadow. Ain't yet earned an eagle feather, though. Means he ain't took enough scalps yet. So he's got somethin' to prove.''

Zach gave the warrior a keen once-over. He wore a bone breastplate on his bare chest, a red breechclout, and leggins with coarse fringe down the outer seams. His side hair was braided, and the forelock was made to stand upright, stiffened with a dressing of clay. A roach of chestnut horsehair had been woven into his own hair in back, and was long enough to brush his mount's croup.

Jagged vermilion thunderbolts adorned his face and upper arms. The same marking was painted on his horse, a high-spirited buckskin, at the shoulder and running from haunch to hamstring. The red thunderbolt seemed to be a personal symbol; Zach noticed that the markings of the other warriors were all different: a bear paw, arrows, a handprint, a crescent moon, yellow rings, three blue horizontal bars.

In the way of weapons, the warrior carried a bow in an otter-skin case and a quiver of arrows on his back. Both quiver and bow case were nicely ornamented with beadwork. Dangling by a rawhide thong from his left wrist was a war club. On his right arm was a round shield. Zach saw that his colleagues were similarly armed; only a few carried rifles, and these were old smoothbores.

Major Henry arrived. "Shadmore, come with me, please." His gaze flickered over Devlin, then fastened on Zach. "You as well, Hannah."

They followed the Major into the fort, away from the prying eyes of the Crows. Seven other buckskin-clad men stood in a group. Among them were Beckwourth, Bridger, and Sublette.

"You men will accompany me to the Crow camp," announced Henry. "I want to have a few words with you before we strike out, and I don't want our Crow friend to think we're plotting some mischief.

"Most of you already know this, but it bears repeating: The Crows are the biggest liars and the worst thieves west of the Father of Waters. Stealing is no sin, in their book. In fact they've honed it down to an art, and think of it as great sport. If they can, they'll make off with all our trade goods before we get to our destination. And if we manage to acquire horses, they'll do their level best to steal them right back. Possession is all ten points of the law with this crew.

"So keep on your toes. Sleep with one eye open. Each of you will be responsible for watching over the goods on one travois. If they try something, don't shoot one of the bucks unless you have to in self-defense. Drop the horse and claim it was an accident."

"Might've been better had we gone down the Yellowstone in bullboats," remarked Beckwourth.

"Perhaps. But they made the offer, and I couldn't refuse. Didn't want them to think I didn't trust them, even though I don't. It will be hard enough to get them to part with some of their ponies."

Beckwourth and several of the others nodded. Buying horses from an Indian was about as easy as pulling teeth, and they didn't give much for their chances. A warrior could not have enough good horses. They were as essential as the air he breathed. He needed them to go into battle and defeat his enemies—a warrior on foot would not count many coups. He needed them for hunting, so that he could provide for his family. He made presents of horses, sometimes bought his women with them. His wealth and standing in the tribe was measured by the quantity and quality of his personal herd. Without good horses, a warrior was not a warrior. He was a nobody. If he traded a good horse for a trinket, he was likely to face ridicule and resentment at the hands of his peers.

The Major recommended that they carry as much powder and lead as they could without being conspicuous about it. Zach repaired to his cabin and filled his shot pouch with Galena "lead pills," his powder horn with glazed Dupont powder, and made certain he had plenty of percussion caps.

He was grateful to the Major for picking him to go

along. Wherever the woman with violet eyes was, he wanted to be. Staying behind would have been unbearable.

Devlin met him at the door of the cabin, blocking his exit.

"Let me go in your place, Zach."

"I can't do that."

"You mean you won't."

"The Major didn't ask for volunteers, Sean. He picked those he wanted to go. He passed you over."

He regretted the words as soon as they'd passed his lips. But Devlin was aggravating him, and he was in a hurry to get back outside; there was only one travois he was interested in guarding, and he wanted to get out there and stake his claim before someone beat him to it.

Devlin's demeanor was dark and resentful.

"I'll give you this," he said, brandishing his money pouch.

"Tyree's stolen money?" Zach was incredulous. "You should know me better than that. Besides, I don't have a say in this. The Major chose me."

Devlin's moods were mercurial. Suddenly the scowling darkness was swept away by a sunny grin.

"You're right, Zach. I'm just hankerin' to get away from this dreary old fort. Need a little excitement."

Zach knew exactly what Devlin hankered after—or rather, *who*.

"No hard feelins?" asked Devlin.

"No."

"Keep your powder dry and your hair on." He gave a sly wink. "And if you get the chance, give her a kiss for me."

Zach grimaced and brushed by.

Chapter 11

They traveled south by west, in no particular order, other than the constant of Major Henry in the van, accompanying the leader of the Crow party, the foremost warrior in the group, whose name was Rides A Dark Horse. The others trailed along behind, each hunter sticking close to the travois that was his looksee.

The squaws led the packhorses, which were weighed down to the limit with the trade-laden travois. Only the ten warriors were mounted. It was their responsibility to scout the countryside. This they did by riding at breakneck speed ahead and to both sides of the caravan, checking every ravine and point of trees for a hidden enemy, climbing every rise to make certain that danger did not lurk in ambush on the opposite side.

Zach got his wish; in trapper parlance, he "floated his stick" with the young squaw who so beguiled him, and her husband, he of the red thunderbolts. The latter haughtily informed him, with sign, that his handle was Tall Wolf. The warrior went on to state, in no uncertain terms, that he was regarded far and wide as a fearless fighter, as well as a peerless marksman with bow and arrow. Zach concluded that Indians were not burdened with anything even remotely resembling false modesty. Tall Wolf sang his own praises as a matter of course. Zach could only respond by tapping himself on his chest and saying his name. Tall Wolf waited a moment, expectantly, and when it became obvious that Zach had no exploits about which to brag, he rode away with a look of absolute disdain on his face.

Every warrior took a turn at reconnaissance, and occasionally Tall Wolf would range far afield. Zach got his courage up enough to seize one such opportunity and venture closer to the woman with the violet eyes. He signed, asking for her name, relieved that he did not have to speak. He doubted he could have pushed a single coherent word past the lump in his throat.

He put the query by holding his right hand palm-outwards, at shoulder height, with fingers extended upwards, and then turning the hand at the wrist several times. This was followed by pointing at her, and finally by placing the thumb and forefinger together, flicking the forefinger out straight. These signs, translated literally, were "What You Called."

Her name was Morning Sky. Zach had some trouble with the first word, as "morning" was conveyed by combining the signs for "day" and "sunrise." Seeing his bewilderment, she patiently repeated the hand movements several times, until finally he grasped the true meaning. Then she smiled, and her smile was so replete with sweetness and light that it knocked the wind out of Zach. Blushing, he dropped back to walk alongside the travois, where he remained for most of the day.

He did his best to keep his gaze sweeping across the country, in that alert and unceasing watchfulness that is second nature to the hunter, but time and again he caught himself staring distractedly at Morning Sky, especially on those occasions when Tall Wolf was off scouting.

More than once she caught him at it, looking over

her shoulder unexpectedly. Each time, Zach panicked and averted his eyes. Never quickly enough, he realized, feeling foolish. A dozen times he resolved to meet her gaze next time, to look her square in the eye like a man. And the next time, helplessly unable to keep the commitment, he would look away.

The country through which they passed was rolling prairie, open but for the trees and thickets embraced by hollows and draws. The land dipped and swelled like a strongly surging sea of russet and amber, splashed with color by the evergreen sagebrush and late-blooming wildflowers: yellow rabbit brush, scarlet paintbrush, purple penstemon.

To one mountain-born it might have seemed a barren land, but in fact it was a land of plenty. Antelope grazed on the hardy sagebrush, where thousands of horned larks nested. The larks swarmed thick as locusts. They flew low to the ground, in a darting motion, folding their wings tight against their bodies after each stroke, looking like they had only half learned how to fly. Far more graceful were the golden eagles and sparrow hawks soaring on the wind, their sharp eyes ceaselessly scanning the ground for prey. Coyotes trailed the caravan at a wary distance, hopeful that its passage might flush a ground squirrel or gopher from cover.

The day was clear and warm, but with the evening came a coolness, a hint of imminent winter, and a panoply of mare's-tail clouds stroked with the majestic brush of sunset. Normally attentive to Nature's grace, Zach paid only cursory notice to this pretty spectacle. Compared to Morning Sky, all other beauty had paled to insignificance.

He could not wholly understand what had happened to him, or how it could have happened so quickly and utterly. He supposed it had to be true love, the kind that makes poets wax eloquent, the kind that happens in a heartbeat. He imagined it must have been just this way for his father and mother, when first they'd met, a force as relentless and irresistible as the banshee wind of a mountain storm.

His attraction to Morning Sky was to more than her physical beauty, was much more than mere passion. It was as though he had found a part of himself that he hadn't realized, until now, had been missing. She touched instincts that before had lain fallow, down deep inside him. He looked out upon the world through different eyes, because he was a different person who saw all things, big and small, in a new way: from the perspective of how all those things related to and revolved around her.

And even while he was happier than he could ever remember being, a shadow of excruciating dread hung over him. There was no escaping the fact that Morning Sky was another man's wife. And while love was evidently not a necessary element in an Indian marriage, Zach saw no evidence to indicate that she was dissatisfied with the present arrangement. Perhaps she actually did love Tall Wolf, had given her heart to him, though how any woman could love a man so overbearing and arrogant escaped Zach's ken.

All Zach had by way of encouragement were a couple of shy smiles, a handful of sidelong looks—thin ice indeed for a man to walk on! He knew it was foolhardy to assume she felt the same way about him that he did about her. It seemed inevitable that they would part company. Zach could not even bear to contemplate the grim specter of that moment.

They traveled thirty miles that day, and made camp near a creek dancing down a fold in the prairie—one did not build his night fires on high ground, for all the world to see. Supper had been bagged during the day; a man could kill enough game during a single day's stroll through this country to feed himself for an entire month. The Crow warriors had killed a number of rabbits and sage hens, shooting the latter on the wing, showing off their fine bowmanship for the benefit of their white companions. Major Henry responded by dropping an antelope at a third of a mile with one shot, breaking the animal's neck with one ounce of Galena lead. This feat mightily impressed the Crows, as the Major had intended.

"Just the Major's way of remindin' these heathens that their bows and arrows and such ain't no match fer our long rifles." opined Beckwourth, as the hunters hunkered around their campfire, roasting choice cuts of antelope on sticks.

"They don't know what to make of our rifles," added Sublette. "They won't generally take nothin' but old snaphaunce smoothbores in trade."

"Why's that?" asked Bridger.

" 'Cause the bullet whines when it comes out of a rifled barrel," replied Sublette. "Any kind of funny noise like that, an Injun'll figure it's a spirit of some kind, and they're mighty bashful when it comes to associatin' with spirits."

Shadmore chuckled. "The Major's spirit-gun sure got their eyes to poppin'. Wagh!"

The squaws unhitched the travois from their horses, which were hobbled and let loose to graze. The warriors kept their own ponies close at hand. The Major organized an all-night guard for the ten travois, two-hour shifts with two men on each shift. He assured Rides A Dark Horse that this was not to be taken as evidence that the hunters did not trust their Crow friends. Everyone knew that the Blackfeet sometimes ventured south this time of year, solely for the purpose of taking Crow scalps. Rides A Dark Horse made some uncomplimentary comments concerning the arch-enemies of his people, and seemed to accept Henry's explanation.

Of course, it *was* the Crows and their time-honored tradition of thievery that the Major was guarding against. He had no reason to believe there was a hostile Blackfoot within a hundred miles.

He was wrong.

Word of the white men setting up shop at the mouth of the Yellowstone had spread through Blackfoot country to the north, and that very afternoon a war party of more than sixty warriors had attacked the fort. Though outnumbered two-to-one, the hunters had laid down such a deadly accurate fire that the Blackfeet soon retired, realizing that the cost of taking the stronghold would be too high.

Discovering the trail of the caravan, and thinking it might be easier pickings, they had struck out in hot pursuit. That night they paused only a few scant miles from the camp of the caravan. They built no fires, hoping to conceal their presence and employ the element of surprise. They eagerly awaited the sunrise, and the spilling of the blood of their enemies.

Chapter 12

The camp was split into two parts, with the Crows around their fire and the hunters around theirs. Not that there wasn't some mingling; by ones and twos the warriors drifted in and out of the hunters' section of the camp. Some just roamed, solemn and silent, their keen eyes roving covetously over every possession of the white men. Others sought boldly after gifts. Zach marveled that men so proud could beg so unabashedly. They asked for whiskey, tobacco, gunpowder, lead, knives—in short, for virtually everything the hunters owned.

Their persistence was aggravating, but the hunters ignored them. Or so it seemed, until a brave was foolish enough to actually touch one of the whites' "possibles."

One such incident involved a hunter named Godin—a moody, taciturn, French-Indian breed with the disposition of a straight razor. Godin had set aside a knife he'd been sharpening on a whetstone, and turned his attention to an antelope hamsteak suspended on a sharp stick over the fire and dripping sizzling fat into the flames. A visiting Crow picked up the knife, on the pretext of admiring the weapon, holding the blade close to his face and turning it this way and that. In fact he was intending to pilfer the knife, as soon as he was certain Godin was sufficiently distracted.

The next instant found the warrior knocked sprawling a good ten feet. Humiliated, he pounced upright, temper flaring. Godin retrieved his fallen knife and squared off, grinning like a starved wolf.

Major Henry interceded, turning Godin away from his recreation. The Crow was restrained by some of his fellow warriors, who made light of the clash. This was a well-advised discretion, as every hunter had coolly laid hand to rifle. The Major made the shamed Crow a gift of some tobacco. The warrior accepted the peace offering with face-saving disdain. Godin looked disappointed as he put away his blade. The altercation demonstrated to Zach that the house of good relations between Crows and whites was built on a shaky foundation.

Zach and Sublette took the first watch. While on his post among the travois, Zach observed the activities of the Crows on their side of the camp. He noticed it was the women who maintained the fire, cleaned and cooked the food, and tended the horses, while the men lolled around the fire and talked.

He paid particular attention to Morning Sky until, toward the end of his shift, as the Crow fire subsided into a bed of glowing orange embers, the men stretched out to sleep. As Morning Sky lay down beside Tall Wolf, Zach turned quickly away, something inside him twisting.

His guard duty done, he retired to his blanket. Sleep eluded him. Try as he might, he couldn't stop imagining what it would be like to have Morning Sky lying close beside *him*. These thoughts turned the night several shades colder. Restless, he twisted and turned, until Shadmore, bedded down nearby, came up on one elbow with a grunting sigh.

"I swear, Zach, you're squirmin' like a feller staked out over an ant bed."

"Sorry."

"Hurts, don't it?"

"What?"

"Feels like somebody done kicked you in the gut. It's enough to make a man grind his teeth down to the nub. It ails you sumpin' fierce, and the fever don't never break. Reckon it's woman-time for you. Happens to the best of us. Taint nary a thing you kin do but grin and bear it."

Zach didn't know what to say. Shadmore's commiseration didn't help at all. Knowing he wasn't the only one to suffer such torment didn't make him any less miserable.

The old leatherstocking lay back down with a long, rumbling sigh. Afraid that he was robbing the other hunters—light sleepers, all—of their rest, Zach forced himself to lie still, mortified by his own inconsiderateness. Eventually he slept, though fitfully, so that he woke exhausted, to face the dawning of a day that turned out to be one of the most important of his life.

Early the next morning, as they were about to break camp, Zach thought he detected a faint drumroll of distant thunder. In reflex, he checked the sky. Nary a cloud was in sight. The sun had not yet peeked over the eastern rim of the prairie. The sky was a delicate shade of blue, harboring the most stubborn stars. The air was cool and crisp, sweet in the lungs. The land was strangely hushed.

While their warriors idled about, most of the squaws were bringing in the horses set out to graze the night before. Morning Sky was among them. The hunters were having their coffee. A small fire had been built to heat a kettle of the strong, fragrant brew. As a rule, these were men who could miss many meals in a row without batting an eye, but they were loath to start a single day without coffee.

Vaguely troubled by the faint sound, Zach looked around at the others. Everyone seemed suddenly to freeze in place, in an attitude of keen listening. With the camp down in a hollow, they could not see very far. Rides A Dark Horse barked an order to one of the warriors, who leaped upon his horse, wheeled the pony about, and galloped for the nearest high ground. Zach watched him go, wondering why he felt as though disaster were about to strike. Then he noticed Shadmore was looking to his rifle, checking cap and load.

"What is it?" asked Zach. "Buffalo?"

Shadmore grunted. "Wouldn't bet my topknot on it."

A shout rose up, followed by a storm of frenzied action. Startled, Zach looked to the rise where the lookout had gone. The warrior was riding his pony round and round in a big circle, waving a war club overhead, and uttering a sound resembling the scream of a panther—a sound that raised the hair at the nape of Zach's neck.

"Blackfeet!" barked Shadmore. "That Crow's makin' a big circle—means thar's lots of the devils, comin' on hard. Git ready, Zach. We're fixing to have us a fracas."

An angry cry burst from several of the Crows, and once more Zach looked to the rise, in time to see the scout topple off his horse, riddled with arrows.

Screaming like banshees, the Blackfeet surged into sight over the rim, sweeping down into the hollow toward the camp.

"Find cover!" yelled Shadmore, and jumped behind the most convenient travois.

The sky was suddenly dark with arrows in flight. A half-dozen speared the ground all around Zach. He leaped after Shadmore. His ears were filled with piercing war cries, the cracking detonation of rifles. The earth trembled beneath the pounding of hard-run horses.

A perfect calm abruptly possessed Zach. His pulse raced, his mouth was dry as dust, but he had a remarkable clarity of vision, and his hands were rock-steady as he settled in behind the trade-laden travois and brought the Hawken to shoulder. He'd never before been in a shooting scrape like this, and had sometimes wondered how he would perform when it happened. Now, a cool and calculating instinct kicked in. Like an old hand, he picked his target, drew a bead, and fired—all in a heartbeat. A Blackfoot, guiding his pony with his knees, was in the process of drawing back his bow to let an arrow fly. Zach's shot hurled him backwards off his horse.

Squinting against an acrid drift of powder-smoke, Zach ducked down and reloaded. He remembered a piece of advice his father—a veteran of the Shawnee wars—had given him. Taking several bullets out of his shot pouch, he popped them into his mouth. Pouring a powder charge from horn to barrel, he flipped one of the bullets into the Hawken with his tongue, then struck the butt of the rifle smartly against the ground.

"Depends on the kind of fight you're in," his father had told him. "Most times it's quick and wild and close in, and you ain't got the leisure to measure your powder or fiddle with patch and ramrod. You'd be wise to learn to pour the proper charge. Don't worry about spillin' powder. Better to lose powder than your life. And the spit'll hold the bullet as well as wadding, in a pinch."

In this way Zach managed to load the Hawken, cap it, and fire again, less than fifteen seconds after his first shot. Another Blackfoot pony galloped by, short a rider.

The Blackfoot attack was like a wave breaking against a rocky shoreline. The mounted warriors streamed past the camp on both sides, and some plowed straight through it, their agile ponies leaping the travois. Many of them were armed with fusils or flintlocks, which they were adept at reloading while on horseback. The morning was shattered by the constant rattle of gunfire and a stunning clamor of savage war cries.

After the initial pass, most of the Blackfeet wheeled their horses and commenced shooting into the camp through a choking, obscuring cloud of dust and smoke. Others jumped from their ponies and tried to close in for hand-to-hand fighting.

Zach came up from behind the travois to fire a third time, dropping a Blackfoot who had dismounted and was sprinting straight for him with war club raised. Another hostile darted in from a different angle, hurtling past him to pounce on Shadmore and carry him to the ground. Straddling the old trapper, the Blackfoot lifted a knife for the killing stroke. Shadmore spat tobacco juice into the warrior's eyes, and followed up with a powerful punch that sent the Blackfoot reeling sideways. At the same time Zach struck with the butt of the Hawken, aiming for the Indian's head but striking the shoulder instead. The Blackfoot rolled to his feet. With an ear-splitting shriek he lunged at Zach, who blocked a knife stroke with a deft downward sweep of the barrel and brought the rifle stock around and up sharply to hammer the warrior off-balance.

The Blackfoot scarcely seemed to touch the ground. He was up and darting in so swiftly that Zach was caught by surprise. He hurled the empty rifle into the Indian's onslaught, groped for the knife sheathed at

his side. The warrior plowed into him, snarling like a
wolf. Zach gasped as cold steel raked his ribs. Only
a glancing blow, but it scared him, and fear stoked a
cold fury in him. Falling, entangled with his deadly
foe, he twisted desperately, so that when they struck
the ground the Blackfoot took the brunt of the fall.

They wrestled, straining every muscle, each trying
to drive home his knife while holding back the blade
of his enemy. Then the Blackfoot whiplashed Zach
with a leg, his knee striking the young hunter a terrific
blow to the head. Zach rolled desperately away, fighting a violent nausea. A rifle spoke, almost in his ear.
Zach got his feet under him, blinked away funny lights
that danced behind his eyeballs. He saw the Blackfoot
spread-eagled on his back, a blue hole in his forehead.
Shadmore stood nearby, reloading his rifle.

"Wagh!" exclaimed the old trapper, with grudging
admiration. "These varmints is tough as old buffalo
bulls, and twice as mean." He winked at Zach.
"Obliged for the help."

"Likewise," said Zach, with difficulty. He still had
a bullet in his mouth, and was surprised he hadn't
swallowed the lead pill.

He sheathed his knife, scooped up the Hawken, reloaded. Casting about through the dust and powder-
smoke, he sought another target. But the shooting had
suddenly subsided. The Blackfeet seemed to be with-
drawing.

Though he could see precious little, Zach could hear
defiant war whoops and the thunder of ponies east of
the camp. He looked around. Godin was bending over
a fallen Blackfoot. Pulling on the dead warrior's side
braids with one hand, the half-breed made a deft cir-
cular incision with his knife, starting at the hairline.
Zach heard a liquid, popping sound as the scalp came
off. He stared with unwilling but helpless fascination.

His stomach performed a slow roll. For the first time it struck him that he himself had taken three lives. He felt sick and shaky, and fought against throwing up.

A woman screamed, off in the distance. A horse galloped past, so close that Zach was pelted with dirt. He caught a glimpse of the rider. It was Tall Wolf, emitting a blood-curdling yell.

"Morning Sky!" gasped Zach, heart lurching in his chest.

He took off, running.

Chapter 13

On the warpath, it was the Blackfoot way to rely heavily on the element of surprise. They were not ones to stand toe-to-toe with their adversaries and slug it out.

This day, a more circumspect approach would have served them better. But, seeing the smoke from the hunters' fire, their lust for blood and glory had got the best of them; they'd ridden furiously across the intervening ground, an indiscretion that betrayed them to the members of the caravan. Pride played a part—they had been stung by their bloody defeat at the fort the day before. Now they were too eager to redeem themselves.

They were stung even more by the hunters' rifles, and to a lesser extent by the Crows. Many Blackfoot warriors perished in the brief but fierce melee, only two or three minutes in duration. Though some of them were armed with guns, they were no match for the hunters in the use of firearms. It was the rare Indian who developed into a skilled rifle shot. Seldom did they possess sufficient powder, lead, or experience to achieve expertise, and their weapons were generally inferior to those most hunters now carried—guns made more reliable by the employment of percussion caps, and more accurate by their rifled barrels. It was as well that most Indians preferred the old flintlock smoothbores, for that was all the majority of white traders were inclined to provide them with. Snaphaunces were cheap to buy, and therefore profitable at resale; and few traders were foolish enough to arm an Indian as well as himself.

Had the Blackfeet held to the high ground and rained arrows and bullets down into the camp, the outcome might have been different. A fair hand with the bow could keep several arrows in flight at all times, and every one accurately shot. Instead, they stormed down into the hollow and learned they had bitten off more than they could chew.

The battle would have been over—except that, as they fled the camp, the Blackfeet discovered the Crow squaws. The latter had been separated from the camp at the moment of attack, and sought shelter in the sparse peachleaf willow and cottonwood lining the creek. Unfortunately for them, the general direction of the Blackfoot retreat was across the creek and through the trees; it was impossible for the Crow women to escape detection.

Here were easy pickings for the Blackfeet: defenseless squaws to slaughter, and packhorses to steal. Warriors of the tribes that populated the mountains and high plains never asked for mercy, and seldom showed any. It was accepted custom to kill the mothers of their enemies. The Crow women knew this was their fate.

As it came clear that the Blackfeet were after their women, Crow warriors like Tall Wolf, who had managed to keep their war ponies close at hand, galloped madly to the rescue. The rest set out on foot, running as fleetly as deer, shrieking ferocious insults at the Blackfeet who swarmed through the trees bent on butchery.

Zach ran with them. Long and lean, he covered the

ground swiftly. The knife wound he had suffered was momentarily forgotten. He was unaware that his buckskin shirt was slick with blood. All he cared about was reaching Morning Sky in time to protect her.

He saw a Blackfoot ride a woman down. The warrior's tomahawk flashed in the day's first slant of amber sunlight. The weapon swept down, came back up dripping scarlet. Zach could produce only an inarticulate cry of rage and fear. The dying woman spun as she crumpled, her skull crushed, and he saw it was not Morning Sky.

A witness to cold-blooded murder, Zach was horrified and outraged. He stopped running, hiked rifle to shoulder, and shot the Blackfoot butcher off his horse. Running again, he reloaded, grimly satisfied. He felt no remorse, and knew somehow he never would. Not for this deed. To fight a man fair and square was one thing. To slaughter women was an unforgivable atrocity. He did not see through the eyes of an Indian—did not see that a dead Crow woman would bear no sons who might one day kill Blackfeet—and it wouldn't have changed his opinion one whit anyway. A man who killed a woman deserved to die. Zach's conscience was clear.

The Blackfeet turned their attention to the Crow warriors and the young yellow-haired hunter, hastening toward the trees. Zach heard the keening whine of a bullet. The ground all around sprouted a crop of Blackfoot arrows. He paid no heed to the danger. A mounted Crow galloped past. The next instant found the Crow falling, riddled with arrows, his pony veering off. Zach hurtled the dead warrior and kept running.

Then he saw her.

She was racing through the trees with the grace of

a gazelle. In hot pursuit were a pair of mounted Black-feet, one some distance ahead of the other, both closing fast. She was quick, but stood no chance. Sensing this, she seized a dead limb, wheeled, and ducked under the vicious sweep of a war club to brandish the limb into the forelegs of the horse with all her might. The horse screamed and somersaulted. The limb was shattered into splinters. The force of the impact struck Morning Sky to the ground. The Blackfoot warrior sailed through the air, arms and legs akimbo, and lay still where he had landed.

Yowling like a wild animal, the second Blackfoot bore down on her. Zach planted himself and prepared to fire. But then Tall Wolf appeared, bent low on his buckskin. The horse seemed to fly through the trees without touching hoof to ground. It collided full-bore with the Blackfoot's horse, and with perfect timing Tall Wolf launched himself at his foe. Men and ponies fell in a tangle. A flailing hoof caught Tall Wolf in the head. The Blackfoot pounced, raising his war club, and with a triumphant cry prepared to deliver the killing blow. Morning Sky cried out. With an expression of surprise the Blackfoot froze, whirled to look at her. At that instant Zach's bullet exploded his heart.

Both horses got up and wandered away, wobbly-legged, leaving the two warriors sprawled in blood-splattered grass. Morning Sky rose, ran to kneel beside the Blackfoot. That struck Zach as odd, but he did not spare it more than a passing thought. More urgent matters demanded his attention. Running full-tilt, he hooked an arm round her slender waist and literally swept her off her feet without breaking stride. She was light as a feather. Straight ahead grew a clump of serviceberry, thick with the purple-black fruit that was a

staple of the Indian diet. He crashed into the thicket
and set her down.

"Beg pardon," he mumbled. Even in the crucible
of a life-or-death struggle, Zach's upbringing ex-
acted an apology for taking the liberty of manhan-
dling her.

Her violet eyes were bright and riveting. Reloading
the Hawken, he marveled at her perfection, and at his
own desire. He was incredulous; how could he have
such thoughts at a time like this? Was he mad? It had
to be a kind of madness.

The fight raged about them, quick and fierce, like the
flash of powder. The hunters were introducing themselves into the fray, to the detriment of the Blackfeet.
Zach felt his blood cool. The fever of battle abruptly
left him. He was done fighting for the day. Crouched
in the thicket, he was content to watch over Morning
Sky until the danger had passed.

The Blackfeet were calling it a day. They'd killed a
few of their enemies, slaking their thirst for blood.
The arrival of the hunters, who could generally claim
a life with every shot fired, was the deciding point.
The Blackfeet cut and ran with a smattering of parting
shots.

As happened in such fights, a number of horses
were killed. It was inevitable: A horse was a much
bigger target than a man, and was often hit by a bullet
or an arrow meant for its rider. Some of the Blackfeet
tried to conceal themselves by clinging to the sides
of their mounts. The hunters weren't foiled by this
artful contrivance, and had no compunction about
dropping a pony just to buy another crack at its
owner.

This was the fate of a horse thundering past the
thicket where Zach and Morning Sky were hiding. Its
rider was pitched violently, and lost his rifle in the fall.

As the Blackfoot sprang resiliently to his feet, not twenty feet away from Zach, the latter drew a bead. Lining up his sights on a Blackfoot already seemed second nature to him.

Before he could squeeze the trigger, Morning Sky clutched his arm, speaking in an urgent whisper. He did not comprehend the words, but he grasped the meaning. She was beseeching him not to shoot. He heard the adjuration in her voice, read it in her expression, and knew what she wanted of him even before she thought to sign "No Kill."

The Blackfoot whirled to peer into the thicket. Spying Zach, he reached impulsively for the knife at his side, and took an aggressive step even though he saw that Zach had him dead to rights. Still Zach hesitated. He was disposed to do anything Morning Sky wished of him. The Blackfoot became master of his own fate. If he turned away, he would live. If he made another hostile move, he would die.

Morning Sky read the situation correctly. She called out to the Blackfoot. Zach was watching him eagle-eyed, saw the surprise on the warrior's face. Morning Sky spoke rapidly, fervently, pressing her point and, ultimately, having her way. The Blackfoot turned and loped away. A riderless horse was careening through the creek-bottom timber. The warrior cut it off, leaped with the agility of a panther onto its back, and splashed across the shallows to join his brothers streaming up the flank of the hollow and out of sight over the rim.

Zach was mystified. Why would Morning Sky want him to spare the life of an enemy of her people? Clearly she had warned the Blackfoot. He had understood—therein lay the key. Zach did not know enough to distinguish Crow from Blackfoot, but he assumed Morning Sky had spoken the latter. And another thing:

She had gone to the body of the Blackfoot who'd been a tick's hair from finishing off Tall Wolf. Why had she done that, when her husband lay severely injured nearby? Did all this mean . . . ?

He signed "You Blackfoot."

Morning Sky nodded.

Chapter 14

Zach had little time to ponder this development. Shadmore was jogging through the timber, calling his name. The old mountain man moved with remarkable spryness for one possessed of so many winters. He paused in his search only to prod a couple of sprawled Blackfeet with his rifle, just to confirm that the Indians were dead and not playing possum.

Signing "Come, Safe" to Morning Sky, Zach emerged from the serviceberry thicket, followed by the young woman.

"Wagh!" Shadmore said. "Mr. Hannah, for one so short on years, you mighty dry behind the ears."

Zach grinned. "And you're a poet, Mr. Shadmore."

Shadmore gingerly peeled Zach's ripped and blood-soaked shirt away from the knife wound in order to diagnose his protégé's injury.

"Well, yule live, I reckon. Won't be the last scar you earn."

Now that it had been brought to his attention, the wound began to torment Zach. Of a sudden, he became light-headed and rubber-kneed. It felt like someone was jabbing a red-hot poker into his side every time he drew breath. His throat was parched; he thought he could drink a river down to the bottom-slime. His burning eyes felt as though they'd been dipped in gritty sand.

"Don't fret none about it," said Shadmore. "We'll slap some tobacky juice on her. Then I'll sew you up."

A keening wail from somewhere off in the trees set Zach's teeth on edge.

"Squaw," said Shadmore, "moanin' the death of her man. Godawful racket, ain't it?" He glanced shrewdly at Morning Sky. "Thar'll be more'n one kickin' up a fuss today."

Zach started walking. Moving listlessly, he was drawn to the spot where Tall Wolf had fallen. He had one burning question that begged for an answer. Shadmore and Morning Sky followed. The former knelt beside the Crow warrior and felt for a pulse at the side of Tall Wolf's neck.

"Gone beaver," pronounced the old trapper.

Zach believed it. The pony's hoof had crushed Tall Wolf's cheekbone, mangled his ear, and left a deep crescent indentation across the temple. His neck and face were covered with dark blood, his hair matted with it.

Zach glanced guiltily at Morning Sky. He was mortified by his own feelings. His first reaction to the news that Tall Wolf had gone under had been a skulking kind of wicked relief. Such an un-Christian sentiment shocked him, and he castigated himself without mercy. Madness, indeed!

Shadmore straightened, once more peering in a coy way at Morning Sky, who was examining her husband's corpse with seamless impassivity.

" 'Pears we got one widow won't grieve too much," he drawled.

Zach leaped to her defense. "You saw how he treated her!"

"I've seen a lot of bucks treat their wimmin worse."

"She's Blackfoot."

"Huh!" Shadmore wore the doltish look of a man kicked in the head by a mule. He spoke curtly to Morning Sky in a lingo Zach could only assume was Blackfoot. She answered, her chin tilted defiantly. Shadmore fired more gibberish back at her, to which she responded at length, softly, but with a steely edge of emotion. When she was done, Shadmore tugged fiercely on his hoarfrost beard.

"What did she say?" pressed Zach.

"Yore right as rain. She's Blackfoot, sure nuff. Half, anyroad. Other half's white, like I thought from the first. A man from the Land of Always Snow, she says. Canada. Trapper, prob'ly, mebbe one of them Hudson's Bay Company fellers. She got herself captured by a Crow war party when she was jist a little punkin. Had she been full-growed they'd've killed her fer sartin. But sometimes they'll take younkers. Try to raise 'em as their own. Reckon her light skin were of special interest. Anything different like that makes an Injun curious as a cat. Her Crow 'father'—meanin' captor— is Black Knife. But he ain't never been much for treatin' her like a daughter. More like a slave."

Zach gestured at the dead Blackfoot. "But this one was trying to kill her."

"Shoot, he didn't know no different. Far as he were consarned she were a Crow squaw, and so fit fer nothin' but killin'. I feel sorry fer her. More'n likely she ain't too well received by the other Crow women, on account of her pedigree. Says Black Knife's squaws liked to beat on her. And the Blackfoot prob'ly wouldn't take her back now no how, seein' as how she's been brought up by the Absaroka, and hitched to one into the bargain."

Zach glanced at her. She was watching him with unblinking intensity. He was stunned by the developments of the last two days. All this seemed unreal, like a dream. He'd seen Morning Sky, had fallen head-over-heels for her. She'd had a husband yesterday; today she was a widow. What Zach had seen as an insurmountable obstacle suddenly no longer existed. She was a Blackfoot; he'd killed five Blackfeet today, but that didn't seem to matter to her. Or maybe it did. He couldn't tell with any degree of certitude what was going on behind those bewitching violet eyes. His first twenty years of life had been tame to the brink of boredom. Now life was rushing at him from all directions at once, hurtling past too quick to grab hold of.

Rides A Dark Horse approached on a cantering pony. He peered gravely at the body of Tall Wolf. His flinty black eyes shifted to Morning Sky. Anger twisted his bronze features. He spoke with icy reproach. She replied with bold defiance, as she had to Shadmore in the beginning. Rides A Dark Horse waxed indignant. He barked back, in high dudgeon. Zach recognized the tone of voice; no matter the language, it was the tone universally used when raining curses down upon someone. The Crow warrior's horse, reacting to the foul mood of its rider, began prancing and tossing its head. Zach sidestepped, placing himself in front of Morning Sky, Hawken held tight against his chest, irritated beyond reason. It was a small move, but with monstrous implications.

"He'd best keep a civil tongue in his head when he talks to her," he warned Shadmore.

Shadmore was amused and a little alarmed at the same time.

"She ain't showin' the proper distress fer a squaw what jist lost her husband."

"They stole her away from her own people. What do they expect?"

Shadmore sighed, spoke to Rides A Dark Horse. He sounded very diplomatic. The Crow warrior looked from Zach to Morning Sky to the body of Tall Wolf, to the dead Blackfoot and back to Zach. Zach got the impression the chief perceived all that was going on behind the words here—understood the situation and all it augured much better than did Zach himself. A ghost of a smile—or maybe it was a grimace—teased the severe corners of the Crow's mouth. He rapid-fired Absaroka talk back at Shadmore. The tension smoothed out of the old trapper's bony shoulders.

"He says you fought very well today. Killed several Blackfeet. The enemy of his enemies is his friend. In fact, he saw you drop this one hyar. Says Tall Wolf counted first coup, but since he's dead, the kill is yourn by right, so he concedes the scalp to you."

"The scalp?" The memory of Godin lifting the dead Blackfoot's hair seared Zach's mind. He felt queasy again.

"By my reckonin' you got five scalps comin'," nodded Shadmore, immensely pleased. During the fight, he'd been watching out for Zach more than he had for himself. He knew that the sum total of Zach's accomplishments had exceeded his own by the margin of one dead Blackfoot.

"If he thinks I'm going to take a scalp, like some bloody savage, he better think again," growled Zach.

"He's jist payin' you a compliment."

Zach was irate. "If he wants this feller scalped, he'll have to do the job himself."

Again Shadmore addressed Rides A Dark Horse. The Crow nodded curtly and vaulted gracefully from his pony. He did the deed with the aplomb of one familiar with such gory work. Lifting the scalp high, he whooped triumphantly at the sky, then sprang back aboard his horse and departed at the gallop.

"He's much obliged," Shadmore told Zach.

"*You* sound mighty pleased."

Shadmore was indifferent to recrimination. "You ain't been out hyar quite long enough, I see. Still wearin' a layer or two of civilization. Iffen you live long enough, yule git shed of that like a snake sheds old skin."

"If I live out here a hundred years I'll never take a scalp."

A halloo from the camp caught their attention.

"Major Henry," said Shadmore, "callin' us in."

They started for the camp. Morning Sky walked a few paces directly behind Zach. He found this disconcerting, kept looking back over his shoulder.

"She ain't likely to run off, if that's what yore afeared of," chuckled Shadmore. "Looks to me like she's latched on to you. Mebbe you shine in her eyes as much as she shines in yourn. Or mebbe she's jist settin' out on a campaign to become yore squaw fer her own benefit. Next to a coyote, ain't nothin' more calculatin' than a woman."

"What does that mean?"

"Most Injun gals'll take up with a white man quicker'n a hair trigger. They got it in their heads we treat 'em better'n a buck gen'ly will. Some truth to it. I've known hivernans what pamper their wimmin sumpin fierce."

Zach decided there wasn't anything in the world he'd rather do than pamper Morning Sky the rest of her days. But every day has a night, and it was thinking on the nights that gave him a peculiar feeling at the base of his spine.

Chapter 15

Two Crow warriors had been killed in the fight, and a third injured. Three hunters, including Zach, had been wounded, but none mortally. A bullet had carved a deep groove in the arm of a man named Bill Williams, and Beckwourth had taken an arrow through the fleshy part of his calf. Zach arrived at the camp in time to see the mulatto break the shaft in two and pull it free. The wound was cauterized with gunpowder set ablaze. Amid the sickly-sweet whiff of burnt flesh, Beckwourth gave a lesson in stoicism.

Of the Crow women, three had been slain. Infuriated by this cold-blooded butchery, the Crow men proceeded to mutilate the seventeen dead Blackfeet. In this instance, scalping was not enough to slake their thirst for revenge. The dead were hacked to pieces, emasculated, gutted like fish. The Crows gloated, howled, danced like dervishes. They spat and urinated on the corpses. Those frontiersmen who paid any heed at all to this grisly work watched with chill indifference.

For Zach, the spectacle was too horrible to ignore. He no longer wondered why some trappers had nothing but contempt for Indians. His own attitude towards them did a complete about-face. How naive he had been, to think they "belonged" to this wild and beautiful country! They were a blight upon it, not an asset.

They weren't noble savages, as some highbrow easterners liked to portray them. They were just savages. Not a few frontiersmen pursued a policy of exterminating Indians as a matter of course. They did so without qualm and viewed it as their solemn duty. In the same way they would dispense of rattlesnakes, and with as little emotion. An understandable point of view, decided Zach, as he watched the Crows commit their atrocities.

His wound required attention. Major Henry produced a small medical kit and a mixture of turpentine and camphor was applied, a more sanitary ointment than Shadmore's tobacco juice. The concoction burned like double hellfire. To his credit, Zach made no sound. He could do no less, after seeing Beckwourth endure a gunpowder cauterizing so dauntlessly.

The Major and Shadmore deliberated on how best to close the wound and stanch the flow of blood. A fire-heated knife or gunpowder cauterization would suffice, if Zach could lay up for a spell and convalesce.

"But we've got ground to cover today," said Henry. "Zach, you'll have to carry your own weight."

"Then we'd best sew him up," said Shadmore. "Otherwise that cut'll open right back up, and he'll commence to bleedin' agin, worse'n a hog on a hook."

A needle was fitted with ordinary thread. Shadmore volunteered to do the stitching. Zach broke out in a cold sweat, wondering how much more pain he could bear. Sublette arrived, took in the situation at a glance, and produced a small silver flask as soon as the Major had moved on to check the other wounded.

"Take a swig, Zach," urged Sublette.

"What is it?" Zach sniffed suspiciously at the contents. "Smells like wood alcohol."

"Dead on. Pure spirits." Sublette threw a sidelong, surreptitious look around. "But don't be lettin' on.

The Crows find out I got some liquid brave-maker, they'll pester me like a swarm of skeeters. And the Major'll give me the evil eye. He and Ashley made it plain from the start we warn't to trade likker or spirits with the Injuns. They're unpredictable enough as it is, without makin' 'em crazy with firewater. I reckon the Major knows some of us brought along a supply of hunnerd-proof panther poison, and he won't muddy our water on account of it, long as we keep it under our hats. Now drink up. It won't kill you. As fumble-fingered as I know Shad to be, you'll need a good healthy shot of backbone-stiffener.''

Zach figured he had nothing to lose, and took a cautious sip. Liquid fire trickled down his throat, making him gasp.

"Don't *sip* the goldurn stuff!" scolded Sublette. "This ain't no front-parlor tea-and-crumpet social."

Zach took a deep breath, swallowed a mouthful. The alcohol exploded in his belly, a ball of flame that sent his senses reeling. He wheezed like a wind-broke nag and closed his eyes as earth and sky began a tilting spin.

Satisfied, Sublette took the flask and nodded at Shadmore, who straddled Zach's legs and set to the task. He pinched Zach's knife-sundered flesh together between thumb and forefinger, ran the needle in and out and drew the thread on through. The lancing of the needle was bad enough, but Zach suffered every flaying millimeter of thread.

Morning Sky's voice pried his eyes open. The day had turned dark. Objects were furry-edged.

"Gal says she wants to finish up for me," Shadmore told him. "Might not be a bad idee. She's for sartin a fair hand, with all the bead and quill work she's sure to have done in her time. I'll jist sit on you, so's you don't go to floppin' around like a sucker-fish on dry land. Don't want to spoil her aim.''

Kneeling, Morning Sky bent over Zach. Her face was very close to his. Her touch was cool. She seemed to draw the pain out of his body through her fingers. He marveled at that, wondered how it could be so. Once she looked up at him, and he was surprised and chagrined to discover that his pain was there in those violet eyes. When she was done she bent lower to cut the thread with her teeth, and her warm breath was like a healing anointment.

"Thar's as handsome a job as these ole eyes have ever seen!" exclaimed Shadmore. "A scar to be proud of!"

They did not tarry long. Rides A Dark Horse sent a warrior on ahead to alert the rest of the tribe in the summer village further up the Yellowstone. There were several hundred warriors in the village, so it was unlikely that the Blackfoot war party would attack it, but you could never tell with the Blackfeet, who were nothing if not audacious. Rides A Dark Horse was confident that the principal chief of the Absaroka, Iron Bull, would send a large contingent of warriors on fast horses to guarantee the caravan's safety the rest of the way.

No one could vouchsafe that the Blackfeet wouldn't attack the caravan again, and it was agreed that the best course of action would be to press on toward the summer village with all possible haste. The Crow warriors heaped scorn upon their Blackfoot enemies, calling them cowards and worse, and proclaimed the day a great victory in the annals of Absaroka history, but it was really only bold talk to bolster their own courage. The Blackfeet were deadly foes, and no one slipped into complacency.

Some of the horses had been killed, others stolen. The Crow braves were loath to relinquish their war ponies for the task of hauling travois, but no alternative presented itself. The Crows were as eager as the frontiersmen to deliver the trade to its destination. This put all but three of the warriors afoot. It was up to these three to scout for the enemy.

The trade goods were not the only burden; there were the bodies of the five Absaroka dead. The warriors whose squaws had been slain were entirely undemonstrative—it did not befit a warrior to manifest grief. Of the two Crow widows, Morning Sky was as composed as any warrior; the other caterwauled pitiably, to the point of aggravating Zach almost beyond tolerance. To establish the full magnitude of her loss, she had taken a knife and cut off the tip of one of her forefingers. All day she shambled along behind the travois bearing the corpse of her husband, loudly lamenting her fate.

The day severely tested Zach's endurance. Every step, every breath, sent spasms of white heat through his body. As the previous night had been a stage for winter's dress rehearsal, the day became a stifling reminiscence of the summer just past. Weakened by loss of blood, Zach was victimized by the heat. He guzzled water, yet never managed to slake a raging thirst. He felt bloated, and a monstrous ache in his belly made him stagger along bent over.

He saw it through by focusing on Morning Sky. He kept his eyes glued to her, the way a shipwrecked sailor drifting on the swelling bosom of the sea might stare at the salvation of a distant shoreline. Just the sight of her gave him the strength he needed.

She seemed to sense his desperate need for her, and her smiles coaxed him. Her many solicitous glances blunted the pain. Without words, with only these smiles and glances, she reminded him that life was worth living.

Zach lost track of time and distance, and eventually resigned himself to the fact that this ordeal was apparently never going to end. But all things end. Late in the afternoon Iron Bull's rescue party appeared, fifty warriors painted for war and heavily armed. The Absaroka chief had thoughtfully dispatched spare mounts, enough so that all could ride the rest of the way.

"Mighty friendly of him," remarked one frontiersman.

"Friendly, hell," was another's mordant comment. "He don't give half a hoot for our miser'ble hides. It's the trade goods he wants to save. Far as he's consarned, ever' last piece of foforraw is already Crow property."

For Zach, traveling by horse was only a marginal improvement. His world had contracted until it was composed of two things: pain, and pain's counterpoise—Morning Sky.

They reached the summer camp of the Crows in the indigo twilight of day's end. Zach was only dimly aware of an eruption of jubilant shouting, mingled with shrieks of anguish, and the snarling-yapping-howling of dogs. This hue and cry stirred the embers of his curiosity, and he forced back the boundaries of his awareness, to see stretched out before him a sight like none he had ever beheld.

Chapter 16

The Absaroka had long been separated into two major bands. The River Crows claimed the valleys of the Bighorn and the Yellowstone, while the Mountain Crows presided most of the time in and around the Bighorn Mountains to the southeast. In the short summer of the north country, the bands traditionally met and camped together on the Yellowstone, above the confluence of that river and the Bighorn.

It was this village, representing almost the entire population of the Sparrow Hawk people, that Zach saw; thousands of men, women, and children, hundreds of lodges in a lush bottomland shaded by oaks and alders, spread out along the river for more than a mile.

Even through a mist of misery Zach could appreciate the beauty of this scene. The Yellowstone was a ribbon of liquid silver, capturing the last light of day. A haze of wood-smoke hovered above the village. Dozens of cook-fires flickered like fallen stars.

Iron Bull rode out to greet his honored guests, trailing sub-chiefs in his wake. The leader of the Crows was decked out in his full regalia. His hair was braided into locks adorned with eagle feathers, carved pieces of wood, and dangles fashioned from shells, bones, and hammered tin. He wore a necklace of grizzly claws, a bone breastplate, and a buffalo skin with the hair side turned in and the hide painted with an abundance of designs and emblems in a rainbow of colors. His saddle was the pelt of a mountain lion.

One might have thought Major Henry and the frontiersmen were the chief's long-lost prodigal sons. The lodges of the Sparrow Hawk people were open to the hunters. They must make themselves at home. All that the Crows possessed was at their disposal. A buffalo hunt had been conducted in anticipation of their visit, and there would be much feasting.

The Major had no intention of permitting his men and trade goods to be dispersed among the Crows. He made it known, as diplomatically as possible, that the Rocky Mountain Fur Company would maintain its own camp on the outskirts of the village. Iron Bull would not hear of it. Major Henry politely insisted. There was a great deal of debate on the subject. Zach prayed for a quick resolution. All he wanted was six feet of ground to stretch his punished body upon, where he could lie absolutely motionless until next spring if he so desired.

Eventually the Major had his way. While the bodies of the dead Absaroka were borne with much ceremony and consternation into the village, the trade remained in the camp of the frontiersmen. As a result, the hunters found themselves inundated with uninvited Crow visitors. Zach was reminded of vultures flocking around carrion—in this case, the carrion being the trade-laden travois.

In his present condition, Zach cared less about trade goods. He slid off his horse and slumped down into sweet-smelling grass, completely spent.

In spite of the treatment of turpentine and camphor, his wound had become infected. A fever took hold of him. One minute he was drenched with sweat, the next racked him with violent chills.

All through the night Morning Sky watched over him. She covered him with a blanket, later adding a buffalo robe to sweat out the fever. She cooled his burning brow with water fetched from the river. She made a poultice and applied it to the wound to draw out the poison. She guarded his rifle and possibles from the Crow men who lurked like coyotes in the night shadow.

Zach slept fitfully, drifting in and out of consciousness. He missed the arrival of Black Knife, who had some sharp words for Morning Sky. He wanted her to return to the village and display the proper distress for the fallen Tall Wolf. She was adamant in her refusal. Black Knife's mood was belligerent, but he made no real trouble, thanks to the intervention of a steely-eyed Shadmore. Black Knife withdrew. Morning Sky remained.

As the night wore on, the village grew quiet. The fires died down. A damp coolness filled the bottomland. The Major set a guard to watch over the trade goods. The other frontiersmen slept with rifles close at hand.

Shadmore spread his blanket not far from Zach. He woke several times during the night, and each time glanced across. Each time he saw Morning Sky, sitting cross-legged, with Zach's head cradled in her lap. And once he saw her bend low and blow gently on Zach's sweat-beaded face.

Zach awoke with the sun glaring in his eyes. He judged it to be an hour after sunrise. Never in his life had he slept this late. He felt like he'd been trampled by a herd of buffalo. Even so, he felt a sight better than yesterday.

The camp was quiet. Two hunters were watching

over the trade—Shadmore and Beckwourth. Everyone else was gone.

Including Morning Sky.

That made Zach sit up—or try to. He got as far as one elbow. Then his wound reminded him, potently, of its presence. Zach clenched his teeth and tried to overcome the pain. An invisible iron hand was squeezing his heart. He couldn't let it keep him from finding Morning Sky.

Shadmore came over, bearing a tin cup.

"Well, looks like yule live after all. You shore wuz shakin' the bark off the trees last night. How 'bout a little water to wet yore whistle?"

Zach's throat was like a desert, but he paid it no mind. "Where is she?"

The old woodsman sat on his heels. He cocked his head to one side and peered curiously at Zach. Zach thought he was smiling out of the corner of his mouth, though it was hard to tell through Shadmore's prodigious whisker growth.

"Yore still ailin', I see. And this is one ailment she cain't cure, seein' as how she's the cause."

Zach wasn't sure what Shadmore was trying to say, and he frankly didn't care. He reached out and grabbed a handful of the leatherstocking's buckskin shirt.

"Damn it, where is she?"

"Why, Zach Hannah, I do believe that's the first time I ever heard you swear."

Obviously, thought Zach bitterly, Shadmore found his distress amusing.

"I thought we were friends," he said, with acid reproach.

Shadmore sighed. He suddenly looked very grave. "Thar you go. Proves my point. Wimmin make trouble."

"I've got to find her." Zach tried to stand. He had

to roll over and push up onto hands and knees first. Just this small endeavor seemed to cost him the day's entire ration of strength. His head lolled, and he tried to breathe without moving his chest, as every movement sent a lancing pain through his side.

Shadmore tossed the cup away and helped Zach to his feet. The ground moved treacherously beneath Zach. He swayed precariously. Shadmore held on to him until the vertigo had subsided.

"She told me to tell you she'd be back. Reckon she don't want you to worry yore fool head none."

"Where'd she go?"

"Into the village. Where else?"

"I've got to find her, Shad."

He took a step, but Shadmore was still holding on, and reeled him back in.

"You cain't go bargin' through thar, hollerin' her name and pokin' yore nose into ever' lodge. You cain't go into a lodge atall, lessen the flap is tied open. Thar's yore lesson for today. Now git yore wits about you! She'll come back. She's as taken with you as you are with her."

"She said that?" whispered Zach.

"Not zackly. But she didn't have to spell it out. I got eyes."

Zach's heart soared. But he warned himself against getting his hopes up too high. He wasn't completely confident in Shadmore's intuition when it came to women.

"Don't reckon yore any more hungry than you are thirsty," said Shadmore.

Zach shook his head. He was barely paying attention. He gazed across the bottomland to the Crow village, praying for a glimpse of Morning Sky. He didn't see her, but he saw hundreds of other people out and about. Most seemed to be moving toward the center of the village.

"Big doin's yonder," remarked Shadmore. "The Major and Iron Bull are goin' to smoke the peace pipe. Then thar'll be some tradin' done. Then a heap of eatin' and dancin' and such carryin's on. But then, you don't care about all that."

"Are you going to let go of me?" Zach's voice was soft, his tone hard.

Shadmore grinned. "Feisty this mornin', ain't we?" He relinquished his hold. "Thar you be. Ask and yule git, like the Good Book says. But my stick'll float with yourn today. Love-blind like you be, you might walk smack into a hornet's nest, without me to look after yore bacon. Ole Beckwourth kin watch the fofforraw."

Zach wasn't listening. He was already headed for the village. Shaking his head, Shadmore picked up Zach's forgotten rifle and followed.

"Wimmin . . ." he muttered.

Chapter 17

Zach was surprised to find his entrance into the village a matter of great consequence to the Crows.

Men came up and clapped him soundly on the back, which, aside from being painful in his condition, was annoying, as he was none too steady on his feet. Older women reverently touched his sleeve and babbled vociferously, while young maidens struck poses at a distance, cutting eyes at him and murmuring to one another behind their hands. Boisterous children tagged along behind. Camp dogs, excited by all the hullabaloo, barked and yipped and howled. They were the scroungiest, meanest-looking creatures Zach had ever seen. Occasionally one would lunge snapping at his heels, but some of the children were armed with switches, which they used with excessive enthusiasm to beat back the mongrels.

"What's going on?" Zach asked Shadmore. "What's all this for?" It seemed as though half the Crow nation were swarming all over him at once, and he found it thoroughly exasperating.

"Yore a celebrity," replied Shadmore wryly. "Big brave killer of them nasty ole Blackfeet."

"What does 'show-dah-gee' mean?" Zach understood none of the chatter directed at him, but that word was prevalent.

"*Sho-da-gee* is Crow for 'howdy.' "

"What's Crow for 'go away'?"

They made their way to the center of the village. Here, in a clearing almost two hundred feet in diameter, hundreds of Crows had congregated. A lodge larger than the others stood on the west side of the clearing, its entrance facing east. It was painted red, and decorated with a great many symbols in a variety of colors—magic totems of strong medicine. Near it stood two poles literally covered with scalps.

"Them-thar's the scalp poles," said Shadmore. "Guess you kin figure that out for yoreself."

"My God," breathed Zach, disgusted. "There must be hundreds of them."

Shadmore nodded. "They like to show off how great they are in battle."

Zach looked closer. A few of the scalps did not appear to have come from the heads of Indians.

"Are those scalps of white men, Shad?"

"I reckon. Which is to say, don't put yore trust in all this smilin' and back-slappin', Zach. Always read the eyes. The eyes don't lie. A Crow war party catches you out in the open all by yore lonesome, they might kill you jist as quick as the Blackfeet would. It's been known to happen. A warrior might come up to you one day friendly as the dickens, and the next time you see him he'll try to bust yore skull with a war club. You see that red lodge yonder? That's the medicine lodge. Ever' village has one. Once inside, a man's safe, even if he's the enemy of the tribe. Blood cain't be shed inside the medicine lodge. That little morsel of knowledge might save yore skin some day."

In the center of the clearing was a large fire, around which sat Major Henry, Iron Bull, and more than a dozen Crow dignitaries. The rest of the frontiersmen stood behind the Major. They appeared calm and relaxed, leaning on their rifles. But very little escaped their keen eyes. Zach and Shadmore joined them, and Zach took his Hawken from the old trapper. Having seen the white scalps on the poles, he had become acutely aware of just how vastly outnumbered the Rocky Mountain Fur Company really was. He did not need admonishment from Shadmore to distrust Absaroka smiles. The lurid memory of Crow warriors mutilating the dead Blackfeet saw to that. What was to prevent these people from falling on a handful of woodsmen and seizing the trade goods?

He looked at the bronze, impassive features of his fellow frontiersmen, and saw not a trace of fear. With such comrades-in-arms, it seemed that odds even this overwhelming could be beaten. These grim, buckskinclad men were not the kind you wanted to tangle with.

Zach couldn't know that this was exactly the Indian way of thinking. As had the Shoshone, the Nez Percé, and the Flatheads, the Crows had already learned a healthy respect for the fighting prowess of the white trapper. Most mountain men were more than a match for a warrior—or even half a dozen warriors. Only the implacable Blackfeet seemed willing to absorb the cost of all-out, no-quarter war with the whites. Some of the village's Crow warriors had contemplated taking the trade by force, but to a man they'd calculated the heavy toll in Absaroka dead that would have resulted from such treachery, and none made a hostile move. Such was the reputation of the frontiersman.

Though apprehensive, Zach's thoughts remained primarily on Morning Sky. His hopeful gaze swept across hundreds of faces. More than a thousand Crows stood about the clearing and among the adjacent lodges. Shadmore interrupted his ardent search with a prodding elbow.

"Pay attention to the goin's-on hyar," advised Shadmore. "You might larn sumpin."

Iron Bull, sitting to Major Henry's immediate left, was holding a pipe fashioned from redstone clay. The stem was three feet long and quite slender. The pipe was decorated with eagle feathers, dyed horsehair, and the bright-colored plumage from the neck and head of a duck—a bird closely associated with the Absaroka myth of creation. The bowl of the pipe was packed with some of the tobacco the Major had given as a gift to Iron Bull. The Crows much preferred the tobacco of the white man to kinnikinnic—cedar bark and willow, shredded and then mixed with sweet grass.

Holding the pipe with reverence, the Absaroka chief pointed it first skyward, in supplication to the Great Spirit, and then towards the ground, to ward off demons. He described a complete circle with the pipe held at arm's length, invoking the tolerance of the elements, lest the "four winds" blow away the smoke of peace. Twice he puffed smoke at the sky. Twice more at the ground. Then he passed the pipe to Major Henry.

That Iron Bull passed the pipe to his right was significant. It set the tone for all that followed. Had the pipe gone to the left, only a "common smoke" would have resulted. This, though, was to be a "medicine smoke." All who sat in the circle and smoked the pipe were obliged to speak truthfully, to say only what was in their hearts if they said anything at all. Iron Bull was also serving notice that he intended to treat the whites in a fair and friendly way, and expected his people to do likewise.

Those hunters who were wise in the ways of Indians relaxed perceptibly when the pipe was passed to the Major. They knew then that they were relatively safe from Crow skullduggery—at least until they left the village and no longer qualified as Iron Bull's honored guests.

The sacred pipe was passed completely around the council circle. Everyone smoked from it, and no one spoke until the pipe was again in Iron Bull's possession. Major Henry could speak the Crow language, but not fluently, and he augmented his words with sign. Zach managed to follow the discussion, as many of the Indians who spoke also resorted to sign, for Henry's benefit.

One of the first queries put to the Major was whether the trade included liquor. In a very sincere and regretful tone, the Major told them that it did not. Only the frontiersmen knew he wasn't at all sorry. Henry was a meticulously honest man, but he wasn't about to come straight out and tell the Crows that the last thing on earth he intended to do was give them liquor.

He had come to trade for horses, and he made this plain from the first. One of the sub-chiefs wanted to know the future plans of the white trappers. Were they going to live where the Yellowstone and the Big Yellow River—the Missouri—became as one?

Only for the winter, declared Henry. Then they would go west into the mountains. They were going to trap beaver, and they needed horses for a successful season in the Teton and Absaroka ranges. The Arikarees had stolen all their horses.

It came as no surprise to the Crows that the Major and his men had come for beaver fur. They were not the trappers the Crows had met. In the past, though, the whites had set up outposts and encouraged the Indians to do the trapping. This was a good arrangement for all concerned. After all, who knew the country better than the Indians? Why didn't the Major stay in his fort and let the Crows bring the fur to him? Even now there was a great deal of fur in the village that the Crows were willing to trade for the goods the Major had brought.

Henry had been expecting this suggestion. Naturally the Crows preferred to have the white interlopers confined to one location, where they could be kept under observation. They were smart enough to sense that no good would come of allowing even a handful of whites to become familiar with the country. The land was like a beautiful maiden; the more the white man saw of her, the more he would desire to have her for his own. Besides, the Crows had trapped a considerable number of beaver this season, with the expectation of finding whites with whom to trade, as had happened in previous years.

The Major was willing to compromise. It was a matter of simple economics. Due to the mishaps that had befallen it along the Big Muddy, the Rocky Mountain Fur Company had lost valuable time, not to mention capital. They had very little fur to show for their efforts thus far, and Henry was not opposed to the idea of acquiring pelts from the Crows. That might cut some of the losses the Company had incurred. But horses had to be part of the deal. Horses were needed to transport the pelts, and to bring more trade to their good friends the Crows.

Zach came to realize that this council of eminent Crows would have to reach a consensus before the trade was permitted. Iron Bull was willing, and he tried to influence the proceedings as much as he could, but he wasn't going to make the decision hastily. He was the principal chief of the Absaroka by dint of personal accomplishment—advanced in years now, he had distinguished himself as one of the greatest warriors of his generation, and a man who had proven himself to be both wiser than most and singularly concerned, to the point of personal sacrifice, with the welfare of the tribe. But the position he held did not carry with it any kind of guarantee. He was chief at the sufferance of the people. If he tried to force his will upon them, he would in all likelihood die by their hand. Indians did not tolerate despotism.

Whether to make peace with the whites—and trading implied the making of a peace—was an issue of great moment, and in all such cases Iron Bull sought council approval. So it had always been when the Crows engaged in commerce with others. For thirty years the Absaroka had traded with the Atsena, who long ago had helped the Crows drive the Snakes from the Yellowstone country. From the Atsena the Crows acquired British goods, including some guns, which the Atsena had procured from the Hudson's Bay Company.

The Crows had recently become middlemen of sorts, obtaining horses from the Flatheads, who were famous for their splendid herds in the valleys of the Bitterroot Range far to the west, and turning around to trade these same ponies to the Mandans who lived further east. This arrangement worked to Major Henry's advantage, although he was unaware of it at the time, for as it happened this year the Crows had what they considered to be more horses than they thought their winter range could support. This was the deciding factor; after two hours of eloquent oratory and keen debate, it was resolved that trade with the whites would be permitted.

The decision ignited a flurry of activity, as the braves dispersed to gather the horses and furs they wished to exchange. The Major returned to the hunters' camp. There he would barter with scores of Crow braves, one after another, a business that would occupy the rest of the day.

"I thought they'd already made up their minds," Zach told Shadmore, "when they came to the fort to fetch us."

"Oh, they war aimin' to git the foforraw, fer sartin," replied Shadmore. "They jist hadn't decided how, until now."

Zach wanted to search for Morning Sky. But the Major ordered all the frontiersmen to stick close to camp while the trading was conducted. Henry was a square dealer—the bargains he struck were hard but fair—yet rare indeed was the Crow warrior who left the camp perfectly satisfied, and many were as temperamental as children, who don't think any deal was fair unless they'd gotten the best of it. The presence of the hunters kept any disgruntled brave from doing something rash.

By sundown, almost all the trade goods were gone. In their place the Rocky Mountain Fur Company possessed twenty-four good ponies, including several Appaloosas, a breed Zach had never seen before, as well as what amounted to eleven packs of beaver and one pack each of buffalo and otter pelts. The trading was halted, as festivities were in the offing in the Absaroka village.

All the frontiersmen were invited, but the Major had not allowed all the fine talk of peace and amity to go to his head; he wasn't about to leave the camp unguarded. Four men would remain behind, a pair to watch the horses and the others to build the packs.

The pelts had been traded individually, and had to be consolidated for transport. There were eighty beaver pelts in a pack. The "plews"—the choicest pelts—were put in the middle of the pack. All the pelts were stacked fur-side inward, and the whole lot was lashed together securely with rawhide. A pack of beaver skins was worth almost two hundred dollars back east. Zach thought the Company had made a pretty good profit off a few hundred dollars worth of trinkets and brightly colored cloth.

No one volunteered to stay behind in camp. Fair-minded as always, the Major settled the matter with a drawing of straws. Zach didn't draw one of the short straws, and was immensely relieved. He'd gone all day without seeing Morning Sky, and he was as miserable as he had been yesterday. A different kind of misery, and if anything more excruciating. He was haunted by the fear that he would never see her again. The prospect was unbearable.

Chapter 18

The Crows held a scalp dance to celebrate their victory over the Blackfeet. Earlier in the day, a messenger had arrived with word from the contingent of nearly a hundred warriors Iron Bull had sent out after the marauders from the north. The Blackfeet were in flight—news which was received with jubilation and chest-beating. The Blackfeet were running like scared deer from the terrible wrath of the Absaroka.

Beneath all this brave posturing ran an undercurrent of vast relief. The Blackfoot attack had shocked the Crows. Never before, in recent memory, had so many Blackfeet struck so deeply into Crow country. Was this raid a harbinger of things to come? Were the Blackfeet becoming even more aggressive and audacious in their incessant squabble with the Sparrow Hawk people?

Some of the Crows privately laid the blame on the doorstep of the Rocky Mountain Fur Company. The presence of white hunters had aggravated the situation. Everyone knew how deep and strong ran the vein of hatred for the whites in the stone heart of the Blackfoot. But most Crows wanted to cultivate closer ties with the frontiersmen. The Absaroka couldn't ask for better allies if a full-scale war with the Blackfeet was in the offing.

Major Henry and his hunters were the guests of honor at the dance, which took place in the clearing at the center of the village. A huge bonfire threw back the night. The dance was inaugurated by a medicine man who shuffled round the fire to the halting rhythm of drums and rattles, accompanied by the eerie, nasal chanting of four singing-girls. He held aloft a white stick adorned with tufts of human hair. He mumbled and moaned, and moved like a person in a trance.

Zach thought he looked a hundred years old. His hair was white as newfallen snow. His skin was like brown parchment. He wore a buffalo robe, and around his neck was a medicine bag and the sacred sack, a gift from the Great Spirit handed down through generations of medicine men. The sacred sack was never opened—to do so was a sacrilege that would visit a terrible calamity upon the entire tribe. It was the wellspring of the medicine man's power.

He was not the only medicine man in the village, but he was the eldest, and the most powerful in his craft. The people revered him, and he held sway in the affairs of the tribe. On this occasion, his ritual called upon the Great Spirit to bear witness to the brave deeds about to be retold.

One at a time, the warriors who had survived the Blackfoot attack danced—and it was unlike any dancing Zach had ever seen. Decked out in full war gear, their faces painted black, the braves leaped and whirled and struck the air with their war clubs and knives, gradually circling the fire. They pretended to fire arrows, and those who owned flintlocks simulated shooting at imaginary foes. Their features were wild, their bodies gleamed with sweat in the firelight. They acted out the fight blow for blow, and with plenty of heroic embellishments.

The audience, over a thousand strong, lapped it up. Their shouts of encouragement and approbation were deafening. The warriors worked themselves into a frenzy, and each ended his performance by proudly displaying his scalps, to the delight of the crowd.

Rides A Dark Horse took his turn, and gave a performance markedly different from those of his colleagues. After an exhibition of his own courageous acts, he drew the crowd's attention to Zach, who sat with the other hunters in a circle around the dance area. Acutely self-conscious, Zach watched while his own feats of bravery in battle were extravagantly depicted by Rides A Dark Horse.

"Wagh!" exclaimed Shadmore, sitting cross-legged next to Zach. "I didn't know you took on the whole Blackfoot nation and won, all by yore lonesome, Zach."

There was a twinkle of mischief in the old frontiersman's sun-faded eyes. He and the other hunters were much amused by this development.

"Lessen I miss my guess," continued Shadmore, "these folks are goin' to want to adopt such a magnificent fighter into the tribe."

"That will never happen," said Zach adamantly.

Shadmore grunted skeptically. "Never's a long time. Almost as long as forever."

After the warriors who had participated in the fight were finished giving their performances, all others who wished to, men and women alike, danced around the fire and the scalp poles. Zach looked for Morning Sky, in vain. The other hunters gorged themselves on a feast served by shy, smiling maidens. There was roasted buffalo meat, succulent roots sliced and simmered in grouse fat, camas root boiled like potatoes, and cakes made of sunflower and grass seeds and sweetened with wild honey, and sausages consisting of blackstrap chopped into hash and stuffed into cleaned intestines. For dessert, they cracked open buffalo bones and scooped the marrow out with their fingers.

Zach had no appetite. He only pretended to be eating and enjoying it, as befit a good guest. Shadmore wasn't fooled.

"You ain't et enough to fill a squirrel's stomach," he scolded.

"You should've been a Roman," replied Zach. "They'd eat and eat, then stick their fingers down their throats to make themselves throw up, just so they could start eating all over again."

Shadmore's bushy brows came together in a frown. "Now whar in tarnation did you hear such a thing?"

Zach shrugged. "I don't know. Guess it's one of the few things I remember learning about in school."

"If that's what they teach in school I'm glad I never got no schoolin'. Don't sound to me like them Romans had much sense. You git in the habit of swellin' yore belly whenever you git the chance, 'cause out hyar you never know when yore next meal might come along. The best thing about wild meat is you kin et all of it you want and not git sick."

Zach noticed Rides A Dark Horse in earnest conference with Major Henry. The Major glanced his way a few times, which made Zach feel ill-at-ease. A few minutes later Henry was tapping him on the shoulder.

"Hannah, I'd like a few words with you, in private."

They worked their way through the crowd. Zach followed the Major, his heart pounding. They did not speak until well away from the festivities, not far from the bank of the Yellowstone. Henry looked very solemn.

"What's wrong?" asked Zach, alarmed. Was Morning Sky gone? Sick? Or, God forbid, dead?

Major Henry was clearly making every effort to choose the right words.

"You seem to have a friend in Rides A Dark Horse," he said. "Personally, I suspect that the friendship has strings attached. Rides A Dark Horse has lost a brother and a father to the Blackfeet. He lives for revenge. Speaks for full-scale war. But he can't convince Iron Bull and the tribal elders. By themselves, the Absaroka are no match for the Blackfoot, I'm afraid."

Zach was at a loss to see how this could have anything to do with him, but he choked down all the questions he wanted to ask, and waited for the Major to explain the situation in his own time.

"The Blackfeet are fairly well armed," continued Henry, "as you saw for yourself the other day. We have the Hudson's Bay Company to thank for that. They're afraid American trappers will encroach upon their territory. The British want to use the Blackfeet to at least delay, if not divert us. So they supply the Blackfeet with guns, goodwill, and ammunition.

"Rides A Dark Horse is a clever fellow. He hopes we Americans will counter this alliance between the British and the Blackfeet by arming the Absaroka. Seeing the way you accounted for yourself in the fight, he assumes you must be a great warrior with much influence in the Company." The Major's smile was pensive. "He wants to get on your good side, Zach. You noticed how he sold you to the tribe during the scalp dance. He has a notion of inducting you into the Wolf Clan, a brotherhood of warriors. He wants to bring you into the tribe, so to speak."

"No thanks!"

Zach's vehemence startled the Major. A discerning student of human nature, he made a good guess at the reason for Zach's outright dismissal of the idea.

"Their ways take some getting used to, I know. I'm not saying I condone the savagery. On the other hand, I believe it is folly to judge other peoples by our own standards."

Zach's eyes turned a darker shade of blue.

"Just the same, the answer's no."

"Then what about the girl?"

"What does she have to do with this?"

"Rides A Dark Horse is prepared to play the role of matchmaker. He wants to mediate with Black Knife on your behalf. Apparently, Morning Sky has a friend in the wife of Rides A Dark Horse, a woman called Moon Singer. I suspect this is all Morning Sky's idea. She put it to Moon Singer, who suggested it to Rides A Dark Horse, who thought it might further his own schemes."

"You mean becoming a member of this tribe is a condition for . . . for . . ." Zach didn't know how to put such a personal matter into words.

"Rides A Dark Horse has one thing in mind: to foster an alliance between the Absaroka and the Rocky Mountain Fur Company. I don't think he'll insist on anything."

"What do you want me to do, Major?"

Henry carefully considered his reply.

"This reminds me of the old custom of arranged marriages. A tried-and-true method of establishing peace between families, clans, even nations. I won't lie to you. It wouldn't hurt the Company's chances to be on friendly terms with this tribe. But even if it did, I would be the last man on earth to stand in the way of love. You *do* love this girl, don't you, Zach?''

''Yes, sir. More than I can say.''

''That's the way love is. Leaves a fellow speechless. Well, fortunately, Indian courtships aren't elaborate or lengthy affairs.'' Major Henry put an arm around Zach's broad shoulders. ''I want to start for the fort tomorrow, so let's see if we can't settle this business tonight.''

Chapter 19

While Mayor Henry went off to find Rides A Dark Horse, who was to serve as their liaison with first Iron Bull and then Morning Sky's father, Black Knife, Zach lingered down by the murmuring river. His heart pounded furiously against his rib cage. His throat was suddenly so parched he could scarcely swallow. The palms of his hand were damp with a cold sweat. He couldn't seem to draw a good deep breath. In a panic, he walked aimlessly beneath the riverside trees.

He knew perfectly well that the problem was: a gut-wrenching, soul-jarring case of double-rectified cold feet. This was all happening so fast. What did he know of the mysteries of the gentler sex? There had been a girl in Copper Creek, the blacksmith's daughter, and for a little while he had thought it was true love, but it hadn't been. He knew that now, because his feelings for that long-ago-and-far-away yellow-haired girl with freckles on her cheeks were nothing like those he had for Morning Sky. The difference was day and night. Life had no allure without Morning Sky in it.

The arrival of Shadmore, accompanied by Jim Bridger, Old Bill Williams, and the half-breed Godin, just made things worse for Zach.

"What in tarnation you doin' down hyar, scout?" asked Shadmore, "when ever'body else is up yonder at the shivaree?"

"Walking," was Zach's sullen response. He had no desire for company.

"Jist come to make shore and sartin you war still wearin' yore hair," said Old Bill.

Seeing the smirks on the faces of all four trappers, Zach conjectured that there was more to this visit than concern for his health. With a sinking feeling in the pit of his stomach, he realized they knew, somehow, about his imminent marriage.

Shadmore put a comforting hand on Zach's shoulder.

"You look plumb skeered to death, Zach," remarked the grizzled leatherstocking. "Now I know it ain't 'cause you seen a passel of Blackfeet skulkin' around in these hyar trees. Blackfeet don't skeer you worth a plugged nickel—you done proved that yesterday." Shadmore turned to his colleagues. "I reckon we were right after all, boys. Ol' Zach's gonna squaw-up."

Zach was grateful for the darkness. His face was hot—he was blushing furiously, and he could only hope the others couldn't tell.

"That shore nuff is sumpin to be skeered about," nodded Williams, with mock gravity. "I'druther face a hunnerd bloodthirsty Blackfeet than to git hitched agin."

Old Bill was a long, gaunt character who had seen about as many winters as Shadmore. Like Shad, he was a tried and true mountain man. This was by no means his first time west of the Mississippi. Tall and thin as a beanpole, he had in his youth acquired the habit of standing hunched slightly forward to compensate for his unusual height, giving him the appearance of being hunchbacked and making him look even longer in the tooth than was in fact the case. But he was as stalwart as any man in the Rocky Mountain Fur

Company, bar none. The bullet wound he had received in the recent fight with the Blackfeet seemed to be of as little consequence to him as a mosquito bite. His gray eyes were as alive and alert as they had ever been, and twinkled now with a merriment that belied the solemn demeanor he was trying, with incomplete success, to maintain.

"Again?" exclaimed the half-breed, Godin. "You mean you found a woman once who was willing to share a blanket with an ugly cuss like you?"

Godin was not the best-liked man in the company. There was something dark and dangerous about him, an underlying malevolence. His humor had a cutting edge every bit as sharp as the knife he was so fond of using, and which had been the source of trouble between the trappers and their Crow allies a few nights earlier.

Old Bill gave the breed a cool appraisal. Zach thought Williams looked at Godin the way he would look at a cur dog nipping at his heels.

"Some of us are ugly as sin on the outside," allowed Williams tolerantly, "while others are uglier still on the inside, I reckon."

Shadmore laughed. Godin was not amused.

"Go ahead, Old Bill," urged Shadmore. "Tell the younker the facts of life. I done tried to, but he warn't in no mood to listen. I got me a fearsome hunch he's more inclined to see reason at this moment than he ever were before, or ever will be agin."

"Like a dog I kin try," said Williams. "Hannah, I spent a handful of winters up amongst the Broken Arrows and the Cut Throats—"

"Them be Sioux tribes," interjected Shadmore, seeing Zach's brow furrow.

Old Bill nodded and went on. "I packed a squaw back in them days, and the onliest excuse I kin give fer that mistake is that I were a lot younger, and that's to say a sight dumber. She were a wolverine bitch iffen I ever seen one, and she pestered me day in and day out fur all manner of foforraw. If it weren't one thing it were another she wanted, and iffen she didn't git it she'd bawl and bellyache like a sick child. Worse still, dang near her whole goldurn family liked to move right into my lodge. Laziest bunch of no-accounts I ever did see. Finally traded her to some poor idjit fur a lop-eared packhorse what died on me the very next winter, and to this day I believe it war the best trade this pilgrim ever made.''

Zach heard a wheezing sound, something akin to the noise a panting dog would make. It was Shadmore, chuckling like a fool.

''Morning Sky isn't like that,'' said Zach defensively.

''Wagh!'' exclaimed Shadmore. ''You got a thing or two to larn still, I see. Wimmin are all the same, hoss. They'll try to run yore life, and that I cain't abide. They'll latch on to a man s'long as they reckon he kin give them what they want and take 'em where they want to go. Iffen he don't or won't, they'll pretty themselves up and go to lookin' fer someone else to latch on to. It ain't fer better or worse with them, I guarantee.''

''That ain't necessarily true,'' objected Bridger. ''Women aren't all the same.''

''The hell they ain't,'' argued Old Bill. ''And all men are the same, too. Way I see it, a man and a woman ain't meant to stay together. Now, you take critters. A male critter and a female critter git together long enough to do what God built 'em to do, and then the male critter goes on about his business and the female critter raises her brood. Was us humans to do likewise we'd buy into a heap less misery.''

"My God," said Bridger, with a laugh. "That's awful romantic, Old Bill."

"Yore purt near as young as Hannah," said Williams. "Don't figger too many wimmin have left their tracks on yore heart, yet. But they will, and come a time yule see the light."

"Younkers have to larn life's hard lessons their own way, Bill," sighed Shadmore. "They don't never listen to the wisdom of their elders."

"These two old coons come down to have fun at your expense," Bridger told Zach. "I come to congratulate you. Morning Sky's some punkin."

"Won't argue that," said Shadmore. "She does shine. But I'druther woman-up with one that's uglier'n a yeller ox. Purty wimmin draw trouble the way a dog draws fleas. I cain't hardly believe the Major's gonna throw in with this. A purty squaw like Morning Sky will scotch things up plenty back at the fort."

"At least I won't have to worry about you and Old Bill," said Zach dryly.

"Nope. It's young bulls like Bridger here yule have to beat off with a stick."

"Not me," said Bridger, lighthearted. "Zach's too good a shot."

"How 'bout you, Antoine?" Shadmore asked Godin. "You aim to keep yore paws off Zach's wife-to-be?"

"Peut-être," replied Godin, with a noncommittal shrug. *"Peut-être que non."*

Shadmore snorted. "That's what I thought."

"Well," said Old Bill, "all this palaverin' done parched my palate and made me hungry all over agin. Reckon I'll mosey back to the big doin's." He turned away, beckoning to the others. "Come on, lads. Nothin' more we kin do hyar. Zach Hannah's done fer."

Bridger and Godin followed Old Bill up through the trees. Shadmore lingered a moment to rest a hand on Zach's broad shoulder, a paternal gesture.

"Knew you wuz in fer it, fust time I seen how you looked at that girl. It's like a fever you cain't shake, and thar's only one cure. This Morning Sky may be sweeter'n molasses, but she's still a woman."

"I love her."

"You want her, or you need her? Thar's a difference."

"I thought you were my friend," said Zach, keenly disappointed.

"I like to think so." Shadmore was suddenly and genuinely serious. "I used to be like you, a younker wanderin' aimless-like, lookin' fer a place to belong. I found it in the high country, what I were lookin' fer, and I have me a hunch so will you. Has sumpin to do with freedom, Zach. Not havin' to answer to nobody, and havin' only yoreself to look out fer. Many a man's thrown away his dream fer love, or what he thought was love, and precious few have thought the bargain a good one at road's end. You were born to be a mountain man, Zach Hannah, I feel it in these ol' bones. Nothin' like wimmin to lead a man off the right path. Don't lose sight of the mountains, hoss. Try not to lose yore way. Jist remember: A woman's breasts are harder'n stone, and no man's ever found sign on 'em."

Chapter 20

Zach didn't resent Shadmore's attempt to dissuade him from getting hitched to Morning Sky. The old leatherstocking was just trying to look out for him. But Zach knew Morning Sky was different from the women who had plagued Shadmore and Old Bill Williams, and he came away from the conversation down by the river more certain than ever that taking Morning Sky for his wife was the right thing to do.

Still, he was as nervous as a long-tailed cat in a room full of rocking chairs as he accompanied Major Henry into the presence of Iron Bull.

The chief's tepee was no larger than the others in the summer camp of the Sparrow Hawk people, and nothing distinguished it from any other except its location at the center of the camp, across from the medicine lodge and the scalp poles.

The entrance was draped with a bearskin, and this was pinned open, an invitation to enter. Zach followed the Major in. They found Iron Bull, Black Knife, and Rides A Dark Horse seated facing one another on buffalo robes around the center fire. The interior of the lodge was smoky and cozy warm. The two white men circled behind Rides A Dark Horse, who sat with his back to the entrance, so as not to breach Indian etiquette by passing between the warrior and the fire.

Zach studied the faces of the three Indians. The chief

appeared solemn, but his eyes were friendly. Rides A Dark Horse looked like a coyote who had just caught his prairie-dog dinner. Here, mused Zach, was a man who expected personal gain from playing the role of matchmaker. Black Knife, Morning Sky's "father," was sulking. Zach guessed he had already voiced objections to the proposed marriage, and that Iron Bull had overruled him.

This conjecture on Zach's part was very close to the truth of the matter. Black Knife was not at all pleased with the arrangement, and had made his feelings known to Iron Bull in no uncertain terms prior to the arrival of the two white men. Morning Sky's happiness was of no consequence to him, she was merely a valuable commodity. Her beauty made it so. Tall Wolf had given many fine horses for her, and Black Knife had been looking forward to the substantial material benefits he would reap by marrying her off to another up-and-coming warrior—as soon as a suitable mourning period had been observed, of course. That Iron Bull's wish was to use Morning Sky in a marriage of convenience with this young frontiersman was a bitter blow to Black Knife. He had rejected the initial overture made by Rides A Dark Horse, resenting the fact that Rides A Dark Horse had pulled strings with Iron Bull to get his way. The chief of the Absaroka Crows had just finished lecturing Black Knife on the advantages the tribe would realize as a result of this union, and had as much as said that it was Black Knife's duty to place the welfare of the tribe before his own.

It was not the Indian way to come straight to the point, and Iron Bull opened the proceedings with a long-winded retelling of the Crow legend. He augmented his narrative with sign, and Major Henry translated for Zach, who was able to grasp less than half of the chief's soliloquy.

Long ago, declared Iron Bull, there had been a great flood, and when it was over, God found only one creature left alive—a duck. God asked the duck to dive beneath the waters which covered the world and bring Him some mud. This the duck managed to do. God waited until the mud had dried, and when it was dust, threw a little to the north, south, east, and west. Suddenly there was dry land all about. God molded the mountains. The duck dived deep once more, returning with more mud, and asked God to make certain things, including the Indians, because he was lonely, being the only creature in the world. God held the mud in his hand until it had dried, then blew it out. From the dirt sprang a man and a woman—and a great many crows.

God called the man and the woman to him. He showed them the antelope, deer, and buffalo he had created to sustain them. He killed a buffalo and cut it open, explaining the parts of the buffalo and their many uses. He showed the man how to make a bow and arrows, and explained to the woman her responsibilities in the propagation of the species.

In time there were many people in the world, and God divided them into the Sioux, the Cheyenne, the Piegans, and the rest. He permitted them to name themselves, and the first man he asked responded, "We will call ourselves after the black birds you created with the first man and the first woman," and so the Crows were brought into being.

Taking the Crows to the Yellowstone River country, God said, "This is your land. The grass is good, the water pure. I have made all this country round about, with you in the middle. All the people around you shall be your enemies." He further instructed the Crows to kill their enemies, take their scalps, and to keep fighting, even if it seemed hopeless. In their darkest hour, when it appeared that the Crows would fall before implacable foes pressing them relentlessly on all sides, God would send help.

God then went to a tree and struck it, and the white people came out of the tree like a swarm of locusts. God told the Crows he would send the whites to show them how to make iron. "Do not fight them," God said. "Shake hands with them. They will aid you against your enemies, and because of this you will prevail."

Iron Bull pointedly turned to Black Knife as he finished. Zach, who had until then wondered what, if any, purpose lay behind this recitation, suddenly understood. The chief was letting Morning Sky's father know that the fulfillment of prophecy was the reason he approved of the marriage. It was a telling argument—one Black Knife was powerless to counter.

Obviously, love did not enter into it; this was purely a business arrangement. Iron Bull and Rides A Dark Horse were interested only in strengthening ties between the whites and the Sparrow Hawk people. And Zach wasn't sure but that Major Henry looked on it from the same perspective.

One of the few lessons Zach recalled from his school days was that in olden times a king often took for his queen the daughter of another monarch, to bind the two nations together. It nettled Zach to know that he and Morning Sky were mere pawns in a power game that Iron Bull and Major Henry were playing. But he was endowed with enough prudence to keep his opinion of the proceedings to himself.

Black Knife realized that resistance to the matchmaking was futile, yet his avarice ran so deep that it compelled him to argue for generous gifts from Zach in exchange for Morning Sky. This, he bemoaned, was the way it had always been—thereby turning the weapon of tradition back on Iron Bull. No one could deny, declared Black Knife, that but for this arrangement he could have reasonably anticipated twenty or thirty warriors vying for Morning Sky's hand. Surely it was not too farfetched to assume that he would have netted several of the finest horses in the Crow nation in exchange for a daughter lovelier than the mountains, as pleasing to the eye as wildflowers, whose alluring gaze was as blue as the sky, et cetera, et cetera.

The chief acknowledged that Black Knife was due some recompense. The sign for marriage, he pointed out, *was* the same as that which signified trade. As Iron Bull made this concession, Zach noticed the covetous way Black Knife was looking at his Hawken rifle.

Rides A Dark Horse came to Zach's rescue. Seeing only Zach's obvious reluctance to part with the Hawken, and afraid that Black Knife's avarice would ultimately scotch the arrangement, he offered to stand as proxy for Zach in the matter of gifts. Black Knife would have five of his best ponies.

Black Knife seemed inclined to insist on the Hawken. It was a far more splendid fire-stick than any Crow possessed. Of course, he was too old to carry the weapon into battle, but everyone would be suitably impressed with the Hawken. It was a gift worthy of his stature in the tribe.

"There is great magic in that rifle," said Rides A Dark Horse, "but it lives only so long as the rifle remains in the hands of our white brother. I have seen it with my own eyes, when our white brother turned the rifle against our enemies, the Blackfeet. To destroy this magic would do harm to our people, for our enemies are the enemies of our white brother."

Black Knife glowered. Once again forced to prove that he placed his tribe's welfare above his own profit, he consented reluctantly to the offer of five ponies from the private cavallard of Ride A Dark Horse.

The deal done, they smoked a pipe to seal the bargain, using tobacco mixed with the inner bark of the red willow.

As he accepted the pipe from Rides A Dark Horse, Zach found his gratitude for the warrior's assistance mixed with strong foreboding. He was convinced Rides A Dark Horse had intervened on his behalf, not out of the goodness of his heart, but for his own ulterior motives. What price would the warrior exact from him in the future? Whatever the price, Zach resolved to pay it. He would have made a deal with the devil himself for Morning Sky.

All that then remained was a certain ritual for Zach to perform.

Taking a buffalo robe presented to him by Iron Bull, and following the chief's instructions, Zach proceeded to Black Knife's tepee. Black Knife had preceded him. It was late, and the festivities had wound down, with most of the trappers back in their own camp and the majority of the Absarokas retired to their skin lodges. Zach kept his head covered with the buffalo robe, for it was part of the ritual that the suitor not be recognized. Those who passed him as he waited, pacing nervously, studiously ignored him.

Zach's agitation was such that he could scarcely catch his breath. He was afraid to the point of terror— he had not experienced anything remotely resembling this degree of fear during the Blackfoot attack.

What in fact were minutes passed like hours. And when, finally, Morning Sky emerged, Zach's heart skipped a beat. She was a vision of pure, unadulterated beauty in the moonlight, and made music when she moved, for her short doeskin dress, as well as her leggins and moccasins, were adorned with at least ten pounds of colored stones and glass beads. Her long black hair was shining in the silver glow of the moon as she stepped close to him.

Trembling, Zach held the robe open. Morning Sky took another step, and he wrapped the robe around her. Her fragrance made his head swim, and as she leaned against him, and he felt the heat of her slender body, his soul began to sing in joyous exultation. He was complete. Content beyond measure.

They stood embracing for quite some time, wrapped in the buffalo robe. Eventually Morning Sky pulled gently away, and Zach felt cold, and knew he would always feel cold without her near. She took a few steps, turned, and gestured shyly for him to follow. Through the camp she led the way, down a footpath through the dark trees to the singing river. Here, in the tall grass, Zach spread the buffalo robe, and sat with his back against a tree trunk. She curled up beside him, laid her head upon his chest so that she could listen to the beating of his heart. He kissed her hair, and when she turned her face up to look at him, he brushed her lips with his. She sat up, startled, eyes wide. Zach remembered that kissing was not a custom familiar to Indians. Had he offended her? She touched her lips with her fingertips, and then smiled. Extending her left forearm, she touched it with her right index finger several times, beginning at the wrist and concluding at the elbow.

"Yes," he breathed, drawing her to him, "I will kiss you many times. I will kiss you forever."

And there they stayed until first light, in each other's arms, serenaded by the river.

Chapter 21

The trappers left the summer camp of the Absaroka Crow the next day with an escort of warriors led by Rides A Dark Horse, who seemed to be Iron Bull's ambassador to the Rocky Mountain Fur Company. Iron Bull insisted this was a gesture of friendship—with a large party of Blackfeet in the vicinity, one could not be too careful. But none of the trappers was *that* naive. They knew that given half a chance the Crows would abscond with the horses and furs Major Henry had just acquired from them in trade. It wasn't personal, and the trappers didn't take it that way; it was accepted Indian practice.

Of the twenty-four horses now in the company's possession, some had to be employed in carrying the thirteen packs of furs. Zach was given the responsibility for a pack animal laden with four hundred dollars' worth of beaver plews. The horse was a handsome beast, a chocolate-colored mare with a blond mane and tail, and still bearing the red bull's-eye symbol of its previous Crow owner. But it proved to be green-broke, and therefore fractious, and Zach had his hands full all the first day. The pony was one minute straining against the apishamore by which Zach led it, and the next trying to take a chunk out of Zach's arm or shoulder with its blunt teeth.

But even dealing with the difficult beast couldn't intrude too much upon Zach's good humor. Mounted on an Appaloosa, Morning Sky rode behind him, smiling warmly each time he looked at her, which was often. Everything seemed right with the world, as far as Zach Hannah was concerned.

Even the weather changing for the worse could not dampen his enthusiasm. The sky became overcast their second day out, a dull silver-gray lid stretching from horizon to horizon. The sun appeared as a nebulous white spot without warmth, and beneath it thin wisps of cloud scudded briskly. An icy wind gusted from the north, cutting into the eyes and chilling to the bone. Men and horses bowed their heads and leaned into it and plodded doggedly forward. The prairie, so fetching in its autumn dress only a few days ago, now looked bled of all life and color.

They made the trek to the fort at the mouth of the Yellowstone without mishap. In spite of the weather, the uncooperative horse, and the wound in his side, which persisted in shocking him with an exquisite twinge of pain at the slightest provocation, the two days on the trail were not nearly as difficult for Zach as the night that fell between.

As usual, the Crows kept primarily to their fires, and the trappers to theirs. Pursued by some good-natured, if ribald, ribbing from his companions, Zach took his blankets and his bride a little distance off from the camp. By the way the trappers were joshing him, he knew it was his only chance for peace and quiet. The trenchant cold and the peevish horse and the long march, coupled with his injury, had taken the starch out of him. And he sensed that Morning Sky was a mite apprehensive, wondering when her new man intended to consummate their union.

Zach had misgivings of his own on that score. He desired Morning Sky, but was just downright afraid.

Trapped and helpless between conflicting emotions, he let fatigue sweep him into sleep.

Later that night he woke abruptly, with her body on top of his. She was naked, her skin hot and smooth under his hands. The camp slumbered—the night rent by the stentorian snores of the trappers. Morning Sky touched his side, near the knife wound, and he read the question in her expression, shook his head. He suddenly felt no pain. He let his hands describe the curve at the small of her back. She touched her lips, which were slightly parted, and he kissed her, gently at first, and then with a consuming passion, and what began as a timid, tender discovery of bodies rapidly escalated into ardent frenzy.

Some time later, as she slept safe and warm in his embrace, Zach stared at the star-bossed sky, feeling unworthy of all the blessings he had received, knowing he had to be the luckiest man alive, and thanking the Almighty from the bottom of a heart so full of love it was bursting.

Major Henry was not a hopeless romantic.

He had consented to the marriage of Zach and Morning Sky for purely practical reasons, hoping it would serve as a stepping stone to cementing good relations with the Absaroka Crows. He was aware that the presence of a woman at the fort, particularly a woman as winsome as Morning Sky, might create problems among his own men. In time, some of the other trappers would "squaw up." That was inevitable. But what concerned him immediately was the possibility that a few of the trappers might try to trespass on Zach Hannah's territory.

The major understood his mountain men. They were a special breed: daring, self-reliant, courageous, and fiercely independent. But there were two sides to every coin, and he also knew them to be thoroughly undisciplined and unhampered by the strictures of society. They lived an uncivilized life, and you couldn't expect them to be gentlemen. They usually took what they needed, regardless of whether the action fit the mold of civilized behavior. Wild and free, these trappers, and there were some who had a tendency to become a little *too* wild and free at times. Antoine Godin was one who came to mind. And young Devlin was another Major Henry deemed it wise to keep an eye on.

"You put one ewe in a pen with a bunch of rams," he told Zach, "and you're going to see some head-butting, sure as the rain is wet."

For that reason, he suggested that Zach and his bride live outside the fort. He went to great pains to make it clear that Zach was not being cast out. He still expected Zach to do his duty as a member of the Rocky Mountain Fur Company.

Zach was content with the arrangement. His entire world revolved around Morning Sky, and if to keep her he had to forsake the camaraderie of the other men, it seemed a small price to pay.

They erected a skin lodge in the shelter of a point of cottonwoods on a shelf overlooking the Yellowstone, below the bluff where the fort stood. A game trail, winding through the trees and up a draw to the crest of the bluff, provided access from fort to tepee.

The poles of their lodge were pine, trimmed, peeled, and then cured to keep them straight. The frame consisted of twenty of these poles, all approximately twenty feet in length. The first three were bound together at the top, a tripod, and the rest were stacked against these, in the same way that soldiers stacked their rifles in bivouac, with the lower ends of the poles forming a circle roughly fifty feet in diameter. The covering was one piece, made of dressed-out buffalo skins sewn together, and the edges were held together with wooden pins, except for three feet at the top for the smoke-hole and three feet at the bottom for the entrance. A spare pole was attached to one edge of the covering at the top, so that the smoke-hole, usually left open, could be covered if necessary. Zach learned that Indians replaced their lodge covers at the end of every summer, using the old ones in the making of a stock of moccasins for the long winter months. By then the skins that made up the covers were perfectly cured by the smoke from countless fires.

Zach was still part of the "mess" that included Shadmore, Devlin, Bridger and the two French-Canadian rivermen, and he was still expected to do his share in the laying in of food and firewood for the winter. In addition, he was obliged to provide for himself and Morning Sky.

Winter would soon be upon them. The abundant signs of this included great flocks of migratory birds winging southward overhead and massive herds of bison on the move. The Crows broke their summer camp and headed for sheltered valleys deep in the mountains.

Crews labored long and hard felling trees and cutting them into firewood, while others bagged buffalo, deer, elk, and antelope. At his makeshift smitty, young Jim Bridger fashioned scythes, which were used to collect vast quantities of prairie grass, laid in as fodder for the cavallard. In the barracks, they put pelts up to cover every inch of cabin wall. Doeskin, cured, scraped thin, then dried hard and made translucent by applications of marrow fat, went up over the windows. When the shutters were left open, the doeskin allowed sunlight into the barracks and turned away the cold wind.

While her man was absent working with ax or rifle,

Morning Sky did her fair share. A Crow upbringing had taught her leatherwork and embroidery, for which Absaroka women were justly famous. She made Zach a tawny buckskin hunting shirt decorated with handsome quillwork across the breast, and for both of them she made buffalo robes. The entire company coveted the golden-brown smoked elk skins she produced. Zach was impressed by the remarkably stout thread she made from buffalo sinew by twisting and shaping it while keeping it moist with saliva. She dried cuts of meat, sliced and laid across green saplings over a willow fire to make jerky.

Morning Sky fried deer tenderloin in kidney fat, and made a delicious soup by heating the marrow from buffalo bones in a pot of blood and then mixing in succulent roots, sliced and sizzled beforehand in butter made from hump fat. She stuffed mushrooms with marrow fat and browned them. Zach developed an almost insatiable appetite for these "buttons," but her "French dumplings" were the real delicacies—minced buffalo tenderloin, mixed with marrow and then rolled into balls that were in turn covered with flour dough and simmered. They became Zach's breakfast of choice.

As a result, they often had company when it came time for victuals. Shadmore was a frequent visitor. The old leatherstocking wanted to make sure all was well with his protégé. Though he had done his level best to prevent Zach from getting hitched, now that the deed was done he treated Morning Sky with flawless courtesy. In time their relationship warmed to the degree that one might have thought the Indian girl was the mountain man's daughter. Shadmore facilitated Zach's learning of the Crow and Blackfoot dialects, while helping Zach instruct Morning Sky in the rudiments of the English language. The graybeard hunter delighted in acting as translator, and he hastened considerably the learning process for both of them.

Bridger and Sublette came around on occasion, and behaved like perfect gentlemen. Devlin, too, made regular appearances. Zach watched him closely at first, not knowing what to expect, and remembering the way Devlin had looked at Morning Sky when they had first seen her, but Devlin did nothing to justify his suspicion. In time, Zach let down his guard. Shadmore advised him to remain vigilant. "Coyote," declared Shadmore, was the perfect nickname for Devlin.

"I wooden trust that pilgrim fer nothin'," said Shadmore. "He ain't nobody's friend. You keep floatin' yore stick with him, Zach, yule wind up in trouble eyebrow-deep, and that's a gold-plated guarantee."

Shadmore had nothing personal against Devlin; he was just watching out for Zach, and Zach appreciated that. But he couldn't help thinking that Shadmore had been wrong about Morning Sky, and might be wrong about Sean Michael Devlin, too.

"Yule see, I reckon," persisted Shadmore. "Coyote ain't the kind to look out fer nobody but himself."

Before long, Devlin had an opportunity to prove Shadmore right or wrong.

Chapter 22

When winter came, it came with a vengeance. Blue northers scoured the high plains, bringing bitter Canadian cold. Zach woke to step shivering out of the skin lodge one morning, and found himself in a fog that glittered like diamonds. Sudden, intense cold had frozen the moisture in the air—he had never before witnessed anything like this haze of frost crystals.

It proved to be one of the worst winters any of the old hands could remember. So severe that it split trees wide open, froze animals in their tracks, and turned the rivers and streams into solid ice from bank to bank and, in some cases, clear to the bottom. Blizzards howled through with sixty-mile-an-hour winds, filling the air so thickly with sleet that any man or animal exposed to it could die with a nose and windpipe filled with ice. Trappers careless enough to lay hand to the steel of gun or knife or trap sometimes found their flesh welded to the metal.

If there were any bison in the vicinity of the fort when the blizzards struck they often sought shelter in the lee of the stockade, and the trappers could kill that day's supper without leaving their cabins. Many were the days when the world seemed reduced to a blinding tempest of snow and sleet, a wind howling like a thousand banshees, and a cold so keen it crept into the bones and made them ache. The high drifts of snow became so glazed with ice that neither man nor beast could take a step without falling.

For days on end, the men of the Rocky Mountain Fur Company could do little but huddle around the fireplaces in their cabins and wait for Old Man Winter to vent his fury. But Major Henry knew the danger of letting his men sit idle too long. They had endured a lot together, and a camaraderie was there, but eventually tempers began to fray as cabin fever set in. "I ain't one to sit in a hole till green-up, like some gol-danged grizzly," groused one man. It was a common complaint. So when the weather permitted, Henry allowed them to venture forth, to hunt and trap a little. His only conditions were that they travel with at least one other, and that they took care not to stray very far from the fort.

Zach was luckier than the rest. He did not mind it in the least when the weather imprisoned him in his skin lodge with Morning Sky.

As time went on he came to realize that his Indian bride did indeed love him every bit as deeply as he loved her. It was said that Indian women took up with white trappers for purely practical reasons, to better their situation. So said the frontiersmen. Zach wasn't sure he could buy into that. He figured there were good husbands and bad husbands, white and red.

Morning Sky had grown up a Blackfoot captive of the Crow, and if anything, was treated worse than the average Crow woman. Had Zach merely been her means of escape? It shamed Zach even to entertain such thoughts, and eventually they ceased to torment him, as each new day brought fresh evidence of Morning Sky's devotion to him. He was relieved to be rid of such doubts, and had anyone suggested that one day they might come back to haunt him he would have scoffed at the notion.

She soon found herself emotionally dependent on him. There was very little chance the Blackfeet would take her in with open arms after so many years, and the Absaroka had never made her feel like one of their own. Black Knife had treated her little better than he would a slave, and Tall Wolf had been an abusive husband. Zach was so different. He was strong, but gentle. Tall Wolf's attraction to her had been purely physical, and he had soon become contemptuous of her. With Zach there was a spiritual bond. The difficulty in communicating verbally they faced at the beginning seemed to nurture in each an ability to understand the other without spoken or signed words. They were like the two sides of the same coin. Different, yet one. In no time at all, Morning Sky had reached the point where she couldn't imagine life without him.

And that very first winter she almost lost him.

One of the French-Canadian camp-keepers, a man named Chavanac, disappeared a week before Christmas.

Chavanac had been moody and reticent of late, and it was the general consensus that he had deserted the company to return to the arms of a scarlet woman who resided in the Vide Poche district of St. Louis. Of course, to attempt such a journey in the heart of winter was nothing short of suicidal. But that, opined Shadmore, was the kind of damage a woman could do. They could make a man crazier than a loon. Chavanac obviously had been bewitched. The other French-Canadians muttered something about black magic. And being cooped up in the fort for weeks on end hadn't helped Chavanac's frame of mind, either.

Major Henry called a council. Most of the men were disinclined to exert any effort to find Chavanac. For the past few days the weather had been fairly good, but who could say how long it would hold? The discontented *mangeur de lard* had made his bed, now let him lie in it alone. No one gave him a chance for survival. If the cold didn't take him, wolves or Indians would. He was gone beaver, for sure. No great loss.

But Henry disagreed. Chavanac had absconded with two horses and a large quantity of supplies, not to mention a pack of furs. The major couldn't let that go unpunished. If he allowed Chavanac to get away without making at least an attempt to apprehend him, how many others would start entertaining a notion of deserting, and taking company property with them?

He had to make an example of Chavanac.

A light snow had fallen the night of Chavanac's departure, obliterating his tracks. Henry called for four volunteers. They would travel in pairs. One pair would follow the Missouri, while the other cut cross-country due south for the headwaters of the Grand River, a tributary of the Big Muddy which joined the latter in the land of the Arikara. The first was the most likely course for Chavanac—he was a riverman, and knowing the Missouri, would feel more comfortable letting it guide him to St. Louis. But the Grand River route, while chancier, was also quicker.

No one was eager to step forward. It was a matter of supreme indifference to most of the trappers whether Chavanac got away, or even survived. A taciturn, brooding character, Chavanac had no real friends even among the other French-Canadians.

Zach was the first to step forward. While loath to leave Morning Sky, he felt a strong obligation to Major Henry, and he could sense how important Chavanac's capture was to the Major. Chavanac's escape would corrode discipline and undermine Henry's ability to command. Zach felt he owed Henry for his present happiness; without the Major's sanction, he could never have married Sky.

When Zach stepped forward, Shadmore moved to do likewise, but Zach persuaded him not to.

"I'd be obliged were you to stay and look after my wife," said Zach. "You're the only one I'd trust. She means more to me than anything, Shad, and I'll rest easy knowing you're here."

Shadmore could not say no.

And then Devlin volunteered to accompany Zach.

"We're blood brothers, remember?" asked Devlin. "And blood brothers stick together through thick and thin."

Bridger and Williams also volunteered. They would follow the river, while Zach and Devlin drew the overland route. The Major gave Zach his compass. As long as Jim and Old Bill stuck to the Missouri, they could not lose their way in even the worst weather. The same could not be said for Zach and Devlin.

Taking his four volunteers aside, Major Henry enjoined them to return to the fort if in three days' time they had found no trace of Chavanac. Zach sensed that Henry did not hold out much honest hope of success. The search for the errant French-Canadian was really being conducted just for the sake of appearances, and the Major worried lest he lose four good men just to prove a point.

Chapter 23

It tore at Morning Sky's heart to bid her man farewell.

They parted in haste. Chavanac had at least six hours' head start. No good could come of giving him more. Zach collected extra powder and ball, flints, and a buffalo robe, while she prepared a pack filled with enough jerky and pemmican to last a month. She also thought to include slices of frozen raw liver. This "mountain bread" prevented scurvy at a time of year when fresh fruits and vegetables did not exist.

Their parting was hard, and Zach made short work of it, not trusting himself to maintain a manly front if the leave-taking were prolonged. As he rode off with Devlin, he felt absolutely dismal. The austere white wonderland into which they were venturing was breathtaking in its beauty, but he did not have eyes for it. He had lost the capacity to appreciate Nature's grace. Once he had desired nothing more than to belong to this land; now his lone ambition was to belong to Morning Sky. Hers was the only form that beguiled him, and he was utterly wretched when separated from her. That first day he came close to turning back a hundred times, and would have, had he known how to face Major Henry with the confession that he was unable to do his duty because it absented him from his Indian bride. It was a disturbing self-revelation, this dependency. He had found his manhood in Morning Sky's arms, and lost it there as well. He scarcely spoke a word all that first day, and Devlin, displaying uncharacteristic prudence, left him alone.

For her part, Morning Sky put on an air of iron stoicism perfected during the years of mistreatment at the hands of first Black Knife and, later, Tall Wolf. But Shadmore's eyes were keen. He saw right through her.

"He'll be fine," he consoled her. "That boy was tailor-made by God Almighty fer the mountains. I knowed it first time I met him. And you know God ain't in the habit of wastin' time nor effort."

Morning Sky could not quite grasp the eccentric logic of this declaration, but she put on a brave face and did her best to quash the fear of losing her man. She prayed that day, and every other, to Grandfather Sun to shine until Zach returned, and to Grandmother Earth to nurture and protect him while he was away.

Yet though her prayers were earnest and proper, she was not sure they would be heard. A lifetime of tribulations such as she had suffered did not encourage her to put much faith in the munificence of the spirits. They had never paid her entreaties much attention in the past. Morning Sky was a fatalist; perhaps this brief interlude of happiness was all she was meant to have.

She knew something bad was going to happen.

Shadmore took very seriously his responsibility to look after Morning Sky. When she refused Major Henry's invitation to move into the stockade for the duration of Zach's absence, the old leatherstocking debated whether to move his gear down to the skin lodge. But that had a taint of impropriety to it, even though everyone knew Shadmore's attachment to Morning Sky was purely avuncular. One had to maintain appearances. He thought it better to sleep in the stockade and call frequently on Morning Sky during daylight hours. He also spread the word through the company that the skin lodge was off-limits, and that anyone who violated that rule would answer to him.

Still he suspected that a mere caveat would not suffice to deter certain hardcases, and figured the best way to get the point across was by making an example out of one of them.

So it was that on the first night he slipped out of his cabin and posted himself in an advantageous spot, wrapped up in a buffalo robe and in his resolute and tough-minded way refusing to acknowledge the discomfort attending exposure to a twenty-below high-plains winter night.

It was Antoine Godin who volunteered to serve as Shadmore's example.

Late in the night, the half-breed stole out of the barracks and crawled through a hatch cut into the side of the west palisade. The main gate, on the south side, always remained closed and, since the Chavanac incident, was guarded round-the-clock. The hatch Godin used had been made for escape in the event the fort was attacked and overrun by hostiles.

Just beyond the hatch waited Shadmore, more patient than Job. Godin exited on hands and knees. Grinning with delight, Shadmore clobbered him sternly on the back of the neck with a stout length of firewood brought along for the express purpose of clobbering. Stunned but not quite unconscious, Godin found himself hoisted off the ground and slammed head first into the stockade wall.

"Thievin' skunks allus use the back door!" roared Shadmore, loud enough to wake the dead.

Frontiersmen sleep light, and Shadmore's holler was enough to rouse the company—which had been his motive.

The old mountain man dropped Godin into blood-speckled snow and stepped back. The breed was a tough specimen, as tough as they came, and was quick to gain his feet and draw the knife he loved to use, and used so well. Growling like a grouchy bear, he lunged at Shadmore. Blinded by a black rage, he was aiming to add Shadmore's topknot to his collection. But Shadmore still had hold of the piece of wood, with which he first deftly parried the thrust of steel and then applied a solid blow to Godin's skull. It was a carefully measured blow, designed to incapacitate Godin until at least first light.

Shadmore waited until most of the company had gathered before delivering his speech.

"I caught this hyar rascal sneakin' out, and I don't need to tell you boys he had black-hearted business on his mind. I reckon he aimed to bend his steps down yonder to a sartin skin lodge whar he didn't have no proper invite and warn't welcome. Now y'all know I'm a peaceable sort, and it pains me sumpin fierce to put the hurt on another human bein', but I cain't tolerate someone who don't live by the Ten Commandments. I mean the one about covetin' another man's wife, in this case. It's true that ever' man answers fer his sins on Judgment Day, but iffen anybody else in these parts has a notion to try a little sinnin' with that Injun gal, just remember yule have to answer to me and this stick of wood fust." He took a deep breath and added, "Here endeth the lesson."

Confident he had made his point, Shadmore stepped

over the fallen Godin and returned to his cabin, where he slept a righteous sleep.

Loneliness preyed on Morning Sky. Often she entertained thoughts of accepting Major Henry's offer, but she stayed in the skin lodge, because it was her duty to keep the home fires burning.

Every night she survived, and every day that dawned clear lifted her spirits. She did her best to keep busy. Idleness was the worst enemy of a lonely heart. And then, on the morning of the third day, there was an omen.

She was sitting cross-legged just outside the skin lodge. The sun on her face offered little warmth, but the fire in the tepee behind her did. As she worked to make an elk skin pliable by rubbing in a compound of brains and fat, she sang a song from her childhood. It conjured vague recollections of a happier time, days of family and friendship and a sense of belonging. She had a splendid voice for singing. Zach, who couldn't carry a tune in a sack but had a good ear, said so.

No sound betrayed the presence of the wolf. She felt its eyes upon her and looked up from her work. Fear paralyzed her. The wolf was sitting on its haunches not twenty feet away. A big silver male—it weighed at least as much as she—with a charcoal-gray saddle, muzzle, and shoulder markings. It was panting, its breath steaming in the chill morning air, its tawny eyes alert and inquisitive and fastened on Morning Sky. They were intelligent eyes, almost human, she thought. It seemed to her as though the wolf knew exactly what she was thinking.

Morning Sky tore her gaze away from the wolf and looked around. She saw no other wolves lurking among the snow-laden trees. That was peculiar. Wolves usually ran in packs, especially in winter.

The lone wolf made no threatening moves or noises. It appeared quite content to sit there and listen to her sing. Morning Sky's thoughts flew to the flintlock pistol in the lodge. One of the other trappers had traded it to Zach in exchange for two elk skins. Zach had left it, primed, for her to use if she needed to. He had shown her how to load and fire the pistol. She wondered if the wolf would attack when she moved. Experimenting, she lifted an arm, just an inch or two. The wolf's jaws clamped shut. It sniffed the crisp clean air, cocked its massive head a little to one side, like a curious dog. Then it started to pant again.

Morning Sky was perplexed. She knew plenty about wolves and wolf ways. This one did not display any hostility. A solitary wolf would not venture so close to humans unless it was sick or mad or starving, and the silver male did not appear to be any of these things. It was a magnificent creature, in splendid condition.

"Are you a spirit?" she asked, pitching her voice barely above a whisper.

The wolf's ears turned, but otherwise it did not move.

Emboldened, she said, a little louder, "Go away. You frighten me."

The wolf stood up and began to walk away.

Supernatural dread sent a shudder through Morning Sky. The creature *was* a spirit! Why had it come to her like this? What did it mean? All such things happened for a reason. Some disaster had occurred, or some good fortune was just around the bend. Spirit visitations were the harbingers of some important, usually life-altering event.

"Zach," she breathed.

At the edge of the trees the wolf stopped and looked back at her, and then it loped away, vanishing into the snowdrifts.

Morning Sky wept uncontrollably. Only later, when the tears would come no more, did she understand why she had cried. Shadmore came down from the fort that afternoon and found her sitting there in front of the skin lodge, a blank look on her face. Her voice dull and lifeless, she told him with dead certainty that she would never see her man again.

Chapter 24

For two days the sky remained clear, but Zach and Devlin knew their luck could not last for long. The high-plains winter was nothing if not capricious.

Even in fair weather there were inherent perils. Sunlight on the snow could cause temporary blindness—to prevent this they chewed tobacco, then rubbed the dark juice beneath their eyes. The second day was unseasonably warm, and the afternoon sun began to melt the powder. That night the cold north wind kicked up and turned the wet surface into a treacherous glaze, inches deep.

When they broke camp the third morning, Zach's horse slipped and fell sideways on sharply sloping ground. The horse rolled down-slope, thrashing, completely over Zach, whose left leg was trapped at an unnatural angle beneath eight hundred pounds of horse, fracturing the bone six inches above the knee. The horse got up, unharmed.

It was a simple fracture, and Devlin set it. He used willow limbs for splints, and cut a blanket into strips and tied the splints to Zach's leg. He tried to inject some levity into the situation.

"If you wanted to go home you could have just spoke up. You didn't have to go and bust a leg."

Feeling utterly helpless, and not liking the feeling one iota, Zach was not amused.

"Think about all the tender lovin' care you'll get from that good-lookin' squaw of yours while you mend," said Devlin. "That ought to ease the pain some. Can you ride?"

"It's a cinch I can't *walk* back," growled Zach.

Devlin grinned. "I could put together a travois. Drag you around like an old woman."

"Just bring me that damned horse."

Riding with a fresh-broke leg was a real test of endurance. Zach found that Devlin's prescription actually did help take his mind off the scorching pain that shot through his body with every step the horse took. He kept reminding himself that each step brought him that much closer to Morning Sky.

The Major's compass was in Zach's keeping, and it distressed them to discover that it had been broken in his fall. As long as the weather held—as long as they had the sun and the stars and their own sign to guide them—this was not a cause for real concern. But they had no faith in the weather.

They made good time across the rolling, snow-clad prairie, backtracking themselves, and camped that night in a cedar bosky nestled in a fold of the earth. Devlin built a crackling fire, and they thawed their hands and feet. A cedar fire was a loud talker, and produced plenty of smoke, but they hadn't seen a sign of another human being for three days.

Devlin cut some more boughs off the evergreens, laid them out on the snow, and spread one of Zach's blankets over them, making a comfortable and dry pallet for his injured companion. Watching Devlin work, Zach decided there was solace to be derived from having a friend around in times like these. He wondered what Shadmore would say if he could see Coyote go to such pains.

Warmed by the fire and dry on his bed of cedar

boughs, Zach was as comfortable as a man in his condition could expect to be. He countered the pain with thoughts of Morning Sky. With luck, he could be in her arms by the end of the next day, or the beginning of the day after.

But that night a storm crept south under cover of darkness. It struck them without warning at dawn. The temperature plummeted. Devlin jumped up and grabbed the horses, which were startled by the violence of the wind. In minutes the world was a frozen hell. Snow and sleet enveloped them, lashing at them from all directions at once. They huddled in their buffalo robes, grasping the reins to hold their ponies close.

The cold cut through Zach like a knife. He began to lose feeling in his hands and feet, then his arms and legs. He could not control the violent shivering of his body, or the chattering of his teeth. Ever so slowly, a seductive warmth spread through him. He thought he might as well lie down and go to sleep. Just in time, he realized what was happening.

He was freezing to death.

"We've got to get moving!" he yelled at Devlin above the howling of the wind.

Devlin helped him to mount his horse. Zach couldn't kick the beast into motion, so he surrendered the reins to Devlin who, remaining afoot, led both ponies out of the cedars.

The sleet slashed at Zach's eyes, making him weep. His tears turned to ice. Bent over until his face was nestled in the horse's mane, he was soon overcome with drowsiness again. Desperate, he dismounted and tried to walk. He felt no pain from the break, yet could not support any weight on that leg. With one hand he grasped the bridle, and with the other held on to the tail of Devlin's horse. He stepped with his good leg, dragged the bad leg along, anchored it in the snow, and stepped with the good leg again. It was a tricky business, and time after time he fell. He was tired after covering a hundred yards, thoroughly exhausted after a quarter-mile. But the exertion kept the fatal lethargy at bay.

The world was a blinding maelstrom of white—he could scarcely see an arm's length ahead of him. So he kept his head down and just held on to the tail of Devlin's horse. Held on for dear life. There was no way to know in what direction they were going. A man could walk in circles for hours in a blizzard and not know it. Zach didn't concern himself with that. All he cared about was summoning the strength to get up every time he fell down. If he didn't get up, he would die.

Every step was a lifetime of suffering, and he reached the point where he could hardly withstand the temptation to lie down in the soft snow and sleep forever. The only reason he didn't was Morning Sky.

He toiled doggedly on, sometimes sinking down into the powder waist-deep, falling a thousand times and a thousand times getting up, one minute cursing the storm and the next sobbing with despair—and, later, laughing deliriously at the frozen hell that was trying to take his life.

After a dozen eternities the wind died, and in place of the blizzard's violence there came a gentle snowfall. Zach's eyelids were frozen shut, and he rubbed them until he could get them open. He and Devlin, in snow to their knees, stared at one another, too stunned by fatigue to speak. Survival astonished them.

In time they found the strength to move on, riding for a while until plodding through the snow had completely impoverished their mounts, then walking a spell. They could not be sure of the time of day—a solid gray overcast completely obliterated the sun. They could not be certain, either, of their direction, for now there was no wind at all, and the empty, white-cloaked plains rolled on without a single landmark to guide them.

Eventually the gray twilight deepened, and they knew night was coming on. They camped among some trees, built a fire, melted snow in a tin cup held over the flames for a drink, and thawed their jerky and pemmican so they could eat it. Zach stayed awake just long enough to eat. He had never in his life been so weary. Wrapped in the warm cocoon of his buffalo robe, he slept like a dead man.

The next day carried on where yesterday had left off—gray sky, no sun, still as death. They did not see a living thing. It was unsettling. Zach imagined that some awful cataclysm had struck the earth, destroying all life but Devlin and himself. The land appeared completely foreign to him. The plains were like the open sea, he thought, inasmuch as those who tried to cross them also needed the sun and stars to guide them.

He calculated it was afternoon when they first saw the wolf pack.

There were about a dozen of them—dark, fleet shapes loping across the snow, a quarter-mile along their backtrail and closing fast.

"They're after us!" gasped Devlin. "They've got our scent."

He stripped the fringed buckskin sheath off his Hawken, checked the priming.

Zach knew something about wolves. They ran the Tennessee ridges where he had grown up. He listened hard for the sharp yelps wolves made when in hot pursuit of prey. But these wolves were running silent.

In his opinion wolves were the most intelligent of the wild creatures. They were unerringly loyal to their own kind. A wolf would fight to the death to protect its family. They were fearless, elusive, unmatched as hunters. Rarely did they attack a man. But they were mightily fond of horseflesh.

"Reckon it's our ponies they're after," said Zach.

The horses thought so too. Zach had his hands full holding both mounts while Devlin got his Hawken ready for action. Their frightened antics yanked Zach off-balance, and the best he could do was sit there in the snow and hold on to the reins for dear life.

Flight was pointless. There was no chance of out-running the pack.

Devlin brought the Hawken's stock to shoulder and drew a bead. He was shaking—the combined effects of the severe cold and a case of nerves—and cursed himself.

"Steady," said Zach. As had happened during the battle with the Blackfeet, a remorseless calm overcame him. "Let 'em get closer." It occurred to him that a different arrangement—with him shooting and Devlin performing the horse-holding chores—would have better suited the situation. But there was no time to change roles.

The wolves suddenly vanished into a fold of the prairie. Devlin sighted down on the crest where he calculated they would reappear, a hundred yards away.

Minutes crept by.

No wolves.

Devlin lowered the rifle, looking this way and that to check their flanks.

"What in blue blazes . . ." he breathed, bewildered.

"There!" cried Zach.

A single wolf had appeared on the crest, precisely where they had expected to see the entire pack. It was a big silver creature—near twice the size of any wolf Zach had seen in Tennessee.

Devlin raised the Hawken, but before he could fire the wolf had disappeared back beyond the rim.

Raised on the river, Devlin could call on a vast variety of curses, and he let loose now with a long and heartfelt string of maledictions. Zach had the sudden urge to laugh. He couldn't resist. Infuriated, Devlin turned on him.

"You think this is funny? You've lost your flamin' mind, Zach Hannah, damn you to hell! You had to go break your damned leg, and now we're lost in this damned miserable wilderness with a goddamn pack of wolves on our trail, and you think it's a laughing matter! By God, I ought to leave you here. You're doing nothing but slowing me down."

Zach stopped laughing. "My pa told me wolves are the smartest creatures God ever made. They know when a man's armed, and that big silver wasn't going to just stand there and wait to see how good a shot you are."

"You think you're a long sight better than I am, don't you?" was Devlin's surly response. "Well, you don't look like much now, sitting there all stove-up."

"Go along, if you want," said Zach. "I've been wondering why you came with me in the first place. You aren't the volunteering kind."

Devlin reddened, and Zach could tell he had struck a nerve.

"So why did you come?" pressed Zach. "You could be safe and warm back at the fort right now if you hadn't."

Thin-lipped, Devlin said, "Because I used to think I wanted to be like you, Hannah." He snorted. "But you're no great shakes, after all."

The revelation stunned Zach. Though he did not

doubt Devlin's sincerity, he found it absurd that anyone would desire to emulate him. He didn't know what to say.

For a long while neither man spoke. They watched for the wolves to make their move. A mournful howl sent shivers of primeval dread down their spines, and in short order they saw the pack, a quarter-mile off, well to the left of the last sighting. It was a fleeting glimpse. The rolling plains quickly swallowed them up.

"Let's get going," muttered Devlin.

"No. You were right. I'm slowing you down. We can't be far from the fort. Go on ahead. I'll make it."

Devlin was furious. "I can't leave you. The others wouldn't stand for it. Don't take me wrong. It's not you I'm worried about."

"I know that."

"Oh, and you'd come out the hero again," fumed Devlin. "Sacrificing himself to save my bacon. Well, to hell with you! I'm taking you back, and that's my final word on the matter."

Disgusted, Zach hauled himself aboard his horse.

This time Devlin deigned to lend assistance, and that suited Zach just fine. He tried to tell himself that people did and said things under duress that they didn't mean. He and Devlin had quarreled. No need to make a big fire out of a little smoke.

But he was too angry and disappointed to take his own advice. One thing was clear as mother's milk: Down deep, Devlin resented him, and that resentment was a cancer relentlessly eating away at their friendship.

Or had they ever really been friends?

Devlin had let him down, and Zach was hurt. He couldn't wait to get back to Morning Sky. At least he could count on her. He didn't really need anything else. They had to be fairly close to the fort. Even if they were off-course they couldn't miss the Yellowstone, cutting east-west across the plains from the mountains to the Big Muddy. Once they reached the river it would simply be a question of deciding whether to turn up or downstream.

But they did not find the Yellowstone before nightfall, and as they slept, the wolves came calling once more.

Chapter 25

Generally, wolves prey on animals that are sick, injured, or in some way enfeebled. The horses of Zach and Devlin fit that bill perfectly. They were in desperate need of rest and fodder, and had obtained precious little of either. Their efforts to paw holes in the deep snow to reach the grass beneath met with scant success, reducing them to the task of trying to strip the outer bark of spruce trees and licking the cambium. Wretchedly weak, they were in a truly extreme fight for survival, and the wolves could sense it.

Led by the canny silver male, the wolf pack crept quite close to the sleeping camp without being discovered. So close, in fact, that when Devlin's horse did detect them and raise the alarm with a shrill whinny, one of the wolves was on it in a heartbeat, leaping for the throat, sharp fangs sinking deep. The horse reared, screaming. The reins that tethered it to a tree snapped in two and the horse toppled sideways, dying. While the first wolf tenaciously savaged the throat just below the gullet, a second deftly avoided flailing hooves and latched on to a stifle, while a third ripped a horrendous bloody hunk out of its haunch.

Zach's horse broke its tether and bolted, three more yelping wolves on its heels. The rest of the pack closed in on the horse already down. The silver male hung back, watching everything, the way a general surveys a battlefield. It saw Zach and Devlin explode out of their blankets, rifles in hand. Devlin fired without taking time to aim, straight into the melee of wolves swarming his dying horse. The bullet struck one of the beasts in the hip. The wolf writhed in the snow, biting at its own wound. Another hurled itself across the intervening ground and lunged at Devlin. Hobbling on his busted leg, Zach fired from the hip and then fell down. The Galena ball caught the wolf in mid-lunge, smashing its skull and killing it instantly.

The silver male barked and slipped away into the night. The rest of the pack followed, some carrying portions of horse meat in their bloody jaws. The wolf Devlin had shot followed in their wake; it would not go far before expiring.

The pack had vanished before Zach and Devlin could reload.

Belatedly, Zach realized that moonlight was streaming down through the stand of evergreens where they had made their camp. This factor, more than any other, accounted for his good shooting. Astonished, he looked up and saw myriad stars adorning a clear and frosty night sky.

Yelling like a madman, Devlin slogged through the snow in the direction Zach's horse had taken. Shouting at Devlin to stop, Zach tried to get up and follow. But Devlin didn't hear him or wasn't listening, and was soon out of sight. Zach got as far as the edge of the trees before falling. He was too exhausted and pain-wracked to continue.

He lay there a while in the snow, catching his breath, letting the pain subside, frozen clear through and yet almost inured now to cold. He couldn't remember ever really being warm. Cold had become a fact of life.

His mind a blank, he stared at the starry sky for quite some time. Slowly, it dawned on him what he was seeing. Sitting up, he got his bearings, a sinking feeling in the pit of his stomach. Again and again he checked the stars that had guided him on so many nights. The harsh truth could not be denied. Despair swept through him. He wanted to throw up. He tried to swallow the lump of fear caught in his throat.

The fear of dying.

He remembered a story his father had told him long ago, of a day up in Kentucky, when Nate Hannah had crossed the path of a hostile bear. Although his flintlock had misfired, Nate had triumphed, but one thing that had stuck in Zach's mind was his pa's admission that he had been so scared he couldn't even spit.

Zach tried to spit now. But his mouth was dry as cotton, and he couldn't.

Way off in the darkness, a shot rang out. Zach struggled to his feet. He used the Hawken as a crutch. It helped some, but not much. He had told Devlin that wolves almost never attacked humans. Yet this very night he had seen one do precisely that. He imagined Devlin being torn apart by the pack. Aided by the moonlight, he had no difficulty following Devlin's trail, which mingled with that of the horse and the pursuing wolves.

To his vast relief, he met Devlin backtracking to the campsite.

"Damned wolves," growled Devlin. "Killed the other horse. Ran off when they saw me. Shot at 'em. Missed."

Zach just stood there, leaning heavily on the Hawken, too busy sucking air into frozen lungs.

"Well, we're bound to be nearly home now," said Devlin, attempting to put the best possible face on the situation.

"We're days away from the fort," said Zach woodenly.

"You've gone addled on me."

"There's the North Star. I reckon we've been headin' mostly west for the past two days. We're probably fifty miles, maybe more, from the fort."

"Fifty miles!" Devlin stared at the stars, then the frozen prairie, and finally the stars again. He was silent a long time. Zach watched the same succession of emotions he had recently experienced parade across the haggard, bristling features of his companion.

"You can make it in a couple of days," said Zach, "without me slowing you down. If you don't object to horse meat, you'd do well to fill your belly with a hot meal before you light out."

"What about you?"

"I'll just settle down here for a spell. Got plenty of fresh meat, thanks to the wolves. You can send back some help."

"Or I could bring it back myself," said Devlin coolly. "Except you're coming with me."

"This won't be held against you. It's my choice."

"The wolves will come back for their kills," insisted Devlin grimly. "And don't tell me they won't go after you. You saved my life just now, and I'm going to return the favor. I don't want to be beholden to you. I'm taking you back, and that's final."

Zach didn't waste his breath on further argument.

Returning to camp, they discovered that the sack of jerky and pemmican and mountain bread was gone—the sum total of the provisions they had brought with them. They searched the churned and blood-flecked snow, to no avail.

"Damn wolves must've made off with it," grumbled Devlin.

Zach concurred; that was the only logical explanation. Drawing his knife—the one Devlin had purchased for him in St. Louis—he turned to the dead horse.

"I don't relish eating horse," confessed Devlin.

"Got to. If we don't, we won't have the strength to make it. You start a fire. I'll see to this."

Devlin fetched his hatchet and went to work. He soon had a handful of shaggy cedar bark for kindling, and an armload of fresh-cut boughs, trimmed down. Putting flint to whetstone, he ignited the kindling. The green wood sizzled and smoked. Devlin patiently coaxed the fire into life.

Meanwhile, Zach butchered out some loin steaks. These were spitted on trimmed boughs and held over the feeble flames. The half-cooked meat turned out to be tough and stringy, but not unpalatable.

"I've heard tell the Comanche Indians like colt meat over any other," remarked Zach.

"And the Kiowas eat dog," said Devlin. "But knowing all that don't make this any easier."

They ate all they could, and then Zach cut some more steaks. He sacrificed one of his two blankets; cutting strips with which to wrap the stock of his Hawken, he halved the remainder, using one half to wrap the horse meat and the other to swathe the barrel of the rifle, which would serve now as his crutch. He secured this makeshift covering with fringe cut from the buckskin hunting shirt Morning Sky had made for him.

Gathering their meager belongings, they set out, heading north by east, the morning sun slanting in their eyes. Devlin went first, slogging through the deep powder, and Zach did his best to stay apace, keeping as much as possible to his companion's footprints.

The miles that lay before them were a daunting challenge. Zach tried not to think about the odds stacked so heavily against them, even though after the very first of those miles he began to doubt his ability to persevere. His was a continual physical and mental battle, beating down the despair that welled up inside him, seeking the strength to take one more painful step, and then another, and another. But through it all he did not once feel sorry for himself. He did not bemoan his fate, as other men might have. Zach wasn't made that way.

In spite of his best efforts, Zach knew he was slowing Devlin down. Devlin didn't complain. Halfway through the day he positioned himself on Zach's left, draped Zach's arm over his own shoulders, and locked in step with Zach, taking upon himself some of Zach's weight. Zach accepted the help without argument.

At day's end they found shelter beneath a rock ledge on the bank of a frozen creek. Nearby lay the bones of an elk. They cracked some of the bones open and scraped out the marrow with their fingers. The marrow had a bitter, rancid taste, but they consumed it, knowing it was a source of nutrition with which to augment their dinner of horse meat cooked over a deadwood fire.

Zach calculated they had covered less than ten miles that day. At this rate it would take four more days to reach the vicinity of the fort. That was not a pleasant prospect. Day after tomorrow they would be overdue. Morning Sky would worry. Zach hated to think of that happening.

He did not share his calculations with Devlin. There was no need. Devlin was moody and silent most of the evening, and Zach surmised he had done some figuring of his own.

"You reckon Major Henry will send out a search party?" asked Devlin.

"I doubt it."

Devlin nodded. So did he. He stared into the dying fire. "Be like throwing good money after bad, wouldn't it? Just as well. It'd like a miracle for them to find us anyway. Guess we're on our own. When it comes right down to it, you're always on your own in this world, really."

"If you believe that, why don't you leave me behind?"

"Already told you why."

Zach wasn't entirely convinced. He wasn't sure what to make of Sean Michael Devlin.

The next day was a repeat of the one previous, a struggle in a frozen wasteland. Now and then Zach would raise aching, bloodshot eyes and search the distance. It always looked the same. Desolate, lifeless, cloaked in a cold winter haze.

Devlin railed against the barren plains, the snow, the cold. He warmed himself with anger. But Zach did not think a man could fight this land. If he tried he would lose. Despite his predicament, Zach had to marvel at the sheer breadth and power of nature. This was truly God's country, upon which He had lavished His most epic blessings, and though it seemed on the verge of killing him, Zach loved it.

They ate the last of the horse meat the third day following the wolf attack. It was their seventh day away from the fort. Zach couldn't believe it had only been a week—it felt more like a year. They had seen a lone bull elk that day, too far away to shoot, and veered off their course to try to get close enough, but the elk fled. To track it meant going south, and neither of them wanted to surrender one inch of ground bought with such grinding travail. Giving up on the elk, they went hungry that day. The next morning found Zach so weak he could barely stand. A man could go a few weeks without food if he didn't exert himself, but Zach and Devlin required sustenance to continue their trek. They chewed the fringe from their buckskins into pulp, swallowing the tanning fluids. They tried eating snow, but it made them sick. Hunger ripped at their innards, sapped their strength.

By the afternoon of the fourth day Zach knew he was finished.

There just wasn't anything left. As darkness descended they could find no decent shelter. A wind was kicking up. Cutting a circle in the frozen crust which always followed a day of sunshine, they hollowed out the snow, making a hole beneath the crust large enough for them both to curl into, shrouded in their buffalo robes and tattered blankets. Windblown snow soon covered them. Zach went to sleep fairly certain he would never wake up. This hole would be his grave. He was reconciled to his fate.

But he did awake, to the sound of a gunshot, and he emerged from his snowy tomb to stare at Devlin, who was dancing a stiff and stumbling jig and screaming like a madman, shaking his rifle overhead. Befuddled, Zach looked beyond Devlin, and saw the dead wolf ten yards away. Off in the distance the rest of the pack was running, swift gray terrors streaking across the snow, blue in the hollows and pink on higher ground touched by the dawn's light.

The snow around the hole was covered with wolf tracks.

"They were right on top of us!" said Devlin, his eyes bright and strange, like the eyes of a man burning up with fever. "They took off when I come up out of the hole. But I got one of the devils, by God!"

Like wild animals themselves, they fell on the dead wolf with their knives. Ravenous, they did not bother with a cook-fire, eating the still-warm meat raw, tearing at the tough flesh with their teeth. When finally their bellies were full, they rubbed snow into their beards to wash away some of the blood, and rubbed the crimson stain off their hands with more snow. It occurred to Zach that a man could afford to concern himself with acting and appearing civilized only when he wasn't starving to death.

A few hours later they reached a river they knew had to be the Yellowstone.

They turned east, and before the day was out they saw the fort way off in the distance. Devlin fired his rifle into the air and yelled himself hoarse. The distance was too great for his shouts to be heard, but the shot brought men at the run.

An overwhelming lethargy suddenly gripped Zach. He had covered hundreds of miles under the most trying of conditions, but he could not summon one more iota of strength, could not manage the last quarter-mile. The ordeal was over, and he couldn't believe it; he was afraid the fort, and the men churning through the powder towards him, were apparitions—figments of his tortured mind. Falling to the snow, he waited with breathless anticipation until Shadmore reached him. He lashed out and grabbed the old leatherstocking's arm, squeezing it, making certain it was solid flesh and bone.

"Wagh!" exclaimed Shadmore, his bearded features twisting with emotion. "I thought you wuz gone beaver, scout, fer sartin."

Zach didn't know whether to laugh or cry. Then his

vision blurred, and the earth beneath him began to spin. He blacked out. With Jim Bridger's help, Shadmore carried him to the skin lodge.

At some point that night Zach regained consciousness to find himself in the arms of Morning Sky, in a warm cocoon of buffalo robes and velvet skin, and he began to weep silently. She kissed away his tears.

Chapter 26

Bridger and Williams had followed the Missouri downstream for three days. Having found no trace of the errant Chavanac, they returned to the fort without mishap. By all accounts Chavanac never reappeared in the Vide Poche district of St. Louis, and it was the general consensus that he had perished en route.

Zach was quick to recover from his ordeal. This was due in part to his youthful vigor, but even more to Morning Sky's tender care. He thought it remarkable that he had lost not even a finger or toe to frostbite, much less a hand or foot. His leg healed nicely, even though his exertions had stressed the fracture. Shadmore made him an honest-to-God crutch, and he was soon up and hobbling about. Still he spent a lot of time flat on his back, recuperating, and so had plenty of idle hours to contemplate his brush with death.

Devlin remained an enigma to him, and he and Shadmore talked it over. The latter admitted that Devlin's constancy during the crisis surprised him.

"I'd've staked all my possibles that Coyote would've pulled his freight and left you on yore own stick when things got to lookin' bleak," said Shadmore.

"There was a time or two I thought he would," said Zach. "But he didn't. The first time, he said he didn't because he didn't want to have to explain coming back alone.''

Shadmore smiled grimly. ''He might've had a tough time talkin' his way out of that one, hoss.''

''The second time, when the wolves killed the horses, I told him to go on without me. But one of the wolves had attacked him, and I killed it, and he said I'd saved his life and he didn't want to be beholden to me. It was my choice to stay, but he wouldn't leave me.''

''Mighty hon'rable,'' remarked Shadmore.

''But then it went from bad to worse. So bad I didn't think honor alone could make him stick.''

''But he did. So, why? Friendship? You've known me purt near as long as you have him.''

''And you and I are true friends, Shad. I know I could trust you with my life.''

''Same goes for me, Zach. But you ain't so shore 'bout Coyote, are you? Even now.''

Frowning, Zach shook his head. He almost told Shadmore about the money Devlin had stolen from the gambler, Tyree, the act which had thrown them together in that St. Louis alley. But it was a dark secret he shared with Devlin—one that, if exposed, would have dire consequences for the thief. And Devlin *was* a thief, no doubt about it. So why, wondered Zach, am I protecting him?

''All I can tell you,'' said Zach, ''is that he told me, in so many words, that he wanted to be like me. I can't figure out why he would, but that sure seemed to matter to him.''

''Huh,'' grunted Shadmore, chewing the tip of his pipe. ''Wahl, you and him wuz cut from different cloth, I tell you, so he's got a heap of work to do iffen he aims to be like you. Now me, I caclate folks are what they are, and thar ain't no changin' 'em. Oh, you kin try till yore blue in the face, but it ain't no more likely than birds flyin' back'ards.

"Take me, fer instance. I had me a wife back east. That were in my younger days. I hadn't set eyes on the Shinin' Mountains yet. She tried her durnedest to make me into some kind a man that I weren't and never would be. She pestered the dickens out of me, scout. Why, it got so's I couldn't do a danged thing right in her eyes. It went on year after year, and I got to give her credit— she never quit. Wimmin are like bulldogs. Oncet they sink their teeth into you they ain't gonna let go iffen they can help it. Nossir, she never quit, but *I* shore did. Took up my rifle one day, walked out the door and bent my steps due west, not once lookin' back. You cain't be other than you are, so thar ain't no use tryin'. I reckon Devlin didn't want to be like you so much as he wants to have what you have."

"What do you mean? What do I have? You mean . . . Morning Sky?"

"Not zackly. Though I don't figger he'd turn it down, twas it thar fer the takin'. No, I'm talkin' about things like honesty and loyalty and just plain backbone. It's 'cause you got all them attributes that you got sumpin else—the respect of others. It'll be a cold day in hell 'fore Devlin gits his hands on *that*."

"I don't know," said Zach. "But there's no stepping around the fact that he stuck with me. I wouldn't have made it if he hadn't."

"Don't sell yoreself short, Zach Hannah. You got more grit than most."

When Morning Sky informed Zach of the visit by the spirit-wolf it gave him a shock. Many nights since his return he had dreamed of wolves. Not nightmares, exactly; in fact, he could never remember them in any detail. But they disturbed him, as though there were something very important about the dreams he needed to be aware of but couldn't quite grasp.

It encouraged Morning Sky that Zach took the news seriously, so she went on to say that, though at the time the visit by the wolf-spirit had filled her with dread, she realized now that she had misinterpreted the incident. The spirit-wolf had come to her on the very morning Zach had broken his leg. That was no coincidence. The spirit-wolf must have come to let her know that her beloved husband would be protected, would survive the catastrophe that had befallen him.

Zach turned this over in his mind for a few days, and later shared his conclusion with Shadmore and his Indian bride. By this time Zach's proficiency in the Crow and Blackfoot dialects had progressed so far that he resorted very little to the expedient of sign language.

"I never before put much faith in spirits and omens and such," he told them, "but I believe what you have told me is true, Sky. At the time, I saw the wolves as a threat. Now I think they may have saved our lives. They killed the horse, and we had fresh meat to get us through the next few days. And when we ran out of horse meat, and faced starvation, and didn't have the strength to go another mile, then the wolves came again, and Devlin killed one, and again we had fresh meat—enough to see us through."

"And the one what almost pulled Coyote's plug might've been tryin' to do you a favor," quipped Shadmore, only half in jest.

"A big silver male led the pack," said Zach. "And it was a silver male Sky saw."

Shadmore shrugged, skeptical. "I seen wolf tracks. Spirits don't leave sign, do they?"

"I don't know. You told me you followed the tracks into the trees, and they just vanished."

"Wolves kin be crafty critters when they have a mind to be," was Shadmore's only defense.

Zach didn't press the issue. He could tell Shadmore was not going to concede that a wolf could be anything more or less than a wolf. For his part, Zach was well on the road to understanding that there was more to life than what met the eye. His folks had been god-fearing, and of course he believed in the Lord Almighty, and in younger days had dismissed the Indian way, with its multitude of spirits, as paganism. Now he wasn't sure but that the two dogmas could be reconciled. In this magical wild country it was easy to conceive of a power beyond human ken that abided in the sky and the wind and the earth itself, in the tracks of a wolf, or the kiss of an Indian girl.

Devlin's stock went up in the Rocky Mountain Fur Company as a result of the adventure. He didn't beat his own drum; in fact, he downplayed the entire affair. The humble approach only served to strengthen the conviction of his peers that he deserved the status of hero. The facts were there in black and white, and no one could dispute them. With his leg broken, Zach Hannah would have perished had he been alone; his impairment had slowed them down considerably, notwithstanding his own remarkable efforts, and Devlin had exposed himself to further peril by remaining with his friend. The facts did not lie.

It was not Zach's nature to begrudge Devlin this acclaim. He had no intention of raining on Devlin's parade by letting it be known that Devlin, by his own admission, had remained with him for less than noble reasons: because he did not want to face the other trappers after abandoning Zach, and, later, because he did not wish to be obligated to Zach for saving his life.

In the weeks following their return, Devlin was very solicitous of Zach. He frequented the skin lodge, and his impeccable behavior in Morning Sky's presence dumbfounded Shadmore. Morning Sky showed Devlin special courtesy. She was not privy to Zach's misgivings about Devlin. All she knew was what she heard, and all she heard was that Devlin had saved her husband's life. She accepted Devlin at face value, as her man's good friend—someone who could be trusted.

The winter had been as severe as anyone could recall, but it did not linger. The chinooks—warm spring winds—came early and often. By the end of February the rivers had begun to run free again, and a succession of unseasonably warm days facilitated the snowmelt. The Missouri and the Yellowstone swiftly began to rise, and early in March leapt their banks. From the wooded shelf below the bluff at the confluence of these two mighty rivers, Zach could sit in front of the skin lodge and watch huge floes of ice crash and thunder downstream. They caromed against the banks and snapped trees like brittle twigs. Sometimes they carried stranded animals on their backs—Zach saw dozens of helpless deer and buffalo ride the river on icy rafts.

Everyone was happy to see the winter go, but none more so than Major Henry. He looked at the fast-coming spring with optimistic eyes. As soon as the ice was gone and the rivers had subsided, Ashley would be back with more men and more horses and more supplies. It was time to start trapping in earnest. Time for the Rocky Mountain Fur Company to begin showing its backers a return on their investment—not to mention a healthy profit for its organizers, Ashley and

the Major. Last year they had suffered setbacks. The
venture had gotten off on the wrong foot with the loss
of the keelboat and the cavallard. Henry figured they
were due a dose of good fortune in 1825.

But 1825 was going to be another bad year for the
company. Trouble came early, when Devlin killed
Mike Fink.

Chapter 27

Having signed on with the Rocky Mountain Fur Company as the man in charge of the keelboat crews, Mike Fink had somewhere along the way decided on a career change. He was convinced the fur trade was the business to be in, and when Ashley had headed down the Big Muddy bound for St. Louis, Fink had opted to stay behind and try his hand at being a trapper.

At the first sign of "green-up," Major Henry sent small parties out hunting for good beaver streams. One of these consisted of Mike Fink, Devlin, and several others, among them a man named Carpenter, who had become Fink's friend.

This small brigade proceeded as far as Great Falls before the appearance of a large party of Blackfeet made them turn and race for home. Eluding the Blackfeet, they fell in with a group of Absaroka Crow, an advance party of several families dispatched by Iron Bull to establish communications with the stronghold of the "hair-faces" at the mouth of the Yellowstone. Rides A Dark Horse was present as the chief's special envoy and ambassador of goodwill. The Crows greeted the trappers like long-lost brothers and accompanied them back to the fort.

Fink and Carpenter had become partners during the winter. Both were inclined to be boisterous, and each had more than a little of the braggart and the bully in

him. Regardless of Henry's injunction against strong
spirits in the ranks, Fink and Carpenter were among
those who always seemed to have access to snakehead.
As the winter progressed, Henry had turned an in-
creasingly blind eye to their shenanigans, aware that
such men could not be kept on short rein for such a
long time.

When sufficiently likkered up, Fink and Carpenter
were fond of dangerous games. They would fill tin
cups with whiskey and shoot them off each other's
heads. This William Tell routine was a source of tremendous entertainment for the rest of the company.
Henry disapproved, but he kept out of it. Both men
were superb marksmen, and never failed to hit the tin
cups dead-center—even when they had slugged down
prodigious quantities of red-eye.

Fink and Carpenter were the type of swaggering
hooligans Devlin could associate with—men who
didn't give a damn about anything or anybody, who
did only for themselves and didn't care if the rest of
the world went to hell in a handbasket. They were the
kind of toughs Devlin had grown up around on the river
and who had been his only role models, so he just naturally gravitated to them. As time passed he leaned
towards Carpenter; Mike Fink made it plain on a number of occasions that he didn't need some wet-behind-
the-ears youngster like Devlin following him around like
a puppy, which hurt Devlin's feelings.

The Absarokas set up their tepees near the fort. It
did not escape Major Henry's notice that the party of
Indians included a number of unattached maidens. He
knew this was no happy accident. It figured that Iron
Bull would scheme to cement the alliance between the
Sparrow Hawk people and the white trappers with a
few more marriages of convenience, modeled after the
union of Zach Hannah and Morning Sky.

The cunning chief had presided over numerous councils during the winter months, and there was a consensus among the tribal elders that the white man was a fact of life and it behooved the Absaroka to make the most of their presence. The trappers would be of some use in their protracted war with the northern Blackfeet. Last year's battle had shown that the whites and the Crows together could whip several times their number in Blackfeet.

Major Henry was an austere man, stern and demanding in all respects, but he could be flexible when circumstances required flexibility. In this case he realized he was faced with something beyond his control: human nature. The women were here, and available, and men were men, and whatever strife sprang from the situation would just have to be dealt with. He could not send the Crows packing, and he could not forbid his men to associate with the Indians—they would do it anyway, some of them, and he would end up with a discipline problem.

But not even Henry was prepared for the kind of strife the Rocky Mountain Fur Company experienced on account of the Crow maidens.

It so happened that Fink and Carpenter set their caps for the same woman, and in no time at all there was a drunken quarrel which would have progressed from fisticuffs to knives had not cooler heads intervened.

The next day, Devlin tried to mediate between the men.

"What the hell," was Fink's response. "Friends shouldn't let nothin' come between 'em, 'specially a squaw."

"Then you'll shake hands," said Devlin, "and it'll be patched up." He was relieved. Like almost everyone else he was leery of the sandy-haired giant, whose reputation for throat-cutting and head-busting was unrivaled. He had approached Carpenter first, and Carpenter had prevailed upon him to make an overture to Fink, and Devlin hadn't been able to back down for fear of shooting holes in his own reputation.

"Shake hands!" The King of the Keelboat Men shrugged massive shoulders. "I'll do you one better. Tell Carpenter we'll seal the bargain by shootin' cups, just like old times. Like nothin's happened between us. Course, we'll have to do it away from the fort and Major Henry. After what's happened, the major wouldn't stand for it now. One hour, let's say. Beyond the north wall."

Devlin communicated this offer to Carpenter, repeating it verbatim. Carpenter had serious misgivings.

"Sounds almost like he's callin' me out for a duel."

"He's talking straight," said Devlin, aware that success in forging a peace between a pair of hardcase hellbreathers like Fink and Carpenter would only enhance his standing.

"Mebbe," replied Carpenter, dubious. Frowning, he thought it over for a while, and finally agreed. "I'll do it, but only 'cause there ain't no future in having Mike Fink for an enemy."

"I'll come along," said Devlin. "If he tries anything, I'll back you up." Certain that Fink had been sincere, he didn't think there was any danger in making such a brave offer.

They met outside the fort at the appointed hour. Most of the men in the company were out hunting or trapping, and the Absaroka camp was on the other side of the stockade, so their business went unnoticed. Fink and Carpenter shook hands. Mike was jovial, setting the others at ease. He seemed in rare good humor. They tossed a coin to see who would shoot first. Fink won. He took his sweet time measuring powder and selecting a "lead pill," and all the while Carpenter watched him like a hawk, looking for the slightest indication of foul play.

Devlin stood to one side as Fink walked off sixty paces. He was impressed by Carpenter's courage. The man had plenty of nerve, standing there waiting for Fink to make his shot, and not knowing for sure whether Fink would aim for the tin cup or his heart.

Fink turned, raised his rifle, and fired in one quick motion.

As the report rolled away across the sunlit prairie, Devlin stared at the fallen Carpenter, aghast. The man was dead, a blue bullethole in his forehead.

A hue and cry arose from within the fort, but Devlin could scarcely hear anything but the blood roaring in his ears.

Deadpan, Mike Fink said, "It was an accident."

Devlin was too unnerved to think before he spoke. "That's a bald-faced lie, Mike!" he exclaimed bitterly, feeling somehow betrayed. "You've made that shot a dozen times drunk out of your head, and here you are stone-cold sober!"

"Mebbe I should've had me a shot of nerve medicine first," smiled Fink.

"It was murder," breathed Devlin.

Fink's eyes narrowed. He knew he had to act fast. Men were coming at a run, and would appear around the corner of the stockade at any moment.

"Sure," he said, his voice pitched low, a deadly whisper. "I murdered him. Now I'll do you the same favor, boy."

He threw down his empty rifle and tugged a flintlock pistol out of his belt.

Devlin had his Hawken cradled in his arm. He brought it down and fired from the hip, almost blind with panic. His bullet caught Mike Fink square in the chest and sent him sprawling.

Fink was the first man Sean Michael Devlin had killed, though he was known to talk a good game about a notorious career of knife duels and gunfights on the river. Looking at his bloody handiwork, he tasted bile and fought against vomiting as the other trappers, Major Henry and Shadmore included, arrived on the scene.

He explained what had happened. They accepted his unvarnished version. They could hardly do otherwise. The tin cup, Fink's just-fired rifle, the pistol in his lifeless hand, corroborated Devlin's story.

An odd hush fell over the men who stood there in shocked surprise and listened to Devlin's explanation while staring at the corpse of the legendary King of the Keelboat Men. Mike Fink had seemed larger than life, invincible. But all it had taken was an ounce of Galena lead to bring home to the trappers how every life hung by a fragile thread.

Devlin was not censured for his actions. Everyone agreed he had killed Mike Fink in self-defense. And those who heard him justify what he had done were impressed by how calm he seemed. They did not know that this aplomb was a facade, as Devlin desperately sought to conceal the turmoil within. His was a masterful performance. The others were now looking at him in an entirely new way. First his heroism in sticking with Zach Hannah during their harrowing winter ordeal, and now this, secured his reputation. He was, after all, the man who had slain the one and only Mike Fink.

Two men were not nearly so impressed. When Shadmore told Zach about the killings, he spoke with disdain.

"Ever'body's makin' a big to-do 'bout Coyote," said the old leatherstocking. "Talk about him like he were David jist back from puttin' Goliath under. Hoss, that's doodly-squat. He was skeered plumb out of his everlovin' mind, I guarantee. It's downright amazin' what a skeered man kin do when his neck's in the wringer.''

Major Henry had strong misgivings about Devlin, too. He recalled the first time he had met Devlin, on that St. Louis wharf. His first impression had not been favorable. Now he wished he had followed his instincts and refused to sign Devlin on.

It wasn't so much that he blamed Devlin for killing Fink. If he blamed anyone, the major blamed himself. He should never have allowed Indian women in and about the camp. Instead he had waffled, and now two good men lay dead.

What bothered Henry about Devlin in the days following the shooting was the way Devlin let all the flattery and deference he received from the other trappers go to his head. That gave the major a handle on the kind of person Devlin was. Immature, unreliable, and potentially as dangerous as Mike Fink had been. Henry fully expected more trouble from him.

More trouble did come, hard on the heels of the shooting, but not from Devlin.

A young adventurer named Jedediah Smith arrived at the fort early one morning. He was a lanky lad, soft-spoken but steely-eyed. The pocket of his hunting jacket bulged with the family Bible he had carried all the way from Boston.

He was Ashley's messenger, and he had come hundreds of perilous miles in a big hurry to bring ill tidings: the details of the Rocky Mountain Fur Company's latest disaster.

Returning up the Missouri from St. Louis with more men and supplies, Ashley had run into eight hundred Arikaras painted for war. Their hostility caught Ashley by surprise, because always before the Rees had been friendly.

"Not with our luck," said Henry with a long-suffering sigh.

Ashley needed help, quick, said Jedediah Smith. Thirteen Rocky Mountain men lay dead, eleven more severely wounded. The boatmen were threatening to desert. Ashley was holding on by the skin of his teeth, on a keelboat below the Arikara village at the mouth of the Grand River. He was counting on his partner, Major Henry, to pull his fat out of the fire. It was full-scale war with the Rees now. Everybody knew that an Indian who had tasted victory was ten times more dangerous. The Arikaras had whupped the white men and they were going to want more blood, sure as shooting, and the most convenient victims were Ashley and his men, cooped up on that keelboat.

The major called all the men together. Zach Hannah was there to hear Henry's speech. It was short and sweet. Henry wasn't one to equivocate. Ashley was in desperate straits. They would go by river to rescue him—and the Rocky Mountain Fur Company. It would be a dangerous journey, and there was a big fight guaranteed at the other end of it. Only a handful would remain behind to guard the fort. He would call out the names of those he wanted to accompany him. Taking a small black ledger from his pocket, he called out the names—eighty in all. Zach heard his name called, and Shadmore's, and Bridger's. Devlin's name did not pass the major's lips.

Zach sought out Rides A Dark Horse and asked that he keep an eye on Morning Sky. He then returned to his skin lodge to say good-bye to his wife. He was sorry to leave her, but he knew he would have been sorrier still if Henry had not thought enough to choose him as one of the rescue party.

"Don't worry, Sky," he said. "I'll come back. I'll always come back to you."

She put on a brave face. She would not worry, she promised, not too much anyway, because she was convinced the wolf-spirits watched over her man.

It was the last they saw of each other for three years.

H

Chapter 28

During the winter, Major Henry had employed some of his men in the building of Mackinaw boats. These were flat-bottomed vessels with a sharp prow and shallow draft, propelled by oar or by sail, the latter a lateen attached to a short, limber mast. The Mackinaw could accommodate fifteen passengers. The quarters were a trifle cramped, and the men were exposed to the vagaries of the weather, but the Mackinaws were nimble river craft, swift and maneuverable.

While journeying down the high-running Missouri, the Rocky Mountain men were made acquainted with the details of Ashley's disaster. The source was Jedediah Smith, and the story passed from man to man and boat to boat. Shadmore relayed what he had heard to Zach.

"Ussens got rivals, looks like, hoss. Bunch callin' themselves the Missouri Fur Company. Got themselves a post jist below the Arikara town. The big augur's a feller named Pilcher. When Ashley showed up, Pilcher warned him that the Rees were actin' naughty. Story goes that Ashley didn't take Pilcher serious."

"The Rees have always been friendly to white men," said Zach. "They treated Lewis and Clark like kings."

Shadmore smirked. "When you gonna learn, Zach?

Injuns are like wimmin. They'll kiss you today and try to lift yore hair tomorrow.''

Zach laughed. ''You just don't have much good to say about anybody, do you?''

Shadmore dismissed that with a grunt. ''You wanna know what happened, or would you rather keep talkin' me down? Anyroad, Ashley wanted to trade fer Arikara horses, and he found the Ree chiefs happy as all get-out to see him. Yessir, I reckon they were grinnin' like cats. So Ashley anchored the two keelboats right near the village and went ashore to haggle with them redskins.

''He had Edward Rose with him, and no man knows the Rees better'n Rose. He speaks the lingo, 'cause he lived in that very village a couple years. Rose is a half-breed hisself. Cherokee, as I recollect. Whilst Ashley was tradin', Rose sat back and watched and listened, and oncet the deals wuz done, and the Injuns invited Ashley to a big feast, he told Ashley he'd do better to swim the horses 'crost the river and put some distance between them-thar keelboats and the village. Reckon sumpin 'bout the way them heathens were actin' didn't sit well with ol' Rose. But Ashley didn't heed him.''

''Why not? Sounds like Rose would know what he's about, from what you've said.''

Shadmore nodded, fiercely mangling the tip of his pipe. ''You ain't never met Rose. I have. He's uglier than original sin. Why, he's got a face not even a mother could love. You'd swear he wuz the boogeyman hisself, when you set eyes on him. He's a man you wooden trust iffen yore life depended on it, jist by the way he looks, lessen you got to know him. Now me, I'd liefer have Rose sidin' with me in a scrape than most anybody, even if he were a Mississippi river pirate in his younger days.''

"I don't understand why Ashley wasn't more careful. He struck me as a smart man."

"Wahl," drawled Shadmore, 'thar's smart, and then thar's Injun-smart. Way I figger it, Ashley thought the bestest way to bluff an Injun wuz to act like he weren't the least bit worried 'bout him—like you ain't skeered of nothin' on this good green earth, least of all a heathen redskin. But that don't float with Injuns, Zach. They call a spade a spade, and they know a fool's a fool, any way you slice it, so's thar no point in playin' games. They won't take offense iffen you don't trust 'em, and you show 'em that you don't, 'cause they know they ain't to be trusted anyhow.

"But Ashley left the keelboats anchored right close to the Arikara village, and, worse'n that, left the horses on the Ree side of the river, guarded by forty men. Next mornin', come dawn, the Arikaras attacked. What made it bad was that them Injuns had plenty of guns. Fusils, mostly, but Ashley had even traded muskets, powder and ball to 'em fer the horses, so's you could say them red savages was well-heeled. Smith says thar were more'n six hundred warriors in the village."

"Six hundred!" breathed Zach. "That's a tall order."

"The Rees hit the horse guard fust. Killed a few of our'n and more'n a few cayuses, right off. Young Smith and his pardners took cover behind the dead ponies. They had them Black Mouths on three sides of 'em and the river at their backs. It wuz a tight spot, fer sartin. Ashley tried to git his boatmen to row a few skiffs to shore so's to bring Smith and the others off, but the boatmen jist flat-out refused. Reckon they thought it wuz suicide, plain and simple, and mebbe they were right. But I don't put much stock in rivermen. They talk up a storm, but they cain't be trusted.

That blowhard, Mike Fink, was a dandy example. And—''

"I know," sighed Zach. "Coyote."

Shadmore smirked. "The truth allus bears repeatin'. Anyroad, the boys ashore gave a good accountin' of themselves, but they all knowed it was hopeless. Their only chance was to swim for the keelboats. So they jumped up and run fer the river. More were kilt 'fore they reached the water. Some got swept downstream and either drowned or had their hair lifted when they washed up on the Arikara side. But the rest made the keelboats, and Ashley cut loose from the anchors and let the boats drift. The Rees ran along the bank fer a spell, shootin' up a storm, but the Big Muddy's runnin' high, and the heathens couldn't keep up with the boats fer long.''

"Thirteen dead, I hear," said Zach. "Surprised it wasn't more.''

"Lucky fer them—and will be fer us—that most Injuns ain't been around guns long enough to git good with 'em.''

"Still, the odds are tall.''

"We'll have help. Y'see, Ashley sent young Smith to us, and at the same time sent one of the boats—the *Yellowstone Packet*—back downriver. Seems thars a new army post near Council Bluffs, and Ashley sent a message askin' them soldier boys fer help in punishin' the Rees.''

"Think they will help?''

Shadmore shrugged, tugging on his tobacco-stained beard. "Dunno. But young Smith says Ashley weren't too shore. It's ussens Ashley is countin' on. He could only git thirty men to volunteer to stick with him. The rest—mostly rivermen, natchly—hopped the *Yellowstone Packet* and hightailed it fer that Army post, takin' the bad wounded with 'em. So don't count on thar bein' more'n a hunnerd of ussen when it's all done. When you talk odds, that's only six to one.'' Shadmore's pale blue eyes twinkled. ''I'd say 'bout even.''

Zach smiled. ''You would.''

No one doubted for a moment that a big fight was in the offing. The Rees had to be whipped, and whipped good. There was no other recourse. As long as the Indians remained hostile, the Missouri was rendered useless—and, as vile and mean as the Big Muddy was, it was the most viable way west into prime beaver country.

Another factor entered into the equation. News of the Arikara triumph would spread like wildfire among the other tribes, and it would diminish the fear of the frontiersmen which had so far kept most of them at bay—with a singular exception being the Blackfoot. If something wasn't done to salvage their reputation as men not to be trifled with, the trappers knew that every tribe on the high plains would start misbehaving.

Sure enough, they had to make an example of those Black Mouths.

Zach had mixed emotions. He was prepared to fight; he felt bound by loyalty to do so. But he did not relish the prospect. It seemed to him that this country was plenty big for everybody. Why wasn't it possible for men to live here in consonance with one another, and with the wolf and the buffalo, the birds of the sky and the fish of the rivers and streams? This land was blessed; it was paradise. Perhaps for that very reason, mused Zach, men were ready to kill or be killed to have it for their own.

It had happened in his father's day. Nate Hannah had been one of the first white men to venture into Kentucky, and Zach could recall his father referring to that land as a paradise. But before long it came to be known as ''that dark and bloody ground.'' Before the advent of the white man, the Indians had revered *Can-tuc-kee* as a sacred hunting ground, and the tribes had arrived at a mutual agreement whereby all could hunt there but none could claim the land as its own private property. An eminently sensible arrangement, in Zach's book. But Kentucky had become a battleground, a place of death and deceit, terror and torture. Paradise lost.

Zach couldn't help but wonder if a similar fate might not befall this land. He had a hunch it would, and the prospect dismayed him.

The notion to put it all behind him—to take Sky and seek haven far removed from the destructive machinations of man—sorely tempted him. But honor tied him down. The very thought of leaving smacked of betrayal.

He kept these thoughts to himself. And when, at length, they arrived at the Arikara village, he joined the others in grimly preparing for a fight. But Zach Hannah's heart wasn't in it.

Chapter 29

Just north of the confluence of the Grand and Missouri Rivers stood an imposing, crescent-shaped bluff. It loomed above the main channel of the Big Muddy, which in turn lay squeezed between a sandbar and the Arikara side of the river.

A case could be made for claiming that the Indian town was in fact two separate villages adjacent to one another. Both were located on the commanding bluff, scarcely a hundred yards apart. The Rees lived in earth lodges which resembled giant molehills, with an average diameter of fifty feet. Each village consisted of approximately seventy-five lodges. The villages were encircled by palisades made of upright logs twice as tall as a man. It surprised Henry's two scouts to find that the Rees had even dug trenchworks outside the stout palisades.

"Why, you'd think they had ol' Bonaparte hisself leadin' 'em, to look at that," remarked one scout.

"Looks like they're right serious 'bout this war stuff," commented the other.

"Ain't no cover worth mentionin'," the first man told Major Henry. "Nary a thing but scrub and buffalo grass on the bluff and the hills behind it. Now there *is* a cornfield in a valley south of the bluff. . . ."

"Nary a tree fer a mile in any direction," confirmed

the second. "Reckon mebbe they cut 'em all down to make their stockade."

"What else?" asked Henry, sensing there was more—something the scouts were loath to speak of.

"They done cut the heads off some of the boys they kilt, Major, and stuck 'em on poles along the river bank."

This atrocious news put the company in an ugly frame of mind, and nearly everyone agreed there was no time like the present for going in and separating some Arikara heads from Arikara bodies.

Major Henry thought otherwise. "There'll be a time and a place for vengeance," he assured his men. "But there are too many of them and too few of us, and we can't afford to lose another fight." He resolved to try slipping past the Arikara under cover of night. They could then join Ashley downriver.

The risk of discovery was great, but Henry did not want to abandon the Mackinaws and take a circuitous route around the villages overland. So they muffled the oars in their locks, primed their rifles, and set sail.

As they neared the villages, towering thunderclouds collided, their blue-black bellies swollen with rain. The June twilight was sultry and lit up by fireflies. Flickering tongues of lightning stabbed at the earth and danced through the angry clouds. The summer storm struck right on cue; as the Rees sat huddled in their lodges, feeling the earth shudder with each mighty thunderclap, eighty drenched frontiersmen huddled in Mackinaws drifting past the bluff on the rain-fed river.

Morning found them safely below the mouth of the Grand River. Though tired, wet, and cramped, they congratulated themselves on their good fortune.

"The Lord A'mighty's lookin' out fer his chillun," Shadmore declared to Zach. "Them cussed Injuns is downright terrified of storms, and they won't git out in one fer nothin'.''

They reached the mouth of the Cheyenne River on the first day of July. Ashley waited behind palisades of his own, Fort Recovery. Thirty days had passed since the Arikara ambush, but the mood of Ashley's men had seen little improvement. This was made manifest to Zach when he and Shadmore shared a friendly cook-fire and a plump roasted prairie hen with Edward Jackson and William Sublette. All of them knew that Henry and Ashley, along with Pilcher, the top dog of the Missouri Fur Company, were putting their heads together that very night in a strategy session.

''Reckon I know what Ashley's sayin','' said Jackson, the sharp edge of acrimony in his voice. ''He done already made it plain he don't hold himself responsible for what happened upriver. He's probably tellin' the major right this minute that if his orders had been obeyed none of it would've happened.'' He hawked and spat into the fire. He did not need words to express his opinion of Ashley's assertion.

''Who's gonna listen to a feller who obviously doesn't have any idea what he's doin'?'' was Sublette's rhetorical question.

''What could he have done different?'' asked Zach. This wasn't taking up for Ashley—Zach was earnestly soliciting the opinions of two wily frontiersmen, both of whom came from a long line of Indian-fighters.

''We could've moved on past the Ree village or dropped back downriver a ways,'' said Jackson.

''In short,'' said Sublette, ''he could have listened to Rose. I reckon thirteen of our friends would still be above snakes if he had.''

''But instead we sat in that damned narrow channel,'' growled Jackson, ''whar the sandbar puts you up close to the shore. And leavin' the horses thar at the bottom of the bluff, right under the noses of them red savages!'' Jackson shook his head. ''That was an invitation to them Black Mouths to try some mischief.''

''I wouldn't trust Ashley to carry my water,'' declared a bitter Sublette.

''So why'd y'all stick?'' queried Shadmore. ''Why didn't you go on downriver with the rest?''

Sublette and Jackson looked at each other.

'' 'Cause I ain't never turned tail in my whole life,'' growled Jackson.

''Goes for me,'' nodded Sublette.

''Them Rees need comeuppance,'' said Jackson. ''We was just waitin' on you boys to show up.''

''Though I'm a mite surprised that young Jedediah Smith got through with the word,'' admitted Sublette.

Jackson was sheepish. ''Lookin' back on it, I guess we didn't exactly do ourselves proud when Ashley asked for volunteers to take the news to Major Henry. All I can say is, we let Ashley know what we thought of him, allus standin' there like tree stumps. Ashley turned red as a beet when nobody stepped forward.''

''Yep, but we got red in the face when Smith volunteered,'' said Sublette. ''For a sapling, he's got plenty of hard bark.''

''Didn't take to him at first,'' confessed Jackson. ''Him with his fancy talk, and gettin' down on his knees to pray ever' evening, like he do.''

''But he's a fighting son of a gun,'' said Sublette. ''Showed as much when he was pinned down by them Arikaras.''

''I would've been down on my knees prayin' myself right then,'' laughed Jackson, ''if I hadn't been so busy tryin' to dig a hole in the ground big enough to crawl down into. I ain't surprised Jedediah Smith got through. He'll make a name for himself 'fore he's through. Mark my words.''

"Reckon the army will throw in with us?" asked Zach.

"Wouldn't bet on it," said Sublette. "But we might see the Yankton and Sans Arc Sioux lend a hand."

"You reckon?" said Shadmore.

"Even money. The Sioux and the Rees hate each other's guts.''

"That's what started this whole mess in the first place," said Jackson, adding another stick to the fire. "See, Pilcher's been tradin' with the Sioux. 'Fore we came along, the Black Mouths ran up on some of Pilcher's men traveling with a couple of young Sioux braves. The Black Mouths wanted Pilcher's men to give the Sioux up—they hankered to torture the boys to death. Nothin' a Ree likes better'n cookin' Sioux flesh over a slow fire.''

"But Pilcher's men wouldn't do it," said Sublette. "There was some shootin'. The Black Mouths got licked good and proper in that one. Then they declared war on the white man. Pilcher tried to warn Ashley, but Ashley's got bone for brains.''

No wonder this feller Pilcher's bein' so all-fired helpful," mused Shadmore. "Sound to me like the Rocky Mountain Fur Company got itself caught smack in the middle of Missouri Fur Company trouble.''

"Pilcher don't have a lot of trappers workin' for him," said Sublette. "But he's gettin' rich off the furs those Sioux bring in. It's a safe bet the Missouri Fur Company's doin' a long sight better'n we are.''

"Shore do look like we been snake-bit," allowed Shadmore. "We lost a keelboat and cavallard and tangle with a passel of Blackfoot last year, and now, when we should be up yonder in the mountain valleys trappin' brown gold, we end up down hyar huntin' Rees.''

''We're jinxed,'' agreed Jackson, long in the face. ''And having a double-certified fool like Ashley callin' the dance don't help none.''

A few restless days later, word spread through Fort Recovery that the army was coming after all. With the soldiers and the Sioux and the two fur companies joining forces, it looked like the Arikaras wouldn't stand a chance.

Zach didn't like the waiting. He was impatient as the rest of the frontiersmen to get the job done, but for a different reason. While the others looked forward to the scrape, Zach just wanted to get home to Morning Sky. With each passing day he found this business more and more distasteful—a petty squabble between two tribes escalating into full-scale war. It was ludicrous.

While lingering at Fort Recovery, he learned as much as he could about the Arikaras. Edward Rose, who had lived with the tribe for a time, was his primary source of information.

He found, for instance, that the Black Mouths were a select group of warriors who served as tribal police. The blackening of their lower faces was a badge of authority. The term ''Black Mouth'' was used indiscriminately by whites to refer to any Ree warrior. Male Arikaras progressed through several bands; young boys belonged to the Fox Band and old men to the Crow band, with the Young Dog Band, Strong Heart Band, and the Bull Band the intermediate levels. The Strong Hearts were proven warriors in their prime.

Generally, males were promoted from band to next higher band by dint of courageous acts. No one seemed willing to dispute that the Arikara were conspicuously brave. It was, however, possible to purchase one's promotion with gifts that often included sharing one's wife with the chief of the band. It appeared to Zach that Arikara women were most definitely treated like second-class citizens. If aspersions were cast upon a maiden's virginity, or a wife's fidelity, she was required to endure a terrible ordeal known as the Test Dance. Those lacking the stamina to weather the test were forced into virtual prostitution—made available to any and all males.

Zach couldn't comprehend the attitude Indian men in general adopted toward their women. He couldn't imagine using Morning Sky as a means to climb the social ladder, or permitting her to be subjected to a painful ordeal in order to satisfy others of her loyalty to him. Of course, Sky would never do anything that had even a hint of impropriety—of this Zach was certain.

At length, the soldier boys arrived from Fort Atkinson. In command was a Colonel Henry Leavenworth, a stern disciplinarian with splendid military bearing and a forceful personality. He was the type of officer who by his very martial appearance inspired confidence in the troops. Already possessed of a fairly distinguished record, he was starving for more glory. He was known to be ambitious beyond reason, and he seemed to believe that a healthy military career required regular baptisms in blood.

For that reason he decided not to wait for permission from district headquarters in St. Louis, starting out at once for Fort Recovery and the field of glory, with six companies of the Sixth Infantry and some artillery on three keelboats.

But the Missouri River was unimpressed with Colonel Leavenworth and promptly sank one of the keelboats, claiming a large proportion of the expedition's supplies and the lives of seven soldiers.

This less than auspicious beginning left the Colonel inconsolable. He had taken the field without specific orders from his superiors, and he alone had to answer for the loss of life, not to mention the loss of property, to the U.S. Army. The mishap put tremendous pressure on Leavenworth, for he realized now that the venture *had* to have a successful conclusion—his career depended on it.

To ensure that success, Leavenworth made it clear to Henry and Ashley and Pilcher that he, and he alone, would be in command. He proved to be about as open to helpful advice as Ashley had been—no one had a higher opinion of the Colonel's expertise and ability than the Colonel himself.

The men of the two fur companies were formed into what Leavenworth christened "The Missouri Legion." He bestowed field commissions: Jedediah Smith was made captain; Edward Rose found himself an ensign; Thomas Fitzpatrick became quartermaster. William Sublette was distinguished with the rank of Sergeant-Major. The remainder were pressed into service as enlisted men.

Leavenworth squandered a few comical days trying to whip his "legion" into some semblance of soldierly shape, only to run smack into an obstacle he could not overcome: the fierce independence of the mountain man. Zach and his colleagues were not impressed by their new status as legionnaires. They expressed supreme indifference to standing in line on parade, or marching in step, or shooting by the numbers. Discipline was lax in The Missouri Legion.

By the end of July the Sioux had arrived, led by Chief Fireheart. Zach decided Leavenworth might have fiddled around all summer at Fort Recovery, but for

the Sioux. Five hundred warriors had come to fight.
They had painted their horses and their shields and their
faces. They had made their medicine and left their lodges
and women behind. So they were in no mood to tarry
until the Time of the Falling Leaves. The company leaders
knew it was high time they had a serious talk with Colonel
Leavenworth.

"Indians don't wage campaigns," Pilcher told
Leavenworth. "All these braves have gathered from
different bands for one quick strike at their enemies.
One battle, and then its home for them, and, they hope,
a big celebration, where they can strut like peacocks
and make a lot of bold talk about their exploits. The
only reason those Sioux warriors are here, Colonel, is
because they think they can do a lot of damage to the
Rees, with our help. That's the way an Indian ap-
proaches war. He looks for the chance to inflict the
greatest damage at the smallest cost. So if we just stand
around here and don't look like we're the least bit interested in taking the Rees on, the Sioux will just up
and go home."

"Why do you tell me what I already know?" said
Leavenworth. "Let them go, if they want. They are
unreliable, anyway. We don't need their help to sub-
jugate the Arikara."

The colonel's attitude alarmed Pilcher. The company's future depended on the good graces of the
Sioux. Leavenworth had invited them to partake in the
chastisement of the Rees, and they had come. Pilcher's
stock would fall if it turned out they had come for
nothing, or if, God forbid, the insufferable Leavenworth managed to insult them in some way.

"I say use fire to fight fire," said Major Henry.
"Use Indians to fight Indians."

"Sure," agreed Pilcher. "You don't have to motivate a Sioux warrior to kill Arikaras. Just point them in the right direction and let 'em loose.''

" 'Cry havoc,' " said Henry, quoting the Bard, " 'and let slip the dogs of war.' "

"Minimize our own casualties," added Pilcher. "The end result should be the same. The Sioux will count their coup, we'll free up the Missouri for our trade, and you'll get the credit."

"Glory is not what I seek," protested Leavenworth.

Poker-faced, Pilcher said, "Of course not."

So, shortly after the arrival of the restless Sioux, Zach Hannah and the rest of The Missouri Legion prepared to pay the Arikaras back, with interest, for their treachery.

Chapter 30

The ninth day of August turned out to be a scorcher. Almost as soon as the sun rose, the sky acquired a brassy hue, and the sweltering heat came hammering at the summer-tanned prairie.

Standing in the scrub on the crest of a hill five hundred yards south of the Arikara villages, Zach had a clear view of the enemy stronghold. Between his hill and the bluff upon which the Rees had built their fortified town stretched a cornfield, irrigated by a series of canals branching off from a creek that fed the Big Muddy. Zach could see the angry, reddish-brown river through the hills to the east of his location. South of him, deeper in the hills, lurked Leavenworth's main force. But he and his fellow scout, Jim Bridger, were more interested in what was taking place to the north and west of them.

Pilcher and two-score mounted men were raising a plume of dust as they circled the Arikara town. Their mission was to cut off the enemy's retreat. To their left, where the valley containing the cornfield widened, they could see Chief Fireheart's Sioux preparing to attack.

It was a sight to behold. Fireheart had arrived at Fort Recovery with five hundred braves, and during the march north, several hundred more had come riding in. Zach had never seen so many warriors gathered in one place. A true wonder, for certain. Now they were chanting their war songs, uncovering their shields, and making ready their weapons. Horses pranced, warriors whooped and shouted encouragement to one another and insults at the Arikaras, and a great dun-colored cloud of choking dust rose up out of the valley to hang suspended in the stifling heat. The noise they made, thought Zach, was not much different, or any less nerve-wracking, than the commotion five hundred coyotes could make yapping at the moon.

"That racket," he told Bridger, "is getting under my skin."

"It's s'pose to get under *their* skin," said Bridger, pointing with his chin at the Arikara villages.

The Ree fortification were swarming with activity. "I guess a surprise attack is out of the question," said Zach wryly, blinking sweat out of his eyes.

"Wonder why we come all this way, if Colonel Leavenworth's gonna hold us back and let the Sioux do all the fightin'."

Zach knew that most of the other mountain men were wondering the same thing. They came, the majority of them, from fighting stock, and it didn't suit their nature to sit back yonder by the river while the biggest brawl in recent frontier history was about to take place within spitting distance.

"Looks like they're done with the hoopla," said Zach, watching Chief Fireheart, in full regalia, ride a high-stepping Palouse to the edge of the cornfield. He was easily identifiable by his war bonnet; while he wasn't the only Sioux warrior to have earned the right to wear one, his was far and away the most spectacular. It was decorated with a set of buffalo horns and ermine skins. The tail-piece was so long it draped the haunches of his Appaloosa.

The other Sioux fell suddenly silent as Fireheart raised his rifle. When he swept it down, pointing the barrel at the Arikara town, eight hundred warriors kicked their ponies into a gallop. The thunder of thousands of hooves rose up from the valley, mingling with the high-pitched war cries of the braves. In their passage, the Sioux trampled the cornfield and surged up the steep slope of the bluff.

To Zach's amazement, the Rees came charging out of their fortifications to meet them.

"Them Arikarees is as brave as all get-out," acknowledged Bridger, "but none too smart. Why'd they get all forted up if they were gonna fight out in the open?"

Fusils and muskets cracked. Dust and smoke obscured the battleground. Zach breathlessly waited for the tide to turn in favor of the Sioux. They outnumbered the Rees, after all. But the Arikaras held their own. They fought with such unbridled ferocity that the Sioux wavered and began to trickle by twos and threes back down into the valley. Their leaders rallied them, and the Sioux charged valiantly again, only to break like a wave against an unyielding shore as they smashed into the Arikaras a second time. Once more the Rees stood fast and the Sioux faltered.

"One of us best go back and tell the Colonel that the Sioux need help," said Zach.

Bridger agreed. "If the Sioux turn tail, then Pilcher and his boys'll catch hell. I'll go fetch the others."

Zach nodded. If the trappers could move up double-quick and get within shooting distance of the Rees, the day would be won. The Sioux had drawn the enemy out of his fortifications. Now it was time for the mountain men to deliver the coup de grace.

Again the Sioux urged their tired ponies up-slope into the Arikaras. Zach figured he was within long rifle range, but he kept his Hawken cradled in the crook of his arm. He could scarcely distinguish friend from foe in that melee, and he wasn't too keen on killing anyway, unless it was in self-defense.

Minutes dragged by. Where was Leavenworth? Zach could sense that the Sioux were cooling fast. More and more of them were detaching themselves from the dusty fracas and drifting away, while fewer and fewer of these were heeding the rallying calls of Fireheart and his sub-chiefs. The dauntless Rees refused to surrender an inch of bloody ground.

Finally the Missouri Legion swarmed through a notch between Zach's hill and an adjacent rise. Looking behind him, Zach spotted the column of Regulars, marching in perfect order, some distance back from the Legion. They didn't seem in any big hurry. Zach had a hunch Leavenworth was determined to limit the Sixth Infantry's losses to the seven soldiers drowned in the river.

As the mountain men rushed forward to join the fray, Fireheart's Sioux began to disengage in earnest, and Zach's colleagues commenced picking off the Arikaras without the worry of shooting through their allies. Zach decided it was time he stopped being the spectator, so he loped down into the valley to join the other trappers. He heard the angry whine of bullets, flinched at the close passage of arrows, as the Rees turned their fire on this new threat. Wouldn't it be bitterly ironic, he mused, to be slain by a bullet fired from one of the rifles Ashley had foolishly traded to the Arikaras in exchange for horses? He raised the Hawken and fired into the mass of Rees halfway up the slope of the bluff. Reloading on the run was a trick he had learned hunting fleet black-tailed deer in the Tennessee high country. But he didn't get off that second shot, for the Arikaras suddenly turned and scampered to their earthworks and palisades.

The mountain men were hot on their heels. Though outnumbered ten-to-one, they had faith that their superior marksmanship evened the odds. The momentum was clearly theirs. Victory was within their grasp, if they could reach the enemy fortifications before the Rees got settled in.

But then several of Colonel Leavenworth's subordinates came barrelling through them on stretched-out horses, yelling at them to halt.

Zach's first thought was that Leavenworth had seen something they hadn't—perhaps they were blundering into a trap. The Colonel was, after all, the professional soldier, the grand strategist. He had a full-scale battle or two under his belt. Surely he knew what he was doing. Zach stopped running. The rest of the mountain men did likewise. They stood a moment, firing up-slope. Taking cover behind their works, the Rees answered back, winging several trappers. They weren't the best shots in the world, but it didn't take the mountain men long to realize that they were getting the short end of the stick, trading lead below the Rees' fort.

So they fell back in good order, keeping up a steady fire all the while, and taking their wounded off the field with them. They withdrew to the high ground across the valley from the villages. Here they caught their wind, soothed their parched throats with a drink of water, checked their weapons, and waited restively for the order to resume the fight.

And waited.

Waited some more.

Shadmore found Zach. The old leatherstocking was scowling like a bear with a bellyache.

"Ashley and Leavenworth," groused Shadmore, shaking his head. "Leavenworth and Ashley. Iffen you could put their brains together you'd still have a half-wit.''

''What happened?''

''If I tell you, I'll strangulate on the words,'' declared Shadmore. But he went ahead and did anyway. ''The Colonel's decided we cain't do nuthin' else till he pounds on 'em with his cannon.''

''But the cannon are way back yonder!''

''Makes no never-mind. Y'see, hoss, the Colonel goes by the book, and the book says you cain't take a fort lessen you shell the dangfool thing fust.''

''Sounds like a book written by idjits fer idjits,'' opined Jim Beckwourth, as the mulatto hunkered down within earshot.

''How long will this foolishness take?'' asked David Jackson, sprawled nearby.

No one had the answer. All they could do was wait and see. Time slowed to a crawl. They had no shelter from the blistering August sun. To while away the hours, some of them traded potshots with the distant Rees. Lead messengers of death screamed back and forth above the trampled cornfield, but with little effect.

The battery of six-pounders did not arrive on the scene until after sunset. There was to be no more fighting that day. Zach and some of the others slipped down to the cornfield under cover of darkness to harvest the multicolored corn. Finding a cheerful voice or visage in The Missouri Legion that evening would have been a difficult task. Zach felt more than a little disgruntled himself. He was homesick for his skin lodge and the loving arms of his beautiful Indian wife, and any delay that prolonged his absence was a source of irritation.

The next morning, Leavenworth began his by-the-book cannonade of the Arikara fortifications. The six-pounder cannonballs bounced off the palisades and inflicted little damage on the mud houses beyond. A sarcastic cheer rose up from the onlooking mountain men when one round knocked over a tall medicine pole in the center of the southernmost village.

Some of the idle Sioux mingled with the trappers, looking for handouts of tobacco or ammunition and, as was Indian custom, hoping to abscond with the possibles of an inattentive hair-face. They were quick to snipe at the ineffectual shelling, ridiculing the white man's way of making war.

Several braves approached Zach and a group of trappers including Shadmore, Beckwourth, and Bridger, and in sign language bragged about their fighting prowess, telling all who would pay attention the details of their heroics on yesterday's field of battle. They lambasted Leavenworth.

"Your chief is old woman," one Yankton brave signed to Zach and the others. "He stays back behind his big guns and makes much noise, but kills no Arikara. Why? He is afraid to fight man-to-man."

The trappers could not argue. They shared the sentiment, and no one stepped forward to defend Leavenworth.

"There is blood on the ground," signed another Sioux. "It is Sioux blood, and Arikara blood. But I can find no white man's blood on the ground."

This kind of talk infuriated the mountain men. They had their pride, and it rankled to take this kind of abuse. It was guilt by association with Colonel Leavenworth, and they did not care for it. An unpleasant ripple of mutinous discontent spread through the Missouri Legion. Some, like Godin and Jackson, suggested attacking the Rees on their own stick, and to hell with sitting around like a passel of turtles on a log, waiting for orders.

Chief Fireheart called personally on Pilcher to air his complaints, and the latter sought out Leavenworth. The Colonel stood on high ground with an entourage of aides, observing the enemy camp through field glasses. Edward Rose stood near at hand, leaning on his long rifle and looking immensely bored with the whole spectacle. It was mid-afternoon, and the big guns were falling silent one by one, out of ammunition.

"When are we going to attack, Colonel?" queried the anxious Pilcher. "Our Sioux friends are getting restless, and so are my men, if the truth be known. They came to fight, and they're a short hair from crossing that valley and taking it to the Rees."

"You will remind your men that they are under my orders," said Leavenworth sternly. "If any man acts without or in defiance of my orders, he will be put to death."

"Good Lord," breathed Pilcher, disgusted.

Chapter 31

"I am meeting with several Arikara chiefs within the hour," announced Leavenworth proudly, as though he had accomplished one of the most extraordinary diplomatic feats of the century.

Pilcher couldn't believe his ears. "What? Are they surrendering?"

Leavenworth scowled. "They wish to talk. Smoke the peace pipe."

Pilcher was suspicious. "Did they ask to?"

"It was my suggestion," replied the Colonel. "They have sustained severe losses."

"Who says?"

"They have suffered a sustained bombardment. That is very demoralizing, Mr. Pilcher."

"For which side?" Pilcher was too upset to be circumspect.

"I will brook insubordination from no one," warned Leavenworth. "Least of all a civilian."

"Least of all? You have no authority over me or my men, unless we give you that authority. And if we do, or if we have, we can take it back."

"I'd advise against testing that theory."

"Colonel, you *can't* call a truce! We lose if you do. The Rees will make promises they have no intention of keeping. They'll laugh at you behind your back.

And then they'll keep on bushwhacking white men whenever and wherever it suits their fancy.''

"Do not presume to lecture me on the ways and wiles of the Arikara nation. There are honorable men among all tribes. You and your kind underestimate them.''

"I'd say you're the one doing the underestimating. And it has nothing to do with honor. Lying and stealing isn't wrong, to the Indian way of thinking. It's just accepted practice. I don't condemn them for it. I know how they think, and I accept it. Colonel, you've got to deal with an Indian the way another Indian would, or he won't respect you. He'll think you're a fool and he'll treat you accordingly.''

A solitary Arikara had appeared in front of the earthworks ringing the villages. He was carrying a strip of white cloth tied to the end of a rifle. Leavenworth summoned one of his aides, a callow second lieutenant, and ordered him to ride forward and meet the Arikara emissary, with Rose along to act as interpreter.

As they waited and watched the junior officer and the mountain man ride down into the valley and up the slope of the bluff, Leavenworth, still provoked by Pilcher's insufferable defiance, said, "Your kind are forever whining about Indian savagery. If you had your way you would wipe them all off the face of the earth. And yet you treat them atrociously. You cheat them shamelessly with your cheap trade goods. You kill them without second thought, as you might a snake or a wolf. It is little wonder to me that they ambushed Ashley in the first place.''

"You're apologizing for them,'' said Pilcher in disbelief. "Facts are facts, Colonel. You've got to whip an Indian before you smoke the peace pipe with him, or the peace won't be worth spit. If you don't make them pay for their attack on Ashley, you put the life of every white man west of the Mississippi at risk. Don't you see? Every tribe from here to the Divide knows what's happening here. They're watching us. We must have retribution, Colonel, or we'll have hell to pay. A little bloodshed now, or a river of blood later. Mark my words.''

"An eye for an eye, is that it?'' asked Leavenworth.

"Worked for the Lord God Almighty, it'll work for me.''

In short order, Rose and the shavetail were back.

"He says they're having some little trouble with a few hotheads who want to fight to the death,'' reported the lieutenant. "Nothing to worry about—they want peace. But they need some more time before the peace council takes place.''

"How much time, Lieutenant?''

"Till tomorrow morning, sir.''

Rose was shaking his head.

"Is Lieutenant Kelso's report inaccurate, Mr. Rose?'' asked Leavenworth brusquely.

"That feller was Little Soldier,'' said Rose. "He's a two-legged snake. Iffen he says sumpin, you'd do well to believe the exact opposite.''

"You suspect treachery?'' scorned Leavenworth. "You think, perhaps, that they will come out and attack us tonight?''

"I don't reckon. Injuns don't keer to fight at night, if they kin hep it. They figure if they die at night, their souls might git lost in the dark and never find the next world.''

"Then what? What harm could come of giving them until tomorrow morning? None, to my way of thinking.''

"The Sioux won't like it,'' observed Rose.

"I did not come to appease the Sioux.''

No, thought Pilcher, only the Arikara.

"Well," drawled Rose, "I don't rightly know what the Rees'll try to pull on you, Colonel, but I know one thing: They don't want peace. Not really. And iffen they do sit down to smoke the pipe with you tomorrow, all they'll be doin' is blowin' smoke in yore face."

"Go back and inform Little Soldier that they have until sunrise tomorrow," snapped Leavenworth. "As for you, Pilcher: Tell your Sioux friend Fireheart I will expect his presence at the peace council."

"He won't show," sighed Pilcher.

"Then to hell and be damned with the whole lot of them."

With a heavy heart, Pilcher returned to Fireheart and informed the Sioux chief of what was taking place. He presented Leavenworth's demand as a polite entreaty, but the disenchanted Fireheart would have none of it. Deeply offended, he held a brief council with his sub-chiefs. Before sundown, the Sioux were gone.

The next day broke to find the Arikaras vanished, as well.

Only an old blind woman, too enfeebled to travel, was found in the deserted villages. Leavenworth ordered a return to Fort Recovery. From there he would proceed back to his post at Fort Atkinson. In his dispatches, he wrote as though the campaign against the Arikaras had been a smashing success. The mountain men knew better. By all accounts, less than thirty Rees had been slain—and most of them by the Sioux. The Legion had lost, not won, and everybody but Leavenworth seemed to know it.

Yet the Colonel insisted a victory had been achieved. Hadn't the enemy retreated? Hadn't they abandoned their lines and skulked away like a kicked dog in the night? Leavenworth had been left in possession of the field of battle, and according to the book, that meant the battle had been won.

Pilcher tried to persuade Leavenworth to at least burn the villages—he realized that attempting to prevail upon the Colonel to pursue the Rees was futile, so he argued for the next best thing. But Leavenworth wouldn't hear of it.

So when the Missouri Legion headed back downriver, their heads hanging in shame at having been participants in such a farce, several of them slipped back and put the Arikara town to the torch. Even that, or so it seemed to Zach, as with everything else in this endeavor, was fruitless. How well did mud lodges burn? The palisades might go up in smoke, but Zach knew, as did the other trappers, that the Rees would eventually return home, when the coast was clear. They would dance a victory dance and laugh with contempt at the white men, and they had every right to do both. They would kill a lot more whites in the future— that was certain—because now they knew they could get away with it. And that would effectively close the Missouri River to fur company travel for the foreseeable future.

This was to radically alter the plans of Major Henry and William Ashley. They had originally taken the method of the Hudson Bay Company, up in Canada, of using Indian trappers to bring the fur to established trading posts, and modified it to cut the unreliable red man out of the picture, replacing him with the hired white trapper. Now they were forced to make a second modification.

"The river road is closed to us, at least for a while," Henry told his men as soon as they'd arrived at Fort Recovery. "We can't maintain the fort on the Yellowstone, or anywhere else for that matter. Besides, the

Indians will be more troublesome than ever, and a fort will be too tempting a target.

"We've decided to split the company into brigades. Each brigade will select its own booshway, and its own trapping ground. The brigades will be on their own. When one spot gets trapped out, or overrun with hostiles, the brigade will move on. Meanwhile, Ashley and I will bring goods to a prearranged location every summer. When the trapping season is over, the brigades will meet at that rendezvous, trade their plews to us for whatever goods they want or need to outfit themselves for the following season.

"You men will consider yourselves employed by the Rocky Mountain Fur Company—that won't change. You'll agree to trade only with us at rendezvous. Of course if you don't like the arrangement, you can float your own stick as free trappers. But we can guarantee to trade fair and square for all the fur you bring in."

Zach thought Henry looked ten years older than when he had first laid eyes on the Major, last year on that St. Louis wharf.

Some of the men opted to become free trappers, but most decided to take Henry up on the deal. They didn't mind being left to fend for themselves. In fact, they preferred it that way. The Arikara campaign had demonstrated to them that they were better off trusting only in themselves, anyway.

"Course," Shadmore told Zach, "Ashley and the Major profit twice. They make boocoo money sellin' the furs we bring 'em once they git back to St. Louis, and then they turn around and make more sellin' us supplies and such at mountain prices."

"I don't care," said Zach. "I just want to reach the mountains. I left St. Louis over a year ago, and I still haven't seen them."

"You figure on joinin' up with a brigade, or bein' a free trapper?"

Zach smiled. "I'll float my stick with yours, mountain man. Just so long as we put this war-waging, and these high plains, behind us."

"Wagh!" exclaimed Shadmore, delighted. "I'm fer that, Zach Hannah. We're all leavin' this godforsaken place tomorrow, headin' overland fer the Yellowstone. Major says we'll try to trade with the Sioux along the way so's we kin get some horses. Mebbe we'll manage to hold on to these, eh? By the time we reach the Yellowstone, we'll have all the brigades sorted out. Then we'll pack up yore little sweetheart and make tracks fer the high country. How's that sound?"

"Best news I've heard all year," declared Zach, Morning Sky foremost on his mind.

Chapter 32

While Major Henry and most of the Rocky Mountain
Fur Company were off on the Arikara Campaign, those
who remained behind at the fort on the Yellowstone
kept busy.

In the mountains and on the high plains, when it
came to trapping beaver, there was an old saying:
"There are three months—July, August, and Winter."
The prime trapping season was short, and winter long,
and those who had been left at the fort had been given
quite specific orders by Henry: their first priority was
to take beaver fur.

Left in charge was an experienced mountain man
named Eli Simpson, who had been with the Major during Henry's previous excursion into the wild country.
Simpson knew his business, but, being a taciturn and
no-nonsense kind of person, he wasn't popular. He
took his responsibilities seriously, and drove the men
hard, which did not endear him to men like Sean Michael Devlin.

Not long after the departure of Major Henry and the
others down the Big Muddy, Devlin found himself
partnered up with Simpson and a younger backwoodsman named Coburn. They set out with packhorses
laden with traps, headed up the Missouri for two days,
and then turned south into the valley of an unnamed
tributary. Here were all the earmarks of excellent

beaver country. There was plenty of sign: slides, dams, felled and "shaved" trees. They commenced at once to setting their traps.

The traps they used were a relatively new contraption, invented only a few years earlier in New York City by one Sewall Newhouse, a blacksmith's son. Made of steel and much more reliable than the traditional snare, the Newhouse trap significantly increased the number of beaver a single trapper could take. Weighing five pounds, the trap was attached to a five-foot chain sporting a swivel ring at one end, which in turn was affixed to a stake or "floater stick."

A trap was usually placed in the shallows at the foot of a "slide," the distinctive path made by a beaver as it entered the water. The floater stick was driven firmly into the bottom mud and usually tied to something on the bank by means of a rawhide thong. The trap was carefully placed with its vicious jaws spread and trigger set. Each trapper carried a vial filled with castoreum. The vial was made from the tip of an antelope horn, and stoppered. The trapper dipped the end of a "bait stick" into the odoriferous "medicine," that appealed so strongly to a beaver. The bait stick was then secured in the mud at the water's edge, so that it angled out over the water directly above the trap. This done, the trapper threw water on the bank to wash out his scent and waded some distance upstream or down before emerging from the water.

Whether attracted by the castor or playing on the slide, a beaver sooner or later fell prey to the cleverly hidden trap. Once the steel jaws had closed, the beaver instinctually dived into deeper water. The swivel ring at the end of the trap chain slipped down to a deep notch near the bottom of the stake, or floater stick, and caught fast. Unable to free itself from the trap, and essentially chained to the bottom of the river, the beaver quickly drowned. Only rarely did a beaver have time to gnaw off its trapped foot and swim free.

It was general practice to skin the beaver where it was trapped. The pelt was cleaned, dressed, cured, and marked. Fresh bait came from the creature's perineal glands, located at the base of the tail. The glands contained the castoreum, a creamy, bitter, orange substance. Trappers removed, smoked, and dried the glands in the sun, then mixed it with alcohol, cinnamon, or cloves, or a combination of the three. The resulting "medicine" could attract a beaver a mile away.

Beaver meat was discarded. Few white men cared for it. It was difficult to prepare, needing first to be soaked at least twelve hours in salt water to draw off the excess blood. Even this did not make it very palatable, and there was plenty of better game.

On the other hand, the beaver's tail was considered a delicacy, when basted with wild goose oil.

Sixty skins made up a beaver pack, which weighed in the vicinity of a hundred pounds. The pelts were squeezed together by means of a scissor-press fashioned from logs and rawhide.

Trapping was hard work, and Devlin did not approach it with much enthusiasm. But in spite of himself, Devlin learned a great deal about beaver. The manner in which they constructed their dams and lodges amazed him. As Zach Hannah would have said, it was a "true wonder" to watch them fell a tree and then cut the fallen timber into lengths of about three feet, which the industrious creatures then transported to the spot where the dam was being built, packing the structure with mud and stone.

Tree-cutting was a family affair. The adult male

and female took turns, cutting round and round the trunk, and going deeper into the side nearest the stream, where they wished the willow or cottonwood to fall. While one cut, the other stood watch. Sometimes the adults allowed their young to try a little cutting. When the tree began to fall, the entire family raced pell-mell into the stream or pond and plunged into the water, knowing that the noise might attract predators.

Dams, Devlin learned, served to create ponds, which, in turn, provided the environment for the beaver family's "lodge." The lodge generally sat in the middle of the pond, like a castle surrounded by a moat. Beaver lodges averaged six feet in diameter and stood three feet high. They were dome-shaped, with very thick walls, and usually sported at least one entrance below the level at which the pond water froze during the winter months. Beaver kept their lodges meticulously clean.

During the summer, the beavers spent little time in their lodges, preferring instead to venture far afield. The end of summer found the entire community back home and busy laying in a winter store of food—the bark of young trees. One or two trees provided a beaver family with enough provisions for the winter.

The beaver was a family-oriented creature, and Devlin learned that if several members of a family fell prey to a trapper's steel, the remainder became exceedingly wary and difficult to catch—or "bring to medicine," in trapper parlance. Devlin saw some of these wily creatures in action, springing traps with sticks, sometimes even stealing the traps, taking the dreadful contraptions to the pond bottom or somewhere in the dam.

The easiest beavers to catch were the ones the French trappers called *les parasseux*. These were the bachelors, the males without families. They made no dams and did not live in lodges. Their homes were tunnels along the banks of a stream or pond. Often they lived alone, though occasionally two or three stayed together. A trapper was always encouraged when he stumbled upon one of these "bachelor halls."

Much as he hated it, Devlin did his part, wading around all day in icy water, scraping skins, and keeping a constant eye peeled for danger. They were not far from Blackfoot country. Already this year the Blackfeet had been making trouble for the white interlopers, along with their new allies, the Gros Ventres. Word was, a number of isolated trapping parties had been attacked.

One day Coburn returned to the base camp with a look on his face that told Devlin and Simpson all they needed to know.

"By God," breathed Coburn, shaken to the core. "I almost lost my topknot, boys!"

"Blackfeet?" asked Simpson, hefting his rifle.

Coburn shook his head. "Gros Ventre, I think."

"Tell me why you think so," said Simpson. He did not entirely trust Coburn or Devlin when it came to such matters—they were young, and new to the country.

"Well, for one thing, they wore their hair all different kinds of ways. Some had braids. A couple had scalp locks. They dress pretty much like Blackfeet, with fringe all down their leggins, but they got rawhide soles on their moccasins, and I recall somebody telling me only the Gros Ventres do that."

"What about their horses?"

"Only a few were mounted. They were poor-looking critters."

Simpson nodded. "They're out to steal horses,

mainly. It's a big thing with them, on account of sumpin that happened not too long ago. They're the worst danged thieves on the plains. Worse'n them pesky Absaroka Crow.'' He clapped Coburn on the shoulder. ''You got a sharp eye, boy. I'd say you got the makin's of a mountain man. If you live long enough, that is.''

''We won't none of us live much longer if we don't make tracks out of here.''

''No call to panic,'' said Simpson. ''How many was there?''

''I counted twenty.''

''No squaws?''

''This was a war party, Eli. They were painted up.''

''They didn't see you?''

''God, no. I'm standing here talking to you, ain't I? I seen them before they seen me. I was standing out in the middle of that crik about a mile from here, just putting down a trap. All I could think to do was swim underwater. Came up for air in a beaver lodge. Lucky for me it was empty. The critters would have raised a ruckus and I'd be dead meat.''

''Which way they headed?''

''West.''

''Over the hill into the next valley,'' surmised Simpson.

''They might change their minds.''

Simpson shook his head. ''They ain't got any idea we're here. If they'd seen sign of us, they'd scour every inch of this valley. I reckon we're safe enough, iffen we keep our wits about us. But just to be safe, we'll mount up and go cut their sign. Follow 'em a ways, to make sure they keep going.''

Coburn was none too enthusiastic about this plan. In his opinion, when you saw hostile Indians and they were turning left, *you* turned right. Devlin was inclined to agree. But neither of them protested. Simpson ran the show.

Being an old hand at the game, Simpson was not one to lose his nerve just because a passel of redskins were in the neighborhood. A war party was an occupational hazard for a trapper, and he knew they weren't going to find any prime beaver country completely free of that hazard.

So they armed themselves, mounted their best horses, and headed for the creek where Coburn had sighted the Gros Ventres.

They found the war party sign. Simpson dismounted to take a closer look at moccasin tracks.

"Yep. Gros Ventre, shore nuff. Only ones I know of sew that rawhide sole on their footwear. Bad news, them coming back up to these parts."

"Back from where?" asked Devlin.

"They come north from a long stay with their kinfolk, the Arapaho. I hear the Kiowa and Comanch' are makin' war with the Arapaho these days, and I guess the Gros Ventre didn't want to buy in. So they come north. And they got crossways with every tribe 'tween here and the Arkansas River doin' it. They left the Arapahoes with plenty of good horses, 'cause the Arapaho steals his ponies from the Spanish, and that's where you'll get the very best horseflesh. But by the time the Gros Ventre got back up here, they'd lost dang near everything they owned. So they're stealin' horses all over the place this year. That ain't to say they won't steal yore hair while they're at it. They be mean and onry critters, believe you me."

"Well, at least they aren't Blackfeet."

"Huh! They'll kill you just as dead."

"Then let's leave 'em be," suggested Coburn.

"We must be sartin they ain't going to double back

on us," said Simpson, mounting up. "So bite the bullet, boy, and let's go have a look-see."

They followed the creek, and a little further on found a dense plum thicket. Simpson checked his horse sharply.

"What is it?" whispered Coburn.

Simpson put a finger to his lips and tilted his head. Devlin listened hard too. Were the Indians lurking in the thicket? Perhaps they had somehow discovered that three trappers were on their trail, and now lay in ambush. Whether or not this was the case, Devlin decided it was the perfect time to beat a hasty retreat.

But instead of retreating, Simpson dismounted and freed his long rifle from its beaded and fringed sheath.

"What are you doing?" asked Devlin in a fierce whisper.

"You boys sit tight," replied Simpson. "I heard sumpin down deep in that thicket, and I aim to satisfy my curiosity."

Your curiosity will get us all killed, thought Devlin. But foolish pride prevented him from voicing a complaint. He was afraid to seem afraid.

Simpson entered the thicket. The fact that he was able to move quietly through the tangle of wild plum was a testament to his skill as a woodsman. He knew there was something, or someone, lurking in the thicket, and he felt it was essential to find out if it was the war party. Whether they had left the valley or stayed would determine what he and his partners did next.

He suddenly found himself in a small sandy clearing, bordered on one side by the murmuring creek.

At the same time, a bear cub burst bleating from the thicket on the other side of the clearing.

"Sweet Jesus," breathed Simpson, frozen in his tracks, an icy dread working its way down his spine.

The grizzly she-bear came plowing out of the thicket after her cub, took one look at the mountain man, and charged.

Chapter 33

Simpson knew it would be pointless to run. No one could outrun a bear on level ground. He had one chance. One shot. He had to make it count.

Grizzlies were extremely hard to kill. About the only shot that did the trick was through an eye or directly behind an ear. Simpson knew of many Indians and fellow mountain men who had been torn to pieces by these ferocious beasts. The grizzly feared no man, and almost always attacked. Indians counted coup on the grizzly, and the rare warrior who managed to slay one of the beasts wore the claws in a necklace. There was no greater badge of courage.

Simpson swept his rifle up and set the trigger, but just as he was about to fire the grizzly batted the barrel with one massive paw. The rifle discharged; the shot went wide. The gun's report and the acrid cloud of white powder-smoke served only to infuriate the grizzly. She struck the trapper with a powerful, sweeping blow. Her claws tore a huge bloody chunk of flesh out of Simpson's shoulder and knocked his arm out of joint. The impact hurled him twenty feet. Before he could get up, the grizzly was on him, clamping down on his thigh with her mighty fangs. Simpson screamed and lost consciousness. The bear savaged the thigh for a moment and came away with a mouthful of man meat. Rearing up on her hind legs, she watched the trapper for a moment. But when Simpson did not move, the grizzly lost interest and turned away, seeking her cub.

Devlin and Coburn heard the shot, the scream, the growls of the grizzly.

"Bear!" cried Coburn.

"Damn!" murmured Devlin. "We've got to go in and help him."

He did not care personally one whit for Eli Simpson. As he dismounted and tethered his horse, he silently cursed Simpson for putting him in this predicament. But he had to go into the thicket simply because that was what Zach Hannah would have done.

Rifles ready, he and Coburn plunged into the tangle.

Simpson was unconscious only briefly. When he came to, his first instinct was to escape. He tried to get up, made it to his knees, but the pain gave him pause, leaving him breathless.

He should not have moved at all. It would have been better to play possum. For as soon as he showed signs of life, the she-bear attacked again with a vengeance.

When he reached the clearing with Coburn, Devlin froze before the most horrible sight he had ever beheld.

The grizzly had clamped its mighty jaws on Simpson's shoulder and was flinging the mountain man around like a rag doll, all the while tearing bloody chunks out of him with its claws.

Devlin's first thought was that Simpson was surely dead, and he might have turned and run from this terrible carnage, had not the she-bear suddenly released Simpson and turned on Coburn and him, rising to her full height. She roared and lumbered towards the two trappers. Devlin and Coburn brought their rifles up in unison and fired.

Both bullets struck the grizzly. The she-bear came

down on all fours, bellowing rage and pain. Bleating, the cub crashed into the thicket. More than anything else, this saved Devlin and Coburn. No longer obliged to protect her offspring from the humans, the wounded she-bear followed the cub out of the clearing.

Devlin and Coburn reloaded and waited breathlessly, wondering if the grizzly would return, too stunned to move. Bears were nothing if not unpredictable.

They eventually concluded that the she-bear was gone for good. As their nerves settled, they ventured into the clearing, approaching Simpson's body with understandable trepidation. It was not a pretty sight. Devlin's stomach did a slow roll. Coburn turned away, bending at the waist and dry-heaving.

"God A'mighty," wheezed Coburn, when he had recovered sufficiently to speak. "He's gone beaver."

"No. I think he moved."

"Dead bodies move sometimes."

"He's alive," insisted Devlin.

"Can't be."

But then Simpson groaned and writhed.

"Oh, Christ," said Coburn.

Devlin knelt beside the injured man. Simpson was drenched with blood, his thigh and shoulder terrible open wounds. The she bear's claws had gashed him in a dozen places. The left side of Simpson's face was gone, and Devlin could see teeth and jawbone.

"What do we do?" asked Coburn.

"Don't know that there's anything we *can* do. Except stay here with him until he dies."

"What about them Injuns? What if they heard the shooting?"

Devlin hadn't thought about that. It was a distinct possibility. He caught himself wishing the grizzly had killed Eli Simpson outright. That would have made everything a lot simpler.

"I say leave him," whispered Coburn. He did not know whether Simpson was in any condition to eavesdrop, but just in case he pitched his voice low. "He's dead anyhow. Why should all of us go under?"

Devlin stalled for time, trying to think. Obviously Simpson couldn't be moved. A man with lesser wounds might survive being transported by travois. But Devlin was afraid even to touch Simpson for fear the shock and pain would kill the man.

"Let's get out of here," urged Coburn, anxiously scanning the plum thicket. "We can't do nothing for him."

I know what Zach Hannah would do, thought Devlin.

"We ought to stick with him for a spell," he said.

Coburn looked at Devlin as he would a raving lunatic.

"What for?" In his desperation, Coburn dropped all pretense and let his true colors fly. "I never liked him anyhow, and neither did you."

Devlin was no good samaritan. Had he been cold-blooded enough, he would have cut Simpson's throat and been done with it. But he just couldn't bring himself to do it. He knew it shouldn't be any different from shooting a horse with a busted leg. But this was a human life. For some reason, you weren't allowed to do the humane thing for human beings.

He was reluctant to abandon Simpson for two reasons. One was the knowledge that Zach Hannah, if placed in this situation, would most certainly stay, regardless of the risks, and Devlin refused to admit to himself that he was possessed of any less integrity and courage than Zach. The second, even more potent, had to do with his reputation. He had learned a lesson by sticking with Zach throughout their harrowing adventure of last winter. Mountain men appreciated that kind of valor, and Devlin had enjoyed celebrity more than anything else in his entire life. While hoping that every breath Simpson drew would be the mountain man's last, he was willing to take certain risks to enhance his reputation even further.

"If it was you lying there," Devlin told Coburn, "you'd be singing a different tune."

"Well, it *ain't* me," was Coburn's truculent response. "I wouldn't have been dumb enough to get into such a mess in the first place. I ain't the one who wanted to follow those damned Injuns. I ain't the one who came meanderin' into this-here thicket just to get crossways with a grizzly bear. And I ain't gonna get kilt on account of Eli Simpson."

"Then go on," said Devlin. "Get back to the fort. Send help."

It felt good, taking a page out of Zach Hannah's book. It was just what Zach had said to him, all stoved-up out there in the snow last winter—big hero talk—and Devlin felt heroic as he said it.

Coburn considered the suggestion, and found it wanting. He did not relish the idea of going it alone across a hundred miles of wild country swarming with hostile redskins.

"Damnation!" he railed. Petulant as a child, he scowled, paced, fumed, and paced some more.

"If you're going to stay," said Devlin, "go bring the horses round by way of the creek."

As Coburn left the clearing, Devlin wondered if he would ever see the man or any of the horses again. He spent some anxious moments until Coburn returned, wading up the creek with the three horses in tow.

"Is he dead yet?" were the first words out of Coburn's mouth.

Devlin shook his head.

"He ought to be," said Coburn, disappointed. "He's lost a couple buckets of blood, looks like."

They sat there for the entire afternoon, saying little, listening stringently for the slightest sound that might indicate the presence of the Gros Ventres in the vicinity, and waiting for Eli Simpson to breathe his last.

As dusk settled in, Coburn's restlessness increased. "How long's the old wolf going to linger?"

Devlin had no answer, so he said nothing. Every hour that passed tested his resolve. The clearing smelled of death. He had a strong sense of impending doom. With morbid fascination, he watched Simpson's shallow breathing, wondering how the man could hold on so tenaciously to life.

In the gray twilight they heard horses beyond the thicket. Later, in the night shadows, they saw the flicker of a campfire through the tangle, not a hundred yards along the creek. Coburn crept over to Devlin, his face a pale portrait of fear in the moonlight filtering down into the clearing.

"Figure it's them Gros Ventres?" he whispered.

Disgusted with this turn of events, Devlin nodded. What good was a reputation when you were dead, your bloody scalp dangling from some filthy savage's shield? He blamed Simpson for this dilemma. The old fool had been bound and determined to stick everybody's neck in a noose by following the war party, then traipsing into this thicket, and now refusing to die.

When Simpson moved and moaned later that night, Devlin lost his temper. Now the sorry old cuss was trying to lead the goddamn Gros Ventres right to them! Devlin crawled over to Simpson on hands and knees and hissed, "Shut your mouth, you stupid old bastard!"

At first light he ventured over to the creek for a

drink. When he glanced downstream, a sight met his eyes that made his blood turn to ice.

The hostiles had broken camp and were crossing the creek not an arrow's flight away.

Devlin lowered himself flat on his belly in the shallows, holding his head above water, watching the Indians cross single-file, a few mounted, most afoot, moving like gaunt, gruesome ghosts in the gray half-light.

They were heading down into the valley, and Devlin felt a new wave of bitterness. The way his luck was running, they would discover the base camp and take the packhorses and possibles and plews. All the tiresome toil he had invested in trapping the past few weeks would end up being for naught.

Simpson lingered all that day—out of pure spite, in Devlin's opinion. He was long past the point of staying out of regard for anything as silly as reputation; he remained in the clearing now because the Indians had come back, and deep in the plum thicket seemed to him the safest place to hide. He didn't know what else to do.

Towards the end of the day, with no further sign of the Gros Ventres, Devlin could stand it no longer.

"We're leaving," he told Coburn abruptly.

"Simpson's still alive," said Coburn, despondent.

"Now you want to stay?" snapped Devlin.

"You're the one who said we—"

Devlin cut him off with a curt gesture. He had already rationalized his change of heart, and now explained his reasoning to Coburn.

"The Injuns do it when someone's too old or feeble, or too bad hurt, to go on. They leave him. It's . . . expected. If he was able, I reckon Simpson would tell us to do the same thing. He won't pull through; he's just too strong and stubborn to die quick. That war party will find us sooner or later. They've probably found the base camp already. My guess is they're searching the valley right now for sign of us. They'd have seen our tracks leading into this thicket, except that made their camp late yesterday and broke it early this morning. But won't be long and they'll find us.''

"You don't have to talk me into it," said Coburn. "I'm past ready to leave. You're the one who was so dead-set on staying."

They got ready to go as soon as it was dark.

"What about his horse and rifle and such?" asked Coburn.

Devlin had already given that consideration. "When we get back to the fort we'll have to tell the others he's dead. It isn't that much off the mark anyway. If we don't, they'll wonder why we left him. And if we say he's dead, they'll expect us to have his plunder with us.''

This was eminently sound reasoning, and Coburn accepted it without question.

One last time, Devlin checked on Eli Simpson. The man was still breathing shallowly, lapsing in and out of consciousness. Flies swarmed in his wounds.

"Just let go, old-timer," murmured Devlin. "It's time to die. We all go under. Might as well accept it. I'd say words over you, but it don't seem proper, you still breathing. Besides, I don't know too many of those words. Except maybe 'ashes to ashes.' '' He sighed, looked around the clearing. On the verge of abandoning Simpson, he felt a sudden twinge of conscience, and tarried. "This is a godforsaken country anyway," he said bitterly. "Let the bears and red savages have it, I say. Wish I could go back to the river. But I can't. You see, there's a gamblin' man name of Tyree, and—"

"Devlin!" hissed Coburn, standing over by the horses. "Come on."

"Rest in peace," said Devlin, and walked away.

Simpson gave no sign he heard. He just kept breathing, the air rasping in his throat, while Devlin and Coburn, the latter leading the third horse, quit the clearing and quickly vanished into the night shadows.

Chapter 34

They made the fort without mishap—in fact, they did not see hide nor hair of a single Indian. The irony of that did not escape Devlin.

The journey took them three days. He and Coburn spoke little. Both men were haunted by what had happened, and by what they had done. The first night, Coburn did not sleep at all. The second night, he woke screaming at a nightmare.

"I seen him coming at me out of the mist. He was all bloody and ragged. His eyes were sunk deep in his skull. They glowed red. He was reaching out for me."

Devlin did not have to ask Coburn who he was talking about. He tried to make light of his partner's nightmare. Still, it bothered him, more than he let on. He figured it was guilt. A conscience was a damned nuisance. He wished he could do away with his altogether.

From then on Coburn kept checking their backtrail. Every few minutes he turned and looked over his shoulder. Devlin knew what he was looking for. Or rather, who.

"You gonna do that the rest of your natural life?" he snapped, perturbed.

"I just wish he'd been dead when we left him," bemoaned Coburn.

"He's dead by now," said Devlin, trying to sound more convinced than he felt.

He spent his time honing the story he would tell the other trappers. The temptation to embellish the facts with a heroic tale of Indian ambush and his own courageous deeds in a valiant yet futile attempt to save Eli Simpson was hard to resist. But in the end he decided to stick to the unvarnished truth, with one omission.

Of course, the key was to make absolutely certain Coburn would corroborate. The night before they reached the fort, Devlin had a heart-to-heart talk with his companion.

"Most important thing for you to remember," he said, "is that Eli was dead when we left him."

"I ain't stupid. I know that."

"Stop acting so jumpy," scolded Devlin. "Stop looking over your shoulder. And stop talking in your sleep. Sooner or later, somebody'll start wondering what wrong's with you. The way you're acting, they'll get to thinking you might have something to hide. You act like a man with something to hide. You've got to stop that."

"I *do* have something to hide," muttered Coburn. "We both do."

"Then hide it."

"We shouldn't have left him. You were right all along, Devlin. I feel . . . ashamed."

"We stayed as long as we could."

Coburn just nodded.

The next day they reached the fort, and Devlin told his story. The Rocky Mountain men accepted it without question. The notion that Devlin and Coburn might have abandoned Simpson while the man still clung to life did not occur to a single one of them. After all, this was Sean Michael Devlin, who had stuck with

Zach Hannah last winter. The trappers grimly shrugged it off, and put it down as just another mishap to befall the company. One of many. The venture had been snake-bit from the start.

In the days that followed, Devlin called regularly on Morning Sky. He behaved faultlessly, never outstaying his welcome. He told the other men he was merely keeping an eye on his friend's woman. They joked about it, made suggestive comments, but Devlin would not take the bait, and even managed to appear nobly offended by their remarks.

Morning Sky was always glad to see him. She cooked for him, and on one occasion mended his buckskin hunting shirt. These were small courtesies she thought it only proper to show the good friend of her husband.

Rides A Dark Horse also came to see her every day. Zach had asked him to look out for her, and he was happy to oblige. He had a vested interest in the success of the marriage. He had engineered the thing, after all.

Morning Sky was polite to Rides A Dark Horse, but remained somewhat aloof. She felt uncomfortable when the Crow warrior came calling, and could not completely mask her reservations. He never did anything untoward. But every time she saw him, Morning Sky remembered her captivity at the hands of the Sparrow Hawk people. It wasn't the fault of Rides A Dark Horse, and she knew it; he had personally done her no disservice during those terrible years. But he was a Crow, and that was all it took. Morning Sky did not want to have anything more to do with the Absaroka. She did not want to go back to her own people, the Blackfeet, either. All she wanted was to spend the rest of her life with Zach Hannah.

Rides A Dark Horse detected her reserve. To his credit, he took no offense. He came, treated her with respect, made sure she wanted for nothing, and returned to the Crow camp up on the bluff in the shadow of the fort palisade. He kept his promise to Zach Hannah and went about his business.

For his part, Devlin envied Zach this home and this woman. What made Hannah so special, that he deserved to have what he and the others did not have? It wasn't fair. Devlin managed to hide his envy, his desire to possess Morning Sky. But the more time he spent around her, the more difficult it became to exercise restraint. It got so he could scarcely sleep at night. He lay in his bunk in the fort and stared at the ceiling, seeing in his mind's eye every supple curve of her slender bronze body. He imagined what it would be like to slip into the skin lodge while she lay sleeping. Imagined her reaching out to him, greeting him with open arms, pulling him to her. Imagined how her body would feel against his. Imagined her hot breath and sweet, intoxicating kiss.

He decided he was in love with her. She was all he ever thought about. It *had* to be love. Problem was, she loved Zach, positively adored the man. Devlin could see it on her face, hear it in her voice. She missed Zach terribly. She asked every day if there was word from him. She talked about him as though he were a god. It made Devlin sick. But he knew he had to be patient. Until he had devised some scheme to win her heart and steal her away from Zach, Devlin would mind his manners. Only by doing so could he remain in Morning Sky's presence.

Maybe Zach would be killed in the campaign against the Arikara. That would be perfect. Then he could step in. He would console Morning Sky. He would provide for her. Gradually he would insinuate himself into her life, until she became dependent on him, until her eyes glowed with warm affection at the mere mention of his name, the way they did now when Zach's name was mentioned. Already Devlin was beginning the process.

As the days passed, Devlin began to forget about Eli Simpson. His conscience, it seemed, was very durable. Coburn had held up his part of the bargain, and by now Simpson's bones certainly had been picked clean. Devlin started to relax. He'd been in a bad spot and had gotten out of it, as always.

Then, two weeks after his return to the fort, a Crow warrior came thundering into the Absaroka camp on a hard-run pony, bearing news of great import for Rides A Dark Horse.

A small party of Crow braves had come across a lone white man wandering across the plains. The man was half-crazy. Hardly more than skin and bones, this man, and his skin bore hideous wounds. He could not speak coherently. At first the Crows had been afraid, thinking he was an evil spirit. But he was just a crazy old white man. They were bringing him in on a travois, and one had gone ahead to bear the tidings.

The Rocky Mountain men wondered who this man could be. Too consumed by curiosity to await his arrival, some of them rode out to meet the Crow party.

Devlin was out hunting when the Crow messenger arrived. As soon as he had returned, Coburn cornered him.

"It's Simpson!" declared Coburn, in a panic. "He didn't die! Somehow he's still alive, and he's coming for us!"

Devlin fought down his own rising panic. "Maybe it's not him. Nobody knows who it is."

"If we wait to find out, everybody'll know we lied.

They'll know we left him when he was still alive. You know what they'll do to us then?''

Devlin shook his head. He didn't know, and didn't want to.

"Come dark, I'm leavin'," said Coburn. "I ain't gonna stick around. I know who it is, and so do you. It's Eli Simpson, damn his eyes!''

It isn't possible, thought Devlin. In his condition, Simpson could not have lived two weeks—could not have traveled the hundred-odd miles that lay between that plum thicket and the fort.

Later that day, Antoine Godin found Devlin.

"Mon ami," said the crafty half-breed, "are you sure Eli Simpson was dead when you left him?''

Devlin almost lost his composure. Almost.

"What kind of question is that?" he asked in righteous indignation, all the while afraid his heart would jump out of his chest.

Grinning like a fox, Godin gave a Gallic shrug. "I wondered to myself why you did not bring the body home.''

"Godin, the place was swarming with redskins.''

"Mais oui, I understand. But perhaps Simpson's ghost, it does not, eh? Perhaps it come home on its own.''

Devlin walked away, suspicious of Godin. What was the wily breed really saying? What was he really thinking? The conversation had been unsettling, to say the least, yet it helped Devlin decide what to do.

Like Coburn, he had to flee.

Once the other Rocky Mountain men discovered that the man the Crows had found was Simpson, Devlin knew they would turn on him with a vengeance. He wasn't sure what they would do. He might be banished, cast out alone into the wilderness. Or their reaction could take a more violent turn. It wasn't that

Simpson was popular; that had nothing to do with it. It had to do with an unspoken rule. Mountain men lived by few rules, but they were inviolable. Devlin and Coburn had broken one of these by abandoning Simpson. Whatever the punishment, it would be severe.

Devlin chose not to accompany Coburn. He had a hunch he would fare better on his own.

He had only one regret: that he would have to leave Morning Sky.

Or would he?

He tried to conduct himself like a man who did not have a care in the world. The Crows escorting Simpson—for he had no doubt the wanderer they had found was Simpson—would not arrive until morning. Devlin knew he could not gather his possibles without raising suspicion. When he left he would leave with only the clothes on his back, his Hawken rifle, and the knife in his belt sheath.

And—just maybe—something else.

At dusk he walked out of the gate, strolling. The guard asked him where he was bound. It was a casual question. The Rocky Mountain men pretty much came and went as they pleased. They weren't the kind of men who would tolerate restrictions. He answered that he was going to Zach Hannah's skin lodge to pay a call on Morning Sky. There was nothing untoward about that. He had been doing it for weeks.

"See you in the morning, if yore lucky," quipped the guard with a sly wink.

As he proceeded down the path through the trees to the shelf overlooking the river, he saw her sitting in front of the skin lodge, nursing a small fire, and he faltered. It was that damned conscience again. What would it do to Zach to return and find Morning Sky gone? Devlin tried to tell himself that it wasn't his look-out. But he knew Zach would be devastated. The man truly loved his Indian bride, with an abiding and unselfish love which Devlin secretly envied, for he was not the kind to give of himself without asking for something in return. But he asked himself what was more important: Zach's friendship and feelings, or Morning Sky?

He walked on. She was surprised to see him. He did not usually come calling at this late hour. His expression was very serious.

"I've heard from Zach," he said.

Her eyes lit up. "Is he near?"

They spoke in English. Thanks to the patient tutoring of her husband, Morning Sky could understand English very well and speak it competently. That was fortunate for Devlin, who lacked the discipline to learn the Blackfoot or Crow dialects, and who was only fair-to-middling when it came to sign language.

"Not far," he replied. "He wants me to bring you to him."

"Is he not coming home?"

"Not right away." Devlin was playing it off the cuff, and didn't miss a beat. "They are building a new post. He must stay and help. We will travel light, and it won't take us very long to get there."

"Yes!" rejoiced Morning Sky, clapping her hands in delight. Then she frowned suddenly, unable to remember the English word that would convey what she sought to know. Forming a circle with the index finger and thumb of her right hand, she held her arm out horizontally, pointing east, and raised the arm ninety degrees. It was the sign for "Sunrise." At the same time, she raised her eyebrows in silent query.

Devlin was unable to grasp what she was trying to say. She repeated the sign several times.

"I don't understand you, girl," he snapped.

"When sun comes—we go?" she asked.

"We go now."

Morning Sky was puzzled, and the notion caused her some disquiet.

"Zach is eager to see you," said Devlin. "If we leave now we can be there tomorrow." Morning Sky nodded.

She kept a paint pony nearby for her use, and Devlin fetched it while she entered the skin lodge to get blankets and a pouch of pemmican. Her heart sang with joy. She would gladly brave the terrors of the night to be with Zach.

With Morning Sky on the paint, Devlin led the horse up the game path to the rim of the bluff. Skirting the Absaroka camp, he got away unseen, and headed west. He had no particular destination in mind. But westward seemed to be his only option. To the north was Blackfoot country. To the east was the Mississippi River and Tyree, and the consequences of past indiscretions. And somewhere to the south and east was Zach Hannah. Some days ago, word had come up the Big Muddy with a couple of free trappers of the fight at the Arikara villages, and news that Major Henry and his men were returning by way of the Grand River route, thence across the plains to the mouth of the Yellowstone. So heading south was out of the question.

The last person Devlin ever wanted to see again was Zach Hannah.

Chapter 35

Early the next day the Crows brought in Eli Simpson.

As he was carried from the travois to a bunk in one of the stockade's cabins, Simpson went from mumbling deliriously to a moment of lucidity. He recognized Antoine Godin, and clutched the half-breed's arm.

"Devlin," he croaked. "Coburn."

Godin nodded grimly. He knew now, as did all the others, what had really happened. A search for the culprits came up empty. One man remarked that the last time he had seen Devlin was after yesterday's sunset, on his way down to the Hannahs' skin lodge. Godin checked the tepee on the wooded shelf below the bluff. He didn't expect to find Devlin, but he went anyway, looking for sign. The sign told him plenty. Devlin and Morning Sky, the latter mounted, had departed the night before.

He returned to Simpson's side. "They are gone, *mon ami*."

Simpson's eyes, sunk deep in blackened sockets, blazed.

"I'll find 'em," he vowed, and tried to rise. But he was too weak to lift himself from the bunk, and sank back with an exhausted sigh, nearly passing out from the exertion.

"Rest yourself," urged Godin. He knew that days,

if not weeks, of food and sleep were all that could be done for Simpson. The man would be hideously scarred for the rest of his life. But he would live.

"I'm gonna kill 'em both," muttered Simpson before lapsing into unconsciousness.

The Rocky Mountain trappers held an impromptu council to decide what, if anything, they would do about Devlin and Coburn. The majority concluded they weren't worth going after.

"Simpson wants vengeance," Godin told them. "He has a right to seek it. I think it is the one thing that kept him alive."

"It ain't our business," said a trapper named Tom Fitzpatrick, by common consent the new booshway at the fort since Simpson's absence. "Our business is trappin' beaver. We can't spend what's left of the season chasin' those two no-accounts all over God's creation. When he recovers, Eli can go after them, with my blessing."

"Today the trail is warm," said Godin, dispassionate. "By the time Simpson is well enough to ride, it will be cold."

"I know you, Antoine. You're tryin' to sound like you don't care one way or t'other, but you'd pick huntin' men over trappin' beaver any day of the week. And I know Eli, too. We've rode the river together. I wouldn't want to be in Coburn's moccasins, or Devlin's either. This country is might big, but not half big enough for them to hide in once Eli gets after 'em."

Godin checked on Simpson after the council had disbanded. Eli was conscious. A camp-keeper was feeding him a rich flavorful broth made of buffalo blood and marrow. When Godin informed him of the council's decision, Simpson just nodded.

"Suits me. Better that you all didn't go after 'em

anyhow. Might be they wouldn't come back without a fuss, and then you could end up killin' one or both. And I'd hate to see that.''

''You would?''

''Damn straight. I don't want anybody else to have the pleasure of killin' those skunks.''

''What happened?''

''Well, I'll tell you,'' said Simpson, feeling much stronger with the blood broth in his belly. He told of the Gros Ventre war party, and his encounter with the she-bear. Even a hardcase like Godin had to suppress a shudder as Simpson related, in a coolly matter-of-fact way, how the grizzly had torn into him. Then, in words that cut like knives, the old mountain man recounted how Devlin and Coburn had abandoned him.

''I am surprised they did not cut your throat,'' said Godin; it was what he would have done.

''They didn't have the guts,'' snorted Simpson, and winced as a wave of pain washed over him. In a moment, he continued his narrative.

He remembered passing in and out of consciousness, and one time seeing Devlin leaning over him, and another time hearing Devlin and Coburn talking. He could not make out the words. It was as though they stood at one end of a vast cavern while he stood at the other end. Their words were garbled and echoed hollowly in his ears. He realized he was in a bad way—in fact, he thought it a genuine miracle that he still lived—and he was grateful beyond measure to his two stalwart companions for sticking with him.

And then one day he had come to and found them gone. Gone, and his rifle and horse gone with them.

''I think mebbe them two coyotes runnin' out on me gave me the will to live.''

Godin nodded. ''Revenge is a powerful motive. More powerful even than love, or greed.''

It had taken Simpson most of an afternoon to drag himself to the nearby creek for a drink. For food he found plums and berries within easy reach. For three days after the departure of Devlin and Coburn he lay there in the clearing, nursing himself back to health. His wrath at being left to the nonexistent mercy of the wild country transformed itself into a slow-burning rage which, if anything, accelerated the rate of his recovery.

Slowly, he tested his punished body. His left arm and leg were almost useless. He washed his wounds in the creek and used his torn, blood-caked leggins to wrap them—a tiring and time-consuming process with but one good arm.

But for the presence of the Gros Ventres in the valley, he might have lingered longer in the clearing.

He'd been wondering if they had heard the shot he'd fired at the grizzly, and had backtracked to investigate. He thought it quite possible that Devlin and Coburn had fled on account of their seeing the hostiles. But he wasn't sure until one morning he heard a gunshot, and then a second, followed by a whoop his old Indian-fighter ears could distinguish as coming from a savage's throat. The gunshots were alarmingly near, and he wasted no time in dragging himself inch by tortuous inch into the cover of the plum thicket. Moments later, a warrior appeared in the clearing. Simpson watched the Indian's dedicated study of the ground.

Two more Gros Ventres joined the first. They engaged in a long, animated discussion, with much gesturing. Their dialect was not one with which the mountain man was familiar. The warriors moved to the creek. One pointed to the tracks of three horses. Not thirty feet away, Simpson lay in the brush with his hunting knife in hand, knowing that if the Indians read the sign correctly he was as good as dead.

''Reckon I ought to be grateful to them two skunks for leavin' me my knife,'' Simpson told Godin sarcastically. ''I'll be shore to thank 'em proper for that small kindness—before I use it on 'em.''

The Gros Ventres did not correctly read the confused sign. They knew there had been a trio of white men in the clearing at one time or another, but they assumed all three had ridden out. As a result of this erroneous conclusion they waded upstream, seeking the place where the three horses had left the creek.

It was a close call, and it convinced Simpson that the plum thicket might not be the safe haven he had hoped it would be. The Indians were still looking for the three trappers they knew had been in the valley. They had the plews and the packhorses and the plunder from the base camp, but they weren't satisfied. They were hungry for blood. They had missed him once, but Simpson wasn't willing to bet his life that they'd miss him again. And now he had something very important to live for.

He spent the rest of the day fashioning a rough-hewn crutch out of a forked willow limb, wrapping the uppermost part with strips torn from what was left of his hunting shirt.

After a few hours' rest and a long drink of creek water, under cover of darkness Eli Simpson left the clearing he had entered more than a week before. Gaunt and covered with gore, he steered by the stars and headed east. His destination was the fort of the Rocky Mountain Fur Company. It was the closest place he could expect to find white men. But even had that not been the case, he would have gone there regardless, because there he prayed he would find the men he was after.

His first priority was to put as much distance as he could, as quickly as he could, between himself and the valley overrun with Gros Ventres. It was all he could do to cover a couple of miles before sunrise. As night surrendered to day, he crawled into a hole behind the roots of a cottonwood perched precariously on the rim of a sandy cut-bank. Curled in a cramped fetal position, he fell immediately into exhausted sleep.

In the days to come, he despaired of surviving his ordeal. Sometimes he could do no better than crawl, dragging his crutch with him, on the small chance he could ever stand again, clawing his way across the plains. Sometimes he could not even summon the strength to crawl. But every time his stamina ebbed and spirits sank, the passion for vengeance nourished him.

Hunger and thirst were constant torments. There was water to be had, but too seldom to suit him, and he had no means by which to carry a supply with him. The first few days the only food he ate were berries and roots and the marrow from some old buffalo bones, cracked open with the pommel of his knife. By the morning of the fourth day he accepted the fact that he needed something a lot more substantial if he was going to make it.

That very afternoon he saw the buzzards, and by sunset arrived at the scene of a recent wolf kill. The pack had brought down an old antelope. Simpson moved right in on them. After what he had been through, wolves held no fear for him. The pack had satisfied their initial hunger by the time he arrived, and they scattered as he approached, uninclined to fight for the meat. There wasn't much left, anyway. Still, Simpson cut as much as he could carry, including the bladder and some of the intestines. While he worked, the wolves sat off a little ways, watching and waiting. Once the mountain man had moved on, they slipped back in to finish their feast.

Simpson ate the meat raw. When next he found water, he squeezed the contents out of the undamaged bladder, rinsed it thoroughly, and used the intestines, also cleaned out and rinsed, to tie off one end. He then filled the bladder with water and moved on.

His gnawing hunger dealt with, his spirits on the rise, he crawled, stumbled and limped onward, ever onward. When he reached the broad Missouri, he sat down and laughed and wept at the same time.

Later that same day the Crows found him.

Telling his harrowing tale took a lot of the starch out of him. "I'm plumb tuckered, Antoine," he admitted. "I feel like I could sleep for a month."

"You could stand to."

Simpson shook his head grimly. "A day or two. That's all I do. Then I'll be after them."

Godin took his leave, thankful it wasn't him Eli Simpson wanted.

He quickly discovered that Simpson was going to have competition in the hunt for Devlin. Rides A Dark Horse came up to him moments after he had left Simpson's side. The warrior was inscrutable, but his voice betrayed the turmoil of emotion within. The bronze mask did not fool Godin; he could tell Rides A Dark Horse was beside himself.

"Morning Sky," said the Crow brave. "She has gone with Coyote."

Godin spoke the Absaroka dialect well, and acknowledged that this was so. The nickname by which Rides A Dark Horse had referred to Devlin had originated with Shadmore, that first night out of St. Louis. Somehow it had been made known to the Crows.

"Where did they go?" asked Rides A Dark Horse.

Godin shrugged, wondering where this was leading.

"Zach Hannah will be angry," said the warrior.

"No doubt."

"Morning Sky must come back."

The half-breed began to comprehend. Rides A Dark Horse believed Morning Sky had shamed him by running off with Devlin. After all, the warrior had been instrumental in arranging the marriage of Zach and Sky. Godin did not know why the warrior possessed such a keen interest in the success of the marriage, but he did, and to the degree that he obviously intended to make every effort to intercept Devlin and Morning Sky and return the latter to the skin lodge of Hannah.

Less than an hour later, Godin saw Rides A Dark Horse and two other Crow braves depart the Absaroka camp on fleet horses. Each warrior led a spare pony. They went down to the skin lodge and picked up the trail. This brought them back up to the bluff, around the camp, and due west across the high plains.

Godin watched them go from the stockade, until they were only dark specks on the vast sea of tan grass, and he wondered idly what would become of Devlin if the Crow warriors caught up with him.

Not that he really cared what happened to Devlin—or to Morning Sky, for that matter. Devlin had been a fool twice: once when leaving Eli Simpson alive and failing to cut the man's throat, and now a second time as he made off with the Indian woman. True, she was desirable, but Godin was of the opinion that Devlin would have done better to use her and then leave on his own. Many men, mused the cynical half-breed, make having a woman more complicated than it needs to be.

As far as Godin was concerned, Devlin deserved whatever he got for making such foolish choices.

Chapter 36

Eventually, Morning Sky began to realize something was wrong.

She was aware, of course, that Devlin was leading her in a westerly direction. That in itself did not alarm her, because she had no idea that her husband was at that moment more than a hundred and fifty miles east and south of the fort. She knew only that he had gone a long way to fight a tribe called the Arikaras, yet Arikara land, and the middle reaches of the Missouri River where that tribe resided, were beyond the boundaries of her world, and she lacked the perspective to know in which direction they lay.

No, it wasn't the direction in which they traveled that worried Morning Sky. Rather, it was the way Devlin acted. He kept watching their backtrail, with the apprehensive air of someone who has stolen something and expects the rightful owner to give chase. And he kept reassuring her that they would meet up with Zach—Zach was always just over the next hill. Yet she never once asked for reassurance. He gave it compulsively, and for a while she puzzled over the reason why. She could arrive at only one conclusion: that it was a lie. A liar worked much harder trying to be convincing than the man who told the truth. Devlin was working too hard.

She tried to persuade herself she was wrong. Why

would Devlin lie? He was Zach's good friend, wasn't he? Maybe she was just imagining things. But as they traveled through the night and all the next day with little respite, and with no Zach Hannah to show for their efforts, she found herself ever more convinced that something was amiss.

Still, she did not question Devlin. She was afraid to. If he was lying, and she let him know that she knew he was lying, he would drop all pretense—and then what? He struck her as being a desperate man who might do desperate things. No, the wiser course would be to play along, pretending that she blissfully suspected nothing. That way, when the time came, and the opportunity arose, she might be able to catch him off his guard and make good her escape. If escape was what she must do.

As the long day finally drew to a close, Rides A Dark Horse and his two companions appeared.

Devlin let them get closer than he should have before noticing them. After twenty-four hours on his feet, he was fatigued past the point of the blind staggers. He was so tired he caught himself sleeping in snatches while he walked. As a result, he grew lax in checking his backtrail just when he needed to be most vigilant.

Morning Sky saw them before he did. She started to warn him, but thought better of it. This, before she was even sure if they were Blackfeet or Crows or even warriors of some other tribe. Her instincts told her to wait, and wait she did, watching closely. In time she recognized them as Absaroka Crows.

She made the decision not to forewarn Devlin without really knowing why. The Crows were not her people. They were not her friends, and never had been. But maybe that was about to change. Morning Sky was thoroughly mystified. She had no idea what was going on. The three warriors were after Devlin—not her, for she had done nothing to them—and they were as desperate to catch up as Devlin was to escape. Their ponies were being run to death. She would have been even more impressed by their determination had she known that these horses were the spare mounts the trio had brought along. The first bunch had, indeed, been ridden to death, the warriors leaping onto their second ponies as the first fell to rise no more.

She recognized Rides A Dark Horse. Wasn't he the one who spoke of her husband as the white brother of the Sparrow Hawk people? Perhaps Rides A Dark Horse was a better friend to Zach than Devlin was or ever would be.

All these thoughts and questions raced through her mind at once. If only she knew what was really taking place here!

The Crow warriors were a mere six hundred yards away when Devlin snapped to and looked over his shoulder. He reacted by leaping onto the paint pony behind Morning Sky.

The paint was weary, too, and the sudden addition of this extra burden did not sit well. The pony humped its back and shook its withers. Morning Sky grabbed hold of mane and halter and hung on. Devlin couldn't. He hit the ground cursing, dropping his rifle. Morning Sky saw her chance and urged the pony into a reluctant gallop.

To her shock and chagrin, Devlin leaped to his feet, scooped up the Hawken, and fired on the paint, killing it.

As the paint went down, Morning Sky was thrown clear. The collision with the ground knocked the wind out of her. Dazed, she managed somehow to get to her feet. She started to run. Devlin was already running. He made a diving leap and tackled her, an arm around her knees. Rolling over, she kicked at him. He absorbed the kick and crawled all over her. Morning Sky gasped and became very still as she felt the blade of his knife at her throat.

"Try to run away from me again and I'll kill you," he said.

She believed him.

Devlin got up and yanked her to her feet. He dragged her back to where the paint pony lay dead, and threw her roughly to the ground.

"Stay there and don't move," he snapped.

She nodded. He turned his attention to the three Crow warriors. They were now only a couple of hundred yards away. Standing there, a look of cold disdain on his face, Devlin reloaded the Hawken, brought it to his shoulder, and fired. When the white powder-smoke had dissipated, he saw that one of the Absaroka ponies was riderless.

The other two warriors checked their horses, turned back to their fallen companion, and dismounted. Devlin reloaded and fired again. This time the bullet whistled harmlessly over the heads of the Crows. One of them returned fire. The shot went wide, but not by much, and it convinced Devlin that he would be unwise to remain standing. Though such bravado had its appeal, staying alive appealed to him more. So he hunkered down behind the dead paint.

He expected a shooting match, but the Crows weren't in the mood for shooting. His first shot had seen to that.

The two warriors had come this far only because Rides A Dark Horse had prevailed upon them to do so. They had no personal stake in Morning Sky, or whether she stayed or went. They had agreed to accompany Rides A Dark Horse because he was a great warrior and well respected by all the Absaroka Crows. To ride with him was an honor. But now he lay dead, and the resolve of the other two warriors melted as the ground soaked up his blood. Mountain men were crack shots, and the pair did not think highly of their chances against Devlin. Little did they know that Devlin was an average marksman at best, and that his had been a lucky shot.

Rides A Dark Horse's pony had wandered far afield, so the two warriors draped his corpse over one of their own mounts. While one rode away leading the horse bearing Rides A Dark Horse, the other jogged alongside. The latter turned once to raise his rifle overhead and yell defiant taunts at Devlin in parting. Devlin answered with a shot that had no hope of hitting anything, a waste of ammunition.

Once he was sure the Crows were gone for good, Devlin relaxed.

"Guess I showed them," he said.

"You have killed Rides A Dark Horse," said Morning Sky woodenly.

She looked at him as she might look at a dead man, with horror and pity.

"Why are looking at me like that?" he snapped.

"All the Crows will be your enemies now. Rides A Dark Horse was a great warrior."

"Not so great."

"The other warriors will want to be the one to take your scalp. It will bring much honor, the scalp of the man who killed Rides A Dark Horse."

"To hell with them," said Devlin gruffly, striving to conceal his apprehension.

"You are not taking me to Zach," she said—a simple statement of fact.

"No. You're mine now."

After a moment's silence she said, softly yet earnestly, "I will never be yours."

He moved as though to strike her, flush with sudden

anger, but Sky did not flinch or cower. He withheld the blow.

"I'll treat you right, Morning Sky," Devlin said, trying a different tack. "I'll treat you better than Zach ever did."

She could only shake her head, mortified by this turn of events. Her happiness with Zach Hannah had been only a brief interlude; now she was a captive once more.

"Yes I will," he insisted. "You'll see. I'll buy you all sorts of fancy foforraw. I've got money." From beneath his belt he tugged the pouch he had stolen from Tyree, the riverboat gambler, shook it so that the coins it contained jingled. He still had almost half of the poke—the rest he had lost in games of chance to other Rocky Mountain men.

She made no response.

"Zach," said Devlin, seething. "You'll never see him again, Morning Sky. So you might as well forget about him."

Suddenly, tears welled up in her eyes. They caught her by surprise. She had taught herself not to cry. Hadn't since childhood, except for that one time when the wolf-spirit had visited her. During her first weeks of captivity among the Crows she had cried, out of fear and homesickness, and from the pain when the Crow women beat her with sticks for not obeying quickly enough. She had soon learned that crying only led to sterner beatings, and did little to dispel the fear and homesickness.

Again tears did her little service, because it made Devlin angry to see them.

"I'm your man now!" he snapped wrathfully. "So you'll do what I say. And I'm telling you to stop sniveling."

She wiped her eyes and held the tears at bay.

"That's better," said Devlin, and reached out to touch her cheek.

She almost drew back, but made herself stay still, letting him touch her.

"Gather your possibles," he said, standing. "We'll move on. Don't worry. We'll make camp for the night soon enough. I know you're tired."

As she got her blanket and pouch of pemmican, Morning Sky worried, not about getting rest, but about what the night would bring. Would Devlin try to force himself on her? If he did try, what would she do? What *could* she do? The prospect almost triggered another flood of tears.

Her fears proved groundless. They walked a couple of miles, stopping in a point of woods. Devlin built a small fire. The timber grew in a depression between two grassy swells, and he did not think the fire would be seen from afar. He gave Morning Sky a few speculative glances while he curbed his hunger with the pemmican. She lay down, wrapped herself in her blanket cocoon, and pretended to fall instantly to sleep, her back turned to him so he could not see her face.

Devlin stirred restlessly for a spell, and every sound he made caused her heart to skip a beat. Yet he made no advances, and eventually slept, on the other side of the campfire.

For a long time, Morning Sky stared out into the night. Try as she might, she could not hold back the tears.

Chapter 37

Zach Hannah arrived back at the fort a week later, with Major Henry and most of the erstwhile Missouri Legion.

Every man had a mount. Using the goods Ashley had brought up from St. Louis, they had traded with the Sioux for good horses.

Ashley had returned again to St. Louis, this time to explain to the entrepreneurs who had invested in the Rocky Mountain Fur Company the new course of action he and the Major had decided upon, and to acquire the goods that would be needed at the first rendezvous next summer.

Godin and Fitzpatrick rode out to meet them long before they reached the gate. Ere they had said a word, Major Henry knew the company had suffered yet more misfortune.

Fitzpatrick began by telling of the Eli Simpson business: how Devlin and Coburn had abandoned Simpson in his time of need, and of Simpson's extraordinary fight for survival.

"When they learnt that Eli was being brought in by the Crows," said Fitzpatrick, "them two headed for tall timber."

"How is Simpson?" asked a grim Major Henry.

"He's on his feet and gone." Fitzpatrick shook his head in wonder. "Never seen nothin' like it. A man

that tore up . . . I tell you, Major, he looked more
dead than alive when he showed up back here. But in
four days he was up and around, and just yesterday he
took out.''

''Where did he go?''

''He swore he'd kill Devlin and Coburn for leavin'
him the way they did. I reckon it was kinda like attempted murder, Major. That's the way Eli sees it,
anyhow, and for one I can't say as I don't agree with
him. They should've stuck with him. Instead, they
took his horse and rifle and left him to suffer and
die.''

Zach and Shadmore were close enough to hear this
conversation, and the old leatherstocking fired an I-
told-you-so look at Zach.

''Coyote's gone and done it now,'' said Shadmore.

Tight-lipped, Zach said nothing. He was dismayed
by the news about Devlin. But somehow, not too surprised by it.

''So Simpson's out for revenge,'' sighed Henry.

''He went after Coburn first,'' said Godin.

''Why Coburn?''

''Devlin headed west and Coburn east,'' said Fitzpatrick. ''Eli had to make a choice. So he flipped a
coin. Coburn lost. Y'see, Major, it don't really matter
to Eli who he gets first. It ain't like he's scairt the other
one will get away. He aims to get 'em both, no matter
how long it takes. The man is obsessed. It's like what
happened to him changed him entirely. He sure ain't
the old Eli Simpson I knew.''

Henry nodded. ''I've known that to happen.''

''For my money,'' said Godin, ''the Crows will get
Devlin before Simpson does.''

''The Crows? What do you mean?''

''Devlin killed Rides A Dark Horse.''

''My God,'' gasped Henry. ''For what reason?''

Godin's eyes swept the faces of the men who had followed the Major on the campaign against the Arikara, searching for and fastening on that of Zach Hannah.

"Because Devlin didn't leave alone. Morning Sky left with him."

Zach kicked his horse forward, bringing it broadside to the breed's pony.

"You're lying," he said, with an icy calm.

"He ain't," said Fitzpatrick hastily, fearing that violence was imminent.

"She couldn't have," said Zach flatly. "She wouldn't have gone. . . ."

"I'm truly sorry, Zach," said Fitzpatrick. "She took off with Devlin. That's why Rides A Dark Horse went after them."

Godin nodded confirmation. "I spoke to the Indian right before he left. He acted like he took it personal. Like she'd let him down by leaving the marriage he had helped make possible. He'd made the match, and he was going to do his damnedest to see it stayed made. Or die trying—which he did."

"When they brought his body back, the whole Absaroka camp was in an uproar," said Fitzpatrick. He made a sweeping gesture. "As you can see, the Crows are gone. I'm afraid our alliance with them is gone, too."

Major Henry swore, loudly and with feeling.

It was the first time any of them could remember hearing such language from the Major.

"They were downright unfriendly when they pulled up stakes," continued Fitzpatrick. "Don't surprise me none. That's the way with Injuns. One feller from one tribe kills a feller from another. Might be over something as minor as who gets the choice cuts from a just-killed buffalo. Then, before you know it, the tribes are at war and a lot of folks are getting kilt.''

"Which is why the Rees went to war against all white men,'' chimed in Shadmore. "On account of Pilcher's boys not giving up a couple of young Sioux braves to an Arikara war party who wanted fresh Sioux scalps to hang on their shields.''

"Devlin was an employee of the Rocky Mountain Fur Company,'' said Henry darkly. "When he killed Rides A Dark Horse, it was the same as if we all had a hand in it, as far as the Crows are concerned.'' He turned to Zach. "I knew in my heart it was a mistake to allow you and that woman to marry.''

Zach couldn't believe his ears. Henry spoke out of bitterness, unwisely. He was about ready to call it quits. Lately he had been longing for St. Louis, and the carefree life of a gentleman of leisure that he had given up for this misbegotten adventure.

But Zach took him seriously, and made no allowances for the Major's state of mind. "That woman'' were the words that rankled Zach the most. He had admired Major Henry, even looked up to him, but he would not brook any man speaking of Morning Sky in such a disrespectful manner.

"Be careful what you say,'' he advised.

There was deadly anger in Zach's voice, and all those present feared for Henry's life if the situation worsened. Lesser men would have taken offense at the threat implicit in Zach's warning, and blood would have been shed. But Major Henry had the grace and courage to admit his error.

"Forgive me, Zach,'' he said. "I spoke before thinking, and without regard for your feelings.''

"Marrying Morning Sky wasn't a mistake,'' said Zach.

Shadmore had eased his horse alongside Zach's. "Easy, scout. The Major done apologized."

But Zach would not relent. He did not seem disposed to accept the apology. Without another word, his expression stony, he kicked his horse into a canter so suddenly that Shadmore's pony snorted and jumped sideways in surprise, almost unseating its rider. Zach didn't look back. He rode straight for the skin lodge. He couldn't accept what he had heard about Morning Sky. He refused to accept it. She had to be at the lodge, waiting for him.

A couple of hours later, Shadmore ventured cautiously down to the skin lodge to check on Zach, and found him sitting in front of the tepee, slump-shouldered. Zach didn't even hear him coming. He just stared at the ashes of the dead fire in front of him. Shadmore sat cross-legged across the blackened circle of stones from Zach and waited patiently for the other's eyes to rise and focus on him.

"She's gone, Shad," said Zach, his voice shaky and hollow.

Shadmore nodded sadly. "I know, son."

"I can't believe it."

"Life has a bad habit of sneakin' up on a feller and kickin' him in the gut when he least expects it. You better believe it. Believe it and accept it and just go on."

"Go on?" Zach's laugh was bitter. "For what?"

Shadmore scowled. "Now listen hyar, Zach Hannah! It pains me sumpin fierce to hear you talk like that. Why, a feller might think you'd never had a broken heart before."

"I guess I haven't."

"Well, now you have. Join the human race. Prob'ly won't be the last time."

''Yes it will.''

''That's crazy talk. Like a broken leg, a broken heart will heal. Might take longer, but it will.''

''I thought Morning Sky—''

''Wagh!'' exclaimed Shadmore. ''You thought she loved you. I reckon she did. Love ain't the sky or the mountains, Zach. It don't last forever. You cain't count on it, for Pete's sake. But it'll come back to you in time. Always. Wimmin!'' Shadmore shook his head. ''I sometimes think thar ought to be a bounty on 'em. You figure a grizzly's dangerous? Or a mountain lion? Zach, thar ain't a more dangerous critter on the face of this earth than a woman. She kin tear a feller to pieces so easy it's downright scary. Lord knows, I tried to warn you.''

Zach's smile was feeble. ''Yes, I reckon you did, at that.''

''*Shore* I did. But you wouldn't listen!'' Shadmore threw up his hands in a melodramatic gesture of exasperation. ''Younguns never do listen to their elders. I reckon they just got to fall in over their heads, and 'bout all you kin do is stand by and be ready to pull 'em out, iffen yore able.''

Zach shook his head and lapsed into silence. It pained Shadmore to see him so miserable. For a while, no words passed between them. Shadmore waited with the patience of Job.

His mere presence was an immeasurable comfort to Zach, who had never felt so alone as he did when he'd stepped into the skin lodge to find Morning Sky gone. And obviously she had departed of her own free will— there was no sign of a struggle or hasty departure. He felt marginally less lonely with Shadmore there, and he was grateful.

He knew Shadmore was right. He had to pick himself up, dust himself off, and go on with his life. Naively, he had thought of Morning Sky as his whole life, the beginning and middle and end. Now he saw how hazardous that was. This was the worst kind of death he was living through. An endless death. A living death.

But Zach Hannah was a born survivor. He realized he could not live long like this. He had to reevaluate the entire affair with Morning Sky. To survive, he had to make himself believe that his life was a straight path to the Shining Mountains. To reach that distant and mysterious paradise had been his goal long before he had known Morning Sky even existed, and so it must be again. He had to understand that she had diverted him from that straight and narrow path. His life, his destiny, lay in the high country. It was there, waiting for him. Morning Sky had delayed his finding it. He hadn't started living his life when he met her. He'd *stopped* living it. Now was the time to start living again.

He could do it, but it would be difficult. He had become too dependent on another person. In retrospect, that shocked him. Before he had always been self-sufficient. What had happened to that happily self-sufficient man? The man who now could not seem to function on his own?

He had to find that man again.

"I reckon I'll be going to the mountains, Shad," he said, more than an hour after they had last spoken.

In that time, Shadmore had reached the same conclusion. The mountains were Zach Hannah's salvation.

"I'm right glad you ain't goin' after her," he said.

"God knows, I want to. But it would just make things worse. Wouldn't it?"

Shadmore nodded. "She's going where she wants to go. Let her go."

"I'll have to tell Major Henry I'm quitting the company."

"He'll understand. He's a good man. And . . . well, I'd be obliged was you to let me come along with you."

Zach's expression was anguished. "I hope you don't take offense, Shad, but I have to go alone. I'm not sure I can explain why."

Shadmore masked his disappointment. "Shore I do, scout." He stood up. "Let's go find the Major."

As Shad had thought, Major Henry understood, and offered Zach his pick of two good horses and a set of traps. Then he offered his hand.

"I pray you will not hold a grudge against me for any hasty words," he said.

Zach shook the hand. He did not have to say anything.

That same day, Zach Hannah left the fort at the mouth of the Yellowstone. He said his good-byes to Bridger and Sublette and a few others he had come to call friends. They did not ask any questions. He saved Shadmore for last.

"Reckon we'll meet agin," said the old leatherstocking, with a brave smile.

"Reckon so," said Zach, trying to inject into his voice a confidence he did not feel. He wasn't going to count on anything anymore. He would have no expectations that might be dashed to pieces by the whims of fate. He would live day to day, and that was all.

As Zach rode away, Major Henry came to stand beside Shadmore.

"My prayers go with him," said Henry. "He is a lost soul."

"He'll find himself."

"I hope so. I hope to see him again. Maybe at rendezvous. But I've known men to ride off into the wilderness who were never seen again. I fear that will happen in this case."

Shadmore shook his head. "Don't you bet on it, Major. Zach Hannah ain't no ordinary man. I've said it before, and I still believe it. Zach'll make a name for himself. He ain't hardly got started yet."

Chapter 38

Devlin had no doubt Morning Sky was right—he was a marked man. Every Absaroka Crow was his mortal enemy. And he was smack-dab in the middle of Crow country. Like a hounded fox he circled to the north, less concerned with the dangers that lay ahead than he was with the peril at his back. He envisioned hordes of vengeful Crow warriors scouring the plains for him.

In a day and half they reached the Missouri River. He stood now at the border between the land of the Crows and Blackfoot country. He did not give much for his chances on either side of the river. But there was no turning back now. Deciding to stick to the river, he headed west. He had the vague idea that he would let the river guide him into the mountains. Perhaps there he could find some remote place where he and Morning Sky could live in peace. It was his hope—albeit a remote one—that most Crows would not venture so close to the realm of their perennial foes.

The fifth day away from the fort, he spied a cabin on the opposite bank of the river, in a clump of dusty cottonwoods. A slender gray thread of wood-smoke trickled out of its chimney. Devlin was astonished. Between it and a nearby corral confining several horses, the ground had been reduced to hardpack, and the clutter of long residence was everywhere in evidence. How had whites survived so long undiscovered by the

Blackfeet? Who were they? They could not be affiliated with the Rocky Mountain Fur Company.

Curiosity got the better of him. He and Morning Sky waited all afternoon, watching the cabin across the river, and when the sun set and dusk stretched long fingers of indigo shadow over the land, they crossed to the other side. It was no coincidence, thought Devlin, that the cabin was located at a point where a brush-covered sandbar split the river into two channels. The channels were deep and the water quick, but at least it cut the perilous swim into two halves.

As a precaution, Devlin tied a rope tightly around Morning Sky's waist, fastening it with a knot she would have trouble loosening, and securing the other end of the rope around his own waist. He wanted to prevent her from plunging into the river and taking her chances in a desperate escape attempt. Of course, he lied when she asked him why he was doing it.

"I'm a good swimmer," he told her. "I learned to swim almost before I could walk. If you get swept away, just hold on and I'll pull you across. Don't want to lose you."

"But if you drown . . ." said Morning Sky.

He grinned. "Then we die together, I reckon. Won't that be romantic?"

Going upstream, he found what he was looking for a few hundred yards from the crossing. A dead tree had fallen into the river who knew how many miles upstream, to be swept downriver until it washed up here.

They pushed the log out into the river. The current grabbed them and hurled them down towards the sandbar. They clung to the log for dear life and swam for all they were worth to reach the middle of the river. The river tossed them onto the western point of the sandbar, pretty as you please. Here they rested for a while before negotiating the second channel. They reached the north bank of the Big Muddy well downstream of the cabin.

Once on the other side, Devlin took the precaution of drying and reloading his Hawken before proceeding back to the cabin. He did not remove the rope that joined him to Morning Sky. By this time it was slapdark. Yellow lamplight leaked around the edges of the cabin door and the shutters on its two windows. Morning Sky followed quietly as he crept cautiously closer, rifle at the ready. As he neared the cabin, Devlin debated whether to knock or barge right in. He was not allowed the opportunity to do either. When he was three strides from the threshold the door swung open.

" 'Bout time you got here," said the man who stood in silhouette against lamplight, framed in the doorway.

Devlin jumped, leveling the Hawken at the man.

The man chuckled. Being menaced in this way was apparently of no consequence to him.

"Go ahead and shoot. Yore shakin' so bad yule miss me by a long mile."

"Don't be too sure," warned Devlin.

The man snorted. "Reckon if you was goin' to kill me, you'd have done it by now, and if not, then yore a fool. You two look like a couple of drowned cats. Come in and warm yoreselves by the fire." And with that gruff invitation, he turned back inside.

Devlin crossed the threshold, wary. He had to drag Morning Sky in after him. She held back, sensing danger awaiting them within. Annoyed, Devlin gave the rope a vicious tug. She stumbled and fell at his feet.

The man was sitting at a split-log table in the middle of the cabin's only room. He was a big character, broad-shouldered and barrel-chested. A black beard almost completely hid his features. In contrast, he was bald on top. He had just finished eating, and shoved a plate aside with one hand while reaching for a jug with the other.

"Beans 'n' blackstrap on the fire," he said. "Help yoreselves."

Devlin saw the kettle hanging by its bale from an iron hook in the fireplace. He was famished, but made no move to accept the offer. He gave the room a slow survey. It was packed to the rafters with trade goods. One entire wall was covered with traps hanging from long pegs. In one corner was a stack of red Nor'west blankets. Old smoothbore muskets were stacked in another. Bolts of cheap, gaudy fabric, crates of trinkets, and kegs of black powder—all this and more Devlin saw. A ladder provided access to a loft.

"Who are you?" he asked.

"Connor's my name. Yore's?"

"Devlin."

"And who's this purty little thing?" Connor's piggish eyes roamed hungrily over Morning Sky.

"She's mine," said Devlin.

"Not by her choice, I see, since you got to keep her tied on."

"That's on account of our crossing the river."

"Yore across the river now."

"In Blackfoot country."

Connor grinned. "And yore itchin' to know how come I'm still here all in one piece." He rubbed the top of his head. "Mebbe 'cause I ain't got a scalp worth takin'."

Devlin shook his head. "You're a trader, aren't you? You trade with the Blackfeet?"

"Have been since last summer. You want to trade that little punkin there?"

"I told you. She's mine."

"Make you a good trade. Been a while since I had me a woman."

"No."

Connor shrugged, took a swig from the jug, and then offered the jug to Devlin. "Top-notch tongue oil. Help yoreself."

"No thanks. Who do you work for?"

"Now ain't you just full of questions? I work for the Hudson Bay Company, what else? How else would I be sittin' here in Blackfoot country still alive and kickin' if I didn't?"

"This isn't the British Possessions."

"That's a matter of opinion."

"This is American soil," insisted Devlin. "What's the Hudson Bay Company doing here?"

Connor tiled his head and squinted at Devlin, as if he were trying to see better.

"You a Rocky Mountain man?"

Devlin knew better than to hesitate. "No." It was immediately obvious Connor wasn't persuaded, so Devlin opted for the truth—or, at least, the partial truth. "Not anymore. I killed a Crow named Rides A Dark Horse."

Connor's furtive eyes flicked to Morning Sky. "Over the squaw, I reckon."

Devlin nodded. "So I had to leave the country." He deemed it wise to omit the Eli Simpson business.

"Rides A Dark Horse," muttered Connor. "Heard of him. The Blackfeet will be right happy to know he's dead. The Hudson Bay Company's been doin' business with the Blackfeet for years. They get their guns and ammunition from us. Last year, we heard about Ashley and his bunch further downriver, so we set up a few tradin' posts like this one in Blackfoot country. With their blessings, of course. Just watchin' over our interests. Now, it ain't that they like us, but they tolerate us, bless their dirty little red souls, 'cause we're the only ones who'll sell fire-sticks to 'em."

"Aren't you afraid they'll turn those guns on you someday?"

"Well, it's true you can't trust an Injun, 'specially a Blackfoot. But I ain't afraid of nothin'. Besides, the best beaver country in the world happens to be smack in the middle of the Blackfoot nation, and we'll take long chances to get them plews. We're the only ones to get 'em, too, since we're the only ones the Blackfeet trade with."

"And in the meantime you keep a close eye on the Rocky Mountain Fur Company."

Again, Connor grinned his yellow grin. "You ain't as dumb as you look. Now, if you killed Rides A Dark Horse like you say you did, yule be one unwelcome son-of-a-gun in Crow territory from now till the grass don't grow no more. On the other hand, yore a hero so far as the Blackfeet are concerned. Seems to me you ought to think about joinin' up with us."

"I killed Mike Fink, too."

Connor lifted his eyebrows. "You? I heard Fink had gone under. Yore the one who put him down? I'll be damned! You done some mighty big killin' for such a youngun. Come on, Mr. Devlin. Smooth down yore hackles, rest yore bones, and have a drink, compliments of the Hudson Bay Company."

Cradling the Hawken in one arm, Devlin drew his knife and cut the rope from around his waist. He sat down across from Connor, the rifle tilted against the table close at hand and the rope still in his grasp. Morning Sky remained on the floor, too scared and exhausted to move.

Taking a sip from the jug, Devlin felt the whiskey explode like liquid heat in his belly.

"That ain't Tennessee sippin' whiskey, Devlin," admonished Connor. "It's good, but it ain't that good. Go ahead and have a man-sized snort."

Devlin did, and managed not to gasp. He slid the jug across to Connor, who drank it like water.

"Yore shore you don't want to trade that purty little gal of yorn for a few jugs of this prime nerve medicine?" asked the Hudson Bay man.

"I wouldn't give her up for all the goods you've got in here," replied Devlin sternly. "So just forget about her."

Connor's grin was lecherous. "How much for just one night?"

Devlin reddened. "Don't push your luck. She belongs to me. I went through a lot to get her, and she's going to stay mine. Understand?"

Connor's grin faltered. He shoved the jug back across the table. "If you say so. I ain't about to tangle with the man who killed Mike Fink and Rides A Dark Horse, believe you me!"

Devlin detected a trace of sarcasm. As he balanced the jug on his shoulder he said, "But I thought you weren't afraid of anything," with equal sarcasm.

When he took a swig, his head titled back, Connor made his move.

The flintlock pistol was on the bench beside him. He brought it up, pointed it across the table at Devlin.

Devlin was ready. He had figured the Hudson Bay trader was up to no good. When he saw the pistol he hurled the jug at Connor with such force that it smashed to pieces against Connor's face. Rising, Devlin turned the table over on the man. The pistol went off, the ball lodging in one of the split logs. The impact of the jug knocked Connor backwards off his bench, and as soon as he hit the puncheon floor the table came down on top of him.

Devlin had to let go of the rope, and as soon as he did Morning Sky scrambled to her feet and bolted for the door. It was a testament to Devlin's determination to keep her with him that, rather than finish Connor off, he turned and caught her before she could get out of the cabin.

With a growl any grizzly would have been proud of, Connor threw the table off him and got to his feet, swaying, his beard dripping with whiskey and blood. He drew a knife from his belt and lunged at Devlin.

Devlin's Hawken was on the floor near the overturned table. He couldn't reach it. But he still had his knife. Even as he drew it, he thought twice about engaging in a knife fight with the Hudson Bay man. He knew he would lose. Instead, he pushed Morning Sky to the floor and dodged to his left. Connor altered the angle of his charge. Devlin grabbed one of the traps off the wall and swung with all his might. The five pounds of sharp-angled steel caught Connor on the side of the head. He went down like a cut tree. Swinging the trap by its chain, Devlin struck again. Connor rolled over and raised an arm. Again and again Devlin struck, battering Connor's feeble defenses. He kept striking until Connor moved no more—until the man's head was a bloody pulp. Then, dropping the trap, he turned away and fell to his hands and knees and dry-heaved.

Morning Sky lay where she had fallen, paralyzed by horror. She had seen more than her share of killing, but never anything quite so brutal.

Devlin slowly raised his head and looked at her.

"I'm sorry," he croaked. It was all he said. He rose and dragged the corpse out of the cabin. He felt numb, exhausted, his mind a blank. Righting the table, he spread a blanket over the bloodstains on the floor. He drank some whiskey, and a little later ate some of Connor's beans 'n' blackstrap. Ladling some onto another plate, he carried this to Morning Sky, but she refused it.

"You need to eat," he said, solicitous.

She couldn't though, not after what she had witnessed, and she wondered how Devlin could be so calm. He acted as though nothing had happened. His attitude frightened her. Her will to escape him, or even to resist him, began to falter. She did not want to end up like the Hudson Bay man.

Devlin sat down at the table, drank some more whiskey, and stared for a long time into the fire. He no longer seemed to be worried about Morning Sky attempting to flee. He hardly seemed to notice she was there. Still, she dared not move—scarcely dared to breathe. Eventually she laid her head down on the blood-spattered floor and slept.

The next morning, the Blackfeet came.

Chapter 39

Devlin was out in the pearly light of dawn, digging a grave for Connor, when they came. They came like wraiths, and he was too wrapped up in his brooding even to notice until it was too late for him to act. He had now killed three men, and he didn't like it one bit.

There were five of them. Their faces and ponies were not painted for war. Several led packhorses laden with plews. Devlin considered making a run for it, realized that was hopeless, and decided he was about to die, all in a heartbeat. As a result he just stood there, blank-faced, which in fact was the only thing that kept him alive. Had he made a break for the river, or lunged for the nearby Hawken, they would have killed him.

A white man rode with the five Blackfeet. He was a gaunt, yellow-haired man with a pock-marked face. He wore a tam-o'-shanter, buckskin hunting shirt, green-and-blue tartan kilt, and leather gaiters above his beaded moccasins. It was the most outlandish get-up Devlin had seen. A bagpipe was tied to his high-backed Blackfoot saddle.

This man was the first to speak.

"So who y'be?" he queried, his Scottish brogue heavy.

"Sean Michael Devlin."

"Y'killed Connor?"

"He tried to kill me."

The man dismounted and walked over to the body, wrapped in a red Nor'west blanket on the ground beside the hole Devlin had been laboring over. He pulled the blanket away from Connor's face. The grisly spectacle did not faze him.

"What in flamin' hell did you use on the poor beggar?"

"He came at me with a knife. I hit him with a Newhouse trap."

The man nodded. "Twoulda been foolishness to let him get in close with a blade in his hand. He was a pure terror with a rib-tickler." He dropped the blanket, turned and faced Devlin. "At least you're burying the poor bastard. Wouldna be easier to throw his remains in the river?"

"I didn't want to kill him. He forced me to. It was self-defense." Devlin shook his head. He knew he wasn't making sense, or answering the man's question. He wasn't even sure himself why he was going to such trouble. It was just something he felt he needed to do.

One of the Blackfeet spoke sharply. The man in the kilt responded.

"What did he say?" asked Devlin.

"That be Standing Bear. He wishes to know if you are one of us. One of us meaning the Hudson Bay Company. If you're not, he'd be obliged if I stood aside and let them kill you."

Devlin's blood ran cold. "What did you tell them?"

"That I wasn't sure who you were, yet."

"Tell them I'm with the company."

"Now why should I do that?"

"Tell them I killed Rides A Dark Horse," said Devlin, desperately.

"Didja now?"

"Yes."

"And might you have the scalp handy, as evidence of your claim?"

"No. Some other Crows carried his body off."

"So we have only your word for it, that you killed one of the greatest Crow warriors in the history of the Absaroka."

"Ask hcr."

The man in the kilt turned to see Morning Sky in the cabin doorway. She was staring wide-eyed at the Blackfoot braves.

"Well, I think I know why you had to kill Connor," remarked the yellow-haired man.

"Are you a Hudson Bay man?"

"Aye. The name's MacGregor. Connor was my partner. Lest that cause you some concern, Sean Michael Devlin, I confess I didna ever really care for the man."

MacGregor started for the cabin, and Devlin followed. Before they could reach Morning Sky, one of the Blackfeet urged his pony forward. He pointed at her and spoke angrily, addressing his companions. Morning Sky shrank back from his prancing horse and menacing gestures.

"Tell him to leave her alone!" exclaimed Devlin.

"He says she's a Crow," said MacGregor. "He can tell by her buckskins that it's so. She is the mother of their enemies."

"She is a Blackfoot herself," said Devlin, fearing for Morning Sky's life. "Taken as a child by the Crows."

MacGregor spoke to her in the Blackfoot dialect, but she did not respond.

"Tell him who you are," Devlin urged her. "Tell him that what I've said is true."

"I cannot!" she cried out, in English. "They will kill me if I do."

"They'll kill us if you don't! Can't you see that?"

She realized it was so. If she claimed to be a Black-foot in captivity since childhood among the Crows, they would kill her for having dishonored the tribe by not escaping or taking her own life. If she denied be-ing a Blackfoot, they would kill her for being one of the Sparrow Hawk people.

Her only chance lay with Devlin. If the Blackfeet accepted him, which they might as the slayer of their mortal enemy, Rides A Dark Horse, she had a slim chance of survival as his woman.

So, in the Blackfoot tongue, she told MacGregor, "What he says is true. I am Morning Sky. The daugh-ter of He Looks At The Sun. My brother is Ten Bows. I was taken by the Crows when very young. Now I am his woman." She could not bring herself to look at Devlin as she said this. "It is true, also, that he killed Rides A Dark Horse, five suns ago."

"But there is no proof, lass," said MacGregor in English, sounding apologetic, like a compassionate judge forced to condemn a defendant to death.

"In time it will be known that Rides A Dark Horse is dead," she replied. "If they kill him now"—she pointed at Devlin—"it will bring great dishonor down upon them later, to have taken the life of one who has done the Blackfoot such a service."

MacGregor tugged thoughtfully on his chin. He seemed more amused than troubled by this impasse.

"It might work," he said, and looked up at the scowling Blackfoot looming over them on his nervous pony. He said something, once again switching to the Blackfoot dialect. Devlin cursed himself silently for having been too lazy to learn the language. The war-rior reacted with an angry tirade, cut short by the ar-rival of the one called Standing Bear. The latter barked at the other warrior in an imperious manner. Sulking, the other turned his pony sharply and rode back to join the three remaining braves. Standing Bear slid off his horse and approached Morning Sky.

"He says he is a friend of Ten Bows," MacGregor said in English. He remembers Ten Bows' sister was taken many winters ago by the Absaroka."

Devlin drew his first good breath since the appearance of MacGregor and the Blackfeet.

Standing Bear turned next to Devlin and spoke. Again, MacGregor translated.

"He says if it be true you killed Rides A Dark Horse, you are welcome among the Blackfeet. But, if it is learned that Rides A Dark Horse lives, you will die."

"Fair enough," said Devlin, relieved.

MacGregor spoke with Standing Bear, then told Devlin to follow him inside.

"And bring your squaw with you," advised the wily Scotsman. "You wouldna care to leave her out here with five Blackfoot bucks."

Once inside the cabin, MacGregor barely glanced at the bloodstains. He went in search of a jug of whiskey, then brought one to the table.

"Standing Bear and the others have come to trade," he informed Devlin, who sat down across the table from him.

"Those are fine-looking plews. Where did they trap them out?"

"Oh, they didna trap them. They took them, from a couple of free trappers. Also took a couple of scalps while they were about it." MacGregor shrugged. "But I don' care where they get the flamin' skins, so long as they bring them to yours truly."

"I should have known," said Devlin.

"Aye. A Blackfoot buck's too busy killing and such

in the summer to waste his time catching beaver. Have a drink.''

Devlin did. Though he thought it a little early in the day for strong spirits, his nerves were sorely in need of medication.

"Now, as to you, Sean Michael Devlin," said MacGregor, "you're late of the Rocky Mountain Fur Company, I wager.''

"How did you know?''

"Simple deduction. You got your squaw from the Absaroka, and the Rocky Mountain Fur Company's been going to great lengths to tie in with them.''

"I was. But no longer.''

"No, I wouldna think so, if you killed Rides A Dark Horse. That wouldna sit well with Ashley and Henry, would it? So, for you, what now?''

"The Hudson Bay Company is short a man.''

MacGregor threw back his head and laughed heartily. "Aye, that it is. Care to be my partner, then?''

"Sounds good to me. As long as you don't insist on trading a jug of whiskey for her." Devlin nodded at Morning Sky, who stood off to one side, trying her best to be inconspicuous.

"That's a deal," chuckled MacGregor, reclaiming the jug. "I wouldna want to make you have to dig another grave.''

Chapter 40

In the mountains he had never seen, Zach Hannah found his home.

From the sagebrush and alkali of the high plains he came to the forested foothills. Summer was drawing to a close, and the hardwoods were already beginning to turn. Their gold and orange and crimson were shot through with strands of evergreen. Beyond the ribbon of foothills he saw them—a majestic cordon of gray granite, snow on the jagged, cloud-wreathed peaks and between the sharp mountain shoulders.

He kept to the Yellowstone, his guide to the high country. Higher and higher he climbed. Often he had to lead his horses, for the way was too steep for riding. The plains tilted sharply up to meet the foothills, and the foothills reminded him of the Smokies he had once called home. The air was thin at this altitude and made his lungs ache; the clarity of the air made objects appear closer than they were. The first range he saw were the Bighorn Mountains, but he skirted these, passing well to the north of them, aimed dead-on for the Beartooth Range. From the time he first saw them in the distance, a jagged cobalt line frosted with the white of snowy peaks, it took him ten frustrating days to reach their base.

Every day the clouds seem to anchor against the high rocky escarpments, melding into ominous thunderclouds with bellies smoky-blue with rain. When the rain came, it did so with a vengeance and vitality that took Zach's breath away. Here, it seemed, Mother Nature never did anything by halves. The water plunged down off the mountains in dancing creeks and magnificent waterfalls, and the Yellowstone raged fast and deep through its canyons.

He saw wondrous sights. Veins of strawberry-pink quartz and slopes of mica captured the sun. The quantity and variety of semiprecious stones was remarkable. Blood-red garnets, purple amethyst, turquoise like teardrops from the sky captured in a stony carapace, lay on the ground, there for the taking. He came across a black crystal shaped like a sunburst, a foot in diameter. Zach did not know that this was a rare specimen of tourmaline; he knew only that it was a true wonder.

The canyon of the Yellowstone deepened. The river roared like a demon, and a damp mist made for treacherous going. The ledges and paths were slick and dangerous, and eventually he found a way to the rim—an extremely difficult and harrowing climb, especially hauling two reluctant horses. He kept the river beside him and soon saw cliffs of black volcanic glass, and beyond these, hot springs and bubbling mudpots that belched the most godawful stench into the air, and even a petrified forest.

Zach had heard stories of such a place—tall tales, or so he had thought. John Colter, who had come west with Lewis and Clark, only to remain behind in the Rockies for a spell when the rest of the expedition went home, had found his way back to civilization with word of a high plateau deep in the Rockies, rimmed on all sides by forbidding ranges. On this plateau, Colter claimed, he had discovered a bizarre landscape. Like hell on earth. Where the streams and lakes were too hot for fish, and the air too foul with sulfur fumes for fowl, and where no animals could sustain themselves. Even the Indians, said Colter, were loath to linger in this unworldly valley.

Few had taken him seriously. He was, after all, a mountain man, a species prone to exaggeration. This was the same Colter who insisted he had been captured by the Blackfeet and, in escaping unarmed and naked, had outrun five hundred warriors less one, whom he had killed with his bare hands. Most people smiled behind their hands and agreed that John Colter had a splendid imagination.

Zach realized he had found the place Colter had described. Some of what Colter had said seemed to be true. There was no sign of Indians. But there was abundant wildlife. The plateau swarmed with mule deer, and he saw entirely too many grizzly bears to suit him. He found a large lake surrounded by a lush forest of lodgepole pine. Elk and moose frequented a marsh of willows and sedge located at one end of the lake. The male elk were in their autumn rut, and staged battles royal for his entertainment. Their bugling war cries echoed against the stern mountain flanks. The surface of the lake was quite warm, but according to Colter only to the depth of two or three feet, and trout flourished beneath this level. With game in such abundance, Zach decided to make his base camp in the pine forest, selecting a meadow adorned with wildflowers of purple, yellow, and blue. It was his intention to spend as much time as possible exploring the plateau, figuring to stay until the first snow. Then he'd have to skedaddle. The mountain ranges encircling the plateau would become impassable in winter.

For days on end he explored. One morning he came to a barren stretch of rocky ground surrounded by wooded ridges. Directly in front of him rose an ash-gray mound, from which trickled a thin vapor cloud. This excited little interest in Zach, who had by this time seen countless mudpots and hot springs and even small geysers. As he neared the mound, it burped up a little water. Then, suddenly, a fountain of steaming water erupted from the crater, shooting skyward a hundred feet with a loud *whoosh!* Drenched by the scalding spray, Zach ran, slipped and fell, got up and scampered for safety.

From a safe distance, the awestruck wanderer sat on a rock and watched the geyser until it subsided, as suddenly as it had come, a few minutes later.

Zach had never seen anything like it. He ventured warily closer, walked all around the quiescent mound, and finally returned to his rock, determined to sit there all year if need be just to witness the miracle again. He was not disappointed. An hour after the previous geyser, the mound produced another just as spectacular. Zach spent the rest of the day there, a rapt audience of one, and every hour on the hour the geyser faithfully appeared.

In the days to come he saw many more geysers, though none quite so magnificent. He decided there could not be any other place on earth so wondrous, and it was with keen regret that he took his leave. But he knew he had to go, as the brief high-country autumn gave way to winter's icy chill. Following a week of raw, blustery wind mixed with rain and sleet, the first snow fell, and on that day Zach rode on, promising himself that he would return to this remote wonderland the following spring.

Major Henry had graciously provided him with all the essentials, among them an ax, and when, a week later, he found the spot he wanted, he went to work felling saplings and constructing a sturdy lean-to shelter beneath a rocky ledge on a shelf overlooking a secluded valley, on the south slope of a sawtooth peak. He killed an elk and several mule deer, stashing the meat in caches high up in the forks of trees, out of reach of most predators. The meat would freeze and keep. He had several blankets and a couple of buffalo robes, and there was plenty of firewood near at hand, as well as a deep, fast-running creek tumbling down off the shelf into the valley.

There he spent the winter, a winter in which a gray cottony mist wrapped itself around the high reaches in the morning, and the hail when it came stung like buckshot, and the creek froze clean to the bottom so that he had to chip ice out with knife and ax and melt it in a kettle over his fire for drinking water, and the snow came sliding down the flanks of the mountain across the valley in thundering avalanches.

He spent these idle months with a book of Shakespeare the Major had secreted, unbeknownst to him, in the plunder he had brought with him from the fort. Additional entertainment came in the form of mountain goats gamboling in seeming reckless abandon on the grim escarpments of the peaks surrounding the valley. When the weather allowed he ventured out for more exploring, eager to acquaint himself with every nook and cranny of his new home.

In this isolated splendor he healed himself.

Now and then a stray memory escaped from that place in his mind where he had locked away all his memories, and he thought of Morning Sky, and the pain was exquisite. But as the weeks passed this happened less and less frequently. Survival took up a great deal of his time and thoughts. The challenge exhilarated him. He was alone, but somehow seldom lonely. Though some days he heard nothing but the wind fluting in the high reaches, and saw nothing living as he gazed across the valley from his lean-to, cozy in his buffalo robes on a soft and fragrant palliasse of fresh-cut spruce boughs, he knew there was life out there, much of it curled up in warm holes, waiting for green-up.

Occasionally he came across the sign of a wolf pack that shared the valley with him, and once he thought he saw them, a mile away, crossing a snowfield. Like the hibernating bear and the prowling wolf, he felt as though he belonged here.

The days came and went in a lazy blur. He waited patiently for winter to end. These mountains would be his home for the rest of his life, so he was in no hurry.

Though wolves were fond of horseflesh, the pack never molested Zach's ponies, intent to roam far and wide in search of deer and elk and even mountain sheep that had become hampered or even trapped in deep snow. In spring they sniffed out dead animals that had been buried under snowslides. The bear did this, too, and Zach witnessed a battle between the pack and a grizzly on the mountain across the valley. It was a contest over the rights to a feeding ground, and the wolves won. Several members of the pack were mauled, but the bear, itself injured, eventually lumbered away. For the first time, Zach saw the big silver wolf who seemed to be the leader of the pack.

At green-up he returned to the plateau near the Yellowstone and reacquainted himself with its magical wonders. He stayed but a few weeks this time, leaving to find a beaver colony.

Zach had no desire to associate with humans, but he was pragmatic enough to realize that sooner or later he would need more powder and lead if he intended to keep hunting for meat to sustain him, and protecting himself from the occasional grizzly or Indian war party. So he set the traps Major Henry had given him, and caught his beaver, and before the summer was out had a pack of fine plews. He could have had more, but that was enough. He spent the remainder of the season exploring, and in the winter he returned to his secluded valley.

In this manner, Zach Hannah spent three years.

He came to know the mountains, from the Bitterroot Range in the north to the Wind River Range in the south, better than any white man then living, and better than most Indians. Unlike the Indians, he spent the year round in the high country. When in the summer they descended to the plains to hunt buffalo he watched them go. He did not care ever to leave the mountains.

Endowed with a faultless memory and the knack of keen observation, he learned every aspect of his new home so thoroughly that he became familiar with each pass in every range, and every stream or river crossing. He knew all the valleys—where he could have had the best beaver trapping, and the best water and graze—but he kept to the mountains.

He came to learn the mountains with the attention to detail a lover bestows upon his partner, because he *did* love them; the high mountain meadows sprinkled with wildflowers; the sapphire lakes that looked like fallen pieces of sky; the mighty waterfalls; the sheer cliffs; the high reaches above the timberline crowned year-round with glaciers; the crystal-clear air that tasted like wine. The mountains nurtured and protected him, and he knew he could rely on them. They would never betray him as long as he did not abuse their hospitality.

He sometimes crossed paths with Indians, though he went out of his way to avoid them. Only twice did he have real trouble, both times with Blackfoot marauders. The warriors who survived these fights returned to their villages to tell of a lone white man who could appear and disappear like a spirit, and who fought with cool skill. Many Blackfoot braves dreamed of being the one to take the scalp of this solitary mountain man. They looked hard for Zach Hannah, but every passing year found him more adept at avoiding them—so skillful that, for the last couple of years, not a living soul had set eyes on him, and many thought him dead.

Zach had become master of the wilderness, the reclusive monarch of a grand and lonely kingdom, and he was content to be that and nothing more.

But it couldn't last forever. Every season, more and more brigades of fur trappers ventured deeper and deeper into his domain. Their clashes with the Blackfeet and the Gros Ventres increased in frequency and ferocity. Zach found himself caught in the middle of a war, and his beloved mountains had become the battlefield. As the fur trade flourished, the trappers were pressured to find new and better beaver country. The Blackfeet and their Gros Ventre allies vowed to drive the hated man from their country.

Zach tried to stay out of it. He told himself he owed no more allegiance to the trappers than he did to the Indians.

But in the summer of 1828, something happened to prove otherwise.

Chapter 41

That spring, a brigade of Rocky Mountain Fur Company trappers prepared to leave their winter camp at the headwaters of the Greybull River, just east of the Owl Creek Mountains. They were bound for the Great Divide and beyond. The Shoshones, who had treated them in friendly fashion, swore there was rich beaver country west of the Wind River Range.

The brigade was comprised of eight mountain men, among them Shadmore, who had been elected by the others to serve as booshway. Accompanying the party were two Shoshone guides. They had high hopes of a successful season, too far south to expect any trouble from the Blackfeet.

Their route took them through South Pass, which the Crows had shown to Tom Fitzpatrick four years earlier. The discovery of this pass had already had a great impact upon the fur trade, providing trappers with easy access into the mountains beyond the reach of the Blackfeet. It had turned the fortunes of the Rocky Mountain Fur Company completely around. No one then realized how important a role South Pass would play in the near future, when a horde of emigrants would use it to cross the Continental Divide on what would become known as the Oregon Trail.

The approach to South Pass was easy going—a gently rolling stretch of desert where, it seemed, only sagebrush and locoweed could flourish. Spring had provided a dash of color to break the monotony of sagebrush gray: scarlet trumpet adorned the slopes, and blue patches of larkspur decorated the bottoms. Game was plentiful. The trappers saw thousands of pronghorn browsing on the sage, and even more horned larks nesting in it.

Once through South Pass, they turned north and searched the valleys west of the Wind River Range. They could not find the prime beaver country the Shoshone had promised. Ashamed, their guides deserted them. They continued north, well aware that by doing so they were drawing ever closer to Gros Ventre territory. But there was no help for it.

They passed a mammoth glacier that filled a cirque two miles across. The glacier's ice-melt was a major source of the Green River. Near the foot of the glacier was a lake with water that was milky-blue due to a high concentration of rock flour. The vegetation was as sparse as in South Pass, but of an alpine rather than desert nature: huckleberry, fleabane and stonecrop. A frigid wind swept down off the glacier day and night, and they were glad to put the place behind them.

Proceeding along the Green River valley, they made good time, and all agreed it was a pleasant march. While the mountains on either side were steep and thickly wooded, the valley floor was remarkably level. The languid river twisted like a snake through lush sedge and marsh grass of a rich amber hue, in eye-pleasing contrast to the deep green of the fir and lodgepole pine clinging to the rocky slopes.

Next they came to the Green River lakes, over which loomed the landmark of a distinctive mountain the Indians called Squaretop. Beyond, the river flowed into a broad valley as it left the mountains. It had been decided last summer that this sagebrush valley would be the site for the rendezvous of 1828.

Shadmore led the brigade onward, pushing north toward the rugged Teton Range. Eventually, in the valley of a Snake River tributary, they found their beaver country. Fifty miles due east were the headwaters of the Greybull River, the site of their winter camp, which they had left almost three weeks and two hundred miles ago. They had made almost a complete circuit around the Wind River Range. Shadmore was in no mood to appreciate the irony of the situation. They had lost valuable time, and now hastily proceeded to place their traps.

Every man in the brigade knew they had to keep an eye peeled for Blackfeet or Gros Ventres. Shadmore paired them off, so that one could constantly be on-guard while his partner worked.

Two of the trappers, Maury and Delaplane, followed a creek along which they found plenty of beaver sign. Five miles from the brigade's base came they stumbled upon a half-dozen skin lodges. Meat on spits cooked over smoking fires only recently tended, yet the brigade saw no one.

Maury rashly decided to venture into the camp. He harbored dangerous contempt for the red man, holding to the opinion that Indians were no better than vermin, and that it was every white man's bounden duty to kill them whenever they were found. Maury cared less what tribe the inhabitants of the skin lodges belonged to; Crow or Blackfoot or Shoshone, he was prepared to shoot first and ask questions later.

But the tepees were empty.

Maury did not have the sense to be alarmed by this development. Instead, he tarried in the Indian camp and helped himself to the meat.

Delaplane struggled with a dilemma. He didn't like

this one bit, yet could not bring himself to desert his colleague. Anxiously he waited for Maury to finish stuffing himself. His anxiety swelled to near panic when Maury began to loot the tepees. Delaplane protested, to no avail, and Maury left the camp with some fine elk skins and several new pairs of moccasins.

Retracing their steps, they made for the brigade's base camp, intending to warn the others of the presence of Indians in the valley. Less than a mile from the tepees, they blundered into an ambush. As they entered a thick stand of quaking aspen, the Blackfeet jumped them.

Most of the warriors were armed with smoothbores, courtesy of the Hudson Bay Company. Seven rifles spoke, spewing hot lead and acrid powder-smoke. Those who did not possess a firearm shot arrows.

The first volley killed Delaplane outright. The French-Canadian took two arrows and several bullets and toppled dead off his horse. Maury took an arrow in the back and a bullet in the leg, yet managed to stay aboard his pony, which he spurred into a gallop, pursued by more bullets and arrows. He looked back once, to see several Blackfeet pounce on Delaplane's corpse and commence to hack it to bloody pieces with their knives and hatchets.

The Blackfeet were unprepared to give chase, having been overly confident in the full success of their ambush. Their ponies had been left some distance from the site in the keeping of their squaws, one of whom had alerted the small summer camp of the approach of the two trappers. The small Blackfoot band had worried that the pair might be advance scouts for a larger party of ''hair-faces.'' The Blackfeet, numbering only ten braves and nine women and children, had slipped discreetly into the brush. Only when they knew the two white men were on their own had they devised the ambush.

Maury made it back to the base camp. Shadmore and one other, another French-Canadian whose name was Baptiste, were there when the wounded mountain man rode in. Bleeding profusely, white from the pain and shock and loss of blood, Maury slipped off his lathered horse into their arms. They laid him down gently, on his stomach. One look at the fletching of the arrow in his back, as well as the symbols of its shaft, told Shadmore most of what he needed to know.

"Wagh!" exclaimed the old leatherstocking, more disgusted than alarmed. "Cussed Blackfeet!"

"Where is Delaplane?" wondered Baptiste.

"Gone beaver," gasped Maury. "They bush-whacked us."

"Whereabouts?" asked Shadmore.

"If you'd pull that damned arrow out of me, I'd tell you," bargained Maury.

Shadmore obliged him. No sooner had the arrow been removed than Maury uttered one last shuddering breath and died.

"Huh!" grunted Shadmore, chagrined. "What d'you know about that? Who would've thought? I've taken purt near a dozen arrows in my time, and not a single one kilt me."

Baptiste shrugged. He was more concerned with the living than with the dead. "I wonder do they come?" he muttered in his broken English, watching the trees from which Maury had emerged.

"We cain't jist cache out of here, if that's what yore gettin' around to. If we kin, we'll wait fer the others so's to warn 'em."

Prepared to make a quick escape, they lingered in the base camp, not knowing if it would be Blackfeet or brigade men who came first.

An hour after Maury's return—one of the most nerve-wracking hours Shadmore could remember—two more trappers rode in on tuckered ponies. They too had seen Blackfeet. At least twenty of the pesky redskins, with squaws and brats and mongrel dogs in tow, some six-seven miles east and headed this way.

"Not the same ones as did for Maury and Delaplane," Shadmore remarked to Baptiste. "Looks like we done picked the wrong valley, boys. Sounds like them Blackfeet is settin' up a summer camp in these parts. Never heard of such a thing, but you cain't hardly argue with sumpin that's as clear as the nose on yore face."

"This is purty far south for them to be puttin' up their lodges," said a trapper named Fletcher.

"The Big Bellies," said Shadmore, referring to the Gros Ventres, "are a mountain over thataway." His nod was westerly. "And they've been sidling up to the Blackfeet like hungry dogs since they come back north. Mebbe that has sumpin to do with this. But I don't aim to stick around and find out."

"We laid out a bunch of traps," said Fletcher. "Didn't bother fetchin' 'em after we seen them Injuns."

"Forget it," said Shadmore.

'But if we leave our traps we'll go to rendezvous without much of a load of plews."

"Better to leave yore traps than yore hair," replied Shadmore. "Gather up yore possibles and let's make tracks. Cleeson and Montez went south. We'll pick them up on the way out."

By the time they'd found the last two members of the brigade the sun was setting, but they pressed on, heading south. It promised to be a difficult climb over steep and broken ground to quit the valley in that direction, especially at night, but the Blackfeet had been seen to the north, coming down from the Snake River. They uttered many a curse at the darkness during the arduous trek, though Shad reminded them that they should be giving thanks for the night's shadows.

Several hours after sunset they saw the fires of a very large Indian camp up ahead. Shadmore crept forward to have a look-see. He returned with the news that the fires belonged to yet a third party of Blackfeet, this one with at least two dozen warriors, and a passel of women and children besides.

"Looks like they're having' a rendezvous of their own," he said dryly, "and we're smack in the middle of it."

"We can try to slip by them in the dark," suggested Fletcher.

Shadmore shook his head. "The way narrows up yonder, where they're sittin'. No, we've got to back up and find us another way out of this cussed valley."

They turned back, and followed a creek tumbling down off the eastern slopes. Dawn found them in a narrow canyon choked with ash and aspen. Their horses were exhausted, and so were they. As it appeared that another steep and difficult climb lay ahead of them, they paused to rest. While the others stretched their weary bones on the rocky ground, Shadmore ventured further afield, scouring the timber for any sign of recent Indian passage.

That was when Zach Hannah approached him.

Shadmore didn't recognize Zach at first. And he didn't hear Zach coming. He just looked up from his study of the ground and gave a start, for there before him stood a dark, gaunt, bearded man, his buckskins almost black with grease and grime. A strap of leather served as a headband to keep long, shaggy blond hair out of intense blue-gray eyes. Behind the man stood a rawboned sorrel horse—a long lank critter whose appearance gave no hint of the iron and grit and cunning that were the keystones of its character. Shadmore simply could not believe that the man, much less the horse, had snuck up so close to him without his knowing it.

"Wagh!" cried Shadmore softly. "I must be gettin' old, stranger, to let you Indian-up on me that way."

"Stranger? Don't you know me?"

Shadmore's eyes widened in surprise.

He knew the voice.

"God bless my worm-eaten soul!" breathed the old mountain man, and tears suddenly welled up. "Zach Hannah! Yore alive!"

Zach nodded. "But you won't be, if you keep on up this canyon, old friend."

Chapter 42

"There's no way out of this canyon," said Zach, "for men or horses. By the time you reach the end and see that what I tell you now is true, it will be too late for you to backtrack and find another way out of the valley. You see, the Blackfeet have found some of your traps, and I suspect they have also come across your camp by now, and they'll be on your trail even as we speak."

"How d'you come to know all this?"

"I've been watching."

"From where?"

"Everywhere."

Shadmore squinted sidelong at this buckskin-clad apparition. There was a lot different about Zach Hannah, and nothing was more noticeable than his flat delivery. The fact that they were in a bad fix, the countryside swarming with hostiles hopeful of lifting their hair, did not seem to arouse one iota of excitement in Zach. He appeared utterly indifferent to danger, devoid of all emotion.

"How much have you seen?" asked Shadmore.

"Enough. I trailed the first bunch of Blackfeet into this valley long before you showed up. I was curious what they were doing so far south of their usual range."

"You could've warned us, Zach."

"I figured you'd find out about them before they found out about you."

Shadmore wasn't sure this was an acceptable excuse.

"Maury and Delaplane stirred 'em up first day out," he said.

Zach nodded. "They were fools. Now they're dead. In these mountains, that's what happens to fools. They rode straight into an ambush."

"You saw that too?"

Again Zach nodded.

"God A'mighty, Zach!" cried the old graybeard, shocked. "Why didn't you he'p them?"

"It wasn't my fight."

"You've changed, all right."

"We're wasting time."

"What d'you care, hoss?" asked Shadmore bitterly. "It ain't yore fight."

"You're my friend, Shad. I owe you that much."

"You don't owe me nothin'."

Brows knit, Zach looked away. He was confused. Shadmore's harsh words cut deep, and it had been years since Zach had experienced emotional turmoil. It was an unpleasant reminder of the pain he had suffered when last he had associated with his own kind, and reminded him why he had sought the solace of the lonely high country in the first place.

"There was little I could have done for those two, Maury and Delaplane," he said.

"You could have tried. You could've at least warned 'em of the ambush."

Zach grimaced. "Maybe. But would they have listened? Would it have made any difference? I doubt it."

"They were my men, Zach. I'm the booshway of this hyar brigade."

"I figured that. You deserve a better outfit."

"What does that mean?"

"They charged right into the Blackfoot summer camp, Shad. They stole some skins and moccasins. The Blackfeet knew they were coming, and had taken to the brush, so the camp was empty. Your men looted it."

"Still," said Shadmore, "they were white men. Yore own kind."

"I belong only to myself, and the mountains."

Shadmore tugged fiercely on his beard. "You've become a wild'un, haven't you? Don't believe in nothin' and nobody. I reckon I shouldn't be surprised, after what happened to you back in . . . '25, warn't it?" The old leatherstocking ruefully shook his head. "Yessir, you done changed a heap. You shore ain't the Zach Hannah *I* knew. Well, Maury and Delaplane might have done what you say. Mebbe they weren't the smartest pilgrims around. But they were still mountain men, and by God, mountain men stick together! If you forgot ever'thing else I tried to teach you, hoss, I'd've hoped you remembered that."

"You see me standing here, don't you?"

"True enough. So you reckon you kin get us out of this mess?"

"I reckon so."

They turned to the others, who were astonished to see Zach Hannah.

"I thought you was dead," said Fletcher.

"In a way," said Zach, "I did die. The day I rode away from the fort on the Yellowstone."

"Dead and come back," said Fletcher. "Resurrected, like Lazarus. I'll be."

"If you want to stay alive," said Zach, "follow me and ask no questions."

He led them out of the canyon, back into the valley. A couple of the men muttered among themselves,

sharing reservations about heading straight into the
jaws of a certain Blackfoot deathtrap. Shadmore si-
lenced them with a severe look. Though Zach had
changed in many ways, Shadmore instinctively trusted
the man.

But even Shadmore's faith was shaken when Zach
stopped on a grassy knoll, far from the cover of any
trees, and slipped off the shaggy, wild-eyed sorrel. He
built a small fire, using dry grass with some twigs he
had broken off the branches of dead trees when last
they had passed through some woods, igniting this
kindling with sparks struck from flint. As soon as the
fire was going strong, he pulled up more dry grass and
fed this into the flame, making smoke.

"Have you lost yore everlastin' mind?" cried
Fletcher. "You'll bring them redskins right down on
top of us!"

"Who's got likker?" asked Zach.

They stared at him as though he were a raving lunatic.

"This ain't hardly the time to sit around a fire and
drink to each other's health," said Shadmore.

"I know somebody's got to have some strong spirits," insisted Zach. "After all, this is a brigade of the
Rocky Mountain Fur Company."

The others looked to their booshway. Shadmore
shrugged. He was at a loss. But he had put his faith
in Zach Hannah, and it was too late to take it back.

Baptiste produced a fancy silver flask.

"Cognac," he told Zach.

"That'll do."

Zach doused a blanket with the contents of the flask,
using every last drop, much to the French-Canadian's
chagrin. Then he jumped agilely aboard the sorrel and
took a long look around.

"Ah," he said finally. "Here they come."

The others looked north.

"Don't see nothin'," confessed Cleeson.

"Just wait."

And then they saw the Blackfeet, at least twenty of them, swarming out of a line of trees a quarter-mile away, their ponies stretched out in full gallop.

"Our goose is cooked," muttered Fletcher.

Zach dipped one end of the blanket into the fire. The fabric, doused with cognac, ignited, and the instant it did, Zach kicked the sorrel into motion. The horse jumped like a jackrabbit and carried Zach down the knoll at breakneck speed. He dragged the flaming blanket through the summer-dry grass, setting it afire.

Shadmore was the first to catch on. Wetting the tip of a finger, he held it up. He'd been so wrapped up in worrying about the Blackfeet that he had failed to notice that a steady wind was sweeping the length of the valley, coming from the south. He barked a laugh. The other mountain men paused in looking frantically to their weapons in order to stare at Shadmore, wondering if perhaps the insanity that had taken Zach Hannah was contagious, since their booshway seemed to have lost his senses as well.

The wind swept Zach's grass fire northward, faster than a man could run, and a dense cloud of smoke soon concealed the mountain men from the Blackfeet. Zach rode two hundred yards before dropping the blanket and turning the sorrel sharply to rejoin the brigade.

"Time to go," he said, and galloped south.

Shadmore and his men followed.

Behind them, the Blackfoot warriors scattered as the grass fire raced toward them.

Zach led the Rocky Mountain men about a mile before angling into a point of trees where the wooded flank of a mountain jutted out into the valley. Down into a ravine he rode, before calling a halt and bidding the others to dismount.

"What are we doin' now?" asked Fletcher, a die-hard doubting Thomas.

"Keep quiet," snapped Zach.

Fletcher scowled. His mountain man independence flared. They hadn't picked Zach to be their booshway, so who was he to talk to them like a scolding father? In spite of his rebellious frame of mind, however, Fletcher kept quiet.

A few minutes later another bunch of Blackfeet thundered past the point of woods, an arrow's flight away from the ravine, heading north to investigate the big smoke.

"How'd he know they was coming?" Fletcher whispered his query to Baptiste, who stood nearby.

Baptiste answered with a very expressive Gallic shrug. He was as mystified as everyone else.

"That's about all of them," Zach informed Shadmore. "Not counting the squaws and little ones, of course. We can ride south now to the Snake River. By the time they figure out what happened we'll be long gone."

Shadmore was grinning. "You outfoxed a whole passel of Blackfeet, and not a shot fired!" he said, admiringly.

Zach's expression was wooden. The praise did not seem to have the least effect upon him. He turned away and mounted up, leading them out of the valley, and out from under the shadow of death.

Chapter 43

By the end of day they were near the mouth of the valley, where the river joined the turbulent Snake. Feeling reasonably safe from further Blackfoot pestering, they made camp. They could see the smoke from the grass fire far to the north, a smudge of gray against the darkening sky. For thirty hours they had been on the move, and now needed rest and food. While the others sat around the campfire, Shadmore and Zach stood off a little ways, out of earshot, and the former brought the latter up to date on the events of the past few years.

The Rocky Mountain Fur Company was finally meeting with success. It had a lot to do with better leadership. Ashley had retired from the field in '27, selling his interest in the concern to Jedediah Smith, Dave Jackson, and Bill Sublette, and returning to St. Louis for good.

The men who were the booshways of the brigades knew their business. Bill Sublette, Tom Fitzpatrick, Jim Beckwourth, Jim Bridger, and even young Jed Smith all had their own outfits. Thanks to the efforts of these men, the rift between the company and the Crows that had followed the killing of Rides A Dark Horse had been bridged.

The decision to let the brigades go on their own way, to meet every summer at some prearranged spot for rendezvous, had been a wise one. The company was still freighting goods out from St. Louis to trade for the furs the trappers brought in, and the investors were raking in their long-awaited profits. For every six thousand dollars the Rocky Mountain Fur Company took from St. Louis in goods, they returned with thirty thousand worth of brown gold.

Aside from trapping beaucoup beaver, the Rocky Mountain boys had done a heap of exploring. Bridger had discovered a Great Salt Lake, and Fitzpatrick had "found" the all-important South Pass with the Crows' help. Young, book-learned Jed Smith, though, had outstripped them all in the exploring department.

Smith had gone all the way to Spanish California in '26, returning the next year through Nevada, only to revisit California and head north up the coast to Oregon. There he and his outfit had been attacked by Umpqua Indians, their furs stolen and, worst of all, Smith's journals, meticulously detailing his explorations, filched as well. The Rocky Mountain men suddenly found themselves in desperate need of help from their rivals, the men of the Hudson Bay Company who were posted at Fort Vancouver at the mouth of the Willamette River.

The rivalry between the two fur companies had been heating up. In '27, Fitzpatrick's brigade had gotten crossways with Hudson Bay booshway Peter Skene Ogden. The Rocky Mountain boys, Ogden declared, had employed underhanded means to steal Hudson Bay business. Ogden used Rockway and Iroquois Indians to trap for him. Fitzpatrick's outfit had plied these fellows with liquor and persuaded them to trade their furs to the Rocky Mountain concern, in violation of their solemn promise to Ogden. No bloodshed had come of *this* affair, but the level of hostility between the companies had increased.

The Hudson Bay booshway at Fort Vancouver was a man named John McLaughlin, who, though not fond of the Rocky Mountain Fur Company, could not tolerate Indian treachery in his bailiwick. Thanks to him, Smith's furs and journals were recovered. The grateful Smith promised McLaughlin that the Rocky Mountain trappers would leave the country north of the Snake River to the Hudson Bay Company.

The rest of the Rocky Mountain booshways agreed to honor Smith's commitment to McLaughlin. This was prime beaver country north of the Snake, but also prime Blackfoot country, and the Hudson Bay men seemed to be the only whites who could get along with that tribe. So Smith and his colleagues hoped that though they were giving up a lot of fur they would gain some peace of mind.

"So that's it," said Zach.

"That's what?" asked Shadmore.

"Why the Blackfeet are raiding so far south."

"I don't follow you, hoss."

"The Blackfeet are a warlike people. They don't want a truce. They like to fight. They hanker after white scalps. So they're coming down here to find you boys. While you hunt beaver, they hunt you."

"Huh," grunted Shadmore. "Well, ain't that special? Them comin' all this way jist fer us."

"It's going to be war," predicted Zach.

"It ain't already?"

"No. It's going to get a lot worse."

Shadmore looked Zach square in the eye for a full minute.

"If so, where will you be?"

Zach gazed up at the snow-capped peaks, silvered in the moonlight. He looked at them, mused Shadmore, the way he had once looked at Morning Sky.

As Hannah lapsed into silence, the gray-bearded

mountain man had a moment to reflect on how much Zach had changed. The young man he had known a few years ago had been full of boyish enthusiasm and innocence, quick to smile, quick to learn, and eager to be accepted. Now there was something cold and hard at the core of the new Zach Hannah, something as bleak and inhospitable as the snowfields way up yonder above the timberline. Zach had found his home, the place he belonged, in the mountains, but he had lost a part of himself in the process.

"It's not my fight," said Zach finally. "I don't want any part of it."

"Hogwash!" snapped Shadmore. "Then why did you float yore stick with us today?"

Zach looked fidgety. "I shouldn't have set that fire."

"It saved our bacon."

Deeply troubled, Zach shook his head. "You don't understand, Shad."

"You'd rather seen us dead and scalped than to have burned your precious valley? That what yore tryin' to say?"

Zach sighed. "What's done is done."

Again there was a silence between them.

Eventually, Zach said, "I wonder what happened to Sean Devlin."

"Heard tell he's with the Hudson Bay Company now." Shadmore didn't know whether to mention Morning Sky. He sensed that Zach wanted to ask about her but just couldn't bring himself to speak her name. Fact was, Shadmore didn't know anything to tell. Whether she was still with Devlin, or even still alive, he had no idea.

"Stick with us, Zach," he urged.

"I belong to the mountains."

"Yore one of us."

Zach rose and took his blankets some distance from the campfire, well away from the other mountain men.

The sorrel horse followed him like a devoted dog and stood over him as he lay down to sleep. Shadmore had a hunch that anybody trying to sneak up on Zach during the night would have his hands full with that ornery-looking cayuse.

The rest of the brigade were listening to Baptiste blow a mournful tune on his harmonica. Shadmore moseyed over and waited for Baptiste to finish his song.

"Boys, I been doin' some heavy ponderin'," he told them solemnly. "I think it's time you picked a new booshway."

The mountain men stared at him in shocked silence.

"We could've all been kilt today," continued Shadmore.

"Wouldn't have been your doin'," said Fletcher.

"I figure it would've been. I should've done some scoutin' afore sendin' you boys off in all different directions like that. The safety of the brigade rests on these ol' bony shoulders, but I was in too big an all-fired hurry to get them traps set. I got plumb careless, and there ain't no way around it. I ain't fit to be booshway any longer, and I don't want the job no more. Truth is, I never did want it."

"You know these mountains better'n any of us," said Cleeson.

The others nodded, murmuring agreement.

"Zach Hannah knows 'em like I never will."

"Well," drawled Cleeson. "He shore fooled them Blackfoot and got us out of a tight spit, purty as you please. I'll give him that."

"But will he do it?" asked Fletcher.

"Ask him in the morning," said Shadmore. "I'm turnin' in. G'night, boys."

Shadmore lay awake a long time, wondering if his plan would succeed. He didn't mind being booshway, in spite of what he had told the others, but it didn't mean so much to him that he wasn't willing to give it up for a good cause.

The cause was Zach Hannah.

Zach had gone too far over the mountain. Another year or two alone in the high country and he'd be too far gone to save. Sure, he'd been hurt. Shadmore could sympathize. But that didn't mean he had to divorce himself from the whole human race. What Zach was doing just plain wasn't healthy, and Shadmore was worried sick.

He had a hunch that deep down inside, Zach wanted to come back. He was just afraid to. Afraid of being hurt again. There was a fair-to-middling chance he would slip away in the night, and that concerned Shadmore. That he'd slip back to his mistress, the mountains, and maybe never be seen again.

But the new day dawned to find Zach lingering in the camp. That, thought Shadmore, was an encouraging sign.

As he hunkered down by the morning fire to pour himself a tin cup of coffee, Zach found himself surrounded by the other mountain men.

Fletcher had been chosen as spokesman. "Mr. Hannah, we'd like a word with you."

Standing in the background, Shadmore suppressed a smile. Fletcher was ten years Zach's senior, but he was being so respectful you might have thought Zach was the President.

Zach just sipped his coffee, inscrutable. It had been a long time since he had tasted any. It was good—real good.

"Shadmore feels like he let us down yesterday," continued Fletcher. "He don't care to be booshway no more. So the brigade's got to pick another. We all picked you."

Zach stood up and dashed the dregs in his cup onto the fire.

"Not interested," he said flatly.

"We need you to lead us," said Fletcher.

"Yeah," said Cleeson. "Join us."

"I won't leave the mountains."

"Then we won't either," said Cleeson. "We're with you, Zach. We'll follow you wherever you want to go."

Zach looked at them one by one. Cleeson, Fletcher, Baptiste, the Spaniard Montez, and a young man named Jubal Wilkes. The latter was a lanky, soft-spoken kid who reminded Shadmore a lot of the old Zach Hannah—of the way Zach had been when he had signed on with the Rocky Mountain Fur Company back in '23. Wilkes was quiet and stayed in the background, watching and listening and learning.

Right now, Wilkes was staring at Zach as he might have stared at God. Zach stared right back . . . and then Shadmore thought he saw Hannah smile, ever so slightly.

"Okay," said Zach. "On one condition. I won't belong to the Rocky Mountain Company. You will all be free trappers. That's not to say you can't trade with the company. But I'll owe allegiance to no man or group of men. I belong to these mountains."

They looked at each other, and nodded.

"So will we," said Fletcher.

Chapter 44

Having Zach Hannah for booshway proved to be of immediate benefit to the brigade.

As Zach had told Shadmore, the Blackfeet were ranging further south than ever this summer, and in greater numbers than the mountain men had ever seen before. They crossed plenty of sign of Blackfoot war parties, but Zach always seemed to be able to elude them. It was a mystery to the others how he did it, and not one among them doubted that, without Zach Hannah, their scalps would have been decorating Blackfoot shields.

He took them to a valley chock-full of beaver, only four days' ride west of the one in which Maury and Delaplane had met their end.

"In four summers I've never seen an Indian here," he told them.

By way of precautions, he went to great pains to cover their trail prior to entering the valley. He led them across stretches of bare rock, and had them walking their horses up and down through chilly streams for hours on end. Where their passage would leave sign he had them scatter in all directions and meet up the next day at a prearranged spot. In short, he made sure there was plenty of confusing sign left for any Blackfoot searchers to read, but none of it leading into the valley—instead, it was designed to lead their enemies astray.

Once the brigade was safely ensconced in the valley, setting what traps they still possessed, Zach left them. He did not say where he was going, but assured them he would return. The mountain men fervently hoped so. Already they had come to rely on his instincts and expertise.

Return he did, ten days later, bringing them all the traps Major Henry had given him. He did no trapping himself, maintaining instead a constant and tireless vigil, spending every day from dawn till dusk scouting for trouble. The others left secure, knowing he was always on the job, looking out for them. As a result they were able to concentrate on their work, and before long the plews were stacking up. It began to look as though they would have a good season after all, despite the inauspicious beginnings.

One day, Zach rode into the base camp after sunset and informed them that they were going to have a visitor.

"Injun?" asked Fletcher, instinctively reaching for his rifle.

"No. White man."

"I didn't get close enough to see if I knew him. He's camped a few miles south of here. He found some of our traps. I think he was looking for them. So he'll look for us now. And we'll let him find us."

Later, apart from the others, Shadmore asked Zach what was troubling him about the stranger.

"Nothing," said Zach.

Shadmore grunted, skeptical. "You never could pull the wool over these ol' eyes, scout. I know you cover to cover, so you might as well come clean."

Zach almost smiled. "I'm not sure, Shad. But

there's definitely something odd about him, that's certain. He . . . reeks of death.''

''What do you mean?''

Zach shrugged, struggling to find the words to convey his premonition. ''Ever seen a rabid dog?''

''I reckon.''

''You can tell something's wrong with it, even at a distance. That's the feeling I get watching this man. He ain't trapping—he carries no traps, and no packhorse. And he's not just wandering. He's hunting something, and I don't mean tomorrow's supper.''

Shadmore wasn't sure he understood, but he knew one thing: If Zach worried, he'd make sure his rifle was primed when the stranger came calling.

As Zach had predicted, the lone rider found them the next morning.

Zach had gone out before sunrise, returning an hour later, answering Shadmore's silent query with a grim nod. Cleeson, Baptiste, Montez, and Wilkes were out working their traps. Fletcher, who was Shadmore's partner, was still in camp, building a pack with a scissor-press.

The site for the base camp had been selected with great care, on high ground with a fine long view all around, and open ground on every side, although a small copse of trees stood on the rise itself, with deadfall providing natural ramparts. There was no way to approach the camp unseen, provided the occupants remained vigilant.

The man came from the south, and even at a distance Shadmore could see what Zach meant about him. He rode crooked in the saddle, bent over, as though he'd spent his whole life reading the ground for sign. As he drew closer, Shadmore could discern that he was a gaunt, heavily bearded character. His buckskins were black with grime, and poorly mended. Most all the fringe was gone. His headgear was a wolf skin, with the muzzle hanging down in front to shade his eyes, and the back half of the pelt draped over his shoulders to keep the sun off his neck. A terrible scar over half his face twisted his features into a snarling rictus.

"Wagh!" exclaimed Shadmore. "I know this man."

"Who is it?" asked Fletcher.

Shadmore squinted, staring a moment longer to be sure.

"I believe it to be Eli Simpson."

"Simpson!" exclaimed Fletcher. "After all these years!"

Shadmore looked around for Zach. Hannah was hunkered down with his back to a log, sharpening his hunting knife on a whetstone. He didn't even look up when Simpson's name was spoken. In fact, he didn't seem at all interested in their visitor.

For his part, Shadmore was wondering if Simpson had accomplished his mission of vengeance. In other words, if Devlin was gone under. And Shadmore figured Zach had to be wondering the same thing.

Without so much as a howdy, Simpson rode into their camp. He checked his gaunt pony and stared at Fletcher for so long that Fletcher began to shift from one foot to another, intensely uncomfortable under Eli's piercing gaze. Simpson next turned his attention to Shadmore, but only briefly. Then he looked across the camp at Zach, and again stared for a long time.

"I'm not the one you're looking for."

When Zach spoke he didn't even look up.

Simpson glanced at Shadmore again. "I remember you." His voice was rough and gravelly, and the words stumbled gracelessly over his tongue, as though he were unaccustomed to speaking.

"And I you, Eli."

"Yore Shadmore."

"That I am. Where you been, hoss?"

"Ever'where."

"Still after Coburn and Devlin?"

"Found Coburn."

He reached for a pouch tied to his saddlehorn. This he tossed to Shadmore, who caught it, then dropped it like it was a hot rock.

"God A'mighty," breathed the old leatherstocking. "What you got in thar, Eli?"

"Look fer yoreself."

Shadmore emphatically shook his head. "I reckon not."

But Fletcher was curious. He bent down, loosened the rawhide thongs closing the top of the pouch, and dumped the head out onto the ground.

With a strangled cry Fletcher jumped backwards, tripped over his own feet, and sat down hard. He stared in horror at Simpson's gruesome trophy.

A few shreds of dry, shrunken flesh, resembling old gray parchment, clung to the skull, as did some tangled strands of hair.

"Thar's that skunk, Coburn," said Simpson with fierce elation. "Found him way down near the Arkansas, in Arapaho country. He'd took up with some dogeatin' squaw. Even had a squawlin' half-breed brat. Took me a year and a half, but I found the sonuvabitch. I said I would. And I killed him fer what he done."

"And now yule be lookin' for Devlin."

"Been lookin'. Nigh on two winters now. Or is it three? I forget. I know he come west after leavin' the fort. I know he kilt Rides A Dark Horse. I figure he's hid out in these mountains. Whar else kin he be? The Crows would kill him on sight, and he ain't fool enough to go off north into Blackfoot country. So I'm workin' my way north through these-here mountains. Checkin' every valley, lookin' for traps and such. Seen yorn, and come on in to find out who they belonged to. Sooner or later I'll come up on him. Then I'll have his head, too.''

"Maybe somebody'll take your head for a souvenir first," remarked Zach.

Simpson stared hard at Zach, but Zach was still working on his knife, and still didn't look up.

"I seen you before," said Simpson. "But I cain't recall yore name."

"Zach Hannah."

"Yep. I remember now. Yore Devlin's friend."

He kicked his horse into motion, heading for Zach.

"Don't start nothin', Eli," pleaded Shadmore. "He'll kill you."

As Simpson drew near, Zach stood up, hunting knife in hand.

The look on his face was the same look Shadmore had seen when Zach had threatened Major Henry, that way-back day when he had first learned of Morning Sky's departure with Devlin, and the disconcerted Major had spoken in haste. As he had feared for Henry then, Shadmore now was afraid for old Eli.

"You want to try to cut my head off?" asked Zach.

"I want to know where Devlin is."

"And when you find him and kill him, what then? You won't have anything to live for."

Simpson scowled. "Cain't worry none about that. Devlin's gotta pay for what he done, and that's all there is to say on that score. Whar is he? Iffen you know, you better tell me."

"I got nothing to say to you, except step down off that cayuse."

"Zach . . . ." began Shadmore.

"Stay out of this."

But Simpson did not accept the challenge. Zach had flung a gauntlet down, but Eli wasn't going to pick it up.

"Don't matter," snarled Simpson. "I'll find yore friend. Iffen it takes me till Judgment Day, I'll find him."

With that, he turned his horse away. Dismounting, he put Coburn's head back into the pouch, handling it reverently, as one would a family heirloom. Climbing back aboard his pony, and without another word to anyone, he left the camp.

Shadmore confronted Zach. He was angry, because Zach had tried to provoke a killing, and that was a part of the new Zach Hannah he didn't like to see. The old Zach would have done his level best to avoid bloodshed.

"What's wrong with you, scout? You achin' to kill somebody?"

"He's the killer, Shad. That's all he lives for. I don't want him wandering around in these mountains."

"You mean *yore* mountains, don't you?"

"He's a danger to everyone he meets."

"I was of half a mind to tell him Devlin was up in Blackfoot country, workin' for the Hudson Bay Company."

"No," said Zach flatly.

"Yore still tryin' to protect Coyote? After what he done to you? I cain't believe that."

"Believe what you want," replied Zach, and would not say more on the subject.

He rode out a little later, and Shadmore knew he was going to track Eli Simpson. What Shadmore wasn't sure of was whether Zach intended to follow just to make sure Eli left the valley, or if he was going to track Simpson down and kill him like a mad dog.

* * *

Shadmore fretted all day. Not much shy of sunset, Zach and Wilkes returned to camp with Cleeson laid out on a travois.

Cleeson was knocking on death's door. He had been shot in the leg. The bullet had smashed the bone and chipped a main artery, and he had lost a lot of blood. Zach had applied a tourniquet, but to little avail.

"My God," said Shadmore, upon seeing Cleeson's condition. "He's halfway acrost the river."

"He's lost the leg for certain," said Zach grimly. "If not his life."

"Who done it?"

"Simpson." Cold fury rippled across Zach's bronze features. "I tracked him. He made like he was leaving the valley. Then he doubled back, moving fast. Snuck up on Cleeson and put that bullet in him."

"Where were you, boy?" Shadmore asked Wilkes. The young man was shaken. "I . . . I . . ."

"He was doing his job," said Zach, coming to the youngster's defense. "Dragging beaver out of the crik. It was Cleeson who wandered off."

"I heard the gunshot," said Wilkes, "and came a'runnin'. When I got there, I didn't see nobody but Cleeson. Cleeson told me it was a man named Simpson who shot him. Said Simpson was crazy. Said he wanted to know where Sean Devlin was. Cleeson wouldn't tell him at first, but then Simpson started kicking him in the wounded leg. So Cleeson told him what he wanted to know, and Simpson rode out."

"I reckon you was right about Eli after all," Shadmore admitted to Zach.

"I'm going after him," said Zach.

"I'll go along."

"No, you tend to Cleeson."

Zach didn't wait until morning. By taking the time to deliver Cleeson to the base camp he had given

Simpson a head start. He rode to the north end of the valley that night, and at first light tried to find Simpson or at least cut his trail. He was counting on Simpson camping somewhere in the valley for the night. If Eli was foolish or crazy enough to do that, then Zach thought he could catch up. But he couldn't find a trace of the man.

He had to return to the place where Simpson had bushwhacked Cleeson. Only then did he discover that Simpson had gone up and over the timberline. Zach realized he had been outsmarted. Eli had surmised that Zach would be after him. Cleeson was part of Zach's brigade, and as booshway it was Zach's responsibility to set things aright. So instead of leaving the valley in the conventional way, he had chosen to go over the mountain, a difficult and dangerous climb.

Giving up the chase rankled, but Zach had to let Simpson go. He realized it might take days, even weeks, to find the man again. Eli was a wily old lone wolf, with as much wilderness savvy as Zach himself possessed. If a man was smart enough, and knew all the tricks of the trade, he could shake off a tracker, no matter how good that tracker was. And Eli Simpson knew all the tricks. He was gone.

Frustrated and angry, Zach returned to the base camp.

They were burying Cleeson when he rode in.

Acting restless, Zach brooded all day long. That evening, the rest of the brigade came in from their trap lines. Sitting around the campfire, they had a long council. Zach took no part in it. Later, Shadmore approached him.

"You want to go after Simpson, I reckon," said Shadmore. "Because of Cleeson, or Devlin?"

"Does it matter?"

"Not really. 'Cause we've all decided to ride with you."

"We'll be going into Blackfoot country."

Shadmore shrugged. "Thar's Blackfeet ever'-where."

"What about the beaver?"

"We got some plews. Enough to take to rendezvous and stock up on what we need fer the winter."

"May not see rendezvous."

"Seen one, you've seen 'em all. We're riding with you, Zach, like it or not. We're free trappers now, and we said we'd stick with you. We aim to do just that."

"We'll leave at first light," said Zach.

Chapter 45

Sean Michael Devlin spent three years with the Hudson Bay Company, and for all that time he was ostensibly MacGregor's partner at the trading post on the upper Missouri River.

In spite of that, the two men never developed a real friendship. MacGregor was a very thorough, conscientious, and honest employee—one of the most trusted men in the company. In addition, he was a very astute judge of character. It didn't take him long to peg Devlin as a rogue—albeit a charming one. A man you couldn't depend on. A man who looked out for his own interests, and everyone else be damned.

That didn't mean MacGregor couldn't or wouldn't work with Devlin. The canny Scotsman was accustomed to working with louts and scoundrels. The frontier had more than its fair share of both. For all his faults, Devlin was still an improvement over that drunkard Connor. The latter had persistently made trouble with the Hudson Bay Company's best customers, the Blackfeet, Bloods and Piegans—he couldn't keep his dirty paws off the Indian women. In that regard, at least, Devlin was no problem. And why should he be, when he had Morning Sky?

MacGregor thought she was a bonny lass, indeed. In his own reticent way, the Scotsman came to love her.

But he was too much the gentleman to wear his heart on his sleeve. Instead, he showed her every kindness.

Morning Sky was slow to respond to him. Her reserve was understandable; he treated her the way Devlin had, just prior to tricking her into leaving her husband. At first she was suspicious of MacGregor, thinking he might have similar motives. Eventually, though, she opened up to him. MacGregor had Devlin to thank for that.

Devlin came to take Morning Sky for granted. He was sure he loved her—he declared that this was so— but had he been capable of honest self-evaluation he would have understood that his desire to possess her had been largely predicated on the fact that she belonged to Zach Hannah, heart and soul. And Devlin wanted to have everything Zach had—his fame, his integrity, his courage, and his woman. He wanted to be just like Zach Hannah.

He had two of the four. Morning Sky belonged to him now. And the Blackfeet treated him with ego-gratifying respect as the killer of Rides A Dark Horse. He went so far as to misconstrue MacGregor's amiable tolerance as fear. After all, he had killed Connor, and the Scotsman was obviously putting up with him, even though he wasn't very reliable. The only reason he could see for MacGregor overlooking his shortcomings was that the man didn't want to end up like his erstwhile partner.

As for courage and integrity, he proved he was lacking in both when he learned that Morning Sky was pregnant.

She was afraid to tell him, but it wasn't something that could be kept secret for long, so she went ahead. His response came as no surprise to her. Devlin struck her. He wanted a beautiful woman to share his blankets; he didn't want the responsibilities of fatherhood.

It was all her fault, of course. She was trying to put a rope on him. Tie him down. It wasn't fair. It wasn't what he wanted. From the moment he learned of its existence, he despised the baby.

His behavior infuriated MacGregor. In the weeks to come, Devlin was downright abusive to Morning Sky. It reached the point that the Scotsman had to intervene. At first he tried to reason with Devlin. That didn't work. The two men quarreled, and the quarrel escalated into fisticuffs. MacGregor won. Ashamed of being bested in the presence of Morning Sky, Devlin stormed off, muttering dark threats.

MacGregor wasn't afraid of Devlin. He figured there was a very good chance Devlin would resort to violence. To redeem themselves, cowards often did. Devlin was one of those men who had reached the erroneous conclusion that killing was the easiest way to solve a problem.

Once again Morning Sky felt real fear. By now she looked upon the Scotsman as a genuine friend—the only true friend she had, and her only protection. If Devlin killed MacGregor, what would he do to her baby?

Somehow she had to persuade MacGregor to take her away.

But where could she go?

She could not find safe haven among the Blackfeet. Her brother, Ten Bows, had come to see her once, accompanied by several other warriors. His attitude had been civil, yet distant. Morning Sky thought he was genuinely pleased to know she was alive, but he wouldn't make his true feelings evident in the presence of his peers. The tribe tolerated her only because they respected Devlin. They would never accept her—she was a pariah, contaminated by her long association with the Absaroka Crows. Ten Bows couldn't take her in even if he wanted to.

Could she go back to Zach Hannah? She had not heard a word about him in more than four years. Her feelings for him had not changed one whit—after all this time her love was just as strong. Thoughts of him still made her heart ache. But she did not know where he was, or if he was still alive, for that matter. And even if he was alive, and she could find him, how would he feel about her now?

She could see how it must have looked to him—he could not know that Devlin had duped her. By all appearances she had left with Devlin of her own free will, and there was no one who could tell him otherwise. Only she could do that, and there were no guarantees she could even find him, much less convince him to take her back.

Especially now that she was pregnant with Devlin's child.

Would Zach's heart be big enough to embrace them both? How much had he changed? How much had what she had done changed him? His heart must have been broken, as hers had been. Broken hearts could change people, and often for the worse.

She decided she would have to try to find him, and hope for the best. If she could locate any of the Rocky Mountain outfit, perhaps she could discover his whereabouts. Word had come to their Hudson Bay post that the fort at the confluence of the Yellowstone and the Missouri had been abandoned, and that Major Henry's men, divided into brigades, had gone into the high country, meeting annually at rendezvous.

So she would search for one of those brigades.

But she couldn't make it on her own, not while carrying a child. MacGregor was the only one who could help her.

A woman knows how a man really feels about her, and Morning Sky was aware of MacGregor's strong feelings for her. But she would not lie to him, or make promises she could not keep. Her only approach was complete honesty.

For the first time she told him all about Zach Hannah—how Devlin had used treachery to steal her away, and how Zach was the only one she would ever truly love. It was past time for her to return to him. Would MacGregor help her? She feared for her child's life if she remained with Devlin any longer.

"Aye, lass," agreed the Scotsman. "As do I." He sighed deeply. "This Zach Hannah is a lucky man. I canna deny that I envy him."

"Please help me."

"I must think," replied MacGregor, and quickly left the cabin.

In spite of his rough exterior, the Scotsman had a good heart, and Morning Sky's tragic story affected him strongly. He realized she could never be his, but that alone was not enough to make him turn his back on her now, in her time of need.

Fortunately for Morning Sky, MacGregor's love was of the purest, most noble sort.

She was lucky, too, that the Scotsman's conscience had been troubled of late by a certain aspect of his work. He did not approve of the Hudson Bay Company trading guns to the Blackfeet.

In the end, this tilted the scales in Morning Sky's favor. Later that day, he sat her down and informed her of his decision.

"I hate to leave the company, lass, but I will. Every time I see the scalps of white men on the shields of our Blackfoot clients, I can hardly sleep at night. And I wouldna mind terrible much to get back to trapping. That's how I got my start with the Hudson Bay Company, and I miss it like the devil. I sometimes feel like a flamin' store clerk. So I'll help you. For your sake, and your wee child's, you must be rid of Devlin.''

''Thank you,'' she whispered, almost overcome with emotion, and squeezed his hand.

He pulled gently free. ''We must hurry. No telling when Devlin will return, or what he'll have up his sleeve when he does. There's no time to waste. Besides, the first snows are not long in coming. If we can't find a Rocky Mountain brigade, I've heard tell their rendezvous this season is in the Green River valley a few weeks hence. We'll have to travel fast to make it there in time.''

Before he left, MacGregor took all the rifles in the post and threw them in the river. He penned a hasty note to the Hudson Bay Company explaining why he had destroyed company property in an ultimately useless gesture, and left a pouch of ''hard money'' with the note. Though the pouch contained his life savings, it came nowhere near to recompensing the company for the loss of the rifles.

They gathered a few possibles and left that very day, following the Missouri west, the route the Lewis and Clark Expedition had taken a quarter of a century ago. They met one small party of Blackfeet four days out, but the warriors knew MacGregor and assumed he still worked for the Hudson Bay Company. The Scot did not disabuse them of that notion. He knew it was too soon for word to get out that he had betrayed the company, and he wasn't above using the company's name as a passport to travel safely through Blackfoot territory.

He kept a careful eye on their backtrail for any sign of pursuit by Devlin, but by the time they reached the Three Forks Country he had begun to relax his vigilance.

"Devlin's a poor tracker," he told Morning Sky. "I don't think we'll have to worry about him anymore."

"I hope I never see him again," said Morning Sky.

"So do I, lassie. I might have to kill the lad."

That night, MacGregor broke out his bagpipes for the first time since leaving the cabin on the Missouri. Morning Sky clapped her hands in delight. She loved to hear the Scotsman play, and play he did that night, the keening wail of the pipes setting off an answering coyote chorus.

The next morning a grim, gaunt man in blackened buckskins and wearing wolfskin headgear appeared in their camp. His eyes blazed when they fell upon Morning Sky.

"I know you," said the stranger.

Morning Sky knew she had seen this hideously scarred man before, but she couldn't remember where.

"Who might you be?" asked MacGregor, his rifle cradled in his arms, primed and ready.

"The name's Eli Simpson. I'm huntin' the man what took up with this hyar squaw."

"Devlin? What would you be wanting with him?"

"He's alive, then!" exclaimed Simpson, exultant. "Good! Good! Where is he?"

Something about Simpson made MacGregor uneasy. He took an instant dislike to the man.

"Are you his friend or foe?"

"I'm his executioner," was Simpson's flatly delivered reply.

"I remember now," said Morning Sky.

Simpson nodded. "Yep. I'm the one Devlin and Coburn left to die alone in the wilderness." He turned to MacGregor again, and stroked his scarred face. "A grizzly got holt of me, y'see. They left me to die in a valley swarmin' with Gros Ventres, Devlin and Coburn did. Took my horse and rifle. But I didn't go under. Devlin will die before I do.''

A glance at Morning Sky confirmed for MacGregor that what Simpson said was gospel. Her expression spoke volumes.

"Devlin works for the Hudson Bay Company now," said the Scotsman. "He's up north of the Missouri somewhere, most likely.''

This revelation startled Simpson. "Blackfoot country? I never thought of that." He frowned. "You know him, and here you are with his squaw, so how come yore tellin' me where to find him?''

"I know him, but we're not mates.''

"Mebbe yore runnin' off with his woman, then.''

"I wouldna think that to be any of your business," replied MacGregor.

"Reckon it ain't." Simpson shrugged. "Guess I'll mosey north.''

"Aye. That would be a good idea.''

"Not a very friendly cuss, are you?''

"Not very," agreed MacGregor.

"So long, then," said Simpson, and kicked his horse into motion.

His departure from camp took him directly past the Scotsman. As he drew abreast, he launched himself out of his saddle with the agility of a panther, bearing MacGregor to the ground. Wresting the rifle from MacGregor's grasp, he bounced spryly to his feet and drove the butt of the weapon as hard as he could against the Scotsman's skull. The impact shattered the rifle's stock. He was raising the rifle to strike again when he noticed that Morning Sky was running, fleet as a deer. Dropping the rifle, Simpson took off after her.

The camp had been made beside a purling creek, and as she crossed it, Morning Sky stumbled on loose stones and fell. Before she could recover, Simpson had pounced on her. Terror wrenched a cry from her lips. Straddling her, Simpson grabbed a handful of raven-black hair and forced her head underwater. She flailed helplessly beneath him. Simpson held her under a full half-minute before letting up. Then he dragged her roughly, still holding on to her hair, out of the creek. Reaching the bank, he pulled her to her feet and caressed her throat with the blade of his knife.

"Don't force me to kill you, punkin," he said. "I need you alive. Yore comin' with me."

Gasping for air, Morning Sky managed a defiant look. Simpson chuckled.

"You got spunk, don't you? I bet Devlin's all fevered up over you. Reckon we'll see iffen he thinks yore worth dyin' for."

Chapter 46

The buzzards led Zach and his brigade straight to MacGregor.

Shadmore was the first off his horse. He knelt beside the Scotsman and checked for signs of life. Waiting for Shad's diagnosis, Zach sat his lanky sorrel and scanned the ground, while the rest of the mountain men studied the surrounding countryside for any sign of danger.

"He's above snakes," declared Shadmore, "but just barcly. Somebody tried to cave his skull in."

Zach nodded. He had seen the rifle in the grass beyond the Scotsman before anybody else and noticed it. The stock was shattered—obviously the instrument used in the attempted killing. He dismounted to take a closer look at the scuffed ground around the cold campfire.

"This man and a woman camped here, night before last," he said. "She's Blackfoot. The next morning a man rode in from the south. A white man." Zach took two strides, hunkered down to peer at a footprint. "It was Simpson."

"You shore?" asked Shadmore.

Again Zach nodded. "There's that notched left hoof again."

"Well, of course yore shore," said Shadmore. "I taught you ever'thing you know."

But the old leatherstocking came over for his own look-see. It was the same sign they had found in the valley where Cleeson had been killed. Three days ago they had come across it again, and the next day lost it. They were on Simpson's trail, though, due in large measure to Zach's uncanny ability to anticipate the most likely route the man would take through the mountains.

"You was right on the money about ol' Eli," said Shadmore gravely. "He shore is a danger to every livin' soul in this country. Now how come you reckon he tried to break that feller's head open?"

Zach pointed to the small moccasin print, which obviously belonged to an Indian woman.

"There's a likely reason."

"A woman?" Shadmore tugged on an ear. "Yep, mebbe so. Wimmin can get a man in trouble in a whole heap of different ways."

Zach walked off to study the ground further from camp. He walked a complete circle around the site. Returning, he continued with his evaluation of what had occurred.

"That woman ran. Simpson caught her in that creek yonder. They rode north, leading one horse."

"Huh!" grunted Shadmore, once more kneeling beside the injured man. "How do you like them apples? Simpson's chasin' Devlin all over God's creation because Devlin left him half-dead and took his horse and rifle, and now here goes ol' Eli done the same exact thing to this pilgrim."

Zach was gazing north. Shadmore knew what he was thinking.

"Well, somebody's got to stick with this man," said Shad. "Mind you, I ain't volunteerin'. It's just an observation."

"Two will stay," said Zach. "Fletcher—you and

Wilkes. I don't care if the whole Blackfoot nation rides through here—you don't leave him.''

"Just keep yore eyes peeled and yore hair on," advised Shadmore as he got back aboard his horse.

Zach, Shadmore, Montez, and Baptiste were gone less than two hours when MacGregor stirred. This startled the two frontiersmen who had remained behind. One look at the man's head wound and both had concluded he was gone beaver.

Wilkes gave him a little water. MacGregor's eyes fluttered open. It took him a while to focus on the young woodsman's face.

"Who y'be?" he asked, so weakly that Wilkes had to bend down to hear.

"Jubal Wilkes, sir.''

"Rocky Mountain man?''

"Yes, sir.''

Fletcher came closer. "We're after the man who done this to you. He kilt one of our own.''

MacGregor tried to sit up, but Wilkes restrained him.

"You'd best lay still, sir. You skull's split open.''

"Morning Sky . . .'' gasped the Scotsman before passing out.

Fletcher's eyes got big as saucers.

"What did he say?''

" 'Morning Sky,' I think," said Wilkes.

"Lord A'mighty," breathed Fletcher. "Jubal, you get on the nag of yourn and ride like Lucifer himself was hot on your heels. Find Zach.''

"What about him?'' Wilkes nodded at MacGregor.

"I'll look after him. You just find Zach.''

"What do I tell him?'' The name Morning Sky meant nothing to Wilkes—he had only joined the Rocky Mountain Fur Company that spring.

"Tell him Simpson's got his wife.''

* * *

Devlin returned to the trading post one day after MacGregor and Morning Sky left.

Since the fight with the Scotsman he had wandered alone and aimlessly, one moment vowing violent revenge and the next feeling remorseful and disconsolate for having behaved towards Morning Sky in such a manner. As he rode up to the cabin on the banks of the Missouri, he had made up his mind to try to make amends with both his partner and the woman he loved.

Finding them gone, Devlin flew into a rage that wasn't spent until he had turned the interior of the cabin into a shambles. Exhausted, he collapsed and wept. Eventually he managed to pull himself together. He read the note MacGregor had left for the Hudson Bay Company. This he destroyed, and confiscated the pouch of "hard money" the Scotsman had left to repay the company in part for the destruction of the rifles. Consumed by a cold and deadly wrath, Devlin left the post, picked up their trail, and followed it west along the river.

He was going to hunt them down and kill them.

MacGregor wasn't going to get away with stealing his woman.

And Morning Sky would never belong to another man.

That afternoon he crossed paths with Standing Bear and a Blackfoot war party numbering eleven more warriors. They shared a camp, and Devlin learned that the Indians were returning to their village after a less-than-successful foray into the mountains. They had been involved in a running scrape with Nez Percé warriors, and had only one scalp, a few furs, and four stolen horses to show for their trouble. Not much, for weeks on the warpath. They were on their way to the trading post to see what they could get for the furs.

After four years of dealing with the Blackfoot, Devlin had learned enough of the dialect to communicate effectively, helping himself liberally with sign language. He told Standing Bear that MacGregor had betrayed the company, destroying many rifles that the company had meant for their allies the Blackfeet. It was his job, said Devlin, to track MacGregor down. Would Standing Bear and his fellow warriors help him and the company in bringing the Scotsman to account for his treachery?

Standing Bear discussed the matter with the other braves. The next morning, three of the Blackfeet headed for their village on the Marias River with the furs and the horses, while Standing Bear and the other eight accompanied Devlin.

This was a stroke of pure luck for Devlin. Without the tracking skills of the Blackfeet, he would not have remained long on MacGregor's trail.

Catching up with the Scotsman was an event Devlin anticipated with vengeful relish. If MacGregor wasn't killed outright, he would let Standing Bear and his bunch torture the man to death. Better still, he would make Morning Sky watch. That would teach her not to run off with another man. Maybe he wouldn't kill her after all.

He made no mention of Morning Sky, but somehow Standing Bear surmised the truth, for one night, as they sat around their campfire, the Blackfoot warrior broached the subject. Devlin had no recourse but to admit that Morning Sky had indeed run off with MacGregor. Standing Bear nodded gravely, as if he had known this to be the case all along.

"We will kill them both," said the Indian, and it

didn't sound as though there were any room for debate.

"No," said Devlin, whose anger had by now cooled. "She is my woman."

"She is no good," replied Standing Bear, adamant. He punctuated this assessment with a sharp gesture, striking a fist against his chest and then sweeping the arm to one side and down, opening the hand. Literally, the sign meant "to throw away," and it signified something that was worthless or bad.

"She's mine!" insisted Devlin, feeling the onset of panic.

Standing Bear shook his head. "She must die. You are brother to the Blackfoot. You will take Blackfoot squaw."

"But Morning Sky *is* Blackfoot," protested Devlin, grasping at straws.

Standing Bear scowled. "No. It will be as I say."

And that was the end of it.

Devlin didn't sleep a wink that night. All he could think about was Morning Sky—and the child she was carrying. *His* child. What a fool he had been! His own stupidity had driven Morning Sky away. And now, in his anger, he had allied himself with those who meant to do away with her. There seemed no way out of this predicament. Yet he had to do something. He couldn't just stand by and let these Blackfoot bastards kill his woman and baby.

Two days later, as they neared the northern reaches of the Big Belt Mountains, they saw in the distance two riders emerging from the wooded foothills, descending onto the open plains.

Standing Bear employed one of his most prized possessions: a telescoping spyglass he'd acquired from the Hudson Bay Company. The instrument was powerful medicine—only strong magic could bring distant objects into such sharp and immediate relief. The warrior brandished the spyglass with a flourish and studied the two riders. Without a word, he then handed the glass to Devlin.

"Your woman," said Standing Bear, sardonic.

True enough. There was Morning Sky. But Devlin spared her only a glance, because the other rider was Eli Simpson.

A strangled sound escaped his throat.

"You know him," said Standing Bear, reclaiming the spyglass.

Devlin wasn't sure if the warrior was making an assumption or asking a question. He shook his head, unable to speak.

"We kill them both," decided Standing Bear, and with a sharp command led the other warriors down into a swale, out of sight of their intended victims. Numb with shock, Devlin could only follow.

He didn't know what to do. He couldn't think. His first instinct was simply to run away. Why was this happening to him? What had he done to deserve this malicious twist of fate? How could he save Morning Sky and his child now? All he could hope for was to save his own skin.

Standing Bear was using the contours of the rolling plains to good advantage, trying to close the distance unseen. The Blackfeet intended to get as near as possible to their prey before attacking.

Bitter tears of frustration burned his eyes, as Devlin waited for his chance. He was bringing up the rear of the party, and when they descended single-file into a serpentine gully, he saw his opportunity: For a moment, all the Blackfeet ahead of him were out of sight around a sharp bend. Devlin reined his pony around and galloped the other way.

Once in flight he gave no thought to concealment,

and as he went up and over high ground Simpson spotted him.

The distance was still too great for Simpson to identify the lone rider, but he could tell Devlin was a white man by his buckskin garb, and it was obvious that Devlin was fleeing, and that was enough for Eli. There weren't that many white men in Blackfoot country, and there seemed to be a better than fair chance that this was the man Simpson had searched so long to find.

Simpson was leading both the spare mount—MacGregor's horse—and Morning Sky's pony. Morning Sky's hands were bound with rawhide behind her back. Eli let the spare horse go and kicked his own cayuse into a gallop, towing his captive along behind.

He had not gone a hundred yards in pursuit before nine Blackfoot warriors seemed to rise up out of the ground directly in his path.

Chapter 47

All the Blackfeet had rifles, and almost all of them fired in unison. A bullet struck Simpson in the arm. He heard the loud *whack!* as the lead impacted flesh, but before the pain came numbing sensation, and besides that, Eli was as tough from heel to hairline as old whang leather. He scarcely took notice of the wound.

Of more immediate concern was the fact that his horse was hit, more than once. The animal dropped dead in its tracks. Simpson already had his feet out of the stirrups. He landed on the run, but had to let go of the reins of Morning Sky's horse.

Miraculously, both Morning Sky and her pony were unscathed. The horse veered sharply away from the onslaught of screaming Blackfeet. She clung with her knees as best she could, bending forward at the waist to present a smaller target. Three of the Blackfeet angled off in pursuit of her.

Simpson made his running dismount with long-rifle in hand. He pulled up, brought the rifle up, and fired. One of the warriors somersaulted over the back of his pony, nailed through the heart. Eli didn't have time to reload. The Indians were on him. The nearest tried to club him with an empty rifle. Simpson ducked under and hammered the warrior with his own weapon. The rifle broke in two pieces. The Blackfoot toppled off his horse. Simpson closed in, snarling like a wolf. He drew a flintlock pistol from his belt and fired point-blank at the fallen brave. The warrior's face disintegrated into a bloody mess. At that instant, another Blackfoot planted his hatchet right between Eli's shoulder blades as he galloped past. Simpson roared and dropped to his knees. The Blackfoot charge surged past him. Four warriors, one of them Standing Bear, turned their ponies and moved in on the mountain man.

Two hundred yards to the south, one of the three Blackfeet in pursuit of Morning Sky drew close enough to leap from his galloping pony and sweep her from her horse. The fall stunned her. The warrior raised a knife to finish her off, a savage, exultant cry bursting from his lips.

A rifle spoke.

The warrior's cry was cut short and he fell sideways, drilled dead-center.

The other two braves had checked their ponies. Now they looked around to see where the shot had come from.

Four mountain men were charging hell-for-leather straight at them. Their rifles spat flame. One of the warriors fell. The third wheeled his pony and made a run for it.

Riding slightly ahead of the others, Zach Hannah yelled Baptiste's name and pointed at the fleeing Indian. The French-Canadian took off after the Blackfoot. While Shadmore and Montez veered off to challenge Standing Bear and his three companions, Zach jumped off his horse and ran to Morning Sky. Throwing away his Hawken, he dropped to his knees beside her, drew his knife, and cut the rawhide that bound her wrists together.

"Zach!" she cried. "You are alive!"

Dead and come back, Fletcher had said. *Resurrected, like Lazarus.*

"I am now," he said hoarsely. "I told you, Sky. I'll always come back to you."

He pulled her to him and wrapped his arms around her. Felt her tears against his cheek. Felt the life flow back into him.

So lost was he in his feelings that he failed to see Standing Bear riding them down until it was almost too late.

The Blackfoot uttered a bloodcurdling war cry. Zach pushed Morning Sky to the ground and rose to meet the warrior as he leaped from his horse. He bore Zach to the ground. The blade of his knife flashed in the sun as he raised it. Zach intercepted the arm as it swept down. His grasp was like an iron vise around Standing Bear's wrist. He still had his own knife in the other hand. He drove it to the hilt in the warrior's side. Withdrew the blade and struck again. Hot blood drenched his hand. Again he struck, and felt the strength ebb out of Standing Bear's body.

But even in death, Standing Bear would not fall. Zach had to roll the corpse sideways to the ground.

Standing, Zach took a quick look around to see if any more trouble was coming his way.

The fight was over. Shadmore was coming towards him, on foot. Beyond Shadmore, Montez was checking the dead. And beyond Montez, several riderless Blackfoot ponies—and Shadmore's cayuse—were trotting off.

Morning Sky flew into his arms, and Zach paid no more attention to the field of battle. He dropped the bloody knife and embraced her.

Shadmore approached, grinning from ear to ear.

"Wagh!" yelled the old leatherstocking.

It was all he could say at the moment.

Baptiste rode up, and Zach saw that the French-Canadian brandished a fresh scalp.

"This brigade," said Zach, "will take no more scalps."

Baptiste was startled, then mortified. He looked at the scalp like he didn't know how such a thing had gotten in his grasp, and dropped it.

Montez came over.

"What about Eli?" asked Shadmore.

"*Muerte,*" answered the swarthy Spaniard.

Shadmore nodded. "He went down kickin'. The way a mountain man should."

Montez and Baptiste were staring at Zach and Morning Sky with unabashed curiosity. With a grimace, Shadmore said, "What are you rascals gapin' at? Let's go catch up all those loose ponies."

"Someone comes," said Baptiste.

They looked south—a lone rider, his cayuse stretched out.

"It's Jubal," announced Shadmore. "Lordy, Baptiste. Here I am twice yore age, and I still see twice as fer as you kin."

In short order Wilkes arrived on his foam-flecked pony. Shadmore took one look at the condition of the hard-run horse and shook his head reproachfully.

"You done rode all the tallow offen that cayuse, boy."

Wilkes' eyes roamed over the dead men scattered in the grass.

"Fletcher told me to catch up fast as I could."

"Well, you missed the shindig by inches."

Wilkes turned to Zach. "I was s'pose to tell you that Simpson had—" He stopped and stared at Morning Sky, The blush started at his collar and traveled up his cheeks. "Well, I reckon it don't matter now."

"Come on, youngun," said Shadmore. "We're off

to catch horses. Looks like yore gonna need a new one.''

They left Zach and Morning Sky in peace. Zach stepped back and laid a hand on her gently rounded belly. He looked deep into her violet-blue eyes.

''Whose?''

She swallowed the lump in her throat. Her chin came up a defiant inch. ''Devlin.''

A smile touched the corner of his mouth.

''Ours,'' he said, and embraced her again.

Way off in the distance, Zach could see a dark speck moving across the rolling sea of grass. It was visible only for a moment, and he was the only one who noticed.

By the year 2000, 2 out of 3 Americans could be illiterate.

It's true.

Today, 75 million adults...about one American in three, can't read adequately. And by the year 2000, U.S. News & World Report envisions an America with a literacy rate of only 30%.

Before that America comes to be, you can stop it...by joining the fight against illiteracy today.

Call the Coalition for Literacy at toll-free **1-800-228-8813** and volunteer.

Volunteer Against Illiteracy. The only degree you need is a degree of caring.